Where There's a Will

About the Author

Beth Corby started out in a small Welsh mining village, and pursued her interest in music through to a PhD. Finding academic writing constricting, she embraced creative writing and fell for comedic storytelling at the first pen stroke. Beth relishes time writing, daydreaming, plotting and capturing those moments when her characters misbehave. *Where There's a Will* is her debut novel.

To get to know Beth better, follow her on Twitter: @BethCorby1.

BETH CORBY

Where There's a Will

HODDER

First published in Great Britain in 2019 by Hodder & Stoughton
An Hachette UK company

1

Copyright © Beth Corby 2019

A CIP catalogue record for this title is available from the British Library

Paperback ISBN 978 1 473 69949 6
eBook ISBN 978 1 473 69950 2

Typeset in Plantin Light by Hewer Text UK Ltd, Edinburgh
Printed and bound in Great Britain by Clays Ltd, Elcograf S.p.A.

Hodder & Stoughton policy is to use papers that are natural, renewable
and recyclable products and made from wood grown in sustainable
forests. The logging and manufacturing processes are expected to
conform to the environmental regulations of the country of origin.

Hodder & Stoughton Ltd
Carmelite House
50 Victoria Embankment
London EC4Y 0DZ

www.hodder.co.uk

For my husband and children

1

You can do this. You're confident and smart, smart and confident. Smile. It's only an interview . . . even if it is the only way to start a career after seven years of studying and temping. God! No, don't think like that. Breathe. Everything is going to be fine . . . although I wish Mr Nailer, my interviewer, would stop frowning at my CV like it's a list of criminal offences.

His eyes briefly meet mine over the top of my CV, but he doesn't smile. Is that a bad sign?

Stop it – you're over-analysing. Breathe and relax.

Uncross your legs and sit up straight.

Smile and assume the calm exterior of a perfect teacher.

Yes, that's better. After all, I've only said 'hello, I'm Hannah', 'yes' and 'thank you'. How can that be wrong? And it's always possible that this is just part of his interview technique – see if I crack under the pressure. Or maybe he's got indigestion . . . or a headache . . . or his wife left him this morning.

'So your first degree was in art history?' he asks, as if it was a degree in dog walking. Although, if I'm honest, there are probably more job opportunities in dog walking nowadays.

'Yes. I actually began with just plain history, but I didn't really enjoy it. In fact, I found it quite boring, so I switched to art history, which I loved.'

'Really?' Mr Nailer eyeballs me coldly. 'I read "just plain history" at university – found it fascinating,' he says, slowly turning his attention back to my CV.

My smile is frozen on my lips. I surreptitiously rub my clammy hands on my trousers and try to swallow.

I mustn't panic. People like different subjects – fact of life. No need to read too much into it, just stay personable, get a place on this teaching course and the future is golden. After all, there's every chance I'll be excellent at teaching. I might stroll into the classroom and find I have a hidden talent for honing young minds into geniuses . . . ? Genii? Or is it like sheep and the same plural as singular? Anyway, I could be the ultimate teacher. It could be like *Dead Poets Society* – the beginning, at least . . .

'Then you had a year in the workplace, with . . .' Mr Nailer runs his finger down the page, his lips moving as he counts '. . . eleven different companies?' His eyebrows almost merge with his hairline.

'Yes, there weren't any jobs going in art history, so I worked as an office temp and having a lot of employers goes with the territory.' I smile reassuringly, but he doesn't look convinced.

'And you are now in your final year of an English degree?'

'Yes.'

'And you want to train as an English teacher?'

'Yes.' I think I sound positive but, if anything, he looks even more doubtful. His qualms must be infectious because I'm really starting to wish I had a Plan B to fall back on.

'And you like children?' asks Mr Nailer, watching me carefully as he places my CV to one side.

My prepared spiel about how much I adore the little darlings suddenly seems naive. Do I like children? Well, not the little toad who lives next door to Mum and Dad's, who throws eggs at their front door even when they give him sweets at Halloween. But maybe that's the point: all children are different. Maybe Mr Nailer's asking if I understand that.

'Are we talking about any children in particular, or children as a general subset?' Did I really just say 'subset'?

Mr Nailer pushes his glasses up onto his forehead and rubs his eyes wearily. 'Hannah,' he begins, with so much exaggerated patience it makes me cringe. 'I am only asking if you like children. It isn't a trick question. But to answer *your* question, I am asking about children in general, children in classes, children on playing fields. I don't know . . .' he waves his hands about helplessly '. . . nephews and nieces, if you like? Surely you understand that, as a teacher, you will inevitably encounter *children*. It's helpful if you like them – even the difficult ones.'

'No, you misunderstand me! Of course I like children. I love children. Children are great. I've always loved children – all children.' Whoa, better rein it in a bit. 'Well, no, not every single child. Of course not! No one can say that, in the same way they can't say they like *all* people. No one says they like Hitler, Vlad the Impaler or Genghis Khan, do they, and I guess they were children once? I bet *their* teachers had a few tricky parents' evenings?' A chirp of laughter escapes me, but Mr Nailer remains unmoved.

'Probably,' he agrees after a painful pause. He flicks through his list of candidates, possibly to check I really am one of the English department's brightest and best, or maybe just to see how many more students he has to intimidate today. 'Let's just say, for the sake of argument, that you like *some* children, shall we?'

I nod meekly.

'Let's run through a few scenarios – they might help us decide what age range would suit you best. Tell me, what would you do if you found a puddle on the classroom floor?' He smiles tightly.

It's bound to be wee. I open my mouth to answer, but hesitate. Will he think I'm immature if I immediately assume it's wee? 'Could you tell me what age I'm teaching?'

3

'Early years.'

It's definitely wee. 'Does it smell of wee?' I ask tentatively.

'You tell me.'

OK, I suppose the roof could be leaking, or a child spilt their drink, so I should treat it as a random puddle to be on the safe side. 'I think I'd ask one of the teaching assistants to sort it out while I continued teaching the class.'

That sounds responsible, but Mr Nailer purses his lips. 'You don't have a teaching assistant.'

I feel a stab of annoyance. Early years? Of course I have a teaching assistant – isn't there some child-to-teacher ratio that means I have to have one? OK then, who else cleans up puddles? 'Call the caretaker?'

'The caretaker isn't available.'

Shit. 'Cleaning lady?'

'She only works after school.'

Damn it, he wants me to clear it up. Fine, if that's what it takes to make him happy. 'In that case, I'd find a mop.' I smile innocently at him.

Mr Nailer gives me a hard look and scribbles something in his notes. I crane my neck, but his writing is as illegible as a doctor's. He glances up with lightning speed, and I look away, my face reddening.

'You are teaching a junior class and notice a rat on the classroom floor. What do you do?' he fires at me.

I stare at him. What's his obsession with classroom floors? 'I assume I don't have a teaching assistant and the caretaker is unavailable?' I check.

'That is correct.'

I knew it. OK, so there's a rat on the floor. Drawing attention to the rat will cause all hell to break loose. Besides, I'm not qualified to catch a rat. Isn't that a job for the council or something? 'I ignore it and report that we have a rat problem to the school office at the end of class.'

'You ignore the rat?' he asks incredulously. 'You have thirty screaming children, some of whom are standing on desks, and one of the boys is kneeling on the floor attempting to make friends with it. He's dangerously close to having his hand bitten. You cannot ignore the rat.'

Oh great, now they're screaming. How convenient. 'I take the class outside?'

'It's raining.'

Of course it is. 'Take them to the gym?'

'There's another class having PE in there.'

There would be. Relaxing my jaw, which is starting to clench, I force a smile. 'Can I smack the rat away with a papier-mâché rocket we made last week as part of a class project on space exploration?' I wait for him to deny the existence of my papier-mâché rocket and possibly the whole concept of space exploration.

Mr Nailer opens his mouth, and an air of self-satisfaction creeps over him. 'Let's follow that thought through, shall we . . .' he glances at my CV '. . . Hannah?' I bristle. 'It's an eco-school and the children have just witnessed you beating their beloved pet mascot, Ratty. They are now traumatised. Parents will write in complaining—'

'But I'd recognise Ratty!' I explode. 'This wasn't Ratty! This was a diseased rodent from the sewers of the disgustingly underfunded and filthy school without a caretaker that I've been assigned to. I had to get the rat away from the boy, and far from being traumatised, the children don't care, in fact they're cheering and whooping with bloodlust and I'm their hero. I, on the other hand, am shaking with shock and desperately need a cup of tea, but have to carry on with the class, because I don't have a teaching assistant. As for the parents, they don't even know yet and are probably too busy working three jobs to keep their little darlings in computer games to worry about something that happened at school.

They don't even care.' I halt, breathing heavily. I think I might have gone a bit far. I might even sound like I'm panicking. Which I'm totally not . . . I don't think.

Mr Nailer leaves a telling silence, his eyebrows descending into a frown. 'Oh no, you are quite wrong – they care,' he says, his voice dripping with calm malevolence. 'Believe me, parents care. They come in, and they complain. Parents always do,' he mutters. I picture an enraged mob of parents brandishing pitch forks as Mr Nailer cowers under a minute preschool desk.

I smother a grin as he assesses his list of questions and, seeming to find them redundant, puts them to one side. He steeples his fingers and starts drumming them tip to tip. 'Entertaining as I'm sure this is, I'm going to be straight with you. Based on today and the frequent changes of career I see in your CV, I don't think teaching is the right path for you.'

'But—'

He holds up a finger. 'Teaching is not a fall-back position, it's a profession in its own right. You need zeal and determination to be good at it. Many think that because George Bernard Shaw said "He who can, does. He who cannot, teaches" they can always take up teaching, but it's simply not true. It's a vocation, and to be frank, I'm not feeling your passion.'

I know this interview hasn't gone brilliantly, but is he really turning me down? What will everyone say? Mum and Dad will be devastated, my sister Lauren will sneer and Grandma Betty's 'runt-of-the-litter, knew-she'd-come-to-no-good' disdain doesn't even bear thinking about. No, I can't leave here without a place. I have to rescue this car crash of an interview. So if he wants passion . . .

'Look, Mr Nailer, perhaps we got off on the wrong foot. I love books, I love reading and, honestly, I'm utterly passionate about teaching English. I know we've discussed early years, but I think I'd be great with secondary school children and brilliant at teaching A level. I loved it when I took it and I'd inspire them, I'm sure I would.' I can see their rapt faces staring up at me as I read out extracts from Dickens, Shakespeare and Wilde. 'I really want this. Honestly, I do! And if you want a quotation showing how I feel about teaching, how about, "The touchstone of knowledge is the ability to teach"? That's from the *Auctoritates Aristotelis*.' I know this because I looked it up when I got fed up of people quoting the Shaw one at me, and I've found that just saying *Auctoritates Aristotelis* shuts most people up. 'Mr Nailer, I want to be a teacher. Please give me a chance.' I sit back, slightly out of breath. Surely he can't refuse me after that.

But Mr Nailer is already shaking his head mournfully. 'The *Auctoritates Aristotelis* also says "Silence is a woman's finest ornament", so are you certain you want to hitch your wagon to that particular text?'

Shit, does it? I feel myself shrink to the size of a gnat.

Mr Nailer takes a resigned deep breath and as he inflates, my heart sinks. 'Secondary schools need staff who can teach all of the children in their care. There is no picking and choosing, and since English is a core subject, and only elective at A level, you must see that the majority of your time you would be teaching younger years with varying abilities and backgrounds. And what's more, the majority of job vacancies are in the less salubrious schools.'

'The ones with wet floors, no caretakers and rats?'

Mr Nailer shrugs and gives a small smile. 'Perhaps those are extreme examples, but children are not all little angels from the best homes with the highest intelligence. Schools are not all like *Malory Towers*,' he says, clearly pleased by his analogy.

I don't know what to say. I stare at the parquet floor, examining its pattern, following its zigzag joints out to the edge of the room, but he isn't finished.

'I know what you said, and I've never actually had to ask this in a PGCE interview before, but do you really want to be a teacher?' he asks gently.

I'm almost tempted to tell him the truth: yes, I'm twenty-five and I want a job with prospects, the holidays sound great, and after all the difficulties over finding funding for a second undergraduate degree I want to put my parents' minds at rest over my six-year, double-university debt. It would also be nice to have a job I can tell people about without their faces freezing awkwardly. But no, I don't want to be a teacher.

'Well?' prompts Mr Nailer.

I hoist a smile onto my face. 'Absolutely. I want to be a teacher, and I'd be really good at it. Really.'

Mr Nailer shakes his head as though I've disappointed him. 'I just don't see it, I'm afraid. Try something else. For your own good,' he adds. With a dull thud in the pit of my stomach, I realise the interview is over.

I shake his hand. 'Thank you,' I say, trying to maintain at least some semblance of dignity. 'It was nice to meet you.'

He manages a tight smile and carefully stacks his papers as I leave, somehow making my exit even more shameful.

Outside, in the waiting room, I sag onto a chair and take a few minutes to recover. I'd love to put my head in my hands and do a bit of wallowing, but two girls from my course are waiting for their interviews. I don't know them that well, and I certainly don't want to tell them what happened, so I collect my coat and try to slide by unnoticed. But then one of them beckons me over. The door's right there, but there's no acceptable way to avoid speaking to her.

'How did it go?' she asks.

I open my mouth with no idea what to say. Dreadfully? Ghastly? Fine? My phone pulses with an incoming text in my coat pocket, giving a credible impression that it's ringing, and I grab it thankfully.

'Sorry,' I mouth, holding it up apologetically. 'Good luck,' I add, and flee out the door. 'Hello? Yes, I've just come out . . .'

I babble on happily until the door is firmly closed, then sigh and run my hands through my hair. Desperate for a distraction, I head outside into the weak February sunshine and take a seat on a wall to read the text from my sister. Just sent email about next week – Mum asked me to tell you.

Next week? What's she talking about? I can only guess it's some family thing Mum has asked her to tell me about in the mistaken belief we're forever gossiping, when really Lauren has as little to do with me as possible.

The truth is, we barely tolerate each other. Lauren is a successful recruitment agent, amassing huge commissions, living the high life, partying and going through men like Tic Tacs, and in her mind I'm a nonentity and a perpetual student. We have a mutual arrangement that started in our teens where Mum and Dad thought we were inseparable and always together when really Lauren was out with friends and boys while I went to the library. Lauren had her social life, and I gained my independence. The downside is that we've had to fake a lot of friendly feelings and Mum gives us messages to pass on to each other.

I log in to my account and read Lauren's email.

To: Hannah Wilson
From: Lauren Wilson
Subject: Don't even think about saying no

Hannah,
The whole family has been invited to a party at Great-Uncle Donald's next Wednesday. Everyone's going. Aunty Pam and Uncle Nigel said even Nicholas is taking a day

off work, so you're coming too – no excuses. Take the train to Mum and Dad's on Tuesday night and one of us will collect you from the station.
Lauren

That's weird – I've never even met Great-Uncle Donald. He and Grandma Betty had a big row years ago, and she's supposedly been keeping us safe from his 'subversive influence' ever since. I wonder what's changed and why we're suddenly going to his party.

I write Lauren a quick text. It will annoy her because, as far as she's concerned, she's passed on the message, job done – so I smile as I send it. Hi Lauren. What party? Why? Hannah.

The reply comes almost immediately. Family thing – everyone meeting Great-Uncle Donald. Just say yes.

I mean, it sounds interesting, but I have an assignment due next week and also it's not all that long until my finals. I suppose I could write the essay on the train. I sigh and tap in a quick message. OK. Will be on train. Tell Mum if she phones.

Tell her yourself bleeps Lauren's reply.

I guess I should have expected that.

I pocket my phone, do up my coat and look up at the department building. My stomach squirms uncomfortably, a curdled mixture of embarrassment and annoyance. How did that interview turn into such a disaster? In fact, beyond causing actual bodily harm, I don't see how it could have gone much worse. I suppress the urge to stick out my tongue at the building before I head back to my digs. What the hell am I going to do now? Something had better turn up, because I'm all out of ideas.

2

It's Tuesday evening, it's already dark, and I'm sitting on the train to Farnborough staring dazedly at the tracery of rain trickling down the window. I've just finished reading a translation of book one of Ovid's *Metamorphoses* and I haven't taken in a single word. In fact, it might as well be written in the original Latin for all the sense I made of it. I put it down and assess my notepad, which is usually covered in doodles, comments and a primitive essay plan by now, but this time is uncompromisingly blank. I pick up my pen, worried I'll have nothing to transfer to my computer later, and write the essay title. I stare at it, then underline it, but it's no use, I simply can't focus. I slump back and tap my pen on the metal edge of the table, earning a pointed throat clearance from the businessman diagonally opposite. I stop tapping. I might as well face it – I'm too worried to write.

The trouble is that, although family get-togethers are always a bit tedious, this one, thanks to my dreadful teaching interview and my complete lack of plausible Plan B, has the potential to be gut-wrenchingly awful. There'll be the usual talk of my cousin Nicholas's medical career and how he sees himself rising through the ranks at breakneck speed, with Aunty Pam and Uncle Nigel looking on proudly as their son waxes lyrical. Then there'll be the enquiries about Lauren's marvellous commissions at the recruitment agency, predictably segueing into which famous companies she's worked with lately and how she's matched people to their perfect jobs, changing their lives forever (bring on the halo and heavenly choirs). And then Grandma Betty will turn to me, asking, 'So, what are you up to these days, Hannah? Another change of career on the horizon or are you sticking with English?' Every time without fail, followed by her falsely sweet titter. And then someone will mention my teaching interview . . .

I score another deep underline into my notepad, almost tearing the paper, and quickly put the pen down before I burrow through to the table.

I know I shouldn't care – they certainly don't, and are much more interested in Great-Uncle Donald than anything to do with me . . . so perhaps if I don't mention my interview, no one will ask.

It's possible.

And if they do remember, I could say I'm still waiting to hear. After all, I haven't officially received a rejection letter. It's not a lie, technically. And it would mean I could enjoy the day, meet Great-Uncle Donald, and tell people later . . . preferably when I'm a hundred and three and feigning senility so no one will believe me anyway.

I sit up straighter, a smile sneaking onto my face. Tomorrow could even be fun. I might find out more about the rift between Great-Uncle Donald and Grandma Betty, and how he made the shedloads of money in London – something that Grandma Betty made a snide comment about a couple of years ago but seemed unable, rather than unwilling, to elaborate on.

I wonder if he has any family? There's always tons of extended family on those lost-relative programmes on TV, so he might have kids and grandkids, too.

The train rocks unevenly as it starts to brake, and that's my cue. I quickly shove my work in my bag, haul it onto my back and stagger up the corridor. The train lurches to a stop, and I topple out onto the icy, wet platform to find it empty. My heart momentarily sinks, but if Lauren's drawn the short straw and is picking me up, she won't come out in the freezing rain to greet me off the train – she'll be waiting in her car in the pickup zone.

I hoist my bag more securely on my shoulder and make for the exit, but there are no cars in the empty spaces directly outside. I peer around, trying to shield my face from the worst of the rain, and finally spot Lauren's car on the other side of the empty car park. Honestly, Lauren could write a book on the art of passive aggression. I trudge across the howling expanse until, soaked through and exhausted, I open Lauren's boot and dump my bag inside.

'Need a hand?' Lauren calls, tapping away on her phone, not even looking up.

'No,' I say, wincing as a trickle of cold water runs under my coat sleeve and creeps up my arm as I close the boot. I get in and lean over to give Lauren a hug. 'Thanks for picking me up.'

Lauren shies away, wrinkling her nose. 'You smell like wet dog,' she says scathingly, and turns on the engine. I sniff my coat collar. It smells perfectly fine, but I'm not opening hostilities this early. Instead I hold my hands out to the hot-air vent, which gives me a much warmer reception, as we pull out of the station.

Several roundabouts and the cinema slide past before I think of anything to say.

'So, how's the latest man in your life?' I ask finally.

Lauren laughs. 'Just dumped him, actually. He turned out to be a bit of a nuisance.'

'In what way?'

Lauren overtakes a lorry on the limited stretch of dual carriageway before the next roundabout. 'Too clingy: always phoning and dropping round.'

'I thought boyfriends were supposed to do that?'

'Not mine. I expect them to be fun, take me nice places and know when to give me some space, not get on my nerves.'

I'm not sure what to say to that, so I look out of the window.

'How did the interview go?' asks Lauren. I'm surprised she's remembered. 'Am I going to have to call my little sister "Miss" from now on?'

I toy with the idea of lying to her as planned, but I can't be bothered. 'Don't tell anyone, but it was a disaster from beginning to end.'

'Everyone says that after an interview,' says Lauren. '"Oh I was awful", "Oh it was terrible",' she mimics, lifting a hand dramatically to her forehead. 'How badly can a teaching interview go? They're crying out for more teachers.'

I bite my lip, already regretting my candour. 'The interviewer hated me on sight.'

'And?' prompts Lauren.

In for a penny, in for a pound. 'And I disrespected his field of study and likened children to Hitler.'

Lauren hesitates. 'Not really? Even you're not that stupid!'

'Well, apparently I am.'

Her voice hardens. 'Jesus, Hannah! You're twenty-five. Why can't you answer a few simple questions like a normal person? Mum and Dad can't support you forever.'

I feel a hot flush of embarrassment, which I quickly bury in a shallow grave. 'They don't support me – they just gave me a loan,' I say with determined calm.

'Loan!' snorts Lauren.

'I'll pay them back.'

'What with?' Lauren gives me a cynical look and we sit in silence for a while.

'What's the plan for tomorrow?' I ask, changing the subject.

Lauren sighs heavily. 'Dad's driving us. Grandma and Grandpa are coming with Uncle Nigel and Aunty Pam. Nicholas is driving himself.'

'And has anyone said why we're going?'

'No, we just all received lavish invitations "requesting the pleasure of . . ." I've seen ours. It's all gold leaf and embossed edges.' Lauren cuts in front of a small hatchback, causing the driver to flash his lights angrily. She holds her middle finger up to the rear-view mirror.

'Why is everyone so keen to go?' I ask, hunkering down in my seat as the other driver overtakes, mouthing angrily and throwing her a few choice hand gestures of his own. 'It's not anyone's birthday or anniversary, is it?'

Lauren shrugs. 'I don't think so. At least, no one's said anything. But Aunty Pam wanted to go, and then Grandma Betty said she wasn't going to have us all listening to Donald's lies and not be there to defend herself, and suddenly we're all going.'

'Is this about the family rift, then?'

'I've no idea. I asked Mum if she or Aunty Pam know what happened, but she said the bust-up took place before they were born, and Grandma Betty's always refused to talk about it.'

'So it's a closely guarded secret, then . . . at least as far as Grandma Betty's concerned.'

Lauren frowns – something she rarely does in a bid to avoid wrinkles – then a smile spreads across her face. 'Hmm, but perhaps Great-Uncle Donald will tell me, if I ask him nicely.'

Probably – men are putty in her hands. 'Maybe, but I'd still tread carefully – I'm guessing it's a touchy subject,' I say, because telling her not to would be counter-productive.

Lauren rolls her eyes as if she's back in her teens, wearing heavy eye make-up and a choke-inducing amount of hairspray. 'Are you seriously telling me you don't want to know what the issue has been all these years?'

'Not if he wants to let bygones be bygones, so we can all be family again.'

'Fat chance! Grandma Betty won't let him back into the fold without a bucket load of grovelling,' states Lauren. She has a point.

Lauren brakes hard and swings around a roundabout towards our parents' housing estate.

'Unless it's her fault . . . and Grandma Betty's the one who should be begging forgiveness,' I add, savouring this novel thought. 'Might we see history being made and watch her apologise?'

Lauren pulls up onto the drive and applies the handbrake. There's a pause as our eyes meet and, in a rare moment of agreement, we admit how unlikely that is.

'Time to face "The Olds",' she says, using the term she favoured for our parents during our teens.

'Happy, smiling faces,' I sigh, which is what Lauren used to say to me when she slipped back in after being out all evening when she was supposed to be babysitting me. She smiles tightly.

While I collect my bag from her boot, Lauren opens the front door with her key and shouts into the house, 'Mum! Dad! We're back!' adding, 'Hannah's teaching interview was a disaster!' I close my eyes, and almost drop my bag back in the boot, climb in after it, and pull the lid closed behind me.

'Lauren! Why did you tell them about my interview?' I hiss as I join her on the doorstep.

'Oh, was it a secret?' she asks, looking impressively contrite. I grit my teeth. 'Well, you were going to tell them sooner or later, so what's the difference? At least I've saved you the trouble of breaking it to them.' Lauren gives me a big smile.

'You're so kind,' I mutter sarcastically. Happy, smiling faces, I remind myself sourly, and follow her into the house.

3

Mum and Dad were a bit tight-lipped yesterday evening, thanks to Lauren's grand announcement about my disastrous interview. As a result, I spent a fretful night trying to come up with a suitably impressive Plan B. Unfortunately, after dismissing becoming a bestselling author, internet sensation or art historian on TV (like Sister Wendy Beckett, minus the wimple), I was left with temping again. Now I'm sat in the back of the car next to Lauren feeling bleary eyed and shiftless, Lauren's on her phone swiping men's photos to the left (as she has been for the past hour), and Mum and Dad are arguing over the correct route through Wiltshire's country lanes.

'I'm sure we should have taken that last left, Steven,' says Mum.

'It was a farm track,' snaps Dad, who's still furious with her for agreeing we would come because he can't stand Uncle Nigel or Grandma Betty.

'But it says in the directions to take the first left.'

'If we'd taken *that* left, Angela, we'd have ended up in someone's field. Unless Donald is a bloody sheep, we won't find him up there!'

'There's no need to bite my head off!' Mum gives me and Lauren an obvious glance. 'Perhaps we should stop and ask Nigel. He's got satnav,' she says, gesturing to the large silver 4x4 following us.

'We are not asking Nigel or his bloody satnav – and if we had taken a wrong turn, he wouldn't still be behind us!'

I bite back a smile. I've never been able to figure out whether Dad's envious of Uncle Nigel's car or whether he just thinks he's a bit of a knob.

Silence falls and Lauren sighs and puts away her phone. She looks over Mum's shoulder at the directions and slumps back into her seat.

'It's called "The Laurels",' she says, unimpressed. 'Sounds like an old people's home.'

'Does it?'

'Of course it does. Fan-bloody-tastic, a day off spent with lots of old biddies sat watching us drink tea.' She mimes shooting herself in the head.

I force a smile. 'We're only there to see Great-Uncle Donald, aren't we? The rest doesn't matter.'

'Whatever,' she huffs, peering out at the countryside.

Noticing Lauren's perfectly manicured claws, I inspect my uneven nails and nibble at a rough edge. She turns back and I drop my hand, curling my fingers under so she can't see them.

'I mean, what constitutes a party in an old people's home?' she bleats. 'More than three people in a room? Cups of tea *and* cake? And what can we possibly have to talk about?'

I cast about for ideas. 'I don't know. What we do? What we like? Isn't that what most people are interested in – gossip and news?'

'I suppose,' she agrees grudgingly. 'I can always tell him about my work. He won't appreciate the intricacies, but people usually understand how successful I am from the commission I make . . . though, on second thoughts, perhaps I should play that down. He might not leave me anything if he thinks I'm loaded.'

'What do you mean?'

'I mean, when he dies I don't want him passing me over because he thinks I'm doing well enough already.'

I gasp. 'Lauren, that's horrible! You haven't even met him yet!'

'No, but he's old and he's family.' She gives me a conde-scending look. 'Don't tell me you haven't thought about it? He's supposed to be rich, and why else would he want to meet us all? Why do you think we came?'

I stare at her.

'Oh, don't play the innocent with me. I know you've thought about it,' she whispers, her eyes narrowing.

'I can honestly say it never crossed my mind.'

A smile sneaks onto her face. 'Of course it has. You're planning to butter him up, just as much as I am. And with things going the way they are for you right now, you'd be stupid not to,' she adds, just loud enough for me to hear.

I stare at her in mute disbelief. I feel sick, both about my own situation and what she's suggesting. It's awful! I turn away and close my eyes. I hope Donald has a brood of twenty grandchildren all lining up to inherit. It would serve her right if he did.

Lauren nudges me hard. 'We're here,' she says.

I must have dozed off, because we're passing between peeling cast-iron gates. There's a hand-painted sign proclaim-ing it's 'The Laurels', and we're plunged into the green gloom of its overgrown namesakes. After a few moments, we emerge onto a large semi-circular sweep of gravel in front of a gorgeous and well-maintained Georgian house that bears none of the hallmarks of being an old people's home.

'Oh,' gasps Lauren. 'Grandma Betty wasn't joking about him having a few quid, then!'

'No, she wasn't,' agrees Dad.

I sit up to see better and the warm brick frontage, sash windows and delicately proportioned portico with classical sandstone pillars practically sweep me into a Jane Austen novel and an empire-line dress. I'm still gaping, sweetshop window-style, as we park and Nicholas and Uncle Nigel pull alongside us in a scrunch of gravel. Nicholas is smiling away to himself in his swanky Porsche, and I suspect he's thinking along the same lines as Lauren. But Uncle Nigel, with eyes only for his massive car, gets out with a polishing cloth and lovingly starts cleaning the bugs off his bonnet and grill.

I open my door to hear Grandma Betty complaining – not that there's anything unusual in that, but she's looking pointedly at Uncle Nigel.

'. . . forgotten his manners. A gentleman should help a lady out of his car.'

'You know what he's like about his Land Rover,' says Aunty Pam, and Dad grunts in moody agreement.

Grandma Betty opens her mouth to reply, but words fail her as she finally takes in the magnificence of the house. She stares up at it, frowning, her mouth slightly open. Her expression adjusts into a look of haughty unconcern and her mouth snaps shut as the front door swings open.

'You've arrived,' exclaims a cheerful old man, roughly Grandma Betty's age, coming out and holding his arms wide in welcome. This must be Great-Uncle Donald. He looks so kind and grandfatherly, and is so clearly pleased to see us despite never having met most of us before, that I can't help responding with a smile of my own.

Lauren comes over to stand by me. 'Yummy,' she mutters, and for one very strange moment I think she's talking about Uncle Donald. Then I see that her eyes are unashamedly locked onto a man standing just behind him. I crane my neck to see better, and to be fair he is rather gorgeous. He's about Lauren's age, dressed in black jeans and a crisp white shirt, and his lazy confidence and slightly over-long hair suggest he's taking a day off from his rock band. As he steps out from under the portico, his eyes lock onto mine. I quickly look away, but his distrustful and piercing glower sears itself into my thoughts.

'Who do you think he is?' I whisper to Lauren, careful to keep my eyes averted.

'No idea. Friend? Grandson, maybe?'

I check to see if there's any other family here, but all I see is Grandma Betty's face etched into lines of deepest loathing as she regards Donald and his haughty friend. Donald's friend smiles at her, but there's a hint of a challenge in his eyes and Grandma Betty's jaw clenches. Just as she's about to speak, Donald claps his hands together, summoning everyone's attention.

'I'm so glad you could all make it – lovely! Do come in, it's much warmer inside.' He beckons to us with a charming eagerness, but before we can make our way forward, Grandma Betty turns on him.

'Still no better than you should be, I see, Donald?' she booms, with a voice projected straight out of Shakespearean theatre. 'Toy boys?' She indicates Donald's friend. 'Really!'

My mouth drops open. Lauren lets out a shocked laugh, but then her eyes flick suspiciously between Donald and the young man, and everyone else seems struck dumb. But far from being offended, Donald's friend hides a smile behind his hand, and Donald regards Grandma Betty with an air of polite bafflement.

'I beg your pardon?' he asks.

'Honestly!' spits Grandma Betty, and strides into the house, not bothering to introduce us. We all stare after her. God, this is excruciating.

Shaking his head as though to clear it, Great-Uncle Donald steps forward, holding his hand out to Grandpa Albert. 'Dear chap, how are you?' he asks mildly.

Grandpa Albert shakes his hand. 'Very well, thank you. Pleased to see you again after all these years.'

'And it's been so many. Betty's on top form, I see?' Lauren and I exchange a look.

'Yes,' agrees Grandpa Albert, shrugging helplessly. 'Not quite her usual ... yes ...' He smiles at Donald, perhaps hoping he'll fill in the rest. 'This is the family,' he says, indicating all of us. I smile and give a tiny wave.

Donald nods. 'So it is, and most welcome. But it's too cold to meet everyone out here. How about we go inside and have a drink?'

Grandpa Albert nods gratefully and leads the way inside. We all follow, venturing timid 'hellos' to Donald and his friend as we pass.

Behind me, and last in the queue, Nicholas holds out his hand, grinning like a crocodile. 'It's most excellent to meet you, Great-Uncle Donald,' he says pompously.

I glance back and just catch Donald's surprised expression before he returns the handshake. 'And you,' he says.

'This all yours?' asks Nicholas, indicating the house, and I hurry after the others, hoping to disassociate myself from Nicholas's mercenary question.

The lovely oak-floored entrance hall with a staircase winding around it is grand in itself, but I blink in awe as I enter the drawing room. Its tall windows let the light stream in, and the furnishings are all soft and tasteful. No one else seems fased by it, though Grandpa Albert is at one window gazing longingly out at the garden. Grandma Betty has made herself at home in an armchair, while everyone else is standing, or else perched uncomfortably on the edges of seats. Nicholas follows me in and makes a beeline for one of the twin sofas. Still standing, I watch Great-Uncle Donald come in. He surveys us kindly, and winks at his friend. Lauren is watching them carefully, so I wonder what she made of that.

'Dear family, thank you for coming.' Donald beams at us, and I grin back. 'I asked you here today because I thought it would be fun to see what has become of you all. And, since I'm sure you are just as curious about me, let's begin with some introductions. I am, of course, Donald, or Uncle Donald, should you prefer. Please leave off the "Great" – I am "great", of course, but it's such a mouthful.' His eyebrows rise, willing Grandma Betty to share the joke, but she's a tough crowd. 'And this is Alec.' Donald's friend gives a stern nod, then folds his arms and leans back against the wall, like a school inspector set to observe rather than participate. 'He is my faithful second-in-command here at The Laurels.'

'That's one way to describe him,' blares Grandma Betty. She's not going to let this drop.

'Would you prefer secretary? Or personal assistant? Maybe right-hand man?' Donald offers, savouring every syllable.

'I call a spade a spade, as you well know.'

'How original of you, but he really *is* my PA,' says Uncle Donald, and the air almost crackles between them.

'Just your PA, or also your PA?' retorts Grandma Betty pointedly, but before Uncle Donald can reply, a waiter and waitress bustle in carrying trays of drinks. Good timing! I'm more than ready for a drink.

'Ah, refreshments! I've always loved a Pimm's cocktail,' says Uncle Donald, breaking eye contact with Grandma Betty to make sure we each take a glass. He pauses and I scrabble for something to say, and clearly everyone else is struggling as well because the silence deepens. Uncle Donald sighs as if we're all disappointing children, and raises his glass. 'To family,' he toasts, and I take a big sip. Wow, that's good. 'And reunions,' he adds, and I take another deep swig.

Lauren whispers something to Mum and laughs, breaking the silence and, as everyone starts to talk, Uncle Donald threads his way over to Grandma Betty. Curious, I follow and take a seat on the sofa by Mum so I can listen.

'Betty, darling, how are you?' he asks.

'Oh it's "Betty darling" now, is it? It's been half a century, Donald. You disappeared, leaving me to look after our parents – left their funerals before I could speak to you. And now you expect me to . . . what . . . chat? Just what is this . . .' I turn my head just enough to catch her flapping her free hand at us all '. . . party of yours all about?'

I get the feeling this isn't quite the verbal assassination she had planned, but she's obviously furious. Uncle Donald perches on the arm of the sofa, next to me.

'Now then, Betty, don't be angry. You know why I had to leave, and after that you didn't want to know me. *You* were the one who returned my cheques – not that it was your place to do so, considering they were meant for our parents.'

'We didn't want your filthy money,' she hisses. 'God knows where it came from. I wanted help, someone to take on the burden of responsibility, not your . . .' she hesitates, '. . . money!' she finishes lamely, but with an immense amount of disgust.

'Money can buy that kind of help,' he points out gently.

I lean back casually to get a glimpse of Grandma Betty, who takes a furious sip of her drink, narrowly avoiding taking in a whole slice of orange. 'It can't buy dignity!' Her eyes fall on me and I lean forward again, busying myself with my phone.

'Ah, that old chestnut: what price dignity? But why quibble? We both know you were more than capable.'

'I didn't have much choice, did I?'

'Of course you did, but you must always make your point.'

I sneak another look. Grandma Betty's gaping like a landed halibut, and before she can recover, Uncle Donald gets up, winks at me, and moves on to introduce himself to Dad. Dad, who can't stand Grandma Betty, welcomes him like a long-lost relative – which, I suppose, he kind of is.

Lauren gets up and strolls over to join them. 'Hi, I'm Lauren,' she says, thrusting her hand into Donald's.

'Lovely to meet you,' he says, smiling back at her. 'So, what do you do, Lauren?'

'I'm a Recruitment Executive,' says Lauren grandly, and Dad, after a moment's hesitation, leaves them to it.

'It's a very lucrative business from what I've heard?'

'Yes,' she agrees, though from what she said in the car, this isn't the way Lauren wants the conversation to go. 'And rightly so, because good employees are the foundation of successful businesses. That's where I come in: helping companies find the right staff to take them forward into the future.'

'Oh? I've met a few people in recruitment in my time,' says Donald, frowning slightly. 'From what I understand, it takes a certain . . . zeal.' That's one word for it.

Lauren laughs exuberantly. 'It takes a lot of hard work, that's for sure. You have to make connections and build relationships with people, but I see what you're getting at – like in every industry, there are good ones and bad ones.' Then she adds sweetly, 'I'm one of the good ones.'

As she starts to describe her work, Grandma Betty bustles up to them. 'We're very proud of Lauren,' she says, interrupting when Lauren pauses for breath. I take a big sip of my drink. 'Tell Donald about your commission,' she prompts, and I struggle to swallow.

'Isn't it vulgar to talk about money?' asks Lauren, her smile tightening. 'What's important is that we match the right people to the correct jobs, set them up for the future and leave everyone happy.'

'Oh, I was under the impression that it's quite a cut-throat industry,' says Donald.

'It can be, but I rely on charm and subtle persuasion.' Lauren smiles coyly.

'Really?' he asks, and I have to hide a smile.

'Of course, and once people realise I'm there to make their dreams come true, everyone's happy,' says Lauren, oozing confidence. 'Think of me as a fairy godmother.'

'I must say, it sounds like it's come a long way since the days when you were referred to as head-hunters. No nasty tactics, underhand negotiations, or devastated companies left without key members of staff?' Lauren's eyes dart about nervously. 'Marvellous! Well done!' he says.

I snort unbecomingly. Grandma Betty turns and I quickly assume an expression of disinterested boredom, but her eyes narrow.

'This is my other granddaughter, Hannah. Have you met?' I start at my name and flinch, wishing Grandma Betty wasn't the one introducing me.

'I don't believe I've had the pleasure,' says Donald, turning to me.

I stand up a little too hurriedly and my drink slops over the rim of my glass. The hand I hold out to him is a little wet. 'Sorry,' I say as he shakes it.

Grandma Betty frowns at me. 'Hannah took history, then changed to art history. And now she's finishing up an English degree.' I try to smile, but I know what's coming next. 'Not quite sure how that will help, but she'll be the most qualified of all of us by the time she's done – ha ha.' I hold very still, waiting for the rest. 'Apart from Nicholas, of course. Yes, it's a shame arts subjects aren't more useful, but there we are. She can always teach.'

'But poor Hannah's teaching interview went terribly,' says Lauren, pouting in mock sympathy. I glare at her.

'Did it?' asks Nicholas, scenting blood and coming to join us.

Everyone's eyes are on me, burning with curiosity, except for Donald's PA, whose expression is one of cold indifference.

Why is there never a cataclysmic, ground-opening event when you need one?

'Yes, it wasn't my best day,' I say, trying to sound like it doesn't bother me at all.

'How did you put it?' asks Lauren mercilessly. 'A disaster from beginning to end? And didn't you mention Hitler or something?' She laughs, putting a sisterly hand on my shoulder. There are times when I wish I knew the Vulcan nerve pinch.

'Yes. I wouldn't recommend doing that,' I agree quietly, pretending it's funny, but I can't quite meet Donald's gaze, and my hands are shaking.

'Honestly!' says Grandma Betty, shaking her head. 'There are some things you wouldn't think needed spelling out.'

'No,' agrees Nicholas, and they're all laughing. I shove my fists in my pockets so no one can see my white knuckles, but I meet Donald's eye for a split second and I'm pretty sure he's twigged how I'm feeling.

'And this is my grandson, Nicholas,' says Grandma Betty, thankfully shifting the spotlight. 'He's always been incredibly intelligent: top in school, head boy, excellent A levels, and qualified as one of the high-flyers in his year in Medicine. Now he works at a hospital healing people. Can there be a nobler calling?' Grandma Betty asks reverently, and I edge my way out of their circle as, full of false modesty, Nicholas admits it's all true.

'Do you like it?' asks Uncle Donald as I slide myself down onto the sofa again.

'I beg your pardon?' asks Nicholas, completely wrong-footed by Donald's benign and yet unusual question.

'I just wondered if you *like* it? Do you *like* working in a hospital "healing people"? Not a germaphobe or anything?'

Nicholas looks confused. 'Yes . . . I mean no. Well . . . I have benefitted a great deal from my time there,' he says, regaining his composure, and wrangling his train of thought back on track. 'But it's not where I see myself in five years' time.'

Donald raises an eyebrow. 'No?'

Nicholas smiles his best granny-charmer smile. 'Actually, I've recently been given the chance to join two university friends in setting up a brand new private clinic.'

Wow. The room falls silent. This must be news to everyone. Lauren gives up trying to be a part of their conversation and plonks herself down next to me, defeated.

'Really?' prompts Uncle Donald. 'That sounds interesting?'

'Yes, it's very exciting,' smarms Nicholas, exuding his usual confidence once again. 'The clinic will have the very best facilities and clientele, with the customer interface being truly twenty-first century in its approach. It'll have all the best diagnostic tools and state-of-the-art treatment. Healthcare is changing,' he explains, and I can tell he's rehearsed this pitch until he's word-perfect. 'NHS waiting lists are lengthening, and people have a right to expect a better standard of service. And if you can pay for it – why not?' He nods sanctimoniously. 'It's an excellent opportunity both career-wise and patient-wise. For our shareholders, it's a superb business proposition, expecting to offer a substantial return on any money invested. It's a win-win situation.'

He's advertising so brazenly, I almost hear a 'ting' and see a star sparkle on his teeth. I try to catch Uncle Donald's eye, desperate to communicate I'm not in on this, but he's not looking my way. I glance involuntarily at Donald's PA – I mean Alec – whose frown has deepened dangerously; his mouth is now a hard line.

'Sounds wonderful. Could I invest?' asks Donald eagerly. I glance at Alec in alarm, expecting him to step in, but instead of intervening he leans back against the bookcase with an amused smirk on his face. Have I missed something?

Nicholas smiles. 'Oh yes, absolutely.'

'And if I invested, would you be my personal physician?'

'Not me, no. My specialism is not your area, but James and Rupert are excellent doctors – some of the best in the country. You'd be in excellent hands.'

Donald assumes a demeanour of polite interest. 'So, what is your area, exactly?'

'I'm a gynaecologist,' says Nicholas, and I suppress my usual shudder at the excruciating thought of him being anywhere near my . . . area.

'A gynaecologist?' muses Donald, his expression brightening. 'Well, I know there's a need for them, dear boy, but what a frightful job. From what I've heard, women dread their visits, and what about girlfriends? What do they make of your work? Must make things very difficult in the bedroom . . . or are you gay?' he adds thoughtfully.

'I'm not gay!' splutters Nicholas, and I let out a snort of laughter. Honestly, I could kiss Uncle Donald!

'Calm down, nothing wrong with it,' soothes Uncle Donald, giving me an alarmed sideways glance as he reaches to pat Nicholas's arm.

Nicholas flinches. 'I'm not gay,' he repeats in a much deeper voice. 'And I don't have a problem with women. Ask anyone.' He turns, appealing to the rest of us, but how the hell would I know?

'But don't girls cross their legs when they find out what you do?' persists Donald. 'If the roles were reversed, it would put me right off! How do you get a date?'

'I have no trouble at all. I'm quite the catch!' protests Nicholas, and Uncle Donald starts laughing. 'I am!' Donald laughs harder. 'Tell him,' he orders his mum, his voice plaintive now, but Aunty Pam shakes her head helplessly, and Donald hoots in delight.

'I bet he just says he's a doctor and flashes his Porsche

keys,' I say to Lauren, just as Donald stops to breathe in unexpectedly, and the room freezes.

Oh God, everyone heard.

Within a fraction of a second Mum shuts her eyes, Aunty Pam, Grandma Betty and Nicholas all turn to stare at me, and Alec's mouth finally breaks free into a massive grin.

Donald, having taken in some much-needed air, roars with fresh laughter and cries out with glee: 'I *knew* there was a reason for the car!'

I stare at everyone, aghast, a bright blush blooming across my face. I wish I could stop it, but it only deepens. Honestly, how evolution ever thought lighting up like a beacon might be useful is beyond me. But as I bask in the heat of my own cheeks, being basted by everyone's accusing glares, Donald's laughter turns into a worryingly intense coughing fit. It's so bad that, despite my disgrace, everyone's attention is pulled to him. We watch, frozen, as he runs out of breath, hovering interminably at the end of his exhale, and Alec rushes to his side.

'Breathe,' Alec orders, his voice soothing yet urgent. 'Come on! Breathe!'

There's a moment's indecision, then Donald inhales loudly, holding his chest, his eyes bulging in alarm. I've been holding my breath too, and let it out with relief.

'Slowly, now. Are you all right?' Alec asks him, and I'm struck by the tenderness in his tone. Lauren seems less impressed by his concern, but I reckon she's still trying to evaluate whether Alec might be boyfriend material. 'Slowly,' Alec reminds Donald.

Donald raises his eyebrows and nods, his face pallid. He takes a moment to recover, but once I know that he's all right, I seize the opportunity to slip out of the room onto the terrace.

I stand for a moment, allowing my mortified blush to recede and breathing in the cool wintery air, then give an involuntary shiver. It's freezing out here.

I wrap my arms around myself and notice Grandpa Albert pottering about in the flowerbed immediately below the terrace – he's an amazing escape artist when it comes to family parties. Taking care to keep away from the windows, I tiptoe over.

'Hello, Grandpa,' I whisper.

He jumps. 'Ah! Hello Hannah.' He gives me a distracted smile and returns his attention to the flowerbed. 'Anyone looking for me?'

'No.' I decide not to mention what happened indoors. 'I just came out for some air.'

'I saw a nice bench down on the lawn, if that helps?' He indicates the direction with a tilt of his head. 'It's in the sun, but take a coat – it's chilly.'

Leaving Grandpa Albert to plunge ever deeper into the foliage, I thank my lucky stars that Dad hasn't locked his car. I collect my coat and, keeping well out of sight of the house, hurry down the garden and find the bench. Making myself comfortable and, determined not to think about whether everyone now thinks I'm a complete bitch, I focus on a robin that's hopping about on the lawn. It flies up the garden, possibly to see if Grandpa Albert has unearthed any worms, and I shift my attention to the clouds, trying to enjoy the peace of the moment.

Hearing someone coming down the steps, I sit very still, waiting to see who it is. But it isn't Mum or Dad as I had hoped. It's Alec. I feel myself redden as he sits down beside me, and risking a quick look at him, he raises his eyebrows in a way that suggests I should explain myself. I look down, knowing that he's still watching me.

'I thought it best if I make myself scarce,' I explain.

'Hmm. So you didn't run away, then?'

'No,' I say, though we both know that isn't true.

'Well, you certainly made an impression. Or was that your intention?' he asks, watching me closely.

'No, of course it wasn't. It was just a stupid joke that I only meant for Lauren to hear, but then the room went silent at exactly the wrong moment and everyone heard.' I let out an exasperated sigh, annoyed at myself as much as anyone, and stare down at my fingers as I remember the chilling pin-drop silence, followed by Donald's roar of laughter. 'It wouldn't have been as bad if Donald hadn't found it so hilarious.'

'You can't blame Donald!'

'I'm not! Not exactly. But you have to admit he made it worse, because now everyone's blaming me for turning Nicholas into a laughing stock.'

I glance at Alec, but rather than showing understanding, his eyebrows have drawn together reproachfully. 'You started it, and you can't expect Donald not to laugh when your cousin's face was such a picture.' I roll my eyes. 'And then there was your grandmother's horror,' he points out mercilessly.

'Oh God,' I say, rubbing my forehead anxiously. Grandma Betty is going to have a field day with this – or perhaps that should be a field decade.

'In fact, I haven't seen Donald laugh that hard in ages. You almost killed him.' Alec frowns heavily at me. 'But then perhaps that was your plan: knock off Donald and inherit his fortune?'

I give him a sideways glare. I assume he's joking, but it's impossible to tell.

'Only an idiot would think I could engineer a lethal coughing fit through hysterical laughter,' I say acidly, and there's a nasty silence. 'Is he OK?' I ask more gently.

'He's fine. Still chuckling every so often, which makes Nicholas blush.' Alec tries to look forbidding, but the corners of his mouth are twitching.

I close my eyes for a second, wishing I could redo the last half hour. 'I'm never going to hear the end of this.'

'Probably not,' agrees Alec, his voice indifferent. He clearly couldn't care less.

'So, why are you out here? Or did you just come out to accuse me of attempted murder?' I ask, glaring at him.

'Actually, Donald sent me. He would like you . . .' Alec sketches a flourishing and yet sarcastic bow in his seat '. . . to be his companion at lunch.'

'Why?' I blurt out, and he stares at me, taken aback. 'What I mean is, I'm not interesting, and if I say anything else, Grandma Betty's going to skin me. Try Lauren,' I offer, and immediately hate myself for saying it.

'He asked for you, not Lauren,' says Alec. 'Although I can't think why,' he adds, then sighs. 'Just say yes,' he says impatiently.

That's easy for him to say. I blow out a breath and gaze at the church spire peeking out from behind the trees and the pretty varied roofs of the village with fields and rolling hills behind them. I suppose Uncle Donald did choose me over Lauren, which makes a pleasant change, and since I'm already in trouble with Grandma Betty . . . My stomach gives a hungry groan.

'What's the problem?' he asks irritably. 'You're only being asked to eat some food and have a chat. You should give him a chance – he's giving you one,' says Alec, in a tone that suggests he doesn't think I deserve it.

I sigh, trying to understand Donald's motives. 'Can I ask you a question?'

'You can ask,' he says, leaning back and regarding me warily.

'Why has he invited us here after all this time?'

Alec's eyes dart to mine. 'That's for him to say, don't you think?'

'I suppose so. I was just trying to figure out why he would want to see any of us.' Alec's eyebrows flick up involuntarily. It seems I've struck a chord. 'What's he like?' I ask, changing tack.

'He's great,' says Alec guardedly. I'd get better answers from the bench we're sitting on.

I persevere. 'I mean, what's he really like, as a person?'

Alec hesitates, then pushes his hand through his hair. He looks out at the view. 'He's honourable, decent, fun, clever, excellent company . . .' As Alec turns, his expression holds a warning. 'He's *the best* of people.'

OK, I get the message. 'What about his great sense of humour,' I ask drily, meeting his eyes and daring him to admit that he's laying it on a bit thick. 'Or his clear naughty streak?' I saw how much he enjoyed baiting Grandma Betty, and I know Alec did too.

Alec smiles, despite his clear intention to remain defensive and annoyed. 'Yes,' he admits grudgingly. 'He can be *extremely* badly behaved.'

I can't help laughing. 'I like that about him – it's refreshing.'

Alec looks at me quizzically and, for a moment at least, we're on the same page. 'What do you make of him?' he asks curiously.

I stare at him. He has very long eyelashes. Not that I'm swayed by looks. I shift my gaze across the valley and collect my thoughts. 'I'm not sure. I think he's clever, because he's seeing through all the rubbish my family are trying to lay on him.' Alec nods. I wait for him to say something, but he just stares at me, a light crease forming between his eyebrows. 'Apart from that . . .' I shrug, looking at the view again. My stomach gives another embarrassing groan, and I have to bolt my jaws together to stop myself from giggling.

'I guess it's lunchtime,' he says, like it was a clock chiming, but just as I think he's going to smile, he gets up and starts to

walk off. 'I'm going, even if you aren't,' he calls without looking back, and I roll my eyes.

'Of course I'm coming,' I say, getting to my feet and hurry-
ing to catch up. 'It's not like I have a choice,' I mutter.

Alec stops and turns so abruptly that I almost bump into
him. 'I'll make sure to tell Donald you *leapt* at the chance to
sit with him, shall I?' he asks scathingly. I glare up at him, but
suddenly we're too close for comfort and he steps back.
'After you,' he says, holding out his hand to show the way.

I adjust my coat and, annoyed by his pointedly excessive
show of manners, stalk past him up the steps, only just
remembering to call Grandpa Albert as I go.

4

Call me a chicken, but I hide behind Alec as we enter the drawing room. I needn't have bothered, because Donald is waiting for us and he takes my arm, folding it into his own, before announcing that it's time for lunch.

'Tell me, Hannah,' Donald says, as he leads me along the corridor. 'What's the story between you and Betty? I couldn't help noticing there was a little friction there.'

I shrug, wondering what to tell him. It feels wrong to talk about her behind her back, but it's not like she makes much effort to be fair to me. 'I'm not one of her favourites.'

'I gathered that,' he says with a small smile. 'How come?'

I shake my head. 'I'm not sure really. I think it goes back to when I was little. Every time Lauren pulled my hair or something similar, Grandma Betty was only ever watching when I did it back. She got the impression I was a bit of a troublemaker.'

'And how does that make you feel?' asks Donald.

'Usually it doesn't bother me that much, but sometimes it can be very irritating. Like today,' I add, feeling hot just thinking about it.

'Yes, but luckily for you, I know her of old!' he says conspiratorially as we enter the dining room. I stare at the massive dining table laid out with enough cutlery and glasses for a banquet. It's how I always imagined royal dinners would be. I sit down in the chair he pulls out for me.

'Though I'm surprised she didn't see through that ruse, considering it was one of her tactics when we were children. Hmm,' he says thoughtfully. 'Maybe she and Lauren are kindred spirits,' he says, taking his seat at the head of the table.

I bite back a smile at the thought of presenting this theory to Lauren, and watch everyone else file in. Alec sits opposite me, fixing me with a look that lets me know he's watching my every move. I give him a scathing glare, and promptly look away as I notice Donald watching us beadily. Mum, Dad, Aunty Pam, Uncle Nigel and Lauren all sit further down the table near Nicholas, leaving the place next to me empty, perhaps shunning the traitor who showed him up. Grandma Betty comes in last with Grandpa Albert, muttering darkly about 'muddy trousers'. She takes the stately chair at the opposite end of the table from Uncle Donald, and Grandpa Albert comes sheepishly to take the empty seat next to me.

Grandma Betty glares at us and picks up a side plate to examine the maker's mark. I can only assume it's a good one, because she mumbles 'so ostentatious' before putting it down and allowing the waitress to pour her wine.

Donald smirks. 'She's certainly fulfilled her potential,' he whispers, nodding at Grandma Betty. 'She's the younger of the two of us, and yet she was always a force to be reckoned with. Bossy Betty – quite terrifying, even at a young age.'

Grandpa Albert picks up his napkin and drapes it across his knee with excessive care. I bite my lip, worried he heard Donald's comment, and watch Aunty Pam nod enthusiastically to the waiter offering her wine. I smile gratefully as the waitress pours some for me.

'To a magnificent lunch!' toasts Uncle Donald when we all have full glasses, and everyone takes a sip. It's nice wine, but what with the Pimm's and now this, I can't help wondering if he's trying to get us drunk. If so, given how the day's going, I'm all in.

The waiter and waitress return carrying bowls of soup and baskets of bread. There are even little dishes of butter curls sprinkled with sea salt. It smells lovely and I'm dying to dig in, but everyone is waiting for Donald.

'Winter squash soup,' he explains, and reaches for his spoon. 'Wonderful on a chilly day,' he says, and as his spoon touches his soup, we all tuck in.

After a few seconds of only the chink of cutlery on crockery, the atmosphere loosens and everyone starts to relax. The conversation levels gently rise and I wonder whether I should be making conversation too. I peek at Grandpa Albert, but he's concentrating on buttering his bread. Alec's eyes are on me, but I think we've talked enough.

'So, having not been politely introduced, how about we start with the fundamentals?' asks Donald, turning to me with a polite smile.

I smile back. 'I'm Hannah, female, age twenty-five, studying English. Lauren's my sister.' I cast around for something else he might find interesting, but can't think of anything. 'What else do you want to know?'

'I suppose that's the real question, isn't it,' says Uncle Donald. 'What do any of us want to know about our fellow man?' He nods thoughtfully. 'How about we start with the fun stuff? What is your favourite thing to do?' There's a subtle challenge in his eyes.

'Reading,' I say, and smile at this innocent conversation stopper. This is usually where people falter, drift away, or talk to people on their other side.

He laughs, and I get the feeling he knows exactly what I'm thinking. 'Where?' he asks. Where? What a weird question.

'Umm, anywhere really?' His eyebrows raise expectantly, and I stare down at my bowl, racking my brains for a more interesting answer. 'Outside, under a tree is nice. Or, if it's raining, on the window seat at the turn of the stairs at my parents' house.'

'What do you like to read?'

'Anything well written: I love the classics, I relax with mysteries, and I even like children's books. It depends on my mood and how robust I'm feeling.' I try to focus on my plate, but it's hard to resist checking how he's taking my answers.

'And what's your favourite book?'

I stare at him in consternation. How can he expect me to choose just one?

He must sense my bewilderment because he chuckles. 'The book you go back to when you're too exhausted to cope with anything new. The book you turn to when you want to hide. Your comfort book,' he clarifies, watching me closely.

'What's yours?' I ask, suddenly curious.

'John Buchan, *The Thirty-Nine Steps*. Boys' adventure! Always loved it.'

'Mine's *Jane Eyre*.'

Uncle Donald nods. 'Displaced, unappreciated, feisty female, celebrated for her intelligence not her looks, and far from being rescued by her beloved, does the rescuing.' My spoon stops halfway to my mouth and I stare at him. I can't believe he's read so much into my answer. And it's all true.

Alec huffs sceptically, and I glare at him, daring him to question my choice. Donald warns Alec with an admonitory glance and continues.

'Good choice. Do you hold grudges?' he asks, catching me off guard with another swift change of topic and easily pulling me back into our conversation.

'Erm . . . not grudges, really, but I'm not sure I always like people very much. What about you?' I say, trying to turn the conversation away from myself, especially since I suspect Alec's listening.

'I'm careful who I trust,' he says lightly. 'What are your goals in life? Betty mentioned teaching?' I freeze, and Donald holds up his hands in apology. 'I know the interview went badly and you don't have to tell me if you don't want to. I just wondered whether that was your dream?' We sit back so the waiter and waitress can clear our bowls, but I can tell he isn't deterred.

'No, it's not my dream,' I say, sitting forward again. 'And I think that might have been the problem. My interviewer knew I was treating it as a fall-back position, and it went downhill from there.' I glance at Donald, and he pats my hand.

'It wasn't meant to be,' he says reassuringly.

'Especially not after I likened children to brutal dictators and recommended animal cruelty as a sensible course of action.'

Donald barks out a laugh. 'I'll take your word for it. So, not teaching,' he concludes, taking a sip of his wine, clearly ready to start up again with his questions. 'So, what *do* you want to do – no holds barred, fairy tales allowed?'

I glance at him, puzzled. Why is he so interested in me?

'Really, truly?' he adds, his smile both mischievous and kind. 'I promise I won't laugh, or judge, and I *definitely* won't tell anyone.' He glares meaningfully down the table.

To my surprise, I actually want to tell him, which is odd because I've never told anyone. But for some reason I trust him. 'I want to be a writer,' I say, so quietly I'm almost mouthing it. Alec's watching us, but I don't think he heard.

Donald leans in a little closer, enthralled. 'What's stopping you?' he asks just as quietly.

It's a fair question and I hunt for the answer. 'Me, I think? I had a bit of a bad experience when I was younger.' My eyes flick involuntarily to Lauren. 'And it took a while for me to start writing again. When I finally had a full manuscript and got up the guts to send it to agents, they all rejected it. It was heartbreaking. The ones who wrote back told me my writing had promise but lacked depth . . . and if I'm honest, they're right. I don't know what it's like to be . . . I don't know . . . blissful, petrified, exhilarated, in love or successful. I just know what it's like to be . . . well . . . me. So I write for myself and I enjoy that.' I can't help frowning. 'I really do, but it doesn't pay the bills, and I doubt it ever will.' I look at Donald, suddenly frightened by how honest I've been. 'Sorry, I've let my mouth run away with itself.'

'No, you haven't,' he disagrees, giving me a sincere smile. 'If anything, I'm honoured that you've told me – you've given me a real answer to a difficult question and I respect that.'

I hesitate, but I might not get this opportunity again any time soon. 'Then can I ask you something?'

'Of course.'

'What's your advice? I mean, to someone in my position.'

'You mean from my position of great wisdom and years?' he chortles.

'If you like.'

'Hmm.' He thinks for a moment and I'm grateful that he's taking my question seriously. 'I'd say be brave. Don't let people make you feel insignificant – always remember they don't have the right. Then I'd say get out there; decide what you want to do and damned well do it. If it's writing, then get any old job to tide you over while you write. If finding out about life will make you a better writer, then do that. Don't settle for a second-rate life.'

'Thank you,' I say, and I truly mean it.

He nods almost imperceptibly and as we sit back to allow the next course to be placed in front of us, I notice Alec watching us with an inscrutable expression. Embarrassed, I examine my carefully filleted fish, draped on an island of wilted spinach in *beurre blanc* and caper sauce – it looks like a dish made in a Michelin-starred restaurant.

Donald clears his throat and I turn my attention back to him, then jump as Grandpa Albert lays his hand on mine. 'I'm sorry to interrupt, Hannah, but she'll come over if I don't.'

The four of us, including Alec, look down the table at Grandma Betty, who's staring at us with alarming intensity. I bet she hasn't blinked since we sat down.

'We're only talking,' I tell Grandpa Albert, and he nods wearily, though I catch Alec's eyebrow darting up sceptically in my peripheral vision. I guess it was quite a deep conversation, but still.

'I realise that, but she doesn't like it. Perhaps if we discuss the food for a moment or two?'

'Of course, Albert,' says Donald magnanimously. 'Tell me, what do you think to my excellent chef? He's on loan from a neighbouring dignitary's household . . .'

The rest of lunch passes peacefully, with excellent food and Donald and I carefully confining ourselves to general topics and including Grandpa Albert. Getting up from the table, and surprised I'm not wedged between the arms of the chair given how much I've eaten, I file out with everyone to congregate in the entrance hall.

Donald claps his hands to get our attention, but rather than drawing nearer, I pull back because Grandma Betty keeps checking where I am, which is unnerving. I find myself next to Alec and Grandpa Albert again. Grandpa Albert grins, while Alec regards me with deep wariness. I glare purposefully at him and his expression hardens into one of suspicion. I feel a dart of irritation. What is his problem?

Donald claps his hands again. 'Come on everyone, there's nothing like a walk to aid the digestion, so let's take a short tour of the neighbourhood. Come, come,' he urges, indicating everyone's coats on the pegs. 'You must see the gardens, and the church is well worth a visit.'

Shrugging into his coat, Donald picks up a walking stick, and Lauren hurries to take his other arm, clamping on like a limpet that's just been told its rock is about to be repossessed. I watch her fawning and preening, and guess she must have been seriously rattled by Uncle Donald's interest in me at lunch, perhaps even experiencing a taste of what it's been like for me for the last twenty-five years, but I can't help hoping Donald sees through her nefarious motives. Lauren laughs exuberantly as they head outside, but as Donald checks to see if we're all following, his eyes meet mine for just an instant. I'm relieved to see them filled with wry amusement at Lauren's behaviour. I smile at him and drop to the back of the crowd. I find myself next to Grandpa Albert and Alec again. I don't seem to be able to shake off the man!

We follow the crowd down the drive, and watch Uncle Donald use his stick to point out various historical features, nearby landmarks and, for Betty's benefit, dense areas of shrubbery. Grandma Betty sniffs irritably, her mouth pinched in disgust as if she's sucking an old fluff-covered sweet from the bottom of her pocket.

'So, Alec,' begins Grandpa Albert as we stroll towards the church. 'You're Donald's personal assistant. Is that an interesting job?'

'It's never dull,' says Alec, glancing at me. Yes, I'm eavesdropping, so sue me!

'I didn't think it would be, but you like working for him? He's a good employer?'

Alec hesitates. 'Yes, most of the time,' he says mysteriously.

'Most of the time?' asks Grandpa Albert with gentle curiosity.

'I'd say about ninety-five per cent of the time it's great. He's in a good mood: full of the spice of life, all ideas and excitement.'

'And the other five per cent . . . ?'

'. . . is bloody awful,' says Alec with a big grin, the smile transforming his face, but then his eye catches mine and his expression falls as if at the flick of a switch. He looks away from me. 'He has these wild schemes, some of which are clearly ridiculous, and if they don't work out, he sinks to the absolute depths of despair and behaves like the worst toddler you've ever seen!'

'Sounds familiar,' mutters Grandpa Albert. We gaze after Grandma Betty, none of us quite daring to comment. 'But you get on?'

'Oh yes, he's been wonderful and looked out for me when people didn't always have my best interests at heart; a generosity I hope I return,' he says, his eyes meeting mine in warning.

What is his problem? It's not my fault that Donald and I got on well. Or is he jealous of any competition? Honestly, I reckon he and Lauren are a match made in heaven. Throwing him one of my dirtiest looks, I hurry in through the church gate to catch up with Mum and Dad.

Strolling alongside them, I focus on Donald's commentary and watch as he strikes out with his walking stick to show yet another item of interest, narrowly avoiding Aunty Pam. Suspecting an element of intent was involved, I pay more attention as Grandma Betty leans over to examine a gravestone, and sure enough, Uncle Donald's stick swipes perilously close to her bottom. He clears his throat noisily before speaking to Uncle Nigel, and I'm certain he's covering up a snigger as he leads us all into the church.

Arriving back at The Laurels, we hang up our coats and I slump into one of the drawing-room chairs. Everyone else gravitates toward a sideboard where afternoon tea is laid out, and they all fall on the wafer-thin cucumber sandwiches, decorated cupcakes and pretty biscuits as though they haven't recently eaten a massive four-course lunch. Though now I think about it, I am a little peckish . . .

It's amazing how much dainty food you can put away. I put my plate aside, feeling like I've swallowed the sofa, and survey the room drowsily.

Everyone is relaxing in the luxury Donald has been careful to provide, listening to his risqué stories, and Lauren is hanging off his every word, but oddly this doesn't seem to bother Grandma Betty. I watch the cake stands empty and the light begin to fade, and I'm almost dropping off when, on the dot of four, Grandma Betty stands up, placing her cup and saucer on the tray, and gives Aunty Pam a meaningful look.

'Yes, it's getting late,' says Aunty Pam, cottoning on. 'Long drive,' she adds, elbowing Uncle Nigel sharply.

'Er, yes,' he agrees, jerking awake.

I pull myself upright, feeling strangely sad about leaving Donald and The Laurels.

'It's been lovely,' says Mum, taking up the refrain and going over to kiss Donald on the cheek. 'Thank you so much for inviting us.'

Donald is clearly taken aback by my family's abruptness, but he recovers quickly. 'My pleasure,' he says as Alec helps him up, and the way Donald shuffles to his feet shows the day has taken its toll on him.

Grandma Betty squares up to him with a forbidding expression, and I suddenly want to put myself between them. 'Well, Donald. I suppose this is goodbye.'

'It could be *au revoir*?' He smiles cheekily.

'I think you and I can agree that we shan't be repeating this nonsense.'

'In that case, perhaps "bugger off" would be more apt,' he says mildly, and I stifle a giggle.

'A simple goodbye will do, Donald,' says Grandma Betty, shooting me yet another disapproving look.

'Then I guess it's goodbye, Betty,' he says, his tone oddly mournful.

'Goodbye, Donald.' Grandma Betty eyes him suspiciously as if waiting for the punchline, but he just smiles blandly, so she humphs and stomps off to collect her coat from the hall.

Of course Lauren rushes forward next, gushing and pouting, and everyone else forms a queue behind her as she kisses him 'mwah, mwah' on each cheek.

I'm one of the last to say goodbye, and I smile at him, suddenly shy.

'Hannah, it's been lovely,' he says.

'Yes, it was a lot more fun than I expected,' I say truthfully, and out of the corner of my eye I see Lauren roll her eyes.

'I'm glad,' says Donald, giving me the merest hint of a wink. 'And I enjoyed our talk at lunch.'

Before I can reply, Uncle Nigel sweeps me aside. 'Thank you for having us,' he says briskly, clearly wanting to get off home, and I turn to find Alec glowering down at me.

'I'm sure we'll meet again,' he says, distaste edging his voice.

'Are you? Why?' I ask bluntly.

His eyes narrow, but he seems lost for words – or polite ones, anyway. I take the opportunity to stroll over to where Lauren is waiting for me.

'What's the matter with you?' she hisses furiously. 'He's gorgeous, and you're being really rude.' She flashes him a seductive grin over my shoulder.

I shrug. 'Manners beats looks every time.'

'So where are yours, then?' she asks, and shakes her head at me before stalking off after Mum and Dad. She may have a point, but I only gave as good as I got.

I turn to find Alec watching me. Concerned he may have heard, I follow her out and get in the car, avoiding eye contact with him as he and Donald come out to see everyone off. I give Donald a small wave, but as Dad starts the engine I gasp. 'Wait! I've forgotten my coat!'

Dad sighs as I open the door and get out. 'Sorry, coat,' I call, rushing past Alec and Donald.

As I come back out they're waving off the other cars, and I head for ours, but just as I reach for the door handle I feel a hand on my arm. I turn and I'm face to face with Alec. He's closer than I expected, and I find myself looking into his eyes. They're as hard as flint, though there's a hint of jade . . .

'Could Donald have a quick word?' he asks, his hand flinching from my arm.

I blink. 'Er, yes?' I say, letting go of the door handle and following Alec back to where Donald is waiting.

'Hannah, I just had to ask: what do you call Betty when she's not around?' asks Donald keenly.

'What?' I ask, feeling awkward. I mean, I know what Donald's asking, but I feel I have to say, 'Grandma Betty?'

He purses his lips. 'Come on. Give it up. What's her nickname? She must have one.'

I glance back at our car to check all the doors are closed and lean in a little closer. 'Lauren and I call her "Blast-off Betty".'

Donald barks out a laugh. 'Marvellous,' he cries. 'It suits her.'

His laugh is infectious, and I can't help laughing too. Even Alec's mouth is twitching.

Donald takes my hand in both of his, looking deeply into my eyes. 'I've really enjoyed meeting you today.' His sincerity surprises me, and it feels like he's trying to fit extra meaning into his words.

'Me too. I've loved it, and I'll bear in mind everything you said at lunch.'

'Please do,' he says. He looks at me for a long moment, then pulls me into a hug. I grip him tight, alarmed by how brittle he feels; like a small bird. I meet Alec's gaze, my anxiety for Donald echoed in his expression.

'Don't be afraid to be magnificent,' says Donald. 'It's the best advice I can give you,' and he gives me one last squeeze before shooing me back to the car.

As I climb in, I wave and Donald waves back. Alec just stares, arms crossed.

'What was that all about?' asks Mum as we pull away up the drive.

'Nothing really,' I reply. 'Just saying goodbye.'

5

It's been more than three months since I was last standing here in front of The Laurels, and the house and grounds look beautiful in the May sunshine. Despite the gorgeous weather, everyone is looking pretty sombre, but that's as it should be for a funeral, I suppose.

Lauren is standing by our parents sniffing daintily and dabbing at her eyes with a hanky. She's leaning into Mum for support, and I suppress a snort – I don't remember her being that distressed during the phone call last week.

'Hannah it's me. Mum asked me to tell you that Uncle Donald died and his funeral is next week.' No preamble, just that. It was like she'd punched me. Lucky my bed was right behind me because my knees buckled.

'Hannah? Did you hear me? Hannah?' she'd bleated through my wave of nausea.

'When?' I finally managed.

'Next week.'

'No, I mean, when did he die?'

'Oh, I don't know. A couple of days ago? Does it matter?'

Of course it does.

Watching her now, I stuff my hands a little deeper into my pockets, and Lauren's scorn flashes back to me. 'Oh, for heaven's sake, Hannah, don't tell me you're upset – you only met him once!'

I drag my eyes away from her.

Grandma Betty is complaining as she straightens Grandpa Albert's tie. According to her, ten o'clock is too early in the day for a funeral. She gives The Laurels a disparaging look. 'And why we have to wait out here instead of in the church, I don't know. I have a good mind to get back in the car.' No one says anything, but I can't help thinking her irritation would have pleased Uncle Donald.

Mum and Dad are staring down the drive, and Mum's arm is around Lauren's waist. She gives Lauren a little comforting squeeze, and I manage to resist the impulse to scowl at them. Instead, I turn my attention to Uncle Nigel, who is polishing his wing mirrors, and Aunty Pam, who's checking her hair in the passenger window's reflection.

Nicholas is the only one who doesn't seem bored. He's leaning against his Porsche looking suspiciously smug, and it's not hard to imagine what he's thinking about. He smirks at me and I give him my best look of derision, but if anything, he looks even more self-satisfied.

The distant clop of horses' hooves draws my attention, and after a few moments a lavish horse-drawn hearse rattles from the shadows of the laurel trees. It's impressive, with plumed horses and black fretwork, reminding me of old Sherlock Holmes films. It makes a circular sweep of the parking area and halts by the front door, but despite its grandeur I can't help noticing the pale pine coffin, my eyes welling with tears. How can a person as vibrant as Donald be in there?

Grandma Betty tuts. I peer up at the sky to stop any tears from falling, but for once she isn't tutting at me.

'It's *white lilies* for a funeral, everyone knows that!' she snaps.

Only then do I notice the beautiful, decadent red roses arranged across the coffin lid. Suddenly certain Uncle Donald chose them to piss off Grandma Betty, I hide an inadvertent grin.

'Driver!' calls Grandma Betty, striding up to the front and pointedly ignoring a small drummer boy who's busy picking his nose at the coachman's side. 'Where are the cars for the mourners?'

The driver nudges the boy and touches the rim of his top hat. 'There aren't any, Ma'am,' he says, quickly reining in the horses which, unsettled by Grandma Betty's strident tones, are shifting restlessly.

'Is there *any* form of transport for the mourners?' she asks, her eyes narrowing, and I have to commend the driver for holding his ground.

'No, Ma'am.'

'Oh, for heaven's sake!' she explodes, shifting her weight awkwardly from foot to foot, suggesting her anger is in part due to her new pinching shoes. She's spared no expense, buying a complete new outfit, but karma seems to have spotted her fake, shop-bought grief and given her something tangible to be upset about. I can't help admiring the justice.

I'm pulled from my musings by Alec's voice. He's only speaking quietly to the driver, but it catches my attention as if he's called me by name. The driver pats him solemnly on the shoulder before passing down a tray of red-rose posies. Taking it, Alec glances at me and I notice the dark circles under his sunken eyes before he looks away. I follow his every move as, drawn and exhausted, he passes between us, handing a posy wordlessly to each woman. Grandma Betty's obvious repugnance of her posy is pretty funny, but it gets even better as Alec leads her, all pursed lips and outrage, to stand behind the coach. He indicates that Mum and Aunty Pam should stand behind her, and that Lauren and I should file in behind them. The men fall in behind us, and as the driver calls 'walk on', Alec follows right at the back, all by himself.

There is something poignant about our stately progress, going back the way we came on our last visit, with the boy walking in front of the horses striking his drum, leading us towards the church. Tears sting my eyes again, but the moment seems lost on Grandma Betty.

'He's made us into a bevy of mourning women,' she hisses over her shoulder. 'And if he expects me to wail and weep and stagger, he's got another thing coming!' She looks forbiddingly at Mum and Aunty Pam. 'We shall carry out this debacle with some dignity,' she declares, and promptly staggers around a large, steaming deposit of manure.

We approach the church in paces measured out by the beats of the drum, and the last stragglers hurry inside. With a final drum roll, we halt in front of the church doors and follow Grandma Betty around the hearse to be greeted by the vicar.

'Good morning,' he says pleasantly. Grandma Betty glowers at him. I'm not sure if she disapproves of the 'good', or if it's just her shoes, but the vicar's smile drops a few notches. 'You may follow the coffin into the church in a procession or take your seats,' he offers.

'We shall take our seats,' declares Grandma Betty, not bothering to consult the rest of us.

'The front two pews are reserved for family,' says the vicar, and hurries away to help the pallbearers.

As we walk in, I almost cannon into the back of Mum as everyone suddenly stops. I look over her shoulder to see what's happened and my breath catches in my throat. The church is full! I had no idea Uncle Donald was so popular.

Grandma Betty recovers first and, hoisting herself to her full height, strides down the nave like she owns the place. Mum and Aunty Pam keep in line behind her. I follow, feeling like I'm on show, but with Lauren gliding gracefully at my side I doubt anyone's looking at me.

I've hardly sat down when the organ starts up and we all stand for the arrival of the coffin. The vicar leads, intoning, and is blissfully unaware of the pallbearers shuffling awkwardly up the aisle behind him. It becomes clear, as they veer to the left, halt, correct their positions and repeat (seriously alarming the congregation on their port side), that the coffin on their unequal shoulders is pulling them off course. Still oblivious, the vicar reaches the front, closes his eyes and lifts his arms in silent prayer. The rest of us hardly dare breathe as, with shaking arms and legs, the unfortunate pallbearers finally make it to the front and lower the coffin safely onto its stand. There's a communal exhale of relief and one of the pallbearers even mops his brow with his tie. I stifle a smile.

Finishing his prayers, the vicar turns to welcome us and now that potential disaster has been averted, everyone seems suitably gloomy. Lauren sniffs into her hanky through the readings and the prayers, and I try hard not to feel annoyed that they're actually nothing special – they don't reflect Donald's personality at all. As the choir starts to sing, I glare down at the kneeler, so it takes me a few moments to realise the gorgeous and haunting tune is actually a choral adaptation of the naval song 'Spanish Ladies'. That's better! I break into a grin, and look down the pew to see Grandma Betty looking haughty and disdainful – which makes it all the more perfect.

The prayers, hymns and readings that follow are pretty traditional, but as Alec takes the dais for the eulogy and surveys us all, I get the feeling something's about to happen.

'Donald was a force of nature. He was both magnificent and shocking. Love him or hate him, you knew when he was in the room.'

There's a general murmur of amused agreement.

'And in all my time with Donald, I don't think I ever had an ordinary day. Even the most mundane tasks were an adventure, and not always in a good way. For example, during one trip to the supermarket, he enchanted a disheartened house-wife in the fruit section, had an argument with the fish counter attendant, and broke a self-service till by smacking it 'for cheek' with his stick. When he refused to hand over his stick, store officials had us removed from the store and after a few of Donald's carefully chosen expletives, they called the police! Luckily for us, the policewoman saw the funny side and let us off with a caution. She even gave Donald her number before we left, and I believe they stayed good friends—'

'Yes, we did!' shouts someone from halfway down the nave, and everyone laughs.

Alec nods. 'Let's just say we didn't get our shopping that day, and I never took Donald to the supermarket again, which I'm sure was his intention all along.' I can't help laughing along with everyone else.

'As if life with Donald wasn't exciting enough, he loved practical jokes. Even preparing for this funeral, Donald tried to convince the vicar to let the coffin spring open at an inappropriate moment . . .' Alec stares hard at the coffin, and so do I '. . . but the vicar said no.' There's a shout of laughter from behind me, and even the vicar chuckles, shaking his head. Grandma Betty glares and tuts. 'He had you going though,' says Alec.

'In the end it all came down to family with Donald. He loved his sister, Betty.' I glance to where she's sitting with her head held high. 'He said she was the most fun you could have without morphine.'

There are a few amused snorts and Grandma Betty's jaws clamp tight.

'As children they were close,' Alec continues relentlessly. 'With Donald valuing her kindness and trustworthiness, confident she would never reveal a secret. He lived life happy in the knowledge that he could always rely on her placid and accepting nature.'

I glance along the pew. This has to be nonsense, and Grandma Betty's livid, twelve-bore glare confirms it. What the hell did she do? What secret did she reveal? I'm almost desperate enough to ask, but Alec isn't finished.

'And I can't fault her for her unrelenting and selfless care of Donald in his final days. They had a blast – often talking for hours.'

Wait, what? Alec's looking straight at me, and his odd annunciation sinks in. He hasn't really put 'Blast-off' into the eulogy! He and Donald have no shame!

'She was a tower of strength,' continues Alec, looking away, 'and stayed up reading him *Lady Chatterley's Lover* and *Women in Love* into the small hours.' Grandma Betty's neck is now a bright and fiery red. 'And after everything,' says Alec, his voice as hard as nails, 'Donald would like me to thank her, for letting him have the *final* word,' and as Alec descends from the dais, the choir starts to sing 'Nobody Does It Better' in four-part harmony. Knowing full well Donald means himself and not Grandma Betty, I stare down at my feet, certain that if I catch anyone's eye, I will laugh.

Collecting the coffin, the pallbearers lead us out to the graveside in a more secure formation, and we file out after them. Grandma Betty's still simmering with suppressed rage. Her steps are slow and deliberate and when Grandpa Albert tries to take her arm, she twitches it away so violently she almost elbows a lady still seated in a pew in the head.

Out at the graveside, the birds sing and the sun shines its blessing on the occasion, but Grandma Betty takes up her position and stands rooted, with teeth clenched, glowering as they lower Donald's coffin into the ground. If he'd ordered a cremation, I feel sure Grandma Betty could oblige him with her eyes alone. Beside her, Lauren is sniffing again, and Dad moves to stand protectively at her side. I bite my lips together.

I almost wish I could summon up a few tears, as Uncle Donald deserves them, but for some reason I can't. I stare shamefully dry eyed into the hole as the vicar recites the committal.

'Earth to earth,' says the vicar, sprinkling soil into the grave, 'ashes to ashes, dust to—'

'Move aside!' The interruption makes me jump, and by the time I've recovered an elderly lady, who must be in her eighties and is dressed entirely in pink, has pushed her way through the crowd and is standing at the edge of the grave. She leans over the hole. 'Your time is up, Donald Makepiece. Now it's my turn. All your dirty little secrets are about to come out, and you can't do a thing to stop it!'

The vicar turns to us with an air of desperation, asking wordlessly if she's an eccentric relation. We all shake our heads, equally bewildered.

'Um, excuse me?' asks the vicar.

The old lady points into the hole. 'He thought he'd won, but he hasn't.' She glares at us all. 'I could tell you some things about Donald that would make your hair curl, and now I'm free to do so!' And with great ceremony, she turns back to the grave and spits in it.

I recoil, and the crowd ripples with shock.

'Now hang on!' begins Dad, starting forward, but the old woman holds up her hands.

'No need. I've done what I came to do. Now, let me through.' She grabs Dad's arm to support herself as she yanks her heel out of the soft grass and after giving a last exultant glance, she walks away.

The crowd closes behind her, and the vicar laughs nervously. 'Well, ladies and gentlemen, shall we resume? Earth to earth—'

'You've read that bit,' snaps Grandma Betty.

The vicar collects himself.

'Looking for that blessed hope when the Lord Himself shall descend from heaven with a shout . . .'

I can't help thinking the 'Lord Himself' will have to wait his turn at this funeral. And I glance about anxiously as the vicar finishes with an 'Amen' and an audible sigh of relief.

I stare into the grave and listen to the inevitable whispers as the congregation start to leave.

'Can you believe that woman spat in the grave?'

'. . . actually spat!'

'I've never seen anything like it . . .'

'Old people are so disgusting!' rings one woman's nasal voice, and I turn to see Grandma Betty standing stock still, her eyes closed in mute mortification.

'Do we really have to attend the wake?' Uncle Nigel asks Aunty Pam.

'Yes, the solicitor is going to read the will afterwards,' she replies and Alec stiffens.

They join the crowd heading back to The Laurels, but I stay staring down at the flower-strewn coffin, trying to ignore the spit and focus on Donald. Alec is looking down, too. He seems deep in thought. I wait silently as everyone wanders away, feeling odd, despite our differences, about leaving him here on his own.

'Do you want to be alone?' I ask tentatively.

Alec shrugs, not looking at me. I glance at the people caught in the bottleneck at the church gate.

'Well, that was certainly different,' I hazard.

'Never a dull moment with Donald,' he says, his voice flat.

'You don't seem surprised. Were you expecting that?'

Alec seems to pull himself together. He gives me a blank look before dropping his gaze to the coffin again. 'No.'

'And the service . . .' I shake my head. 'I've never heard of retribution by eulogy before. Clever, if a little mean, but I expect Grandma Betty deserved it.' Alec doesn't reply. I sigh heavily, wondering what to say next. A light breeze disturbs the tall, uncut grasses around us. I stare down at the finality of the pine box holding the lovely man I met at the party. 'I wish I'd known him better.' And without warning the tears come. No sobbing or sniffing, just big, fat tears dripping off my chin. I wipe my face on my jacket sleeve, and take a few deep breaths. Here I was wishing for tears, and now I feel a bit silly.

'Sorry,' I say, but Alec just gives an infinitesimal shake of his head.

'Emotional day,' he says, excusing me with a businesslike austerity that cures me of any sentiment. I'm tempted to walk off, but I stay, caught by my own fascination over what happened.

'Who *was* that woman?' I ask.

Alec shakes his head. 'I honestly have no idea,' he says quietly.

'She certainly picked her moment.' Understatement of the century, but Alec surprises me by smiling sadly, though his forehead keeps its frown.

'Donald would have liked that.'

'Really? You don't think he'd have been angry?'

Alec sighs and hesitates, as if he's frustrated that he has to explain it to me. 'Donald would have loved the drama. He'd like that no one will ever forget his funeral . . . or confuse it with someone else's.'

I stare at the coffin, and realise that he's right. 'He didn't arrange it, did he?'

Alec dismisses this idea with a scathing look. 'Of course not. He wouldn't have wanted to upset Mrs C.'

'Mrs C?' I ask.

Alec looks at me, as if he's trying to puzzle out why he's even bothering to talk to me. 'Our housekeeper. God, you don't even know that!' he says incredulously, and I almost see the mental shutters come down. His eyebrows draw together. 'You should get to the wake,' he says harshly.

'There's no rush,' I say gently, unsure what I've said to upset him.

'No, I suppose not, given that the will reading isn't until *afterwards*,' he says nastily.

A spasm of anger flashes through me. 'Aunty Pam said that, not me, and why would I care? I'm not expecting anything.'

'Of course you're not,' he sneers.

'Well, I'm glad we've cleared that up,' I retort.

He glares at me and, turning his back, stalks off across the graveyard with his shoulders hunched and his hands stuffed deep in his pockets.

What is his problem? If he's unhappy with how Donald left his affairs he should have taken it up with Donald, not mope about resenting everyone.

Giving Donald's grave one last look, I follow Alec at a discreet distance, and I'm only marginally surprised to hear swing band music and raucous laughter coming from The Laurels. Inside, there's barely room to move.

I push my way in, and thankfully I don't see Alec anywhere.

I assess the mass of people and see Grandma Betty fending off a well-wisher who's obviously taken the eulogy too literally. I can't see Grandma Betty's face, but the well-wisher hastily backs away with a stunned expression.

Relieving a passing waiter of a glass of wine, I head out into the garden and find the bench I sat on at the party empty. I sit down and close my eyes against the sun.

'Hello. It's Hannah, isn't it?'

My eyes snap open to find an elegant woman who looks to be in her mid-to-late sixties standing beside me. I feel caught out and flustered, but I shift up so she can sit down.

'Yes. I'm sorry, do I know you?'

'No, Donald asked me to introduce myself. I'm Lady Jane Forester. Call me Jane,' she says warmly, holding out her hand.

I shake it awkwardly.

'Donald suggested you might need a friend,' says Jane.

'A friend?' I bridle a little that he thought I didn't have any.

Jane smiles. 'Yes, I know it sounds a bit odd and I'm sure you have your own friends, but if you need one of Donald's then call me. Any time,' she adds, taking a pen from her purse and scribbling her number down on the back of her order of service. 'I'm aware this sounds cryptic, but it's all I can tell you right now. I do mean it, though.'

She hands it to me and I get a funny feeling that something important is happening. 'So you're saying I might need you at some point?' I ask.

'Perhaps.'

'Well then, I guess . . . thank you?' I say, failing to keep the confusion out of my voice.

'You're welcome,' says Jane, getting up. 'Day or night,' she adds, and then walks back to the house.

Day or night? I stare down at Donald's picture on the front of the order of service. He's obviously up to something – but what? I fold it carefully, making sure I don't put a crease across his photo, and slip it in my pocket. I take a sip of my wine.

What on earth is going on?

6

Now that the wake is over, the catering company are clearing up. Alec, my family and I are all idly watching the clearing up happen around us, sipping the last of our wine, while waiting for Mr Sanderson, the solicitor, to be ready for us.

'Please come in,' he finally calls, and we troop into Donald's small study, crowding around the desk with Grandma Betty and Grandpa Albert sat in front, Nicholas and Uncle Nigel grabbing the two fireside armchairs and the rest of us standing. I'm pressed up against a bookcase, and Alec is leaning against the doorframe, his strong arms folded tightly across his chest, his expression dark. Behind the desk, faced with us all, Mr Sanderson seems a bit overwhelmed, and I don't blame him.

He clears his throat and looks up nervously. It's amazing how quickly everyone falls silent, but I suppose we're talking money here. I glance around wondering who out of all of us is expecting anything. My money's on Grandma Betty, Nicholas and Lauren.

'This is the last will and testament of Mr Donald Makepiece of The Laurels, dated three months ago. Let all previous wills be retracted and considered null.' Mr Sanderson squints up at us, clears his throat and launches into a long list of small bequests, and one large bequest of three hundred thousand pounds already settled on a Mrs Crumpton, who's not in the room with us, but who I assume is Alec's mysterious Mrs C.

There's a ruffle of discontent, but this abruptly ceases as Mr Sanderson says, 'And now we come to the family.' Mr Sanderson glances nervously at Grandma Betty, and to be fair she is looking pretty formidable just now. '"To my dear sister, Betty, I leave the sum of two thousand pounds . . ."' He pauses, and nervously clears his throat again, '". . . to let her know that she is forgiven for the great wrong that she did me".'

Grandma Betty inflates with outrage. 'The wrong I did *him*?' she demands.

What 'wrong'? Who did what? And it seems everyone is thinking along the same lines because we're all staring at her.

But Mr Sanderson ploughs on. '"To Betty I also leave one genuine police truncheon – an appropriate addition to any expression she chooses to adopt".'

Betty's mouth falls open, and I share a quick scandalised yet gleeful glance with Lauren.

'"For her husband, Albert, I have procured an allotment within easy walking distance of their home"—'

'An allotment?' cries Betty. 'What's Donald trying to insinuate – that Albert needs some sort of . . . refuge? How dare he! Albert needs no such thing! Tell him, Albert. Tell him that you don't want it!'

Grandpa Albert glances nervously at us all, his eyebrows raised, but there's unmistakable delight on his face. 'Actually, my dear, I've had my name down for one of those allotments for three years. They are very difficult to come by. I wonder how he managed it.'

Mr Sanderson takes advantage of Grandma Betty's flabbergasted silence to continue. '"I have set aside a sum of money to be used to build a shed upon this land, complete with tea-making facilities for his use the year round. And to my sister's blood relatives, I leave five hundred pounds apiece",' adds Mr Sanderson quickly.

Dad and Uncle Nigel aren't included, then. But there's an uncomfortable silence, and a shift of attention that seems focused on Nicholas.

'Who told him?' Nicholas demands, his eyes locking onto mine, and I feel a flicker of alarm. I glance anxiously at Dad. What exactly does Nicholas think I've said?

'It's just a legal turn of phrase,' Dad assures him. 'After all, how could Donald know you're adopted?'

A hush falls and Lauren and I stare at each other. Adopted? We look at Nicholas who glares back, his expression defiant and angry.

'Absolutely, just legal jargon,' Mr Sanderson confirms hurriedly. 'In situations such as these, adopted children have the same rights as natural-born children. There's more,' Mr Sanderson calls over the increasing noise levels as everyone starts to ask questions. The room quietens down.

'"That is all ... with the exception of a small matter concerning my great-niece, Hannah, for whom I have left specific instructions with my solicitor. After that undertaking has been completed, the remainder of my estate shall pass to a list of charities, the details of which have been left in a separate document".' Mr Sanderson shuffles his papers anxiously. 'So, if I could ask to see Hannah, please?' He peers around anxiously until I raise my hand. 'Ah, yes. If possible, I would like a word in private?'

I nod, feeling a blush creeping up my neck as everyone looks from Mr Sanderson to me and back again. Then everyone starts talking at once.

Grandma Betty is ranting at Mr Sanderson, but his answers send her sinking back into her chair, as if poleaxed. Mum and Dad appear pleased, but then Aunty Pam, Uncle Nigel and Nicholas start demanding answers from them. Lauren just stares at me incredulously, while Alec watches me with an air of grim resignation. Grandpa Albert is the only one who seems happy. He's sitting amid the uproar with a smile on his face. I think he's picturing his allotment.

Mr Sanderson clears his throat noisily, but everyone completely ignores him. 'Excuse me!' he shouts. 'If you could all please wait outside? Thank you!' he says sternly, and everyone finally starts shuffling out, giving me chilling side-long glances. Alec is also watching me like a hawk, but if he thinks I had a clue about this, he's deluded.

'Now,' says Mr Sanderson as Alec leaves, his eyes fixed on me until he closes the door between us. 'Let's get down to business. I understand that you are just starting your finals?'

'Yes . . . sir,' I add, unsure of the etiquette with solicitors.

'Then I think perhaps it would be best if you visit my office when you are done? That way we can get you started on everything Donald has planned for you. Do you have employment after your degree?'

'No,' I say, happily shelving my plan to sign up for more temping work.

'Good.'

'Could you tell me what this is about?' I ask. 'What has Donald got planned for me?'

Mr Sanderson frowns. 'Ah, well, this is a highly unusual bequest,' he says. 'Let me read you the codicil to this part of the will. Ah yes, here: "For my great-niece Hannah I have prepared a series of tasks to be completed within six months of the date of my death, under the supervision of my PA, Alec. Should she complete them, she shall inherit an undis-closed reward. Should she not complete them, the reward will pass to my list of chosen charities".'

'A "*series of tasks*"?' I ask. 'What kind of tasks?'

'Well, there's the question,' agrees Mr Sanderson. 'I'm afraid I am not at liberty to say just yet, but Mr Makepiece has requested that you either accept or decline immediately.'

'What? Really? Without knowing any details? Just that there are tasks?'

Mr Sanderson nods.

'But what if they're ... I don't know ... dangerous or humiliating ... or just downright odd?'

'His exact words were, "She will know what to do based on our conversation at lunch".' This obviously means nothing to Mr Sanderson, but it finally gives me something to go on. 'And you can back out once you start,' he adds, 'so I don't believe you have much to lose by trying out a task or two?'

I bite my lip. 'And the "undisclosed reward"?'

'Remains undisclosed until you are done.'

'And if I fail even one task?'

'No reward,' says Mr Sanderson, shaking his head sadly. 'To be honest, the best person to ask is your uncle's PA. He will be administering the tasks.'

Oh great, that's the last thing I need – a surly onlooker, hoping I fail. 'And I have to decide right now?'

'Yes,' he says sympathetically. 'Though it does seem like very little to go on. Alec?' he calls loudly and Alec, who must have been waiting outside, comes in and carefully closes the door behind him. 'I have explained to Hannah about the need to accept or decline Donald's offer, but she is understandably tentative. Can you offer any advice?'

Alec looks me in the eye. 'I'd accept,' he says surprisingly. 'If I know Donald, you won't regret it.'

I look into his eyes, trying to understand why he's encouraging me. Does he want me to try and fail, or is he being loyal to Donald's last wishes? It's definitely not because he wants to spend time with me. Pulling my eyes away, I turn back to Mr Sanderson.

'Then I suppose I accept,' I say, a mixture of excitement and apprehension curdling in my stomach. Alec gives a small nod, more resigned than enthusiastic.

'Excellent!' says Mr Sanderson. 'In that case, please visit me at my office in the village as soon as you have finished at university.' He hands me his business card. 'And on that occasion we will run through how this is going to work.'

'That's it?' I ask.

'For now,' agrees Mr Sanderson.

I have a million questions, but he's already packing away his papers.

'Ready to face everyone?' asks Alec, his hand on the door handle.

'Absolutely,' I say coolly – and dishonestly.

Alec opens the door and Mr Sanderson sweeps past us – I think he's trying to get away before Grandma Betty can speak to him again. I walk out, leaving Alec to straighten up the study.

In the hall, Aunty Pam and Uncle Nigel fix me with such a stony stare, I thank my lucky stars Medusa isn't anywhere on our family tree. I hurry past them to find Mum and Dad, but have to stop as I come face to face with Nicholas in the corridor.

'Well done, Hannah,' he says, before I can get past. 'Sold me out to great personal profit – six bedrooms is it?'

'Five,' I say, correcting him before I can stop myself. 'And I'm not getting the house.' I start to turn away, but he takes hold of my arm and pulls me around the corner towards the kitchen.

'Nicholas, what are you doing? Get off me!'

'Why did you tell him?' he demands, his nostrils flaring.

'What?'

'Why did you tell the old man I was adopted?'

'I didn't! I didn't even know!' I try to pull my arm away, but his fingernails are digging into my armpit. 'You're hurting me,' I say through gritted teeth, trying to convey more anger than fear.

If anything, his grip tightens. 'Of course you told him. How else could he know?' He shakes his head at me. 'I've always known you were a sly one; all quiet and watching us, playing the "poor little me" card.' I blink. Is that really how he sees me? 'But now you've taken a step too far, selling me out like that. You've put yourself in a tricky position. The family won't help you when Uncle Donald—'

'Let her go,' Alec says quietly, but firmly, from behind Nicholas.

When Uncle Donald – what? But Nicholas just gives me a nasty look, his grip slackening only slightly.

'Just offering my congratulations,' he says smoothly, finally letting go as he turns around.

'Of course you were,' says Alec watching me rub my sore arm, but when his eyes meet mine there's no sympathy there.

Nicholas smirks. 'I must say, I'm surprised *you* didn't do better,' he says, shaking his head at Alec. 'Buggered you twice daily, did he, and all for nothing? Bet Donald's laughing now.'

I glare at Nicholas, disgusted, but Alec only raises an eyebrow. 'Oh, he's laughing all right, but not at me.'

Nicholas flushes and, giving me one last venomous glance, stalks off after his parents.

'Nice comeback,' I whisper to Alec.

Alec's still staring after him. 'Stay by your parents. He's angry, and I don't like the look of him.'

'Neither do I.' I never have.

'Did he hurt you?' Alec indicates my arm.

'Not really. I'm fine.' I stop rubbing my armpit, and cast around for a change of topic. 'What happens to you now? Do you stay here?'

'For the time being. Donald instructed me to administer the tasks Mr Sanderson told you about, and since I don't have much choice in that matter, I'm obliged to stay.' Even knowing he doesn't like me, that one stings.

'I'm sorry for the inconvenience, but in case you hadn't realised, I didn't exactly ask for any of this,' I remind him icily. 'I'd better find my family. Thanks for intervening,' I add stiffly. Not that I couldn't have freed myself with a swift knee to his groin – Nicholas should be the one thanking Alec, really.

'No problem,' Alec says, his eyes boring into mine as if he's trying – and failing – to understand Donald's choice. His intensity is unnerving, but also weirdly mesmerising in a cobra–mouse kind of way, and I have to force myself to turn away and find Mum and Dad.

Alec follows me out and stands under the portico, probably making sure we all vacate the premises. He nods to me as I get in the car, and as I sit back in my seat I notice Lauren watching me. I bet she's dying to know what Mr Sanderson said.

'I didn't know Nicholas was adopted,' I say before she can ask.

'No,' agrees Lauren, transferring her accusing gaze to Mum.

Mum turns around to us both as Dad pulls away. I glance at Alec once more, but he's not looking my way. 'No, well, Pamela asked us not to say anything,' she says.

Lauren and I wait. Dad focuses on the driving, clearly not wanting any part in the conversation, so Mum sighs and gives us the bare facts.

'Pam and Uncle Nigel had problems conceiving. No signs of a pregnancy for two years. They did tests, but the doctors said they couldn't always tell why some couples have problems. They tried various methods, but nothing worked. In the end, they decided to adopt. They got Nicholas. Neither of you were born, so there didn't seem any reason to tell you.'

I bite my lip anxiously. 'Nicholas thinks I told Uncle Donald about him being adopted.'

'Of course you didn't, darling. You didn't even know.'

'No,' agrees Lauren, but the look she gives me is far from certain.

Silence hangs in the car. It's a long drive and I take the opportunity to close my eyes and feign sleep while trying to make sense of what has been a very peculiar day.

7

After three weeks of exams, a great deal of celebrating and a couple of weeks spent looking into temping and other career possibilities, I buy an ancient Volvo from a friend moving to teach English abroad, and head home. I try not to admit it, but returning home feels like a backwards step and it's odd being back. My room feels smaller, and although I appreciate my parents' attempts to look pleased that I've returned, they're artificially cheerful, and none of us quite know what to do about my being here. After only being home a day, I make an appointment to see Mr Sanderson, and after only three days, I climb into the Volvo to tackle the two-hour drive to Wiltshire to go and see him.

My Volvo has age and wisdom on its side, but not much else, so I amble along in the slow lanes of the motorway and dual carriageways, baking in the early July sunshine, wishing I had air con. It's sweltering, but as I turn onto country lanes, I crank the windows right down and turn up the radio to lose myself in being 'Happy' with Pharrell Williams. After a couple more songs, I almost relax, but as I reach the village, my nerves come flooding back.

Thankfully, Mr Sanderson's building is easy to find, and I go into the reception area and find him waiting for me. 'Ah, Hannah!' he says, showing me straight into his office and indicating a seat opposite his desk. We both sit and I smile at him expectantly. 'We are waiting for Alec,' he explains.

'Oh,' I say, my smile becoming fixed. 'I didn't realise he was coming, too.' Though, if he's administering the tasks, perhaps I should have guessed.

Mr Sanderson checks his watch, looks at the door and checks his watch again. 'He really should be here.' He picks up a piece of paper and starts to read, stopping quite quickly to glare at my foot, which without my knowledge is tapping against the chair leg. I stop tapping and hunt for something to say.

'So this is all quite unusual, isn't it?' I ask. 'I mean, how this will is arranged.'

'Yes,' agrees Mr Sanderson. 'I would go so far as to say it's highly unusual, but then I suppose it represents the eccentricities of the testator.' A pained expression crosses his face. 'I did, however, once act as an executor for a will that contained a contest. It ended badly, but what can you expect when you involve a cat?' He smiles, as if this explains everything. 'Perhaps I should tell you about the challenge we received to your great-uncle's will?'

'Let me guess,' I say drily. 'Nicholas?' I mean, who else could it be?

'Ye-es.' Mr Sanderson gives me a long look followed by the briefest smile. 'Your great-uncle suspected your cousin might take issue with his arrangements and left a letter, which we have despatched as per his instructions. On the plus side, it mentions your cousin's five hundred pounds, so that has been approved. Beyond that . . . well, you had better read it.' He holds out a copy of the letter, and I hesitate. 'It's quite within your rights,' nods Mr Sanderson.

I take the letter reluctantly and read it.

My Dearest Nicholas,

I see you have lived down to my every glorious expectation of you. I would have been disappointed if you hadn't, as ever since we met I have longed for the opportunity to tell you how highly amusing and wonderfully appalling I found you. You are an example of awfulness in your own class, and I would happily hang you at the Tate Modern with an inscription saying 'Beware my Porsche'. I admit you would not be alone in my exhibition, as I have met people who could serve as a whole host of warnings. My favourite was a general who demoralised his men and divorced his thankful wife, declaring her to be 'sub-standard'. (She moved in with a milkman who enjoyed candle making.) The general's inscription would have read: 'Medals maketh not the Man!'

And now to the nub of the matter, the very reason I have written this letter: your unimaginative attempt to pervert my will. Let me make it clear to you that you will not receive a penny beyond your £500. I consider this sum generous given my dislike of you, but I cannot deny that your hilarity-factor should earn you something. But know this – I have left explicit instructions that you will not receive even that should you contest my will any further, particularly should you try to suggest that I am not capable of making sound decisions. Don't waste your time. My solicitor has a witnessed affidavit from a leading psychologist that confirms I am of sound mind. He is willing to testify to this in court. I am lucky in my friends, you are not. Do not persevere.

In thanks for giving me this opportunity to tell you in frank terms what I think of you, and as a final gift, I offer you three pieces of advice. I am well aware that these will thoroughly annoy you, which is probably why I give them so freely, but they are still worthwhile.

1. You seem to have devoted your interest to the wrong end of women. Try the other. They are infinitely more fascinating than you give them credit for.

2. Sell the sports car. It bespeaks a lack of imagination and a desperation to show wealth, where there is, at best, only mild affluence. No one is deceived.

3. Take a pin and deflate your ego. You are not God's gift: none of us are. It takes humility and interest in others to be pleasant company. Save conceit, vanity and self-aggrandisement for old age – it wears better then!

I fully expect you to ignore this advice, but before you dismiss it, know that it is more valuable to you than my entire estate.

With the greatest enjoyment (and thank you for almost giving me the gift of dying laughing),

Yours delightedly,

Uncle Donald

I stare at Mr Sanderson, gobsmacked.

'Quite,' says Mr Sanderson. 'Expressive, wouldn't you agree?'

'Brutally so.'

'But, like I said, it does mention the five hundred pounds.'

It also clears me of telling Donald about the adoption, but still . . .

There's a knock at the door, and Alec comes in dressed in an old Guns N' Roses T-shirt and ripped jeans. It doesn't look like he's shaved in a while, and the dark circles under his eyes have become almost bruise-like. He looks exhausted. He takes a spare chair from against the wall and sits down next to me, mumbling apologies to Mr Sanderson, but sparing me only the smallest and most dismissive flick of his eyes. Any sympathy I might have felt dries up and flakes off like old paint.

Mr Sanderson turns frostily businesslike. 'Now that we are all finally here, please witness . . .' Mr Sanderson holds out an envelope to me with great ceremony '. . . the first letter.'

The envelope is labelled 'For Hannah – The Beginning'. After reading Nicholas's character assassination, I'm a little apprehensive. I glance at Alec for reassurance, but he's staring at the wall morosely. Still, this is what I'm here for, so I prise up the flap and take out the letter.

My Dearest Hannah,

Writing my will proved to be a far more irritating problem than I ever anticipated. I always thought I would name an heir and that would be that. But when it actually came to it, I realised there is no satisfaction in just throwing money at someone – not when you want to make a difference and be remembered and hopefully a little revered for all that you have achieved. I discussed the matter with Alec, but he was no help, so I consulted a solicitor expecting him to have no end of ideas. Unfortunately Sanderson gave only dingbat suggestions about charities and such – please tell me how naming a hospital wing after someone ever changed anything?! Still, deciding where there's a will, there must be a way – and after a lot of wrangling – we came to the conclusion that I should use my assets to help someone. This was all well and good in principle, but when we sorted through my friends, there was no one for whom I could make any real difference (it's an odd moment when you damn your friends for being too happy), so we reached an impasse. We spent weeks rattling around various options, and in the end, somewhere out of the conventions drummed into me in my youth, came the conviction that I should try and help my family. The trouble was I didn't know my remaining family (a situation of my own choosing, I admit) and I didn't want to reward someone repulsive, so, as Alec pointed out, I had to meet you all. This was the reason behind the party you attended.

Though it was a bizarre, manufactured occasion, meeting you has been one of the great pleasures of my recent years. (Watching Nicholas squirm came a close second.) Your person-ality, position and need to experience life – not for the sake of it, but to facilitate your ambition – fascinated me, and our discussion at lunch inspired a scheme. A scheme intended to fulfil both your need to widen your experience and my need to make a difference and be truly known by someone delightful.

Here is my plan. You shall complete the tasks I have set for you and at the end of each task you will receive a diary entry that will enlighten you as to my colourful and most interesting past. It will not always be easy or nice, for that would be dull (be delicious, be delightful, be disastrous, but never, dear girl, be dull – free advice) but persevere and it will all be worth it. Not only will you receive an undisclosed reward of my choosing, but I fancy you will have built up the wealth of experience that you currently feel is lacking in your life and in your writing.

As for tackling the tasks – you will not be alone. Alec shall accompany you and my dearest friend, Jane Forester, has kindly offered to escort you on the occasions where a female companion would be better.

I would like to assume that you have accepted my offer and will persist through to the very end, but my solicitor informs me that you have the right to decline or cry off at any point. Why you would wish to do so, I cannot imagine, but if you do, know that I shall be baffled and disappointed beyond belief. I'll have you know that I have taken a considerable amount of trouble over these arrangements. Should you decide, however, that this wonderful challenge demands too much of you, Sanderson has insisted I tell you that the reward you were to receive shall be disposed of and in no way settled upon you or your family.

With my greatest respect and sincerest hope that you will enjoy the experiences as they are intended.

Yours, most expectantly,

Uncle Donald

'No pressure then,' I mutter, refolding the letter and slotting it back in the envelope. I lift my eyes to find Mr Sanderson and Alec watching me. 'So he wants me to learn about his life and carry out some tasks?' I clarify.

'Yes,' they nod.

That doesn't sound so bad on the surface, but I can't help feeling concerned. 'What if I'm not the person Donald thinks

I am?' I ask quietly, not meeting anyone's eye. 'What if I can't manage the tasks?'

Mr Sanderson defers to Alec, who shrugs dismissively, irritating the hell out of me. 'Donald wouldn't have chosen you if he didn't think you could handle it, and there's nothing in the tasks beyond your capabilities.'

Mr Sanderson starts putting some of the papers away in a file. 'How about you try the first task and see how you get on? You can withdraw at any time,' he reminds me. 'There are provisions for that instance.'

I bite my lip. There's so little to go on, but if I can back out at any time . . . 'How do we do this? How long will it take? Do I apply for jobs at the same time, or might I still be on an island somewhere trying to retrieve the lost Ark of the Covenant this time next year?'

Alec glances at Mr Sanderson, but he's back to putting his papers away. Alec sighs and rubs his eyes as if I'm being deliberately obtuse. 'Donald will support you as long as you are doing the tasks, and if you come and stay at The Laurels we can probably get through everything in a couple of weeks. If you're at home or at college, it will take longer.'

Stay at The Laurels with Alec for a few weeks? That possibility hadn't even crossed my mind. It would be like a holiday in a gorgeous country house. Except it would be with Alec – a man who clearly dislikes me and has made it abundantly clear that he would rather get on with his grief in seclusion without a gold-digger gallivanting about like a child on a hobby horse. Even so, it's got to be better than going home every evening and facing everyone's questions . . . especially Lauren's. I stare at my fingers, and stop myself from picking at a hangnail.

'I suppose I *could* stay at The Laurels,' I agree tentatively.

'Mrs Crumpton will be there most of the time, so we won't be alone,' says Alec, but I don't know if he is trying to reassure me or scare me.

Mr Sanderson hands Alec a thick brown envelope. 'Give her the allotted tasks at your convenience,' he says. 'And let me know when they are completed.' Alec takes the envelope and stands up with bleak acceptance.

'But what if I can't complete them?' I ask desperately.

'Any questions, ask Alec. He'll contact me if he needs to,' replies Mr Sanderson, standing up and holding out his hand. 'In the meantime, good luck.' Glancing at Alec's moody face, I reckon I might need it. I get up and shake Mr Sanderson's hand, and allow Alec to escort me out.

Outside, Alec and I stand on the sunny pavement and he looks down at me with eyes so tired he can't even keep up his hostility. 'How soon can you start?' he asks.

'A few days? I just need to sort out my university stuff, and do some washing,' and field questions that I still don't know the answers to, 'that sort of thing.'

He nods. 'Well, you know where we are. And here's the phone number.'

He jots it down on the back of the envelope I'm still holding.

'Come to The Laurels when you're ready. We're not doing anything else at the moment,' he says, and with that, he walks off.

After a few seconds I realise I'm gazing after him, watching him trudge up the road like a lonely figure in the Arctic. Shaking off the thought, I get in my car and crank down the windows, firmly reminding myself that he thinks I'm a gold-digger, and he doesn't deserve my pity.

Starting the engine, I turn my mind instead to what I'm going to tell Mum, Dad, Lauren and Grandma Betty. I can't imagine how they'll react to the idea of me staying at The Laurels, but I suppose I can only tell them the truth. Trouble is, I'm not sure how realistic it sounds:

'No, I don't know what's going on.'

'Yes, I am moving to The Laurels.'

'No, I don't know how long for.'

'Yes, Alec will be there.'

'No, I didn't find out what the reward is.'

I have a feeling it's going to be a long couple of days.

8

A few days later, I pull up in front of The Laurels and look up at the house. It seems a lot more imposing without everyone else, but I try not to let that faze me. I get out and ring the doorbell, bracing myself for my first encounter with the mysterious Mrs C. Alec opens the door and looks down at me. He looks a little less drawn – the clean, ironed shirt helps – but he still looks tired and gaunt, and he's regarding me with all the resignation of finding yet another baby on the orphanage steps. We stare at each other awkwardly.

'Hi—'

'Do you—'

We break off, and there's an uneasy silence. I gesture for him to go first.

'Would you like some help to bring in your bags?' he asks, making some attempt at civility.

'Oh, that would be great, thanks.'

'Mrs Crumpton has made up a bedroom for you,' he says as we walk over to my car.

'That's kind of her,' I say, though I find his continued use of her surname worrying.

'You didn't meet Mrs C at the funeral, did you?' he asks, and I shake my head. 'She's been here since before I came. She's . . . formidable.'

Is he trying to put the wind up me, because how hard is it to find one positive thing to say about someone?

I open the boot and hand him a bag and, when he indicates he can take more, a box.

'You'll see what I mean,' he says. 'She's a wonderful cook, though. I hope she likes you,' he adds doubtfully. I hate to admit it, but if he's trying to scare me, it's working.

I pick up my remaining bag and follow him in, and he leads me up the staircase that winds around the sides of the entrance hall forming a balustraded walkway in front of the bedrooms. It's all so elegant. Alec opens a door to reveal a stunning dual-aspect room, complete with a four-poster bed that, with a few more mattresses, could be a convincing set for the *The Princess and the Pea*, and my breath catches in my throat. I gaze at the original fireplace and mouldings, and what's possibly a Persian carpet. There's even a beautiful writing desk under the far window – not that I feel up to the Brontë-style writing it looks like it deserves.

Alec plonks my things on the bed and I do the same. It's so lovely, I can't help touching the curtains strapped to the bedposts. I wonder if it's possible to draw them all the way round and completely cocoon myself? I make a mental note to try it out later. I spot Alec watching me and let my hand drop. Suddenly shy, I head for the nearest window, which has a window seat and a view of the garden.

'OK then . . .' he says, slightly less abruptly.

I glance at him, but he's still frowning. 'Thanks for bringing my things up.'

'No problem. Mrs C has made some celeriac soup and homemade bread in case you're hungry?'

What's celeriac? 'Great.' I risk another glance at him, but I can't think of anything else to say and an uncomfortable silence falls.

'I'll see you downstairs,' he says, and he's about to leave when I realise I've had enough of his attitude.

'Look, I know that you don't want me here, that you think I'm a gold-digger and that I somehow tricked Donald into whatever this is with the will.' I pause, and Alec doesn't disagree. 'But the truth is that's not the case at all. We have these tasks to do, and it was what Donald wanted, so can we please try to work together amicably?'

Alec regards me for a long moment, his distrust of my motives finally giving way to resignation. 'I suppose that's fair enough to ask,' he agrees.

I relax a little. 'Good.'

He nods and giving me one last glance, he leaves.

As the door clicks shut, I let out a sigh of relief, and turn to look at the room. My belongings look paltry against Donald's antiques, and I feel just as out of place as they look. I head for the wardrobe mirror, and take a tissue from my pocket. I wipe away the smudged liner from under my eyes and stare at myself appraisingly. My mid-length, mousy-brown hair is a mess, blown about by the air coming in through the open car windows, so I root around in my bag and find my brush. I pull it through my hair and feel a little better. I consider putting on some more make-up, but since I don't usually wear much, it might look odd if I reappear looking made up.

I stand back and look at my reflection wondering, not for the first time, what Uncle Donald expects of me. And why assign Alec to run the tasks when he's so obviously against the whole idea?

Unable to make sense of any of it, I square my shoulders and frog-march myself down the stairs, because right now, I have to face Mrs Crumpton.

As soon as I enter the dining room, Mrs Crumpton's shrewd eyes land on me, and I return the favour. She must be well past retirement age, but I still wouldn't like to cross her. Her short, neat haircut suggests a no-nonsense attitude, and though her apron depicts buttercups, wild flowers and a welcoming summer meadow, her expression is anything but sunny. I'd find the contrast amusing if her thunderous look was directed at anyone but me. As it is, I try a tentative smile, but it hits stony ground, so I sit in the place set for me opposite Alec and do my best not to cower as Mrs Crumpton ladles soup into sturdy bowls, carves doorstops of warm brown bread and pours us some strong tea with the solitary word 'Milk?', glowering the entire time. Not sure what to do, I accept everything she hands me, and breathe a sigh of relief when she finally leaves the room.

She's left the door open and I can hear her reprimanding someone in the kitchen.

'Well, it seems you've made an impression,' says Alec.

How? I didn't even say anything. 'Did I?'

'Oh yes, she's cross.' I examine his face to see if he's winding me up, but he seems less hostile than before, and there's even a slight crinkling of amusement around the corners of his eyes, so perhaps he is making an effort. Still, it's difficult to know what to say to that, so we fall silent and listen to more scolding from the kitchen.

'Who's she talking to?' I whisper.

'Donald,' he says shortly.

'But he's . . .?'

'Oh yes, but that doesn't stop Mrs C. She thinks he's hanging about somewhere near the kitchen ceiling, and she gives him what-for just the same as if he was here.'

She sounds mad, in every sense of the word. 'Really? Is she . . . you know . . . all there?'

'More than any of the rest of us,' says Alec. 'In fact, it wouldn't surprise me if she's proved right one day, and Donald materialises just to answer her back.'

I love that idea.

'Come on,' he says, his face taking on an impish expression. 'If you're going to be here for a while it's best if you understand, but don't be upset by what you hear.' He gets up and I follow him on tiptoes to the door. We peer down the corridor to the kitchen, and I can just see Mrs Crumpton removing a steamed pudding from its basin.

'Just look at 'er. I don't know what you were thinkin'!' she tells the kitchen ceiling. 'I dare say you thought yourself very clever, what with all your plans and your tasks, but I could've given you a dozen better ideas. I mean, what if she gets scared, or fed up? I'm tellin' you now, she'll be off before mornin', and then where will we be, eh?' Alec and I glance at each other uncomfortably. Mrs Crumpton clatters about in a cupboard looking for something – possibly a mace – but eventually comes up with a pan. 'And don't go expectin' Alec to pick up the pieces. He's been mopin' about 'ere like a wet weekend. You didn't think this through, did you? No! Well then.'

Alec jerks his head to indicate we should go back and he looks thoughtful as we sit back down. Strangely, her words don't bother me. At least she only criticised my likelihood of getting scared, which is better than I thought, and Alec had an equal share in her scorn. I don't think he was expecting that.

'Sorry about that, but it is quite funny,' he says apologetically.

I smile at him, glad the truce seems to be holding. 'So does she do that a lot?' I ask. 'With the ceiling, I mean.'

'Yes, ever since Donald died. I think she misses arguing with him, so the ceiling gets it.'

'Did they argue a lot?'

'Like cat and dog. They loved scoring points off each other, but it was always done good-naturedly. I think it gave their day extra meaning. Trouble is, the ceiling hasn't mastered the art of answering back and it certainly doesn't have the grace to look ashamed.'

We both pause to listen to Mrs Crumpton's ranting, but there's an ominous quiet coming from the kitchen. Alec's eyes widen in warning, and we both dig in to our lunch.

Just as we're scraping our bowls clean, Mrs Crumpton comes in to replace them with bowls of steamed jam-sponge pudding and custard, which she dumps unceremoniously on the table. Alec catches my eye and I feel the sudden urge to laugh, but manage to hold it in. Mrs Crumpton regards me imperiously before leaving with the tray of dirty crockery.

I let out a breath, relieved I didn't disgrace myself.

'Is she like this with everyone?' I ask, wondering if she's just annoyed about Donald's will.

Alec snorts. 'Yes, everyone! You have to earn her respect, but until then, from her point of view, you need watching. It's odd, but that's how it works with Mrs C. Her cooking *is* great though, isn't it?'

I have to admit it is. It's not exactly cordon bleu, but it's brilliant comfort food. 'Yes, but her glares make it a little hard to swallow.'

'That wasn't glaring. Not by her standards. Some of the looks she gave Donald deserved medals, but he loved it. Laughed like a child,' says Alec reminiscently. 'They had a strange relationship.' He pauses for a second, staring into the distance. 'But it worked. Speaking of Donald, how about you take a look at your first task after lunch? I brought it down with me.'

My heart leaps into my mouth. I'm a little afraid I might not do it justice.

'OK,' I say, hoping I don't sound nervous.

'It'll be fine,' he says, so I obviously haven't hidden my anxiety that well. 'How about we set up deckchairs in the garden, and you can read it in a nice relaxed environment?'

'Are you going to bring panpipes or do you prefer whale song?' I ask, to show I know he's patronising me. But since I

84

don't want to be left alone with Mrs Crumpton, who's berating the kitchen ceiling again, I get up and indicate he should lead on.

Outside, I finally succeed in unfolding my deckchair, and Alec hands me a white envelope marked 'Task 1'. I lower myself into the chair and watch as he turns his own deckchair over, frowning as he struggles to unfold it from the other side.

I peel open the envelope and hide my smile behind Donald's letter.

My Dearest Hannah,

You accepted! I knew you would. How dare that dingbat Sanderson even suggest you wouldn't! So, let the story of your mysterious Great-Uncle Donald unfold.

I was born in a village not that far from here, near the end of the war in 1944. My mother lay comfortably in bed and was ably assisted by a midwife – such an uninspiring start, don't you think? No bombs going off, no hunkering down under a kitchen table. My father, unlike those of so many of my friends, was at home due to having had polio as a child. He served his country in every way he could: Home Guard, air-raid warden, etc. etc., but this did not alleviate his feelings of guilt, or the envy of those who lived with the day-to-day fear of telegrams concerning their menfolk.

Betty and I are too young to remember the war, but I remember growing up with my father around, where so many didn't. Generally, he was sullen and quiet. My mother, while wonderful and loving to us, was wary of other people. I remember her as kind, but distant.

Despite continued rationing and other post-war problems, I believe Betty and I had an idyllic childhood. We played with our friends, ran in the fields and had everlasting summer holidays. We had solid friendships and learned the valuable lesson of who and why to trust and what and when to risk. We saw nature, lived danger and learned how to handle the sharp smacks of contrition.

I don't expect you to truly understand. Today's children see television, live computer games and learn how to handle all their affairs though mobile phones. It's a very different time. I can, however, show you what I mean. And there you have the basis of the tasks. Not only are you going to read about my past, but you are going to experience it – an excellent idea of mine that should both broaden your mind and make you a better writer, while letting you really get to know me. Utterly brilliant, don't you think?

And so, to your first task – a fond childhood memory of mine and a good way for you to experience a healthy dose of fear: scrumping apples. You must enter someone's garden, pinch five apples and leave with your booty. Once clear, you must eat one of the apples.

Alec will help you and has his own instructions. Please bear in mind that, if you do not do this, you may not continue on to the next task.

Good luck. Don't wear black or go at night – that's just not cricket!

Pilferingly yours,
Uncle Donald

'Scrumping apples?' I ask in disbelief, dropping the letter to my knees.

'Yep,' says Alec, closing his eyes against the sun.

'Not tightrope walking, jumping off a moving train or learning to fly, but a criminal act. Stealing.' I try to keep my tone matter-of-fact, but I can't help feeling disappointed in Donald.

'Technically, I suppose, but hardly criminal.'

'It is, actually. What if I'm caught?'

'You won't be caught – I'll make sure of it.'

Really? Well pardon me for not being reassured.

I stay quiet for a while, picturing a set of increasingly illegal tasks leading up to my drilling a hole into the basement of the Bank of England. 'Is this the start of a slippery slope?' I ask. 'Because if I'm being groomed for a life of crime, I'm out.'

'You're not being groomed for a life of crime, you're just picking some apples!' he says, exasperation creeping into his voice.

'That's easy for you to say. You're not the one doing it.'

'I still have to come with you.'

I stop myself from saying that's not the same and try to think calmly. 'Donald said he left you special instructions?'

Alec laughs and hands me a Post-it note. 'It was stuck to the envelope,' he explains.

'Take Hannah scrumping,' I read out. 'Get at least five.' I sigh heavily.

'Oh, come on. It isn't difficult. First we find an apple tree, then you pick some apples and finally we run away.'

I glare at him. 'What about the owner? What about the stealing? What about the trespassing? This isn't a nice thing to do and it isn't even like we have the excuse of being children!'

Alec sits up, and I can feel him struggling to hold on to his patience – so much for our truce. 'Donald had his reasons for asking you to do this. Does he say what they are?'

I reread the letter. 'Something about the sins of television and wanting me to experience "a healthy dose of fear".' I hand it to Alec to read.

'Well, there you are then: he wants you to experience moments from his life and . . .' Alec frowns slightly as he hands it back. '. . . fear, apparently. So let's get it over with and move on.'

I sink back into the deckchair, knowing my mum would be both disappointed and worried. Dad would be furious. I dread to think what he'll say if I'm caught. I picture him bailing me out, looking livid.

'Can't we pick some from a hedgerow?'

'That would hardly be within the spirit of the task,' Alec scoffs.

'So you think we should actually go into someone's garden, pick fruit they have cared for on trees they have grown from a seed, and then run away?'

'Yes.'

'In that case we disagree.'

'OK then,' says Alec, lying back in his deckchair and closing his eyes again.

'What do you mean, "OK then"?' I ask hotly. Isn't he at least going to call me a 'chicken' or something?

'I'm not going to force you. It seems a shame,' he says, 'but if you don't consider Donald worth a bit of scrumping, then who am I to argue?'

I slouch back and wrap my arms around myself, annoyed. He's got me, but I still think I'm right: what if someone calls the police? I suppose I could always explain about the will; even show them the letter. Uncle Donald would probably say that 'isn't cricket', but I'm not about to spend the summer doing community service over some stupid apples.

I glance at Alec again, who clearly thinks I'm being uptight. I scowl at a butterfly flitting between the urns and sigh. What annoys me most is that Alec is watching me from between his eyelashes, and it's like he knows I'll agree in the end. It's so irritating. I glare at him and he opens his eyes.

'Shall we find some apple trees?' he asks.

Feeling thoroughly outmanoeuvred, I'd love to say something cutting, but nothing springs to mind.

'I'll get my car keys,' I say getting up. And while I'm at it I'll put away my moral code. Alec props the deckchairs against the wall as I stalk back towards the house, and I get the feeling he's laughing at me.

As I drive, I am acutely aware of Alec sitting next to me. He's lounging lazily in the passenger seat, looking out of the open window as the smell of wild garlic and baked grass floods the car. Every so often he calls out directions, and as we approach a village, I catch my forefingers tapping the steering wheel with increasing speed. I stop tapping and hope Alec hasn't noticed.

We drive into the village, and my fingers start tapping again. Gripping the wheel, I glance at Alec, who is calmly scanning the passing gardens for apple trees.

'Could you slow down a bit?' he asks.

I'm tempted to plunge my foot onto the accelerator, but I reluctantly do as I'm told, turning when he suggests we try up a slight hill.

'Bingo!' says Alec. 'Park on the verge.'

I pull onto the grass, muttering darkly to myself as we get out and peak over a garden wall.

In the cottage's small orchard there are several short, gnarled apple trees and a few taller pear trees, but it's the enormous tree at the bottom of the slope that catches my eye, with its beautiful strong limbs heavy with giant apples.

'Now that's an apple tree,' I breathe, pointing to it.

Alec gives me a funny look. 'That's a Bramley,' he whispers.

'A what?'

'Cooking apples,' he explains. 'No good for eating. You want the little trees.'

I can feel a blush creeping across my cheeks. How embarrassing. Not that I care what he thinks. 'Now we've found them, shouldn't we go before we're spotted?' I ask, but he ignores me.

'Here's the plan,' he says, getting down to business. 'We get you over the wall, you climb a tree, pick five apples and we leave. If you're quiet, the owners won't even know we've been. So, be *very* quick and *very* quiet.'

I nod. 'When shall we do this?'

Alec stares at me. 'Now?' he suggests, and his sarcasm stings.

'Or we could come back at twilight or even when it's completely dark? Or, we could send them tickets to a show or something, so they're out? Or we could just hang about until they *are* out.'

'You want to buy theatre tickets or stalk these people so you can pinch five apples? Yeah, that's exactly how small boys do it!' He shakes his head in disbelief and clasps his hands into a makeshift foothold. 'Get over the wall.'

I glare at him.

'Hurry up,' he hisses. 'This doesn't look good, you know.'

I glance along the road. It's true – it looks terrible. Flustered, I put my foot in his hands and feel myself propelled up the wall with more haste than care. I scramble over and land heavily on the grass on the other side. I immediately dismiss the woefully bird-pecked fruit on the ground – there's no way Alec would let me get away with that – and run to the nearest tree. Just as I reach it, a flock of geese and chickens, which I hadn't noticed, start gabbling in alarm. The geese, furious at the intrusion, charge across the grass towards me, their wings spread. Shit – I'm sure I heard somewhere that they can break your arm. I'm not sure how – leverage? Teamwork? Or am I confusing them with swans? I clamp my arms firmly to my sides.

'Hurry up,' urges Alec, landing on my side of the wall, and despite his tone I'm glad he's here.

I clamber up the gnarled bark of the nearest tree, grab five apples and a few scabby leaves and shove them down my top for safekeeping, hurriedly tucking in the hem before they fall through.

'Ow, ya buggers!' cries Alec, fending off the geese, and no longer quite so sardonic about the whole experience. 'Jump,' he calls, holding out his arms.

Just as I'm about to launch myself into the air, the back door of the cottage opens and an old gent steps out. He immediately grasps what's going on, grabs a stick and makes his way across his vegetable patch. 'Bloody hooligans!' he shouts.

'Jump,' shouts Alec again, and I jump, feeling him stagger as he steadies my landing, and the apples thump against my chest.

The old man shakes his stick at us. 'Shame on you, scrumping apples at your age! Go somewhere else to relive your childhood. Better still, buy your own damned apple trees!'

Alec and I run for the wall. 'It's not *my* childhood I'm reliving!' I hiss. Alec gives me a quick boost over the wall, before vaulting over after me.

I can still hear the man ranting above the noise of the geese as we run for the car. 'I spray and prune these bloody trees only for you to—'

My hands shake as I try to fit the key in the door lock.

'You locked it?' asks Alec incredulously.

'Yes! Because some other idiot might have a will telling them to go joyriding!' I snarl.

Alec laughs, seriously testing the bonds of our delicate truce, as I wrench the car door open, and I'm almost tempted to drive off without him. I suppress the impulse and lean over to unlock his side. I'm faster starting the engine and within seconds we're off. I speed up the hill, my heart beating louder than the engine, and quickly turn the corner.

'Slow down,' he says, his voice slightly higher than usual, and I notice he's clutching the sides of his seat. I glance at the speedometer and am surprised by how fast I'm going on the tiny back lane. I ease my foot off the accelerator and let the car slow.

'Would you like me to take over?' he asks, in a way that makes me have to bite my tongue.

I ignore him and carefully assess how I'm feeling. Although my heart's still running the Grand National, now that we're out of sight of the house, I think I'm fine. I take a deep breath and the apples shift uncomfortably around my middle.

'No,' I tell him. 'But I do want to get these bloody apples out of my top.'

We drive along the lane until there's a passing place, then I pull to the side and turn off the engine. I untuck my top, letting the apples tumble into my lap and throw them onto the back seat. It seems very quiet with the engine off. I close my eyes for a moment, but my heart's still racing so I get out and walk around the car, taking some slow deep breaths.

'That didn't quite go to plan,' says Alec mildly as he joins me.

'Oh, I don't know. "Take Hannah scrumping. Get at least five",' I quote, mimicking Donald with all the derision I can muster.

'True,' agrees Alec, leaning against the Volvo and looking out across the fields.

'Oh God! Do you think he saw my number plate?' I ask, images of the old man on the phone to the police vivid in my mind.

'No!' laughs Alec. 'There was a wall in the way. And they're not going to take DNA samples or question the neighbours either. It's only a few apples. It's hardly the crime of the century. God, you're so uptight. Calm down.'

I stare out at the fields, biting back a thousand expletives.

'Try an apple,' he suggests, reaching into the back seat and selecting two. He hands me one.

I pick off the leaves, polish its surface and bite. 'Yuk! It's not even ripe,' I say, spitting it out.

'No, it's too early for them to be picked,' agrees Alec, seemingly savouring the bitterness. 'But that's the taste of a scrumper's apple.'

I take another bite, ready for the sourness this time.

'You're hurt!' Alec points at my legs, and I twist and see a raw scrape across my underarm and then feel the surge of hot pain from more scrapes on the backs of my legs.

'Ow! I wish you hadn't said anything. They hurt now.'

'Sorry,' he says absently, checking the damage. 'We'd better get something on those. Are you still OK to drive?'

I nod. We throw our apples into the hedge for the field mice and get back in the car.

We set off, but the seat rubs against my scrapes every time I change gear. I can't believe I didn't notice the pain before – it's so sore.

By the time we reach The Laurels, my legs are really stinging and every contact with the seat is torture. Alec, seeing me struggle to get out, comes around to my side of the car.

'Let me help,' he says firmly.

'I'm fine,' I say, warding him off with one hand and clutching the door frame with the other. But as I pull myself upright my head reels and I clutch at Alec's hastily proffered arm. He puts one arm around my waist, leaving his other free to open doors, and as he holds me closer so he can unlock the front door, it takes all my self-control not to let my eyes close and my head tuck itself comfortably under his chin. It must be the shock. I try to ignore the heady scent of aftershave and apples, and stay upright as he leads me carefully to a sofa in the drawing room.

Alec leaves me lying on my stomach, gathering my scattered thoughts. I mean, I know he's attractive, but he's also judgemental, rude and has shown barely any civility, and since I don't believe in the old adage 'treat them mean, keep them keen', I shouldn't be acting like a heroine in a Victorian melodrama. But he did smell good . . .

Alec comes back with a first-aid kit, and hands me Donald's next letter before kneeling down to inspect my grazes.

'Read this while I clean you up,' he instructs. His voice is hard but, as I glance back, I see concern in his eyes. He takes out some wipes to clean up my bare legs, and I clear my throat. This all feels oddly intimate, but his calm expression and assured movements give nothing away. I'm probably just over-thinking this. I turn back to the letter and tear open the envelope, grateful for the distraction.

My Dearest Hannah,

Bravissimo! You have succeeded. How did you find it? Did you run until your heart pounded in your ears? Did you feel relief flood through you like a tide? I hope you tasted success, guilt and that strange tang of unsweet apple . . .

'Ow,' I say involuntarily as Alec cleans my scrapes with something that really hurts.

'Sorry,' he breathes.

. . . You should now understand why small boys risked a beating to steal almost inedible fruit. These days, children won't even look at fruit, but add an element of sport and risk and who knows? Parents have missed a trick here, I feel.

I remember the thrill of scrumping as if it were yesterday. It was so exciting and it engendered a high degree of comradeship when done with friends – television and computer games have nothing on it.

Of course it wasn't all success and apples. I was once caught by old Mr Rogers. He dragged me home by the scruff of my shirt – a very difficult way to walk, I can tell you – and he told my father to beat me. My father agreed, and thanked(!) Mr Rogers. He smacked me ten times with a slipper. The slap of that slipper came a whole second before the sting. I didn't scrump from Mr Rogers' trees again (well, not unless it was a dare and therefore a case of chicken or good egg), but I can't say other people's trees were safe.

I acknowledge there is greater guilt associated with doing such acts in later life, and although I needed you to do this task to feel the thrill of fear and danger, let integrity be your watch-word from now on. By all means live for adventure, but listen to your moral barometer. I've lived by mine, and stand by it, though many may say I have done things I shouldn't . . .

I think of Grandma Betty's condemning scowl, and smile even though Alec seems intent on scouring my legs to a sparkling finish.

. . . So, onto the next task. For this one you must build a go-kart. Please construct it out of an old pram and bits of scrap. In other words, properly *– none of this shop-bought rubbish. Alec will help you – and make sure he does because it will do him good.*

When it's complete, ride it down Tor Hill, top to bottom. Alec knows where that is, and make sure you don't dig your heels in all the way down. This task is supposed to be a lesson in exhilaration.

Good luck and with high hopes,
Yours, descending at speed,
Uncle Donald

Building the go-kart is clearly a team task, which is probably a good thing considering I have no go-karting knowledge whatsoever – I wouldn't even know where to begin.

I wince and inhale sharply as Alec smears some antiseptic cream on my legs. God, that stings! I drop my head onto my arms to hide the fact that tears are leaking from my eyes. 'We have to build a go-kart,' I tell him from between gritted teeth.

'Really?' asks Alec. 'You'll enjoy that. Right, you're done,' he says getting to his feet. 'Ready to see what Mrs Crumpton has cooked us for dinner?' He holds out a hand to help me up.

'No, *we* have to build a go-kart, *together*,' I say, taking his hand, and struggling not to get antiseptic cream all over the no-doubt priceless sofa.

'Oh. Well, we can do that,' he says, more willing than I expected to spend time with me. I follow him into the dining room and carefully perch on the edge of a chair.

'So, didn't you know about us making a go-kart?' I ask.

'No,' he says frowning slightly. 'Donald told me about some of the things he had planned, but when I asked him for details he kept telling me to "hold my horses" and that I'd find out when the time came.'

'Isn't that a bit odd, given that you're supposed to be helping me?'

Alec shrugs as Mrs Crumpton comes in with a tray, and as she puts our plates on the table, he tells her what we've been up to, from the geese, to the scrumping and about my locking the car. Wishing to forget the whole experience, I zone out and mull over why Donald didn't tell Alec everything. I'm brought out of my ruminations by Mrs Crumpton's horrified voice.

'That's shameful!' she declares in the tones of a hellfire preacher, glaring at me and Alec with equal amounts of condemnation. 'There's no other word for it – and you bein' educated and such! Shameful!' she says again, shaking her head at us.

I instantly feel just as awful as I thought I would before the task.

Alec laughs. 'Oh come on Mrs C, spirit of youth and all that. Hannah didn't want to do it. She was under orders from Donald.' I'm surprised he's defending me, even if it isn't having any effect on Mrs Crumpton.

'Actin' under orders may be a defence in the military, Alec, but it ain't no defence in manners, law or under God! As for Donald, he's payin' the price wherever 'e is, the old rogue.' But her last words don't contain the vehemence of the rest and, unless I'm very much mistaken, there's a trace of affection there.

'Eat your dinner before it gets cold,' she orders, shooting me a hard look before she leaves the room. I stare at the delicious food she has made for us, but I'm suddenly not as hungry as I thought I was.

9

I pick up the clock by my bed and stare at it. It's 5 a.m., and I've been awake for a while. I turn over, but when I close my eyes I keep seeing the old man struggling across his vegetable patch, desperate to stop me pinching his apples. What he must have thought, seeing a grown woman up his tree, and a man in his garden, I don't know.

'Bloody hooligans!'

That about sums us up. It doesn't help that Mrs Crumpton's 'shameful' keeps ringing through my head like a persistent banshee.

If only I hadn't gone to bed so early, I wouldn't be awake now. But with Alec disappearing off to the study, leaving me – the unwanted guest – to go to my room, there wasn't a lot to do. I tried sitting at the beautiful desk and wrote some tedious and unimaginative first lines as I attempted to describe the day, but soon scrubbed them out, leaving the word 'inspired' mockingly marooned amongst the scratched-out ideas. Then I went to bed, still feeling guilty about the scrumping, and read.

I check the clock again. 5.02. How can only two minutes have gone by? I can't remember the last time I was up this early, but last night I hatched a plan, and seeing as I'm apparently not going to get any more sleep, I might as well put it into action.

I dress, careful not to make any noise or rub my scrapes, grab my purse and car keys and let myself very quietly out of the house.

*   *   *

Thankfully, the 24-hour supermarket had a good selection of fruit and a pretty basket, in which I've arranged everything artistically, but now that I'm parked up outside the cottage with the apple trees, my nerves are kicking in. *And*, I now realise, I've forgotten to buy any paper! A quick search of the glove box yields nothing suitable for an apologetic note, and writing a note on the fruit receipt would look like I was claiming expenses or something. I rest my head against the steering wheel, annoyed at this glitch in my otherwise perfect plan.

I get out, dragging my feet like I'm back in junior school, and stand by the wooden gate looking down at the cottage. The lights are on, so someone's awake, and it's now or never. I open the gate, wincing at its slight squeak, and tiptoe up to the front door, planning to leave the basket on the doorstep. I glance back at the gate, but as I consider this cop-out I realise my own stupid conscience won't let me off. I have to apologise in person, even though the idea of meeting the owner turns me cold.

I close my eyes and knock.

I instantly regret it, and hearing footsteps, I feel an almost irresistible urge to bolt. I only just manage to hold my ground, bracing myself as the latch lifts . . . and a comfortable-looking woman with a friendly face opens the door.

'You're up early,' she says pleasantly, and I almost don't hear her over the blood pounding in my ears.

I thrust the fruit basket at her. 'It's for yesterday,' I say, unable to meet her eyes. Coward. 'I'm so sorry.'

'Bless you, sweetheart,' says the woman. 'You'll be wanting Jim.'

I definitely don't want Jim! It takes all my courage not to turn tail as she disappears off to find him, but I manage to stay put.

Jim comes to the door, drying his hands on a tea towel. He's the man from the vegetable patch, and I open my mouth to apologise properly and sincerely, with an extra helping of heartfelt woe, when he beams at me. 'Hannah, is it?'

My voice sticks in my throat. 'Ye-es?' I answer, my mind frantically spooling through the possibilities: police checks, number plates . . . private detectives?

'Thought you'd be along. Come in for a spot of breakfast.'

The woman nods behind him, giving me an encouraging smile.

Trying to banish *Hansel and Gretel*-type thoughts of ending up in a scrumpers stew, I step into their small, warm cottage with its ancient beams and flag-stone flooring and follow them through to the kitchen. Dominating the room is a large hearth and range with herbs drying above it in bunches. An easy chair holds two sleeping cats, and the room smells of dried thyme, toast and strong tea. Jim's wife points to a crochet-cushioned seat at the table and I sit as she pours a mug of hot sweet tea.

'Get that down you,' she says, pushing it towards me. 'Thought you was going to pass out,' she laughs, and I have to admit I am feeling a bit wobbly. 'We saw you at the funeral,' she explains. 'Did Alec tell you about us?'

I shake my head.

Jim puts the fruit basket on the table and chuckles. 'He wanted to see what she'd do, I reckon. Nice of you, that,' he says, nodding at the basket.

I stare at Jim, light dawning. Oh God, the scrumping was all a set-up, which means Alec watched me be a scaredy-cat for nothing. Bloody Alec! I can't believe he put me through all this!

'Now, I think there's some explaining to be done,' says Jim. I could tell him who needs to do some explaining, but I assume a polite expression. 'I'm Jim and this is my wife, May, and we liked your uncle a great deal.'

I sip my tea, feeling like Alice rammed head first down the rabbit hole, and though I don't usually take sugar in my tea, it's helping.

'He used to come by,' continues Jim, 'and we had many a lovely evening over a bottle o' something. One evening when he was here, Donald explained about his will and such and it was our idea that you scrump apples from my trees so that you didn't get into any trouble. It's no skin off my nose . . .' Jim looks uncomfortably at my scraped arm, '. . . and I was more than happy to be a part of things. I just hoped I'd be here when you came, to add a little spice and dramatic effect. I think he would have been pleased with the show I put on. Bloody hooligans!' he shouts, grinning proudly.

'Well, I believed you!' Enough to give me nightmares.

'Grand,' he says, pleased with my good review. 'Never expected this though,' he says, indicating the fruit. 'Most kind, that is.'

'I wanted to make amends,' I explain.

'Well, that'll do nicely,' says May, putting two boiled eggs and some toast in front of me, and I suddenly realise I'm ravenous. She puts a mug of cutlery in the middle of the table and I take some. 'How's Alec?'

'Fine.' Not that he'll stay that way when I get my hands on him. 'Asleep, I hope. He doesn't know I'm here,' I add, knocking the tops off my eggs and buttering my toast.

'Not to worry. I'm sure he'll guess.' I think May's trying to reassure me, but it only makes me all the more determined to get back before he wakes up now that I know the extent of his treachery. I smile at May, who pats me on the shoulder.

'Did Donald tell you that we only met once?' I ask, dipping my toast in the perfectly gooey yolk.

'He said you were a lovely lass and made him feel young again,' says May, spooning more eggs out of the pan. 'Quite taken with you he was, and excited as anything about his plans. Never seen anyone take so much happy interest in their own demise, but here you are and I see why he was so pleased. How are you getting on with them tasks he was telling us about?'

'All right, but I've only done one so far.' I swallow a mouthful of toast. 'I have to build a go-kart next.'

'A trip to the dump is what you want,' says Jim. 'Rare old treasure chests those places can be if you're good at the old lateral thinking.' He taps his head.

'There are posh ones now called "reclamation yards",' says May, rolling her eyes.

'True enough,' agrees Jim, shaking his head sadly. 'Same stuff, bigger prices. Make sure you use enough fixings, screws and such, so that it holds together over rough ground. Terrible punishing, gravel can be.' He swallows his last bite of eggs and toast and looks sadly at his empty plate. 'Well, that's me done. I must go and feed the chickens and geese. You'll remember them,' he says, chuckling.

'Yes, indeed,' I say grimly. I get to my feet and shake his hand, taking this as my cue to leave.

'You're always welcome, same as he was,' says Jim. 'See that whisky bottle up there?' He points to a half-full bottle of single malt on top of the dresser. 'That's there so he knows he can come by any time.'

May nods. 'He can haunt us whenever he likes.'

It's wonderful to think you can always be welcome somewhere. I smile at them both. 'Thank you for giving me breakfast, and again, sorry about yesterday.'

'Just pleased to be part of it,' says Jim, clearly proud of his amateur dramatics. He'll be auditioning for *Macbeth* next.

'You don't have to go just because Jim's off out,' says May. 'You can always stay for another cup of tea?' I'm tempted. She's such a lovely, comfortable and warm person, I already know I could tell her anything.

'I'd love to, but I want to get back before Alec wakes up,' I say, and May nods. I can see she understands.

'Be no stranger,' says Jim, putting on his boots, while May walks me to the door.

Before I can say my usual 'bye, then', May pulls me into a proper hug. I'm surprised, but it's so genuine, I feel a lump in my throat. Everyone I know hugs like a cardboard cut-out.

'Thank you,' I say as she lets go. I walk down the garden path with her waving at me until I am out of sight. As I get in the car I almost want to run back and ask for another hug. I think she'd happily give me one, too, but I start the engine and head back.

Barely twenty minutes later, I'm back at The Laurels and find Alec sitting on the stairs with a newspaper in one hand and a cup of coffee in the other. He gives me a smile that tells me he knows exactly where I've been, and he's blocking my escape route up the stairs.

'Nice time at Jim and May's?' he asks.

I cross my arms and glare at him. 'Yes, thank you. So it was all a set-up?'

'Yes,' he says, grinning like the Cheshire Cat and sipping his coffee.

'And you let me believe it was all real?'

'Yes.'

'Even though you could have given me a heads-up and saved me a whole lot of soul-searching.'

'If I had, it would have ruined Donald's plans.'

'Which were to make me look a fool!'

'No, they were designed to give you the real experience without exposing you to danger. Where's your sense of humour?'

'So, you're telling me that you didn't enjoy leading me along, pretending it was all real, and watching me get scared?'

'I'm not saying that.'

'I didn't think so!'

He's smiling at me and my mouth twitches involuntarily.

'So, did you have a nice time?' he asks again more gently.

'Of course I did,' I huff. 'They're delightful.'

He bites his lips together, clearly amused that I'm still annoyed. 'Yes, they are, aren't they?' he says conversationally, and takes another sip of his coffee.

'Very accommodating,' I agree frostily, but he's so obviously almost laughing that I pick my way around him and stomp up the stairs. As I round the corner I see his shoulders shaking.

In my room, I plump down on the bed and fall back into the covers with my arms spread wide. I'm still angry, but I'm starting to see that Alec's right – I did have a real experience. I did experience fear and feel the blood pounding in my ears, the thrill of success and the guilt, and all within a safe environment. I even felt a hint of the comradeship Donald mentioned, and I think Alec did too. And he laughed. Shame it was at my expense, but at least he's cheered up a bit. I wonder if Donald set this task to be a sort of ice-breaker? If so, it's clever.

I raise myself up on my elbows and survey the room. Mrs Crumpton is clanking pans down in the kitchen, which reminds me I have another issue to deal with. I head back down the now empty stairs to find her making porridge.

She looks at me with a cocked eyebrow. 'It'll be five minutes,' she says, nodding at the kitchen table, so I take a seat.

Shameful!

I stroke the side of my thumb across the wooden grain of the table's scrubbed surface. Trouble is, I'm quite scared of her and I don't know how to start. Sound confident, and don't show fear. Like with horses. Picture her as a horse.

'Mrs Crumpton?' I venture bravely.

She raises an eyebrow at me, and I manage to keep hold of my courage despite it trying to slink off.

'I went out this morning to visit the people from the apple scrumping and I gave them a basket of fruit to say I'm sorry.' Mrs Crumpton's eyebrow is still raised. 'It turns out that they're friends of Donald's and he arranged the whole thing with them . . . about my scrumping their apples I mean, and honestly, it's fine. They're happy. They have the fruit I bought in return for what I took, and we're all friends.' I'm staring at her, willing her to accept my explanation, but there's an unexpected glint in her eye . . . and suddenly it dawns on me.

'You knew, didn't you?' I exclaim. 'You bloody knew! And you said all that just to be . . . Oh!' I'm so riled up I could swear a lot more colourfully, but I don't quite have the nerve. 'Ooh! Right at this minute, I could really *hate* Uncle Donald!'

Mrs Crumpton nods at me with satisfaction. 'He takes us all like that sometimes,' she says. 'He'd say 'e was teachin' you to stand by your principles, but I know he'd have loved bamboozlin' you.'

I can even picture him smirking as he planned it. 'Bloody, bloody man!' I mutter, still fuming.

Mrs Crumpton ladles some porridge into a bowl and nudges it towards me. I decide to forget about my breakfast with Jim and May, and pick up my spoon. The porridge is heavenly, and I eat more greedily than I'd have thought possible. Adventure seems to have increased my appetite, as well as my temper.

Alec strolls in and sits down. 'Morning, Mrs C,' he says. He grins at me, still amused by our earlier encounter, and I narrow my eyes at him.

'Elbows off the table,' she says in greeting, and ladles porridge into his bowl.

He spoons liberal amounts of honey and cream over it. 'She's an alchemist with food,' he whispers to me. Mrs Crumpton must have heard, but she gives no sign.

I smile at her, but just as I think I've been snubbed, she gives me the merest flutter of a wink and I flush with pleasure. I even grin at Alec, though he doesn't deserve it.

Mrs Crumpton heads off to the sink with the porridge pan giving me a small nod as she goes. I think I've proved myself, and I get the feeling that once she's your friend, she's a fierce and loyal one.

Alec stares from her to me, then scrapes his bowl clean. 'Right, go-kart,' he says, somehow drawing a line under everything to do with the scrumping, which is a good idea.

'Go-kart,' I agree, propping my chin up on my hand. 'Where do we start?'

He rubs his hands together, his face shining. 'We need something with wheels; a pram or a trolley is best.'

'Do you know how to get either of those?'

'No, we need to track one down.'

'How about we try scrap yards and reclamation yards?' I suggest, remembering what Jim and May said.

Alec pushes his bowl aside, and gives this some thought. 'Maybe, but prams aren't as common as they used to be. People value them.' Far from being discouraged, Alec seems pleased by the challenge.

I stack my bowl on top of his. 'We could try the Internet – maybe one of those free-cycling sites will have something?'

'Good idea,' he agrees. 'And we should try the council recycling centres as well. Let's make a list of the things we'll need and then we can look for a few other parts as we go.'

Mrs Crumpton takes our bowls and places a pen and paper in front of Alec.

'Thanks Mrs C.' Alec writes 'Go-kart', then underneath writes 'pram (if available)'.

I have another think. 'Wood?'

Alec nods. He adds 'planks, wooden box? Lots of screws, and maybe some U-bolts' to the list.

Jim's comments about making sure it holds together over rough ground spring to mind. 'What about the bits that connect the wheels?'

'Axles? I'm hoping they'll come with the pram, but I suppose that depends on the state of it, and whether we even find one. Rope!' he says, scribbling it down. He writes 'axles' underneath. He reminds me of a kid writing a list for Santa, and I can't help wondering where all this enthusiasm comes from.

'Have you built a go-kart before?' I ask.

'Yes, a long time ago. Do you understand the basic principles?' he asks. I shake my head, so he turns over the page, sketching a go-kart as he explains the mechanics. 'Three planks in a capital H shape, wheels at each of the outer corners – that would travel in a straight line, like a toy car. But if you put a pivoting bolt in just here, through the right end of the H's cross bar, and attach a rope to the ends of this right-hand plank, here and here, you have steering, similar to the reins on a horse.'

I can see what he means, but there's one vital element missing. 'How do you brake?'

'No brakes,' states Alec. I stare at him. 'You don't need them. You choose a hill with a flat end-zone and come to a natural stop, or you stick your feet down and hope you don't ruin your shoes.'

'So . . . brake shoes?' I ask dubiously.

'Exactly.'

'Why don't you just choose a shallow hill?'

Alec looks baffled. 'Where would the fun be in that? Half the point is being out of control.'

Oh great. While Alec collects his laptop, I pick up the pen and fiddle with it, because if I'm honest, I'm not great with anything on wheels. Cars are fine, bikes are OK, though I never did more than master the basics, but anything else ends in disaster. I tried a skateboard once and broke my coccyx, tried a wheelie shoe (just the one) in a shoe shop and knocked over an entire boot display, and when I was at university my friends thought we should all try roller-blading – big mistake! It turned out they had all had roller-skates as children and when I stupidly tried to keep up with them down an underpass I managed to remove several layers of skin from my hip bone, shoulder and chin despite wearing all the protective elbow and knee pads. I've been a bit nervous of speed ever since. Still, perhaps it's time to get over that, and at least a go-kart is low down.

Alec comes back and sits down next to me, using his laptop to check the local swapping and recycling sites. 'No prams,' he says after a few minutes.

'What happens if we can't find one? Do we have to buy a go-kart instead?'

Alec's mouth drops open and he stares at me in consternation. 'You have to *build* the go-kart,' he says emphatically, as if he's talking to a particularly clueless village idiot, 'and the go-kart has to be made from scrap. That's literally the task.'

I raise my eyebrows at him. 'But isn't that just making life difficult for ourselves?'

'No.' He turns to face me impatiently. 'You see, if you buy everything, there's no spirit in the machine, and you only get half the experience. There's no pride when it works. No beating the odds.'

'But I thought the point of building a go-kart was so you can go fast down a hill?' Now I'm the baffled one.

'That's part of it,' he agrees. 'That gives you the hit of adrenaline; but there's so much more to it than that. There's the joy of making something work and improving on it when it breaks.' Alec frowns. 'Making it from scrap is a long-lasting accomplishment. It's . . .' he's struggling to find the right word, '. . . better. Fixing it, making it faster and getting it right can become an obsession.' No kidding – it's like a secret society, with its own set of distinct rules.

'So, we're not buying one,' I conclude. 'Should we try junk shops, then?'

Alec nods, satisfied I'm starting to understand, and as he looks them up, I carefully jot down their addresses. We also note down any nearby antique shops, though they might prove to be out of our price range.

Closing his computer, Alec frowns. 'So, no pram yet, but we might find some parts in the shed.'

'I didn't know there was a shed?' I say, perking up – I love rummaging through old stuff.

Pleased at my enthusiasm, Alec grins and beckons with his finger. 'Follow me.'

We head through the kitchen, past Mrs Crumpton, who is punishing the porridge pan with a scourer, and leave the house by a small side door. I was expecting a little wooden shack, but nestling in the laurel bushes is an old-fashioned garage with wooden double doors. It obviously hasn't been used as a garage in a long time as the brambles have streaked across the concrete in front of it and fingers of ivy are snarling up the hinges.

Alec tugs open one of the doors. It stutters across the cracked concrete, and its hinges creak in protest as they grind on their rust. As light floods in, I can see parts of an old mangle, an ancient electric cooker, some rusty bicycles whose chains have welded to their teeth, a decrepit chaise longue and some rolls of old carpet. I stand in the doorway and marvel at it all – it's a proper treasure trove.

Alec rushes over to examine some planks leaning against the side wall. 'Some of these will do,' he says, looking along their length to check they're straight.

I crouch down and touch the carpets. The top bits are all off-cuts, but the bottom ones, from their reverse patterning and fringing, look to be genuine old Victorian ones. I'd love to take them outside and unroll them, but the carpets won't help the go-kart. I leave them, with one last longing glance, and pick my way to the small side window where there are some promising small boxes on the windowsill. I pick them out from amongst the cobwebs and dead flies and lift their lids.

'Screws and nails,' I call, holding them up victoriously.

Alec's checking another piece of wood, examining its profile like it's a particularly handsome dog at Crufts. 'Great, if they're not too rusty, we'll use them.'

I grin at him. 'Or we could buy some new ones if these aren't long enough?' I say. His head snaps up and he directs a frown at me. 'Just kidding!' I call in a sing-song voice, and his face relaxes into a genuine smile that softens the harsh lines of his face, while lending him a raffish charm. It makes a pleasant change after all the times he's scowled at me.

'It seems ill-advised to tease the person engineering your go-kart,' he says with mock-solemnity.

'Did you study engineering?' I ask curiously.

'Actually, I studied computing,' he says more seriously. 'But I'd have loved to study engineering . . . or English,' he adds thoughtfully.

'They're hardly similar. And you shouldn't cross the arts/science boundaries – very dodgy,' I say, shaking my head, pretending to be shocked.

He nods. 'But there are some similarities.'

'Such as . . .?'

'I like to see how things work, whether that's sentences or machines, and you can take both apart and put them back together again with varying results.'

'That's true.' I'm surprised by how insightful he is.

'And they're both creative and inventive, and involve learning a lot of basic principles so that they don't stall.'

I hold up my hands laughing. 'OK, you've convinced me – English and engineering are exactly the same. Perhaps you should consider philosophy while you're at it,' I add.

He picks up another plank and grins at me. 'What about you? Do you miss university?' he asks.

I shrug. 'Not really. It was very different the second time around.'

'How so?'

I struggle to put into words how I no longer felt dazzled by the intoxicating freedom of being away from home, how I was never impressed by drinking and casual sex, and that the constant and stringent need to budget got on my nerves. 'I seemed to have a different mindset to everyone else: taking the assignments more seriously, more worried about my prospects, that kind of thing. I was ready to move on ages ago, I just wish I knew what to.' I frown, feeling oddly vulnerable, and I'm pleased when he returns his attention to his stack of wood.

I perch on the dusty chaise longue to watch Alec sort happily through the last few planks, and it suddenly dawns on me how clever Donald has been. Not only are the tasks helping me and Donald achieve our goals, they're also keeping Alec, and perhaps even Mrs Crumpton, from brooding by keeping them involved. Even Donald's friends, Jim and May, are keen to know what will happen next. Everyone's on their toes, waiting for Donald's next move, and that's keeping them going. I think I'll let Donald off for making me look a fool with the scrumping, given the good it's done.

'Ah-ha!' says Alec, holding up a third plank like a trophy, before stacking the rejects back where he found them. He climbs over the carpets to the window and starts sorting through the selection of screws I found.

'Finding a pivoting bolt and fixings to hold the axles might be tricky, but these are a good start,' he says. 'If we use enough you should be fine.'

'I'd have thought that was a given?'

Alec shakes his head. 'It's never a given,' he says, a hint of glee in his voice. Pulling the list from his back pocket, he strikes through the entries for planks and screws. 'We've made a good start, but we still need to find a pram.' He beams at me without reservation, and I'm struck again by the change a simple smile can make.

'I was hoping it'd be a few more years before someone said that to me.'

Alec looks confused, but I don't enlighten him. I walk back to the house to fetch the list of business addresses and my car keys, and we set off to visit the closest town.

10

We've climbed around every rusty junkyard and badly organised antique shop within a ten-mile radius. I've scaled everything from small hatchbacks to tallboys, and even climbed under a kneehole desk, but all we have to show for it is some rope, a big hex bolt and nut that 'will be fine after some WD-40', and some pipe-retaining clips that should hold the axles 'at a pinch'.

We return to The Laurels tired, dirty and pramless.

After a quick wash, we sit down at the table to eat our lunch, but Alec hasn't said a word since we got back. He seems downhearted and I suspect he's missing Donald. Yesterday, I wouldn't have said anything, but now that we're getting on a bit better, it seems wrong to ignore it.

'This is nice,' I venture, taking a mouthful of the ham, salad and boiled potatoes Mrs Crumpton has cooked for us.

'Yes,' Alec says distractedly. I lean into his peripheral vision and wait for him to surface. 'Sorry, miles away.' He shakes his head as if to clear it.

'Are you OK?' I ask.

'Yes.' He sighs heavily and forces a smile. 'It's funny the things we're doing at Donald's instigation, isn't it?'

'Yes,' I agree. 'But I guess that's the point – he wants us to experience new things.'

Alec nods and I nudge a potato around my plate, unsure what to say next, because I don't actually know much about Alec.

'What do you see yourself doing after this?' he asks casually.

'I'm not sure. I guess it depends on how much Donald's will changes everything.'

'In what way?' asks Alec, a slight edge coming into his voice.

I look at him, trying to understand what's made him uneasy. 'I don't know, but there might be a few new possibilities.'

'Because of your "unspecified" reward?' His tone is mocking and his forehead is creased, and I see what's happened. The merest hint of the mention of money, and he's back to the distrust-the-gold-digger stance he had yesterday.

'No, that's not what I meant,' I say patiently, holding his gaze and not afraid to show that I'm hurt that he would even think that. 'I was wondering if Donald might give me the confidence to try . . . something new.' I'm not confiding my hopes of becoming a writer with him in this mood! 'Though the reward is something to think about,' I concede, because, let's face it, it is, and it would be stupid to deny it.

'What are you hoping it will be?' he asks slightly less coldly, but his eyes are still watchful.

'I haven't a clue, but whatever it is I reckon Donald will have thought long and hard about it.'

'And if it's money?' he asks, the sour edge back in his voice, and I look down at my plate, coming to the limit of my ability to take this kind of questioning.

'Then perhaps it can support me for a while, or more likely, go some way towards paying off my university debts.' I frown at him, and he's the one who looks away first. 'Though that seems dull,' I admit, returning my attention to my plate. We eat in silence for a while, and I leave it to Alec to speak next.

'Would you like to go travelling?' he asks, tendering an off-white flag.

I assess his expression, and he seems to have let go of whatever offended him, so I consider his question. I imagine travelling by myself, taking selfies, and staying in youth hostels. 'Not really. I think I'm past that now – I just want to get going with real life, whatever that means. What about you? What do you see yourself doing after this?'

'Not sure. I've loved working here, and I can't imagine anyone else being as much fun as Donald, but I expect I'll apply for some posts and see what happens.'

'What about Mrs Crumpton?'

'Retiring, but I'm not sure she's happy about it.' I glance at Alec questioningly, and he shrugs. 'Donald suggested she retire a few years ago, just after her husband died, but she gave him a flea in his ear – went on about stagnating and dropping off her mortal coil from sheer boredom and no one noticing. She's considering it now though, and since Donald left her a nice nest egg . . .'

Alec pauses as the lady herself comes in to exchange our empty plates for bowls of jam roly-poly and custard, and in the silence I remember my family's shock at the sum of three hundred thousand pounds left to someone who wasn't even at the will reading.

'Neither of you will be here, then?' I ask once she's returned to the kitchen. Alec shakes his head, and I feel a stab of sadness for them both. 'Will you be sad to leave?'

'No, not with Mrs C and Donald gone.'

'But the house?'

Alec's smile doesn't meet his eyes. 'It's just a house, somewhere to live,' he says after a brief pause.

I glance incredulously at the gorgeous Georgian dining room. 'If you think this is just "somewhere to live", your parents must have been rich!'

Alec looks down at his plate, his jaw muscles contracting, and I realise I've struck a nerve, though how, I don't know. I dig my spoon into the jam roly-poly and cast around for a change of subject.

'So, go-karts . . .' I say, and carefully lead him back to discussing the last few avenues we can try for a pram.

It's been a long afternoon and my bum is almost numb from sitting on the stairs with the laptop open on my knees, telephoning every single flipping dealer, estate-clearance company and reclamation yard within a fifty-mile radius. I suggested to Alec that he could take over at one point, but he firmly reminded me that this is my task and therefore my job. That rankled, but he has stopped by every ten minutes or so to see how I'm doing. So far there's been no luck, and I've listened to endless dealers telling me how I'll have trouble finding one of those these days. One even told me I'd have more luck finding a Fabergé egg, though how he expected me to ride one of those down a hill, I have no idea.

Mrs Crumpton, who's passing through, stops to listen as I explain yet again what I want to an antique shop owner, over thirty miles away. The refined gentleman gives me another teeth-sucking negative and starts to say that he hasn't seen one of those for—

'Did you say "pram"?' asks Mrs Crumpton.

I put my hand over the mouthpiece. 'Yes, one of those old-fashioned ones with a hood and big wheels. I don't suppose you've seen one, have you?'

'What's it for?' she asks suspiciously.

'A go-kart – Donald's making us build one.'

Mrs Crumpton throws back her head and laughs. 'The old fool! It must've been three months ago that I saw 'im trying to get one of them things up the stairs. He said you'd need it. I thought 'e was losin' his marbles and said you'd be wanting one of them new-fangled three-wheelers.' She shakes her head, still tickled by Donald's antics. 'I'd try the attic if I was you. Alec will show you,' she adds, sweeping past Alec, who looks at me questioningly.

I thank the antique dealer over the top of his pram-related reminiscences and hang up, shaking my head in disbelief.

'What?' asks Alec.

'Mrs Crumpton says we should try the attic. She says she saw Uncle Donald take one up there.'

Alec bites his bottom lip, I think to stop himself swearing. 'I guess I should have thought of that, really.' He takes the stairs two at a time, and I follow hard on his heels as he heads through a slender door (which I thought was a linen cupboard) and races up a narrow flight of stairs to the attic. By the time we reach the top I'm feeling the thrill of the chase, excited by what we might find. I stare about in wonder. The attic, far from being dark and dingy, has a row of small dormer windows along one side, probably thanks to its servants' quarters past. I look around at the tempting dusty boxes, trunks and old furniture and see, over to one side, a dilapidated old-fashioned perambulator – perfect for our go-kart.

'Ooh!' says Alec, stumbling over some boxes in his hurry to get to it. Who would have thought a manky old pram could make us so happy?

I climb over a chest and unpin a note from its hood: 'For Hannah – The Holy Grail!'

'He knew it would be difficult,' I say, holding it up for Alec to see.

'Hmm,' he agrees, assessing the pram and its all-important wheels. 'Let's get it downstairs.'

We carry the pram down into the hall, then roll it out onto the terrace. In the proper light of day it looks even more raggedy than in the attic. In fact, it's no use for anything but a go-kart – there's certainly no way you'd put a baby in there.

'Were we supposed to find it sooner?' I ask.

'No, I reckon he'd have liked the thought of us struggling for a bit so he could swoop in and save the day. But I can't help wondering how long he had to wait on the stairs for Mrs Crumpton to walk by.'

'Hopefully ages!' I say, rubbing my bum, which is still tingling with pins and needles.

Alec snorts and leaves me on the terrace massaging myself while he goes to unearth some tools and collect our other finds.

I take a seat on a stone bench under one of the windows and close my eyes. The sun bakes my eyelids and as I start to relax, I realise I'm actually enjoying myself. The tasks are fun, and spending time with Mrs Crumpton and Alec isn't so bad now that Mrs Crumpton has decided she likes me and Alec has managed to put aside (most of) the chips he's been carting about on his shoulders since he met me. And I'm really enjoying staying here – the house is gorgeous. In fact, I'm not sure I've ever loved being anywhere as much as this, and it's all because of Uncle Donald.

I feel a shadow pass over me, and I open my eyes to find Alec standing in my sun. With planks tucked under one arm and holding a tool box with his other, he's the picture of a hunky handyman. I shade my eyes, and he gives me a hard look.

'You're not leaving me to do all the work, you know.'

I grin as if that had been my intention, though it wasn't really, and heave myself up. I come over to where he's laying everything out and sit cross-legged on the warm paving stones beside him. He takes out a cordless drill and pulls the trigger, revving its motor – boys!

'Ever used one of these?' he asks.

'No,' I say, shaking my head.

'OK. Lesson one: how to use a drill.' He hands it to me and using the stub of a pencil, he marks a cross where I should drill a hole. I look at him uncertainly. 'Give it a go,' he says. I put the drill on the mark, gently depress the trigger and skitter straight off the piece of wood, leaving a deep scratch.

He smiles, but not unkindly. 'Try again, but this time keep your weight over it.' I put the drill back on the mark and he casually reaches over to pull me into position, but as his fingers touch my bare arm it's as if hot ice courses through me. My eyes snap to his and he yanks his hand away like he's been shocked. Even though he's no longer touching me, my heart leaps about erratically. I try not to blush, but it's no use.

'The key is to pull the trigger slowly while holding the wood still with your other hand.' He's pretending nothing happened, but his eyes are still locked onto mine.

'OK,' I say, discomfited.

'Carefully,' he warns, and looking down, I focus on drilling a neat hole. 'That's better,' he says, and as he examines the hole, I slowly let out my breath, trying to hide the fact that I've been holding it.

I sit back as he drills the remaining holes. There's obviously some kind of attraction lurking beneath the surface, on my part at least, but Alec? Rude, suspicious, determined to think the worst of me . . . I mean, he struggles to remain civil half the time, and even now he's looking irritated! What am I thinking? Of course he doesn't fancy me.

'Hannah?' he asks, breaking into my thoughts. 'Did you get that?' He sounds annoyed. I look down at the drill now sporting a screwdriver head and realise I've missed something.

'No, sorry,' I say, pushing away all my disquieting thoughts, forcing myself to focus.

Over the next few hours we cut planks, screw the frame together, soak the large bolt in oil and deconstruct the pram, laying out the parts across the terrace and making a pile of scrap, while always keeping a careful distance from each other. Alec's been a bit abrupt, but after adding the wheels and axles, the go-kart trundles in a satisfyingly straight line across the terrace, and I can't help thinking we've done well.

'I'm not sure the wheels will stay on, but it looks the part,' he says.

'Great – give me confidence, why don't you?' I scoff, pleased we're able to joke again, though I have to admit it feels a bit forced.

'It's a go-kart. What do you expect?' He pokes his finger in the cup of oil to see if the bolt has loosened up.

'Not to die, for a start! Perhaps you should do the gentlemanly thing and do a test-run.'

'No way!' he says, giving me a satisfied grin. 'We haven't built it for my weight. Besides, I'm sure that goes against Donald's wishes.'

'You're just saying that because you don't fancy risking getting on it yourself.'

'You're probably right,' he admits. 'OK, let's get down to business. If we're quick, we can finish it tonight, and then you can race it in the morning.'

'Great,' I say. Though, if I'm honest, I'd rather have a glass of wine.

It's been an odd evening. We finished the go-kart and had dinner, but after clearing up and discussing our plans for tomorrow, Alec became monosyllabic and I got the impression he wanted some time alone. Not sure what else to do, I said I'd have an early night and came up to my room. I read for a while, but then finally taking my courage in my hands I took out a pen and a pad and sat down at the beautiful writing desk. I wrote for what must have been well over an hour, surprised to find myself more inspired from the last few days than I have been in years. But now it's late, I'm lying in bed and, even though I didn't get much sleep last night, I'm not at all tired.

If I was at home, I'd make some hot chocolate, but Mrs Crumpton doesn't strike me as a hot chocolate kind of person. She might have some cocoa for baking, though. I'm willing to give that a go. I grab my dressing gown and pad downstairs, hoping not to disturb Alec, but I needn't have worried – there's a light under the study door and, tiptoeing over, I can just make out someone sniffing inside. I hesitate, then tap gently on the door.

'Mm hmm,' he says, and I push it open. Alec's sitting at Donald's desk with red-rimmed eyes and there's a bottle of whisky and an almost-empty tumbler in front of him. My heart goes out to him, but I'm not sure if my being here is just going to make things worse.

'I'm sorry; I didn't mean to intrude – I saw the light on. Do you want company, or would you prefer to be left alone?' I smile sympathetically.

Alec wipes his eyes and tries to smile back. 'No, you're all right.' He indicates the empty seat in front of him and I tiptoe in and sit down, feeling oddly formal across the desk from him. 'Can't you sleep?' he asks.

I shake my head, but I'm more concerned about him. 'Is it Donald?' I ask, and he dips his head in acknowledgement.

I hesitate, remembering Grandma Betty's assessment of Alec and Donald's relationship. Were they more than employer and employee? I really don't know. I bite my lip, wondering if it would be better to have it out in the open. At least then he could talk about it. I stare down at my hands. 'It must be hard losing Donald, what with him being your employer and friend, and living with him and everything . . .' I hesitate, unsure whether to continue. '. . . and you don't have to tell me . . . and it may not be the case, but I was just wondering if . . . if he was more than that to you?'

My eyes dart to his, wondering if I've guessed correctly, but the hurt in his red-rimmed eyes has morphed into anger and incredulity, and I wish I'd kept my mouth shut.

'You think I don't have the right to be this upset unless we were . . . lovers, or something?!' he asks, his voice dangerously quiet.

'No! That's not what I—'

'If we weren't, you think I should maintain a stiff upper lip. Is that it?' I shake my head, wishing I could disappear into the floor. 'I have the right to mourn a friend! A *good* friend! A *decent* and *honourable* man!'

'I know that, I just thought that if you needed—'

'I don't,' says Alec firmly. He takes a gulp of whisky and shakes his head at me. 'And I certainly don't need anyone to judge!'

'I wasn't, I—'

'You were just suggesting that if I wasn't his lover then I'm over-reacting,' he says, getting to his feet. 'Well, you can go to hell,' he says, his voice icy. He turns on his heels and walks out, slamming the door behind him, leaving both it and me reverberating. I sit very still, my mind frantically going over what I just said. Maybe I was a little clumsy, but I didn't mean it like that.

Still shocked, I reach for his whisky and take a sip. It scours my insides and I wince. So I guess they weren't lovers, then. But why did I even ask, and why does it matter to me, anyway? I mean, I know my reactions to him over the last couple of days have been a bit erratic, but it's not like I'm actually interested in him in that way.

I tuck my feet up under myself and finish the last sip, holding it in my mouth for a moment so it burns my tongue. The door opens behind me, and I swallow. I don't need to turn around to know it's Alec. He sits down, this time in one of the fireside armchairs, and I pick up his empty glass, grab a second as well as the bottle, and sit in the chair opposite him. He pushes his hands through his hair and I pour us both a drink. As I hand him his, he finally meets my eyes, and in his I read both a wariness and an entreaty for me to understand.

'You asked me earlier if my parents were rich,' he says.

I nod, grappling to keep up with this unexpected opener.

'Yes, they were rich, and their parents before them, and their parents etc., on and on into the dim and distant past.' Alec gives me a long look. 'Let's just say, they're not like me. They're military.'

I picture stuck-up generals and people barking orders and pull a face, but hastily rearrange it into what I hope is an expression of polite interest.

'No, you're right to look like that. Grandfather thought all his offspring should go into the army. My father and his brothers thought the same, so my cousins and I were all packed off to military training as soon as we finished university. As it turns out, everyone else was officer material and I wasn't.' That explains some of his prickliness. 'I couldn't stand it and . . . well . . . I dropped out.' He glances defiantly at me, daring me to comment, and I force my face to remain neutral. He downs what's left in his glass, and pours himself another generous measure. 'My family, feeling I'd ruined our reputation for military excellence, disowned me. I left home and tried to get a decent job, but without references no one would touch me. So I did some menial jobs: labourer, shelf stacker and, well . . . I ended up living in a squat.' He glances at me to gauge my reaction, but I have only sympathy. 'It wasn't all bad,' he adds defensively. 'I learnt to play the guitar so I could busk – just a few chords, nothing special.' I swirl my glass and take a sip.

'Then one day, my grandmother – she was wonderful by the way – came and found me. She pulled up outside the squat in her chauffeur-driven Jaguar, and took me out to lunch. While we were eating, she pulled out a cutting from one of her society magazines and handed it to me. It was in *The Lady*, I think, and it gave the job details for a personal assistant's post in the country serving an old bachelor. "Interesting people only need apply", it said. I remember that,' he says, and even though he's looking down I can hear the smile in his voice. 'She told me I was exactly the right person for the job. She was surprisingly insistent about that, and she made me promise I'd go. She then took me to a barber, bought me a suit and dropped me off at the train station with money for a ticket. She told me to get on with my life and make myself proud. Anyway, that's how I came to work for Donald.'

The whisky sits in my stomach, warming my body, and my eyes are starting to feel pleasantly bleary. 'What happened when you got here?' I ask, taking another sip.

'Donald took one look at me, said "My God!", and sent all the other applicants away. I was exhausted and not very clean under my suit, so he sent me upstairs for a hot bath and told me to come back when I'd eaten something. I promptly went down with the flu and Mrs Crumpton had to look after me for a few days before he could even interview me. She's had a soft spot for me, ever since.'

I stifle a giggle. 'You'd never know. How long ago was this?'

'I was twenty-one, so nearly eight years ago. We got very used to each other.'

'You were good friends,' I say, finally understanding.

'Practically family.' His voice cracks.

I reach out to him, letting my fingers touch his, and there's a tingle of static. Alec looks down at my hand, then back at me and smiles slowly. I'm close enough to see the silvery trace of a small scar on his upper lip, which I've never noticed before. I almost want to reach out and touch it.

'I think you should go to bed,' he says, retrieving his hand from mine. 'I expect you'll sleep now,' he says, nodding at my empty tumbler.

My eyes hold his for just a second.

'Good night, Hannah,' he says and, draining his glass, he gets up and leaves the room without looking back.

II

I didn't sleep well. I kept picturing a precipitous mountain littered with jagged rocks, and me speeding through them on a disintegrating moth-eaten plank. I woke up tired and achy, and at breakfast I had to struggle to eat any of my scrambled eggs on toast, but since neither Alec nor I knew what to say to each other, chewing seemed the easiest option. Now that we're driving up the lane to Tor Hill with the go-kart wedged firmly in the back, I'm not sure the scrambled eggs were a good idea.

Alec gestures to a flat area of grass and I park. As he gets out, I gaze up at Tor Hill. Thankfully it doesn't look too enormous – we're probably talking a five-minute yomp to the top. It's also neat, with even slopes and no jagged rocks, just a circular stone building at its top. Around its base is a flat area of grass, then a dry stone wall, which seems perilously close and unyielding to my self-preserving eye.

I go around to where Alec is wrestling the go-kart out of the back seat, and stand uselessly beside him, examining the cycle helmet Mrs Crumpton handed me at breakfast. She borrowed it from her neighbour and though I can tell Alec doesn't approve of it, I guess Mrs Crumpton must be warming to me. Or, at the very least, doesn't want me to sustain a major head injury. Which is nice of her.

Finally freeing the go-kart, Alec gives the helmet a disparaging look and strides off. I scuttle after him, putting on the helmet, noting that as we approach the hill it looks a lot steeper, while the go-kart in Alec's arms seems more rickety.

Alec puts the go-kart down in front of me and folds his arms. 'Donald wouldn't have worn safety gear,' he says, as if he hadn't already made his feelings abundantly clear.

I look him in the eye, too nervous to mince words. 'Either *I* go with the helmet, or *you* go without – your choice.'

'Helmet stays,' he agrees, holding up his hands. 'Are you sure you don't want safety goggles and steel-toed boots, too?' he asks, raising an eyebrow.

I do my best to look dangerous. 'If I had steel-toed boots, you'd need shin pads.'

He flashes me a grin. 'Fair enough! Ready for your first run?' and with him pulling the go-kart up the hill, I follow, still fiddling with the helmet straps. I'm relieved when he stops a third of the way up.

'Try from here. That way you can get a feel for the steering,' he suggests.

It doesn't look *that* far to the bottom. I lower myself onto the go-kart while Alec holds it steady, and it creaks alarmingly. I look up in panic.

'I told you it wouldn't take my weight,' he says smugly.

'Are you sure it will take mine?'

'There's only one way to find out.'

Digging my heels into the grass, I picture the entire thing falling apart on the way down, and my breaths come faster.

Alec sighs. 'Kids have been doing this forever. What's the worst that can happen?'

'I crack my head open and die?' I suggest, my voice unnaturally high.

'Not going to happen: helmet,' he says, rapping the top of it.

I still don't lift my heels. The slope stretches out in front of me, and I feel like it's got steeper in the last few minutes. The steering rope is rough in my hands and I'm wishing I'd brought gloves – and given that the planks are already digging into my bottom, perhaps a cushion, too.

Alec crouches down beside me. 'Look, the most dangerous element of go-karting is cars.' He shades his eyes and peers around like a mariner. 'No cars. No sheep. Not even a dog walker.'

I frown at him and he sighs impatiently, making me feel pathetic. I take a deep breath and lift my heels.

To begin with, the kart moves slowly, then gravity remembers what it's doing, and I gather speed. The wheels turn too freely. The air swooshes past my face, and the bottom of the hill rushes up to meet me. I press my feet into the plank in front of me, but nothing happens.

'Turn!' Alec yells from behind me.

The gradient lessens, but the dry stone wall is still hurtling towards me incredibly fast. Shit!

'Turn!' yells Alec again, and my mind finally kicks into gear. I yank the rope, slewing the cart around, but too roughly. I lose my footing on the front plank, fall sideways, and cling to the rope, jerking the kart after me. As I roll, the go-kart follows, and as I come to an abrupt halt it smacks me in the helmet.

'Ow!' I yelp, more because of the noise than because I'm hurt. I stay perfectly still and concentrate on my breathing to make the nausea subside. Alec skids to a halt beside me.

'Are you OK?' he asks, panting a little after running down the hill.

I blink and prop myself up on one elbow. 'I think so. Just a bit . . . surprised.' I rub my knee.

We look at the upturned go-kart.

He frowns. 'Perhaps the helmet *was* a good idea,' he mutters. 'Why didn't you turn? Did the steering fail?'

'No, I just . . . forgot.' That sounds so lame.

'You forgot? How could you forget?'

'Easily, as it turns out! It's not like I've done this before.'

'No, but it's a fairly basic part of go-karting!'

I give him a hard look. 'Well, you do it then!'

Alec shakes his head, and I can tell he's starting to find it funny. 'OK, OK, you forgot,' he concedes.

'And it won't happen again,' I say firmly.

'You'll go again?' he asks with insulting incredulity.

'And I'll remember to turn,' I assure him. I get up slowly, brush myself down and stomp off up the hill. Alec gives the go-kart a quick once-over and follows.

We start from the same point, but this time, as I sit on my plank, I feel a bit braver. I lift my feet and set off down the hill. This time I feel the exhilaration as I gather speed and the wind on my face makes my eyes water. I can't help squealing as I bounce over a hummock, and my stomach flips. What's more, I remember to turn and come to a stop with me still on the kart! Alec's cheering, and I get up beaming with pride.

'See, I told you I'd remember,' I say as he comes down to meet me.

'Do you want to try a little higher?' he asks, and I nod eagerly.

Over the course of the next hour we start further and further up the hill, and I'm managing it better each time. By the end, I'm looking down the length of the entire slope.

This is the big one. This is as good as it's going to get.

Alec's talking seriously, pointing out various bumps and dips. 'So keep it steady, and turn gradually from where we made the first run.'

I nod, taking my seat on the now all-too-familiar plank.

'You will be going quite a bit faster,' he warns, 'so put your heels down if you need to.'

I nod.

'Ready?' he asks. I give him a racing driver-type salute and lift my feet, excitement gripping my stomach as the kart gains momentum.

He's right, I'm going quite a bit quicker than last time and it's the most intoxicating feeling in the world. I have to narrow my eyes against the wind, and my whole body is tingling as the world rushes past. But something's wrong. The plank I'm sitting on is juddering and I can feel the kart pulling to one side.

Before I can think what to do, a bump catches the left rear wheel and yanks it backwards. The kart veers violently to one side, and suddenly I'm no longer on it. Thanks to my first run, I remember to let go of the rope, but I'm tumbling faster and faster and can't slow myself down. I'll break something if I stick my arms out, so I tuck myself tighter and close my eyes, hoping against hope that I don't hit the wall at the bottom. The grass is rasping against my helmet, alternating with Alec's shouting for what seems like an age, until I come to a stop on my back, thankfully without hitting the wall. I lie on the grass with my eyes closed, because when I open them, the world won't stop spinning.

'Hannah? Hannah, talk to me!' yells Alec, falling to his knees next to me. He clutches my hand.

I stare up at him for a few dazed seconds, watching him weave about.

'Is Uncle Donald trying to kill me?' I ask, and Alec lets out a relieved laugh and rocks back on his heels.

'Get your breath back. Does anything hurt?' he asks anxiously.

I blink several times. 'I don't think so, but that's enough death-defying stunts for one day.'

'Agreed,' says Alec, sitting beside me and running his hands through his hair. His hands are shaking. 'I don't think the go-kart can take any more, either.'

'Great.' I shield my eyes from the sun and release the helmet clip.

Alec reclines, propping himself on one elbow and starts picking grass out of my hair. It's unnervingly intimate, and I can't seem to pull my eyes away from his. 'Can you sit up?' he asks.

I carefully raise myself to a sitting position, but I still feel dizzy. 'I'm going to ache tomorrow. And,' I add wincing, 'I think my scabs have come off.' I look over at where the go-kart is lying twisted and broken. 'God, I want a cup of tea.'

'You've earned one – and a new task!'

'So I've passed, despite the helmet?' I ask, taking it off.

'After today, I shan't let you out without it.'

'Wow, thanks,' I say, examining it critically. 'It really goes with all my clothes.'

'Women!' he says, and pulls away from my half-hearted punch. 'Come on – let's collect our wreckage and see what Mrs C has rustled up for lunch.'

'And then we can find out how Donald intends trying to finish me off next,' I say brightly. 'I hope it's with cake.'

Mrs Crumpton insists on checking me over in the kitchen after lunch. She tuts disapprovingly at the state of my legs and suggests I head up for a bath, which sounds amazing. As I shuffle gingerly up the stairs, I hear her ranting at the kitchen ceiling.

'Look at the state of 'er! She's hardly been 'ere five minutes and she's a mess! She's not had all your years of bein' a schoolboy, you know. You look after 'er, you hear?'

I grin as I pass out of earshot, and hug her concern to myself as I run my bath.

The water is hot and I can't help wincing as I lower myself in and it bites into my scrapes but, after a few seconds, the warmth starts to soothe my muscles and I stretch out and relax. I hadn't realised how tense I was, but then I suppose facing your fears will make you feel a bit on edge. Not that I think this task was just about that.

Remembering Donald's insistence that Alec help me, I think he's working on pulling Alec out of his grief, too. I lie back and slide deeper into the water. Whatever else Donald intended, I certainly experienced the exhilaration he hoped I would feel, and I loved it, despite the crash. I let my eyes close, allowing myself to unwind. And Alec did join in, and even he would have to admit that at times he was really enjoying himself.

Realising the water's almost cold, I get out, wrap myself in a towel, and pad back to my room.

There's an envelope on the bed – Alec must have been in and left it there while I was in the bath. Keen to see what Donald has to say next, I quickly towel-dry my hair, put on a long T-shirt, and climb under the covers before tearing it open.

My Dearest Hannah,

Well done: another task under your belt. That's my girl! Did you build a good go-kart? Was it fast? I bet it was! Did you feel the thrill of speeding down the slope as well as the joy of seeing something through from its conception to its conclusion – and perhaps even destruction?

When I was young, I was very proud of my go-kart. It was the best in the neighbourhood. It had room for both me and my friend, Jimmy Bartle, who had a pair of motorbike goggles. We thought we looked the business as we raced down our local hill, dodging cars and being shouted at by the locals. It's a miracle we weren't killed, but somehow, through good steering no doubt, cars and go-kart never actually met. Needless to say, our parents didn't approve, but then karting would never have been so much fun if they had.

Well, one day, Betty got it into her head that she wanted to ride my go-kart. I'm not sure what brought this on, but with arms folded and pouting like a milk jug she demanded a turn. I told her it was absolutely out of the question because she was both too little and a girl. (Don't start, she was!) She stamped her foot and threatened to tell our parents if I didn't let her have a turn. So, after a lot of arguing, and Jimmy storming off, I concluded that I had to agree (first mistake).

Being a responsible older brother, I dragged the go-kart to a field. There were brown cows in there, but no bulls or cars, so it was comparatively safe. I hauled the kart up the hill and explained the rules to Betty – no standing, no touching the steering rope and no leaning. We got on and it began well. We set off at a sedate pace down the incline, with Betty sat in front and me behind (second mistake), and with the cows watching us. All seemed fine until Betty, laughing hysterically, took it into her head to grab for the steering rope. We tussled for possession, but despite my best efforts, Betty finally caught hold of one side and yanked it as hard as she could, causing us to head straight for the herd of cows. I tried to correct our course, but Betty still had hold of the rope and I had to hit her hand to make her let go. I then quickly turned, but rather than heading for the dry grass I had originally aimed for, we sailed straight at the gate. The cows had trampled the ground there into watery mud, and as soon as our wheels hit the mud, we bogged down and slammed forward. I kept a tight hold on Betty to stop her hitting the gate, but in the process impaled my knee on the rough wooden side of the go-kart.

Betty instantly started howling because her dress was spattered with mud and, most likely, cowpat. Apart from that, she was unharmed. I, on the other hand, was bleeding and my knee was really starting to hurt. We struggled free from the kart, hid it in a hedge and hobbled for home – a very sorry pair.

On the way, well aware of the trouble I would be in, I tried to convince Betty to say we had slipped down the riverbank – mud and injuries accounted for. No one would be in trouble and we would be one-up on the parents, or so I thought (third mistake). But as soon as we entered the house, Betty ran screaming and crying to our mother, telling her that I had forced her to go on my go-kart and purposefully ruined her dress. She continued to say that I had hit her and told her to lie about falling in the river.

I stood in the hall fuming, while trying very hard to summon up a shamed face for my mother. The telling off that followed barely penetrated as Betty's smirking face peeked out at me from behind our mother's skirt. My father's punishment, however, was far more injurious, for my go-kart was collected, mounted on the chopping block out back and shorn of its essentials as dramatically as if it were on Tower Green. I wept as he destroyed it and Jimmy Bartle didn't speak to me for a week! After that, he kept saying 'what did you expect from that little sneak?', and I'm afraid he was right.

Jimmy forgave me, and my knee did heal, although I still have the scar. My relationship with Betty, however, was damaged beyond repair. Before then, we'd roughed along together, but after that day, I loathed her. It was the turning point in our relationship, which is why it has earned its place in my history.

On a more positive note, Jimmy and I built another go-kart and even raced it in that same field. On one occasion, Jimmy was butted clean over the hedge when the farmer exchanged the cows for a bull. I could only wish it had been Betty.

Implacably yours,

Donald

PS I almost forgot to give you your next task. You must go swimming in a river. 'Wild swimming' they call it now – stuff

and nonsense. Swim in the sunshine and swim in the rain.
They are quite different experiences, and nothing like the swim-
ming baths. Take Alec.

I sink back into the soft pillows. So that's why Uncle Donald
and Grandma Betty don't get on. I can't help feeling a bit let
down. I thought there'd be more to it than a go-kart shorn of
its essentials, and when I think of what Lauren did to me, I
can't help feeling my dislike of her is more justified. I bury
the thought since it doesn't belong here at The Laurels, and
roll out of bed.

Swimming, though . . . I like the sound of that, especially
in the sun. But with Alec, again. I mean, he's a lot more
friendly than he was, and he's certainly been supportive
when I've hurt myself, but . . . I don't know . . . it feels complicated, somehow, in a way it didn't just a few days ago.

I dress quickly and trot downstairs. Alec's in Donald's
study, busy with paperwork and I lean on the doorpost,
unsure whether to interrupt him or not. I knock, trying not to
feel awkward after our conversation in here last night.

He starts, but then smiles when he sees it's me.

I hold up the letter. 'The next task is swimming,' I say with
a tinge of excitement.

'Swimming?' He stretches. 'OK. Any stipulations, specifi-
cations or suggestions?'

'He wants us to swim in a river, in the sun and in the
rain.'

'Shouldn't be a problem. You said "us"?' My stomach
flips. I hand him the letter and take a seat while he reads.
'Makes sense,' he says, handing it back. 'Particularly since I
know the area and I can make sure you don't drown.'

The cheek! Just when I thought he was starting to see me
as more than a gold-digging child he needs to babysit. 'I can
swim,' I tell him frostily.

He regards me appraisingly. 'Good – I hate to think what Mrs Crumpton will do to me if I bring you back damaged again.' His frown deepens and I smirk. 'There's a nice little place out near Attscombe,' he says, his eyes on me. 'It has shallows, depths and an island with trees that dip their boughs in the water. It's a beauty spot – when it isn't covered in inflatable dinghies.'

'Sounds perfect.'

'And if Mrs C makes a picnic, we could make a day of it?' he asks, watching me closely.

I hesitate, but there's no time to figure out how I feel about spending a whole day with him – and at his suggestion. 'Great,' I say lamely.

'How about tomorrow?'

'Fine. Do you know what the weather's going to be like?'

'You have to swim in the sun and the rain, so does it matter?'

It's an annoyingly good point. 'Let's hope it isn't just cloudy, then.'

'Or hailing,' agrees Alec, his mouth quirking at the corner. 'But chances are we'll be able to tick off one or the other.'

I tip my head in agreement, and look at the paperwork spread out in front of him. There's a lot of it.

'Stuff for probate,' says Alec sadly, and I can't help remembering how vulnerable and honest he was last night.

'How are you doing today?' My voice has a tenderness to it that surprises even me.

'Better. Are you keeping an eye on me now, then?'

I blush, not sure if I've crossed some line. 'No, I was just wanting to make sure if . . . well, you know . . . if you wanted to talk, then . . .'

'No, I'm fine. Difficult times,' he says quickly. 'I'm just busy.' He bends over his paperwork and I take the hint.

'OK, I'll leave you to it,' I say, getting up.

He nods. 'Thanks for letting me know about the swimming.'

I run back upstairs to check if I have my swimsuit. I don't, so another trip to the 24-hour supermarket is needed, but I might ask Mrs Crumpton if I can borrow a towel.

12

Last night, after a quick trip to the supermarket and finding myself once again left to my own devices, my writing started to flow in a way it hasn't for years. It was so utterly absorbing that I lost all sense of time, and when I finally looked up at the clock it was very late. Tired but elated, I got ready for bed and lay in the darkness. I heard Alec come upstairs and not long after, the gentle sound of an acoustic guitar made its way from his room. It was lovely: pure, tender and slightly mournful. I was surprised by how well he played – he was obviously being modest when he said he could only play a few chords, and I drifted off to the sound of his playing. I had the deepest sleep I can remember in a long time.

This morning I feel properly refreshed, and as I pack my new swimming costume, with my toes crunching into the sun-baked carpet, it feels like it's one of those summers that will stretch on forever. I skip down the stairs, leaving my bag next to Alec's rolled towel on the bottom step. Then I double back and move it up one step in case it looks like wishful thinking, and join Alec in the dining room for breakfast.

He gives me a quizzical look as I cheerfully plonk myself down at the table. 'Good morning. Sleep well?' he asks as I drizzle honey on my porridge.

'Very well! Near death experiences seem to suit me,' I add quickly, not wanting to admit I heard him playing in case he gets embarrassed.

Still regarding me with perplexed amusement, Alec indicates a large wicker picnic hamper that wouldn't look out of place on the set of *Downton Abbey*. 'Mrs C has prepared us a picnic,' he says with suitable awe.

'Wow. It's enormous!'

As she comes in, Mrs Crumpton gives me a curt nod, which from her is the equivalent of sweeping me into her arms and dancing in circles. I grin at her.

'Catering for the week, Mrs C?' asks Alec, indicating the basket.

'It'll all go. You'll see,' she says, and walks out.

'If we eat all that, we'll sink like stones,' Alec whispers.

It is ridiculously huge. 'Or get cramp. Will she be very offended it we don't eat it all?'

'Heartbroken,' says Alec.

Scraping the last of the porridge from my bowl, I put down my spoon and go over to try and lift it.

'Blimey!' Mrs Crumpton is stronger than she looks. 'No one's upset her recently, have they?' I ask, suddenly suspicious.

Alec snorts and comes over. 'You think the postman's in there?' He lifts the basket with both hands. 'Bloody hell!' he says, putting it down again. 'I think he might be!'

'Shh!' I giggle, checking Mrs Crumpton isn't within earshot.

Alec flexes his muscles for dramatic effect. 'Don't worry milady, I'll manage, though mi' back ain't so good.' He lets out a comedy wheeze as he picks it up. 'Open the car! Open the car,' he shouts as he staggers out into the hall. I'm so surprised by this new, silly side of him, that I almost don't follow him out. Then, as his words sink in, I hare off after him, hoping to open the boot before he makes it to the car.

Attscombe is a gorgeous village. We drive through it, the river sparkling on one side and shops, tearooms and wobbly cyclists passing by on the other. We skirt around parked cars, taking it in turns with the oncoming traffic to make headway along the crowded street, and drive out of the other side of the village. Just as we're leaving all the houses behind, Alec tells me to pull into a busy, tree-shaded lay-by.

'We're heading through there,' he says, pointing to a farm gate. 'The river's at the bottom of that field.'

Leaving the picnic in the car, we grab our swimming things and stroll across the field to a grassy bank full of people sunbathing. Below us the river has formed a large pool where children are splashing about. Given the amount of ducking going on, their parents don't seem to be keeping much of an eye on them.

Alec inspects the ground, spreads out his towel and sprawls on his side. I unroll mine and sit down next to him, hugging my knees.

'Good?' he asks simply.

'Lovely,' I agree as he gets up again, and pulls off his T-shirt.

He's surprisingly well muscled, and I can't help staring. I turn slightly so it's not so obvious I'm looking. My eyes are drawn to his torso, which isn't quite a washboard, but more like the ripples left etched in wet sand as the tide goes out. The annoying side of my brain wants to run my fingers over them. As he folds his T-shirt and drops it onto his towel, his strong shoulders battle with his torso for my attention. Feeling hot and flustered, I can't help but watch as he removes his shorts. Luckily he's wearing swimming shorts underneath. I have to force myself to look at the water before he catches me staring.

Damn it, I realise with a jolt. I should have changed before we came, too – I hate fumbling about under a towel. I take out my suntan lotion and rub some into my legs, stalling. Alec stretches and, walking over to the edge, climbs down the bank and steps into the water. I watch, trying to gauge how cold the water is. From the way he rushes determinedly forward, splashing squealing children, and plunges straight into a confident front crawl, I get my answer – it's bloody freezing. After a few strokes he turns and laughs.

'Wow! That's refreshing!' He flips his hair off his face like he's in a Diet Coke advert. 'I'd forgotten what this is like.' He waves for me to come in. I smile back, not entirely sure what I'm feeling. 'Come on,' he calls. 'It's fantastic.'

I am feeling quite hot, so I struggle into my swimming costume inside the towel Mrs Crumpton lent me – which definitely isn't big enough to serve as a changing room – and pick my way to the river's edge. Everyone – including Alec – can see my sun-shy body together with contrasting grazes, but despite feeling self-conscious, I'm still not sure about getting in. The water looks muddy, and my mum, having nearly drowned as a child, always kept us away from any open water not fully patrolled by lifeguards. Though personally, I always found the idea of skinny-dipping by moonlight quite romantic.

I stare at the murky river bottom, wondering if the reality could ever live up to my cinematic expectation, and slither inelegantly down the muddy bank. My feet disturb the silt as they hit the water and I almost slip over, but I grab at a clump of long grass and just about manage to stay upright. Heart beating fast, I look up to check no one saw. Alec is facing the other way, thank goodness.

'Ugh!' I whimper as mud oozes up between my toes. No, the reality could never live up to the dream.

'What's the matter?' asks Alec, looking over at me.

'It's slimy and slippery. And cold.'

'Get in quickly, then, or it'll be torture,' he laughs.

'Great advice, thanks,' I mutter, and take a few tentative steps. My God, it really is cold! Torture is absolutely the right word, and as the water hits the back of my knees, I yelp. I wrap my arms around myself, feeling the goosebumps prickle.

'Why am I doing this again?' I ask as something, hopefully just waterweed, tangles around my ankle. I kick it off.

'For Donald,' calls Alec, swimming to the far bank and turning back to see if I've got any further. I haven't.

I frown at the water. I can't see the bottom any more; it's gone all cloudy. 'Are there any shopping trolleys in here?'

'I shouldn't think so. Eels, fish, maybe the odd crayfish, but they won't bother you if you lift your feet.'

'Wait, what?'

Alec laughs and does a little duck dive. I inhale sharply as two boys run past, splashing me. Shit, it's freezing. The only solution is to submerge myself, so I count to ten, take a deep breath and plunge into the water right up to my neck.

'Bloody hell!' I gasp, much to the children's delight and the sucked-in irritation of their parents. 'Sorry!' I call through chattering teeth, then set off, swimming like fury. Alec swims up beside me, doing a lazy backstroke. 'Shouldn't it be warmer?' I pant. 'My body's almost in shock.'

'You get used to it after a while. It feels warm to me now.'

'If there were prizes for being smug,' I growl, but even as I'm saying it the screaming sensation is wearing off, leaving only numbing cold. I swim further out and tread water, watching some boys failing to climb into a dinghy. After a while I head back, surprised to find that the water is actually warmer nearer the bank.

I swim a little circuit out and back in again and, now that I'm used to the cold, I start to appreciate how different swimming outdoors is to swimming in a pool. It's lovely not to taste chlorine, and the wind and sun on my face is so refreshing. I stop and watch the wind blow ripples across the surface of the water, and listen to the birds chirruping in the trees. I lie on my back and float, staring up at the clouds, feeling like Millais' Ophelia – until a large yellow dinghy bumps into me, the three squealing children inside all trying to turf each other out. Just before they upend it I swim to the bank, and, sitting on a half-submerged rock, I let the sun warm my body and laugh as the kids try to right themselves. Alec is on the far side doing hand-stands with some of the older children. They accept him with-out question, and it's fun to watch him with his guard down, being so easy-going and patient with those around him. It would be great if he could be like that with me, but then I suppose I was foisted on him, and it's not like he could turn down Donald's last wishes, though I'm sure a lesser man would have tried. Perhaps I should be thankful to Alec. Even in the mires of grief, he's sticking by his promise to Donald to help me through all this, and without him, I'd be fighting through these tasks by myself. If I'm honest, I'm not certain I would have made it past scrumping.

Feeling something tickling my toes, I snatch my feet out of the water, and look down to see hundreds of tiny fish. I slowly lower my feet back in and watch their small bodies converge on them, their scales shimmering in the water. It's funny to think people pay for this, and here they are, just swimming in the river. But then I guess it's like so many things that people pay vast sums of money for; going to resorts, visiting spas, always hoping to buy happiness, forgetting that so much can be experienced for free. Maybe that's part of what Donald wanted me to take from this task . . .

The fish scatter as a boy runs past with another mud-spat-tered child in hot pursuit, interrupting my musings. The second boy is holding a handful of gunge to his shoulder.

'Jackson!' cries a sharp parental voice from above us. 'Put that down or we're going home!'

The filthy Jackson lets the mud dribble away between his fingers. His target laughs and Jackson, his face puce with rage, barrels towards his opponent who's standing very near me. I escape up the bank just before the splashing starts.

Wrapped in my towel, I rummage in my bag for my book and roll onto my stomach to read.

I'm almost asleep when a shadow passes across my page and I peer up to see Alec standing over me looking lithe, happy and – there's no denying it – completely sexy. I shade my eyes to get a better view.

'Enjoying yourself?' I ask, pointedly wiping away the water he's dripped on me.

'Yes,' he says, towelling his hair vigorously and lying down with a thump beside me.

I can't help smiling. 'Are all boys the same when it comes to water?'

Alec assesses the kids in the river, play-fighting and using their dinghy as a shield. 'Pretty much. I'm starving,' he adds after a moment's thought. 'Shall I get Mrs C's food bunker?'

They're probably the same about food, too. 'Sure. Need any help?'

He shakes his head. 'Just give me the keys and I'll get it.'

I hand them over and watch him set off up the field. He doesn't look half bad, and I feel myself blush. I carefully bury myself in my book for a few pages, and look up again just as he's trying to negotiate the hamper over the gate. He balances it on top, steadying it as he climbs over, then lunges suddenly as it starts to slip, rescuing it by the handle. As he strolls back, I can tell he's struggling not to show how heavy it is. He waves briefly, and I chuckle as he quickly reverts to carrying it with both hands.

A sudden urge to get up and meet him brings me up short, disturbing my composure for a second. I stare at Alec, trying to understand my feelings, but they're too unsettled. Deciding just to enjoy the moment, I make sure I'm reading my book again by the time he reaches me.

'Lunch is served,' Alec announces grandly, putting the basket on the ground and opening it up. We gape at the contents. It's a proper old-fashioned hamper with flatware neatly clipped into the lid and, as we start to open the Tupperware pots, we find Mrs Crumpton has packed sandwiches, a quiche, three types of salad, apples, a large fruit cake, ginger ale, cupcakes, sausage rolls and homemade biscuits.

'Wow!' says a boy, pausing on his way past to stare. Other children run over to gawk, ignoring the disapproving looks and calls from their parents.

'Wow, is right,' Alec agrees, and undoes the plates, finding both crockery and paper ones. Glancing up at our increasing crowd of spectators, I suspect Mrs Crumpton foresaw this exact moment. Giving me a grin, Alec hands me the crockery, and starts to share out food to the rabble on the paper plates. I find a knife and chop up the fruit cake.

The children run off giggling with sandwiches, cake and biscuits, only to be sent straight back by their parents to say thank you.

'Thank you,' sing-song the younger ones, while the older ones are gruff with embarrassment. Alec's trying not to laugh, and I bite my lip as I serve out food for us. Once the last child is gone, I hand Alec his plate and we recline on our towels and eat, staring out at the river and watching the children who have finished head back into the water.

It's idyllic and, just as Mrs Crumpton foretold (for she is the oracle), all the food is eaten. I pack up the hamper and read while Alec frolics about in the water again, and it's not long before I notice that the clouds are covering the sun for longer and longer periods, and the people around me are starting to pack up. I watch as they organise their children into carrying their inflatables, and they wave to me as they set off back to their cars. I'm staring up at the sky when Alec comes back.

'Is there anything Donald didn't organise for you?' he asks, as the first raindrops dimple the water.

I picture Donald herding clouds with his stick. 'It would seem not.'

We pack up our things, tucking our towels inside the hamper, and take shelter under the trees as the last few people leave. The rain intensifies and the leaves billow, showing their silvery under-sides as the wind gusts across the river. The water darkens, turning pewter-grey and hiding what lurks beneath.

'Time for another swim?' asks Alec, hanging his T-shirt on a branch.

I stare at the water. It doesn't look so inviting now.

'Oh, come on! Poor Donald's made it rain for you. What more do you want?' cries Alec.

I watch him climb down the bank before I strip off my top and follow him down into the water. At least I am ready for my feet to sink into the mud, and this time, Alec is waiting for me with his hand out. As he leads me into the water, it feels softer than before, somehow. It's still cold, of course, but not so shocking and he holds my gaze, his eyes challenging me to something I can't quite fathom, as he takes me further and further out, until I am swimming. I count out ten strokes and the cold magically recedes. I turn onto my back and look up at the bank. There are blackbirds searching the grass for worms, or possibly Mrs Crumpton's cake crumbs, and a few pieces of rubbish are the only sign that there were dozens of people lounging there only half an hour ago.

It's funny that it should make such a massive difference, but Donald's right: the rain has changed everything. It's stripped away all human intrusion, giving everything back to nature. Also, I'm aware of so much more – how the leaves nod as they drip rain, the force of the river flowing around and past us, and how the wind is turning the air in great folds and brushing the trees and water with its fingers.

I turn to find Alec watching me. I push my hair off my face self-consciously.

'Different, isn't it?' he says, his expression inscrutable.

'Very,' I agree.

His shoulders suddenly tense, and he puts a finger to his lips and beckons me towards him. I swim over to him as silently as I can and he pulls me into the shallows under the trees. The warmth of his body radiates into mine, and I have to resist the urge to huddle closer. Alec points: there's an enormous grey bird stalking about in the shallows down-stream. My heartbeat quickens.

'Heron,' he mouths.

The heron halts and stares into the water, poised on one scrawny, stilt-like leg. It's perfectly still; a living statue. I stare at the bad-hair-day feathers that bristle on the top of its head, bouncing slightly when raindrops catch them. I hardly dare breathe. The bird suddenly stabs the water and its beak emerges clasping a small fish. It raises its head to swallow it down and then resumes its vigil, clearly not satisfied. It stabs again. The bird's beak opens wide to accommodate this much larger fish and, lifting its head to the sky, its throat undulates as it swallows. It's nature at work right in front of me, and it's beautiful.

I don't think I've moved – in fact I've hardly breathed – but the heron notices us and gives us a hard stare. It crouches and springs into the air on heavy wing-beats, heading further downstream, and I experience a pang of loss.

I let out my breath and laugh, and Alec looks down at me, his eyes reflecting my delight. As I look into his face, his expression changes until he looks almost stern. He takes a step towards me in the water, slides his arm around my waist and pulls me to him. His hand pushes my hair off my face, his eyes on mine the whole time, and he slowly leans in until his lips meet mine.

His mouth is warm and almost hard as it collides with mine, but as the initial shock dissipates and the blood surges through me, his lips soften, and we are kissing more passionately than I have ever kissed anyone in my life. My head is swimming and there's none of the awkwardness of my previous kisses. It's like a movie kiss, all sensation and hunger, and as our lips part I feel no hesitation in wrapping my arms around him and pulling him closer so that every part of me possible is touching him, everything burning, everything swirling—

He freezes.

It's like I've wrapped myself around a tree trunk. I remove myself from his suddenly unyielding body and look up at him. He is staring at me, his eyes wide with alarm. I stare back, unsure what to say, waiting for his reaction, an explanation, anything that might give me a clue as to what just happened – but there's nothing. Nothing except a look of utter horror on his face.

Dropping my arms, I take a step back. Alec forces a smile. 'Another task complete,' he says too brightly, and before I can say anything he turns and swims back towards the bank as if a shark were after him. Perhaps I'm the shark. I stay very still as he gets out of the water, and can just about hear him muttering, 'Shit, shit, shit, shit, shit . . .'

What? Why 'shit'? Surely I wasn't that bad? I thought it was amazing . . .

He climbs up the bank, shoulders slumped. Then he straightens up, takes a deep breath and turns around with another forced smile. 'Cup of tea?' he calls.

Are you fucking kidding me? Tea?

I stare at him across the water, completely lost for words.

'I left a flask and some biscuits in the car,' he says, as if this explains everything.

What does he expect me to say? 'Oh yes, tea would be lovely, thank you'? I don't think so. I can't forget what just happened. I can't pretend he didn't just 'shit, shit, shit, shit, shit' all over our kiss. But he's waiting for an answer.

'OK.' I swim slowly back across, my mind as numb as my body in the freezing water. He helps me up the bank, dropping my hand as soon as I have a safe footing, as though he's worried I'll ravage him at the first opportunity. He should be so lucky.

He towels himself roughly, but I can't see his face. I touch my lips, which are still tingling. He glances at me, his slapped-on smile faltering, and starts to throw on his clothes. I pick up my towel and start drying myself, but quickly give up as it's still raining. I struggle into my damp T-shirt, my skin catching on the fabric, and stuff the rest of my clothes into my bag. He watches me for a moment, but if he's about to say something, he clearly thinks better of it. He grabs the hamper and sets off across the field. I stumble after him, hopping briefly to pull on each shoe, and only catch up with him at the gate.

I open the car boot so he can put in the hamper and, while he pours the tea, I pull on my shorts in sharp movements. Neither of us says anything, and I get in the driving seat and stare resolutely ahead. He gets in beside me and the steaming cups of tea he puts on the dashboard mists up the windscreen. I crack open a window.

Explain! Tell me why you kissed me. Tell me why you broke it off. Come on!

Taking my tea, I sip it, burning my tongue. The pain makes my anger swell into something that wants to rear up and shout and scream.

And still Alec says nothing. I blow on my tea, willing it to cool down so that I can drink it and be on the move. I finally drink it even though it's scalding my throat. I wordlessly hand him my cup, and suddenly I'm furious. How dare he! You can't kiss someone like that, then pretend it never happened!

I glance at him, but he looks so wretched that my anger shies away, embarrassed, and canters off.

How did we end up at this point? I didn't even like him a few days ago. He's been rude and condescending, judgemental and superior – not to mention downright insulting. How can I even be interested? And it's certainly not a good idea when we've got all these tasks to do. One thing's for sure: it's going to be awkward as hell after this. I glance at Alec, but he's just staring through the windscreen. I start the engine and go to pull out of the empty lay-by, but I stall. Normally he'd say something sarcastic, but he says nothing, which, if anything, is worse. I close my eyes to hold back the tears. I don't even look at him as I get the car properly into gear and start the drive back.

13

To say I'm tense as we pull in through the gates of The Laurels is an understatement. Alec hasn't said a word the whole way back, but as we emerge into the parking area and see a chauffeur-driven Mercedes waiting by the front door, I glance at him. His eyes meet mine, but he's clearly as mystified as I am.

I park up and we get out, avoiding each other's eyes again. We skirt our way around the Mercedes to find Mrs Crumpton waiting for us in the hall. She's looking anxious, a worrying sign from someone who would normally make a kraken quail.

'Prepare yourself – the Devil's in the drawin' room,' she whispers. 'Show no fear,' she adds, and stalks off to the kitchen.

'The Devil?' I ask Alec, tendering a tentative truce.

He shakes his head. 'No idea,' he says, 'but I've never seen Mrs C rattled before.'

We head cautiously to the drawing room and as we cross the threshold, I stop short. Sat in an armchair, with tea laid out in front of her, is the woman who spat in Donald's grave. She's wearing the same shade of pink as at the funeral, and a small, white, bug-eyed dog nestles on her knee, staring up at me.

'Ah,' she says. Her beady eyes pass across every detail of our shabby appearance, wet swimming costume outlines and all.

'Can we help you?' asks Alec politely.

'Let's hope so,' says the woman, her tone indicating we'd better. 'Tell me whom I am addressing?' Wow. Anyone that determined to use the word 'whom' is unlikely to be a friend of mine.

'I am Alec, Donald's PA, and this is Hannah, Donald's great-niece. And you are . . .?'

'Mrs Jennings.' She regards us glassily, purposefully not granting us lesser mortals her first name. 'Donald must have mentioned me.'

'I'm afraid not,' says Alec, matching her condescension blow for blow.

'Really?' She seems a little disappointed. Her attention shifts to me. 'As his only relation present, I'm assuming you are Donald's heir?'

'Just one of many,' I say quickly.

'How so? Who is the main benefactor?' Her eyes return to Alec, but neither of us has an easy answer.

'A charity?' I hazard.

She sighs, irritated. 'Who gets the house? Who gets his money?' she demands.

I open my mouth to say that I don't know, but Alec interrupts. 'I'm not sure I see how that's any of your business.'

Mrs Jennings smiles like a cobra about to strike. 'No, I don't suppose you do . . . yet. But let's just say it is about to become abundantly clear. You see, Donald owes me.'

'Then apply to his solicitor. I can give you his number—'

She waves her hand dismissively. 'He owes me a greater debt than money, and has done for many years.' She strokes her small dog absently, reminding me of a Bond villain. 'And you are going to make sure I am repaid.'

'What kind of debt?' I ask. I know curiosity killed the cat, but I can't help myself.

Mrs Jennings focuses on me, her mouth pinching at the corners. 'A long time ago Donald let me down; he sabotaged my plans regarding an event that was very dear to my heart and as a result ruined my social standing.' She pauses, her jaw clenching in anger momentarily before she continues. 'It was totally inexcusable and I'm not the forgiving type. An eye for an eye seems a most excellent policy to me, so I'm here for my "eye".'

God, I hope she doesn't mean literally, because I wouldn't put it past her to have a pantry filled with jars of eyes all staring in different directions. I suppress a shudder.

'How, exactly, are you hoping to retrieve this "eye"?' Alec asks, sounding formidable, but I'm unable to look away from Mrs Jennings.

'He ruined my plans. I'm sure he has plans concerning his last wishes, and I'm here to make sure they are just as ruined as mine were. Fair's fair,' she says.

'What makes you think we'll let you undermine everything he's worked for?' asks Alec.

Her beady eyes hone in on him. 'You won't have much choice. You see, I know things,' she says simply. 'A lot of things . . .' she looks pointedly at me '. . . about Donald.'

'What kind of things?' I ask, hideously fascinated, and immediately wish I hadn't.

'Seedy secrets, hideous acts, terrible truths; things you wouldn't want made public. There'd be quite a scandal, I assure you. So let's just agree that you should refuse all involvement with Donald's estate, and likewise any friends and family who've been favoured, and we'll say no more about it.'

'And if we don't?' Alec's expression is becoming more dangerous by the second.

'I'll contact the tabloids.'

'Why would they even care?' I ask, trying to share a disbelieving look with Alec, but he's fixed on Mrs Jennings.

'It's not always *what* you know that buries your reputation, but rather *who* you know. Did you know that Donald was once involved with the wife of a prestigious member of parliament? You'd know her name if I told you and I can assure you that the merest hint of a scandal involving either her or her husband would have the paparazzi slavering.'

'So you're blackmailing us?' I ask tentatively.

'Of course!' She laughs, amazed at my dim-wittedness. 'An eye for an eye, I said. Oh, you didn't think Donald was above using blackmail, did you? That's so sweet! You've quite made my day. But how do you think he kept me quiet all these years – by asking nicely?' She purses her lips, shaking her head at my naivety. 'Your problem is that, now he's dead, you have no idea what leverage he used or the damage I'm capable of causing. That leaves you with two options: reject Donald's will, or accept the consequences.' She takes a sip of her tea, watching me closely.

'But what are you threatening to reveal, exactly?' I ask. 'Surely you can tell us that?'

Mrs Jennings laughs. 'Why should I? It'll be far more interesting for you to find out along the way.'

'But you could be making all this up?'

'I could be,' she agrees. 'But I have evidence, witnesses, times and dates. This isn't an idle threat.' She gets up with relative ease, despite her age and the dog in her arms. 'I'll leave you to think about it, but don't take too long. I might get bored waiting. I'll show myself out,' and after a last self-satisfied smile, she strides out without looking back.

Alec and I stare at each other, the kiss not forgotten, but temporarily overshadowed by Mrs Jennings' threats.

'Is she serious?' I splutter as the front door bangs shut. 'She seems serious. And what was all that about Donald's secrets?'

Alec shakes his head slowly. 'I have no idea. Donald and I didn't talk about the past.'

I stare at him. 'Why not?'

A flash of irritation sparks in his eyes. 'Look, we just didn't, OK? I think we both had things we didn't want to revisit, and we respected each other's privacy.'

Alec glowers moodily, propping his chin on his hand like Rodin's Thinker. I frown, feeling perhaps a little more annoyed than is fair. But honestly, if they had been a bit more open with each other, or if Alec had perhaps shown a bit more interest, we might know what we're dealing with.

'So what *do* we have to go on?' I ask, trying to keep the impatience out of my voice.

Alec shrugs. 'Donald's letters? Isn't he gradually unveiling his past?'

I bite my thumbnail anxiously, suspecting they might prove to be a dead end considering he wouldn't even discuss this stuff with Alec. 'You really think he'll tell me, when he hasn't told you?'

'Maybe not. What about Mr Sanderson?'

'The solicitor?' I ask. 'You think Donald might have told *him*?' It seems unlikely to me.

'There's only one way to find out.' Alec checks his watch. 'He should still be in his office. I'll call him and then get you the next letter.'

'I suppose Donald might have left a letter to be fired off in Mrs Jennings' direction, like he did with Nicholas?' I smirk at the memory of Donald's blistering put-downs. 'It would be another chance for Donald to tell someone what he thought of them.'

'Yes,' agrees Alec without amusement, demonstrating all too clearly, as if I needed the reminder, that our carefree easiness is a thing of the past. Something has definitely broken between us.

Alec takes out his mobile and selects Mr Sanderson's number, his eyes meeting mine coldly, and despite wanting to know what Mr Sanderson says, I realise I can't bear to be around Alec right now. I follow the sounds of roughly handled crockery to the kitchen.

Mrs Crumpton frowns at me. 'She gone?'

'For now.' I blow out a sigh and rub my face anxiously.

'Tea?' she asks.

'Please.'

She nods at the table and I sink down onto a chair. I feel as beaten as a blacksmith's anvil and I wince as, after pouring hot water in the teapot, Mrs Crumpton clanks the kettle down onto a cast-iron trivet.

'Complications,' she says, shaking her head resignedly. 'I knew, when 'e started on all this, there'd be complications. I told 'im,' she says, gesturing at the ceiling.

She collects some mugs and pours the tea, and I wrap my hands around the mug she nudges towards me. I'm completely exhausted. 'Mr Sanderson will know what to do,' I say.

Mrs Crumpton gives me a world-weary smile and sits down. 'I doubt it, but whatever happens, we can't let Donald down.'

'We won't,' I promise automatically. Though, with Mrs Jennings in the mix . . . We sit in worried silence, sipping our tea. 'I heard Alec playing the guitar last night,' I say to fill the silence.

'Did you?' Mrs Crumpton nods her head thoughtfully. 'I thought 'e was lookin' better.' She pats my hand and gives me a smile. 'Keep doin' what you're doin',' she advises, but before I can ask what she means, Alec comes in with an expression that doesn't inspire confidence, and she withdraws her hand.

'Any tea left?' he asks, and Mrs Crumpton pours him a mug before heading off purposefully with a vacuum cleaner.

'Mr Sanderson is worried,' says Alec, turning his mug around by the handle. 'He's concerned that we don't know anything about Donald's past or what Mrs Jennings is threatening. He says that, until she makes her threats more explicit, there's very little he can do, but advised we look into Donald's history.' His voice is stiff – he clearly wants to be talking to me as little as I do to him.

'So, how do we find out what happened?' I ask, though I'm no longer sure I want to know.

Alec looks down at his tea. 'I'm not sure. Might your grandmother know?'

'Grandma Betty? I asked Mum about their relationship after we visited here in February and she said Grandma Betty and Uncle Donald stopped speaking after he left home. Beyond maintaining how terrible he was, seeing him at a funeral and returning the generous cheques he sent for their parents – which was how she got the idea he was rich and found out he was in London from the postmark – she had nothing to do with him until we all came here. She probably knows less than we do.'

'Well, Mr Sanderson wants us to find out as much as we can.' Alec hesitates. 'He also said you can stop doing the tasks while we sort this out. He said you've been given plenty of time to complete them—'

'But what if Donald's letters tell us what we need to know?'

'I said that, but Mr Sanderson said it isn't fair to expect you to continue when your reward is at stake, which I suppose it true.'

I sip my tea, contemplating Mrs Crumpton's 'we can't let Donald down', and Donald's rant in his first letter about how he went to a lot of trouble over arranging the tasks. I have to carry on, and I want to carry on, even if I am a little worried about what I might find out.

'Donald wanted me to do the tasks, so I'll do them.'

Alec raises an eyebrow. 'Even if there isn't a big fat prize at the end?'

Not this again. I press my lips together and close my eyes for a second to stop myself swearing at him. 'Haven't we spent enough time together for you to realise I'm not a mercenary bitch? I'm here because I liked him and I want to find out more about him.' Alec's expression doesn't lighten. 'Doing the tasks is what's important to me. Please try to accept that.'

'Good to know,' he says coldly, sounding unconvinced. 'I'll get you the next letter, then. And I'll check Donald's study, just in case there's something in there that can enlighten us, though I doubt it.' He walks out, and returns a few minutes later with Donald's letter. Without a word, he places it in front of me and heads off to the study. I pour myself another mug of tea and take it into the drawing room. Settling into an armchair and, trying not to let the hurt take over, I begin to read.

My Dearest Hannah,

This letter will be slightly different to my previous ones, but I am determined to give you a fair depiction of myself – both the good and the bad. Never an easy undertaking, but I must do it; in sickness and in health and all that. So, where do I begin?

I'm sure you saw the difference between swimming on a hot summer's day and a rainy one – unless I was lucky and outlived my doctor's predictions, in which case you may have had to brave the swim in autumn or even winter. Perhaps you swam in the snow in a wetsuit? I have never done that and perversely now want to. Perhaps I can persuade Alec to shave the freezer and shake the crystals over my bath?

I digress. I was hoping you'd see how weather can change all things. I expect that is why so many people emigrate. My message is not to emigrate, but to feel free to enjoy life, no matter what the weather, as you may encounter unexpected delights even in the least promising of circumstances.

I picture the heron and its careful watch on the water, almost feeling the water lapping around me, and then Alec pulling me close, his hands on my face, then one arm circling my waist, his other pressed between my shoulder blades. The heat and surprise of Alec's lips on mine as the wind swirls the trees. Even now, just the thought of it makes me light-headed. It's the most romantic thing I've ever experienced outside of a book – and then it all fell apart and I've no idea why. I close my eyes for a moment, then read on.

There is only one rule – keep 'sense' as your watchword. If you don't, things can go awry very quickly.

In the summer of 1955, my friends and I swam almost every day. In those days our parents didn't expect to see us between breakfast and supper, and we would take our towels and sandwiches and head for the river. We swam, dived, raced and made dams and rafts. We would jump in from the bank or off trees, and one place had an excellent high rock over a deep pool that swallowed you whole and spat you out in bubbles. Wind, rain or shine, we swam until we were pruny and cold, then took shelter or lay in the sun to eat mangled sandwiches. Every day was different and we loved it, or at least we did until the accident.

One night there was a great storm and a lot of rain fell. The rain soon stopped, but the water kept coming down from the hills and the river became brown and swollen as it tore through our village, carrying much debris with it. My friends and I stood on the bridge to watch the torn leaves and branches course under its single arch. We knew the river was too dangerous to swim in, but as we leaned over the low wall we boasted that we could do it if we wanted to. We told each other that if we swam on a diagonal upstream we could easily make it across to the far side. We said it with such confidence. We postured, we pushed each other, we bragged about how good we were at swimming . . . *Bravado hung around us like a fog, but none of us ever meant it for even a second.*

The trouble was, we were not the only ones listening to our inflated talk that day. There was a boy called Billy. He was a year younger than us and, being large and a bit of an oddball, had few friends. He trailed after us, pretending to be part of our gang, hankering after our attention and working on our trademark swagger. We had long ago lost interest in him, but we always spoke just a little louder when he was around, perhaps to make ourselves feel bigger, or maybe just to put him in his place – I'm not sure which. He sauntered up to us. 'I could swim in that river,' he said. 'No, you couldn't,' jeered one of my friends. 'You're too small,' said another. 'You'd be an idiot to try,' I said, and we laughed, thinking no more about it.

Later that day, Billy went missing. The alarm went up that evening and the adults mounted a search. It was early the next morning that they found his body downstream, tangled in the branches of a fallen tree.

No one knew how he came to be in the river. There were no witnesses to him entering the water, but he was in his swimming shorts when they found him, which made me start to wonder – was it because of us? Was he trying to impress us? Was he attempting to join our gang? Did our comments egg him on? Or was he stupid enough all by himself, because surely he should have had the sense to stay out of the water?

My friends and I never spoke of it, but I've often wondered whether they had the same questions – why did he go in, and was it really our fault? And I often wonder if it would have even happened if I'd told my friends to stop being so ridiculous, that not even a grown man could survive in that current, and told them to stop laughing at his boasts.

Then there is the question of whether I should have told someone of my suspicions. Back then I thought his parents, our parents and the village would blame us for something that wasn't necessarily our fault, and that my friends would definitely blame me for blabbing. I could see no good coming of it, for it wouldn't help Billy's parents or bring him back, but I still loathed myself for not doing so.

Billy died the same year as Albert Einstein, James Dean and Alexander Fleming. Any mention of them reminds me of Billy and inevitably leads to a sleepless night. In penance, each year on the anniversary of his death, I toast his memory and warn myself against the dangers of arrogance, because of everything I have ever said or done, that day of pointless boasting is my one regret. That is why I speak my mind and risk offence rather than puffing up other people's egos. That is why, horrible though it is, Billy is a fundamental part of who I am. If I am to trust you with knowing me, then this is the reality. Everything else is stamped with my own special brand of integrity, even if it falls far below everyone else's moral threshold. This, however, is the exception. This is my conscience. You see, I do have one.

Yours irrevocably,
Uncle Donald

The letter falls from my fingers, but I'm too exhausted to pick it up. In fact, if I had any energy at all, I'd use it to cry.

I stare at the letter on the floor, exhausted by everything that's happened. On the plus side, if Donald can tell me about Billy, he's unlikely to hide anything else from me. On the minus side, I no longer think I want to discover what Mrs Jennings is hinting at.

I cover my face and take a few moments, but though my eyes ache, no tears come. I let my hands drop.

I wish I could go home and bury myself in books, but I've told Alec and Mrs C that I'll carry on. I'm sure they wouldn't expect me to if they read Donald's letter . . .

But they won't read it. It's private – a gift of trust, albeit a horrible one. So here I am, stuck as Donald's heir in more ways than I ever thought possible.

I haul myself out of the chair and go to the kitchen to make myself a sandwich. Mrs C will have left us some dinner, but I can't face Alec again tonight. Taking my sandwich and a glass of water, I head for my room, and as I dig about in my things, I thank heaven I have packed my copy of *Jane Eyre*.

14

'Hannah! Wake up sleepyhead. Can I come in?' A voice scythes through the door, and I turn on my back and prise my eyes open as I struggle to place it. Oh God, Lauren – what the hell is she doing here?!

'Yes,' I call as brightly as I can, realising the only reason Lauren didn't stride straight in is because she's in a strange house.

'Still favouring the university way of life, I see,' she says, coming in and plonking herself down on the end of my bed. She looks at me reproachfully. 'I've been up for hours and you haven't even cleaned your teeth!'

'What are you doing here?' I ask, already irritated.

'I came to keep you company, stupid.'

I stare at her disbelievingly. She's never kept me company in her life. 'Why?' I ask, suspicious.

Her eyes shift involuntarily towards the door and I have my answer: Alec.

'Oh, you know,' she hedges, not quite meeting my eye. 'I want to make sure you're OK, see if you need any help with the tasks – and besides, I was owed some time off at work and this is such a lovely house.'

And a free holiday. Shit. I rub my eyes, trying to force my brain into gear. 'So how long are you staying?'

'A few days,' she says vaguely, and rearranges her face into a smile. 'So, tell me your news. How's everything going?'

I climb out of bed and push the door closed so I can get changed. 'Fine.'

'Oh?' says Lauren, grimacing as I pull on the jeans I've left draped over the back of a chair. 'And the tasks?'

'Fine. I had to go swimming yesterday.'

'And that's a task?' she asks, pulling a face when I nod. 'Oh, well that's disappointing. Have you found out what you are inheriting, yet?' she asks, already losing interest in the tasks.

'No. I only find out at the end,' I say, pulling my head through a top.

'But you must have some idea?' she persists.

I shrug. 'Not really. I'm guessing I'll get the same as you, or perhaps something to remember him by, like a vase – or his stick.' I smirk, remembering how close Donald came to smacking Grandma Betty's bottom.

'If it's a vase, have it valued. It might be Ming or Lalique, and knowing you, you'd stick it on a windowsill with cheap carnations in it.'

I roll my eyes. 'I didn't mean a literal vase, but there's a real chance the tasks are basically it. And I'm fine with that,' I add.

'Really?' She doesn't sound convinced. She gets up and wanders over to the dressing table, her mouth pressing into a disapproving line as she picks through my make-up. 'So, what's Uncle Donald written in his letters?' she asks casually – not that I'm fooled by her relaxed manner. In fact, I'm starting to feel like I'm being given the third degree – and I haven't even had breakfast, yet.

I keep my voice carefully even. 'Just childhood reminiscences, nothing groundbreaking.'

She turns, her gaze pinning me to the spot. 'Can I read them, then?'

I hesitate. 'Lauren, they're a bit like a diary – kind of personal? They're not supposed to be handed round. But there's nothing to get excited about.'

She watches me for a second, measuring me for weakness. 'OK,' she says, shifting aside so I can pick up my washbag.

'I should get ready,' I prompt, but instead of leaving she gestures that I should get on with it. I head to the bathroom and clean my teeth as fast as I can, but when I come back I can tell she's been rummaging through my things – everything's slightly out of place. There's no point saying anything as she'll just accuse me of being paranoid. I bite my tongue, go over to the dressing table and pick up my hairbrush. I barely glance at the window seat, but the cushions don't look disturbed, so Donald's letters are probably still safe in the recess under the hinged seat. 'So, what's the news from home?' I ask, pulling the brush through my hair, and listen to the family minutiae as I finish getting ready.

I herd Lauren down the stairs in front of me and spot a worryingly large suitcase parked in the hall. I reckon it's about a week's worth of luggage, and my heart sinks.

'You've found her, then?' Alec says, coming through from the kitchen.

'She was still in bed!' Lauren shakes her head and, annoyingly, Alec laughs and smiles warmly at her, which is odd given that they weren't on particularly friendly terms at the party or the funeral.

'Well, I've told Mrs C you're staying and she said you can have the first bedroom along the landing.'

'Does she mind?' I ask, since this doesn't sound like Mrs Crumpton at all.

'No, she's fine with it. Just said "it's like Piccadilly-bloody-Circus round here".'

Lauren purses her lips. 'Well, she can take my case up when she's ready.'

Alec and I both stare at Lauren's enormous bag.

'I'll take it up for you,' he says, and Lauren puts her hand on his arm.

'You're such a lamb,' she murmurs intimately, and as Alec starts up the stairs, I point Lauren in the direction of the drawing room. She doesn't immediately follow, though, preferring to hang back and give Alec a lingering look. 'He's so handsome; I don't know how you keep your hands off him,' she says loudly. 'But then again, he's not your type – and I wouldn't imagine you're his, either,' she adds, giving me a disparaging look. Wow, thanks Lauren.

Going into the drawing room, we both spot the letter I dropped on the floor last night. Of all the letters for me to leave lying around!

'Oh, is that one of Donald's letters?' she asks, bending down, but I snatch it up before she can touch it and stuff it in my pocket. 'Possessive much?' she sneers, her eyebrows arched.

There's an awkward silence, but as Alec comes in Lauren switches on a full-beam smile and he grins at her. Alec seems genuinely pleased to see her, and I get an uneasy feeling in my stomach. I'd have thought with Donald seeing through her, Alec would have had some reservations – but apparently not.

'So, how are you finding chaperoning my little sister?' Lauren asks, purring into action like a well-oiled machine. 'She's a funny little thing, isn't she? So absorbed in her books,' she says, ruffling my hair like I'm about three.

Alec gives me an inscrutable look, and I feel my mouth twist in consternation.

'It's been going really well, actually. We've completed three tasks already,' he says, thankfully glossing over all the friction. I smile, playing along. 'Which reminds me, Hannah, what's the next one?' he asks, like we're on a sitcom.

The next task? I pull the letter from my pocket, skimming its intense emotions and mentions of Albert Einstein and James Dean. 'It didn't say!'

I pick up the envelope from the side table. Inside there's a slip of paper that I must have missed last night. Resisting the temptation to shield it from view, I silently read it through.

My Dearest Hannah,

How brave you are to keep going with the whims of a dotty old bachelor. I commend your tenacity. As a reward, you will attend a dance class, after which I'm sure you will be hooked. You shall waltz, rumba and tango with the best of them. Don't be afraid, for you conquered the go-kart, and this will be even better.

The dance teacher I've chosen is a lady of repute (not the best kind, in my opinion, but she is a first-rate teacher). I have asked Lady Forester to accompany you. She is an excellent dance partner and my plus-one for any social occasion. It's a real pity her husband doesn't dance – he is missing out.

Now go and experience the success of mastering something new. It will be well worth your time, for in my opinion dancing is an extra-curricular necessity.

Jivingly yours,
Uncle Donald

'A dance lesson,' I tell him, surprised by the change of pace after all the Boys' Own adventure stuff.

Alec nods, unsurprised. 'Donald left me the name of a dance teacher, so it should be easy enough to ring up and book us a lesson.'

'No,' I correct him. 'I'm supposed to go with Lady Forester.'

'Oh.' Alec's staring at me, his expression unfathomable.

'Oh my God, you're so lucky!' says Lauren, making me jump. 'Is this what all the tasks have been like?'

'Not exactly. There's been apple scrumping, go-karting and swimming,' I say, counting them off on my fingers. She wouldn't have been so interested in those.

'And now dancing? I thought the old man was going to make you visit the elderly, or confess your sins, or something. I can't believe you get an inheritance *and* tons of great things to do.'

I glance at Alec, who's nodding sympathetically as if what she's saying is genuine, and I suddenly flush hot and cold. Surely he doesn't believe she *is* genuine? Does he like her? And was he so annoyed at the funeral and will reading, not because of Donald's plans, but because Donald chose me and not Lauren? I feel like someone's slapped me.

'It's not even like you're any good at dancing,' Lauren is saying.

'That's sort of the point,' I stammer. 'They're supposed to be challenges – things I haven't done before,' I try to explain, but Lauren isn't listening.

She looks miserably up at Alec. 'I love dancing. If only Donald had chosen me.'

'We could all go,' he suggests, looking deeply into her eyes. 'Hannah has to dance with Jane so you could be my partner.' His eyes flick to mine.

Lauren rests a hand on his arm, drawing his attention back to her. 'I'd love that!' she gushes, looking up at him with all the devotion of a Disney princess for her Prince Charming.

'Great!' I add weakly, my stomach sinking to my shoes and tugging at my smile like an anchor. 'Anyone for a cup of tea?' I ask, suddenly desperate to get away, and I don't wait for their answer before beating a swift retreat.

I sit at the kitchen table and sink my head into my hands.

'Your sister, is it?' asks Mrs Crumpton, chopping the heads off carrots as if she's Madame Guillotine.

I nod, not lifting my head from my hands.

'Pushin' 'er way in where she 'as no business?' she asks, taking a tea tray from the side and clonking it down on the table. 'Hmm, I saw her when she first arrived. That type is never 'appy unless they're the centre of attention.' She pours hot water into the pot.

I let out a sigh, relieved someone understands. 'I know I should be pleased to see her . . .'

'But you know her of old and you can't choose your family. It's a pity, but there it is,' she says, and I can't help agreeing.

'Is her visit going to put you out?' I ask.

'Not me. You, on the other 'and . . .' She leaves an ominous silence. 'Let me know if she needs ousting.' I imagine Mrs Crumpton taking Lauren by the scruff of the neck, and feel a little better. 'Take this through,' she says indicating the tray.

I get up, but before I go I pour her a cup, and she nods appreciatively. 'Lunch in a bit.'

'Thanks,' I say, and I don't just mean for the tea and lunch.

'And that's another thing,' I hear her tell Donald as I walk away. 'You didn't take into account that sister of 'ers, now did you? There's trouble there, you mark my words.'

She isn't kidding.

Things get even more uncomfortable over lunch. We're sitting at the table, with Mrs Crumpton bringing in the food, when Lauren announces, 'I could get used to having staff.'

My mouth drops open. Even Alec looks startled, but luckily Mrs Crumpton isn't fazed. 'Could you, now,' she says, dumping our plates in front of us without ceremony.

Not having eaten breakfast, I dig straight in to the cottage pie, peas, carrots and gravy, almost sighing it's so heavenly, but Lauren looks from me to Alec and back at her plate.

'This is practically school dinners,' she says in a stage whisper. 'I thought after Donald's party it would be a bit more—'

'Cordon bleu and silver service?' interrupts Mrs Crumpton, and Lauren jumps. I don't think she knew Mrs Crumpton was still within earshot.

She colours slightly, but hastily adopts a haughty expression. 'Well, frankly, yes!'

'That wasn't me.' Mrs Crumpton fixes Lauren with a look that could cause blisters. 'That was hoity-toity outside 'elp. I do good plain cookin', and no mistake.'

'It's really delicious,' I say quickly, after swallowing another mouthful. 'Try some.'

Lauren lifts a forkful of mashed potato and meat filling and inspects it. 'I hate to think how many calories are in this,' she says, letting it splat back down.

'The food at the party was stuffed with cream and butter,' I point out.

'But that was a treat.'

'So's this,' I insist. Lauren looks at me like I'm mad.

'Starve then,' says Mrs Crumpton, stalking out.

'I suppose I shall have to,' says Lauren, and picks at the peas and carrots.

15

After spending an exhausting afternoon watching a sunbathing Lauren flirt and flaunt about in next to nothing, I've decided to push everything to do with her and Alec to one side and focus on the tasks. After all, that's what I'm here for. I actually feel quite good as I peer into the wardrobe mirror, eyeliner in hand, getting ready for the beginners' dance class Alec has booked us all into this evening. I've found a pair of pumps that I can dance in, and I've dug out my favourite top and a pretty skirt, which work surprisingly well together. A small thrill of excitement even pulses through me as I try to imagine what the dance class will be like.

'Ready?' asks Alec as I trot downstairs. He's looking gorgeous in a black shirt with rolled-up sleeves; he's shaved and I catch a hint of aftershave on the air. I smile at him as I step around Lauren, who's sat on the bottom step doing up her shoes. She gets up and gives us a twirl to show off her floaty designer dress and strappy high heels.

'What do you think? Will I do?' she asks Alec.

'You look wonderful,' he tells her. 'As do you,' he adds, nodding at my clothes after a pause.

I twist a smile onto my face, feeling about twelve. 'Thanks. So, shall I drive us?'

Lauren snorts. 'No, we'll take my car.' She wobbles over to Alec like a newborn colt and he offers her his arm.

I stare at her shoes. 'Surely you can't drive in those?'

'Of course I can! Driving isn't a problem, but gravel . . .' She sighs dramatically and pouts at Alec. 'Help me out to the car? And you'd better sit next to me for the directions,' she adds. So I guess there's no calling shotgun, even if I want one.

I follow them out, pretty sure that the baby giraffe thing is an act – 'Oh Grandma, what wobbly legs you've got.' 'All the better reason to grip your arm, my dear.' I know Alec isn't Little Red Riding Hood, but I doubt it'll be long before Lauren has her teeth in him.

'It's good of you to drive,' says Alec, gallantly opening Lauren's car door for her.

'I like to make myself useful. Plus, my car's more comfortable than Hannah's.'

She pulls her seat forward so I can climb in the back. With one leg in and my bottom presented to them like a horse, I beg to differ. I shift into my seat and try to relax as Lauren follows Alec's directions out of the village.

We draw up outside a converted chapel. Lauren hops out, suddenly agile in her troublesome shoes, and pulls her seat forward. I clamber out and see Lady Jane Forester opening the door of the VW Golf we've parked behind. I give her a little wave and hurry over.

'Thanks for coming. Nice car,' I say.

'I like it,' Jane agrees. 'I wanted a bumper sticker saying "my other car is a Bentley", but my husband's vetoed it. Alec,' she says, greeting him as he joins us, and then smiles at Lauren.

'Lady Jane, this is my sister, Lauren. Lauren, Lady Jane Forester,' I say formally.

'Delighted to meet you, Lauren, but do call me Jane.' She shakes Lauren's hand. 'Are you joining us?'

Lauren takes Alec's arm. 'Yes, we're going to be partners.'

Jane glances at me, the hint of a question in her eyes, and I work hard to keep my expression neutral. 'Excellent,' she says. 'It's an open class for beginners. Our teacher Madame Jacky is small, but don't be fooled – she's a big character.' Jane takes my arm and I'm happy to be claimed. 'I think you'll like her,' she says to me.

'I'm sure I will,' I agree, and it's odd, but Jane already feels like an old friend.

We walk into the chapel and find a few other nervous beginners clinging to the walls. From the way they look glued there, I suspect they've been dragged here by their partners. They all seem to be wearing some variance on a court shoe, except for the men of course, and I look down at my pumps, hoping they'll do. Lauren, now walking with all the poise of a catwalk model, touches Alec's arm lightly and whispers something in his ear. She glances over at me, and even though I don't know what she said, Alec's air of uneasiness as he follows her gaze makes me blush uncomfortably.

A petite, formidable-looking woman in her late fifties with spiked plum-coloured hair strides across the room towards us, skirts billowing, heels tapping and swathed in a bright tasselled shawl. She regards me for a moment, then turns to assess the rest of the class.

'Onto the dance floor, everybody,' she shouts in a surprisingly broad Yorkshire accent. She claps her hands briskly. I'm suddenly nervous, but Jane pulls me with her, and Lauren and Alec follow. Seeing a few other all-female couples, I feel a little better, and Jane smiles at me.

'Good,' says Madame Jacky, and sets about teaching us the waltz as if we're at a barn dance.

It's actually quite fun. After five minutes, I've mastered pacing the edges of my own little box-shape, and I've never been able to do so much as a two-step before. Ridiculous as it might seem, I'm proud of myself.

'Partner up,' Madame Jacky shouts, and my confidence vanishes. 'Quick, quick,' she claps.

I scurry over to Jane. 'What do I do?' I flap my arms ineffectually, trying to figure out where they should go. Jane raises her eyebrows and I let my hands drop. 'Sorry,' I mumble.

'There's nothing to worry about. Now, I'm the leader . . .' she moves my left hand to her shoulder, and takes my right hand in her left, '. . . and you're the follower. No need to panic.' I nod anxiously.

Madame Jacky turns on a CD player and Strauss plays thinly throughout the hall. '*One*, two, three! *One*, two, three! Do just as I taught you. *One*, two, three!'

'Take your time, and remember to breathe,' Jane says gently, and after a few false starts and a lot of counting in, we finally start to sway around a small patch of floor.

After a few minutes, Madame Jacky, who has been walking round checking on people, gets to us. She lifts my chin with a bony finger. 'Don't look at your feet!' she snaps, and I instantly forget what I'm doing and step on Jane's foot.

'Oh my God! I'm so sorry!'

'It's fine,' Jane says, but I can tell it hurt.

'Start again,' orders Madame Jacky, and walks off to derail another couple.

'I'm so sorry, I can't do this.' Embarrassed, I try pulling away, but Jane keeps a firm grip on my hand and waist.

'Don't be silly. Of course you can do it,' she says, holding tight.

Alec and Lauren sweep past doing a perfect gliding waltz. My eyes follow them involuntarily. All they need is half the feathers off an ostrich and a tub of fake tan and they could compete on *Strictly*.

'You two,' shouts Madame Jacky, pointing at Alec and Lauren. 'Lovely, but *not* in this class. Try Intermediate or Advanced!' She points to the door.

Lauren looks smug, but Alec, shamefaced, tugs at her

hand and pulls her out through the double doors. I stare after them, dithering.

'Get dancing,' Madame Jacky calls at us. 'You won't learn anything standing still!'

'OK,' I agree weakly, and Jane releases me so I can wipe my sweaty hands on my skirt. I hold them up again. 'OK, *one*, two, three . . .' I step straight on Jane's foot.

'Damn! I'm sorry.' How bad can I be at this?

'Calm down and take your time,' advises Jane. 'Just remember, we all have to start somewhere. I was lucky enough to have a wonderful teacher who twirled me around the bedroom floor until it became second nature.' Her eyes briefly lose focus, then spring back to mine. 'Familiarity is key.'

'But I've never been good at dancing. I don't have the coordination. I knocked over five other girls in a ballet lesson. One even wet herself.' Jane laughs. 'I'm not kidding, Mum took me swimming after that. She said at least if anyone wet themselves in the pool, no one would notice.'

'How old were you?'

'Five.'

'Well, Hannah, I'll make you this deal. If you can make any of these lovely people wet themselves, I'll buy you a diamond bracelet!'

A smile creeps onto my face and Jane takes me in a determined grip. She counts us in and we start dancing. I concentrate really hard, paying careful attention to what my feet are doing while trying not to look at them.

'*One*, two, three, *one*, two, three,' Madame Jacky repeats insistently. 'Much better,' she says, tapping me on the shoulder. '*One*, two, three. Oi! You two are about to hit the wall!' she shouts at another couple.

Jane winks. 'You see? You're getting better already. Let your shoulders relax.'

I waggle them, but still make damn sure I know what my feet are doing.

'Right you lot, cha-cha time!' shouts Madame Jacky, turning off the CD player, and though my shoulders are aching, I'm almost disappointed.

'I was just getting the hang of that,' I tell Jane ruefully.

'Good! Don't worry – you'll like this one,' she whispers. 'Just imagine you're in a bar in Cuba, and you'll be fine.'

As we stand in line again, I see why Uncle Donald partnered me with Jane and not Alec – she's fun and there's no pressure.

Madame Jacky claps to get our attention. 'Right, everyone, follow me! One! Two! Cha! Cha! Cha!' she booms, demonstrating the moves slowly, and I have to concentrate so hard that I forget all about being nervous or clumsy.

I squeeze Jane's arm as we leave the chapel. 'That was fun!'

'Wasn't it!' she agrees enthusiastically, but we come to an abrupt halt as we find Lauren and Alec waiting for us. A smiling Lauren is hanging off Alec's arm, and while Alec starts off with a smile, it turns into a frown as his eyes meet mine.

'Hello,' Jane greets them.

Alec shifts slightly, breaking Lauren's grip. 'How did she do?' he asks.

'Incredibly well, actually – I'm impressed.' Jane glances at me. 'Though I think we should practise the moves before the next lesson. Practise, practise, practise,' Jane says to me, imitating Madame Jacky. Lauren snorts, and I glare at her. 'How do you feel about meeting up to go over the steps?' Jane continues.

'I'd love to, but can your poor feet stand it?' I ask.

'Of course they can! There were only a few missteps and thanks to your sensible shoes, I'm fine. Honestly, you were brilliant. How about 10 a.m. tomorrow? That way we can try it again while it's still fresh in your mind. I'll clear the living room?'

'Lauren's staying,' I say regretfully. 'Perhaps in a few days?'

'Don't stay in on my account,' Lauren butts in. 'Alec's happy to keep me company, aren't you Alec?' He nods, his face impassive. 'You can show me the house. There must be priest holes or something?'

'Sorry, no priest holes: wrong era,' he explains, 'but I'll show you what there is. You didn't see the kitchen, or the attics. Don't worry, Hannah. I'll look after Lauren.'

He's being so nice to her; really making an effort. I fight a flash of jealousy.

'In that case, tomorrow would be lovely,' I say, turning back to Jane and hoping my enthusiasm doesn't sound forced.

Jane jots down her address and some directions on the back of a dance leaflet and hands it to me. 'Pleased to meet you, Lauren. Alec,' she says, and she gets into her car and drives off, leaving me with Fred and Ginger.

Lauren unlocks her car and pulls the seat forward so I can climb in. 'Who'd have thought we'd be thrown out of the class for being too good?' she laughs, pushing the seat back and getting in.

'Well, it was only a beginners' class,' says Alec, closing his door and pulling his seat belt across. Lauren does the same at precisely that moment and their hands meet at the seat belt clips. She looks up at him. He pulls back and gestures that she should go first – ever the gentleman where she is concerned.

'I suppose so, poor things. But you'd think they'd appreciate seeing what they're aiming for as they lurch about like a hen party of drunken zombies.' Her laugh tinkles to soften the blow, but I know exactly what she's doing.

I frown. 'So what did you do after you left?' I ask, subtly reminding them I'm still back here.

'We found the funniest little pub, didn't we Alec?' Lauren touches Alec's knee, and he turns to face me briefly before looking back out of the windscreen.

'It was a local pub, clearly only used by locals.'

'And when we arrived there was a deathly hush, like in those old westerns.' Lauren shakes her head in disbelief. 'Everyone fell silent. It was priceless! And when I ordered a cocktail it was like I was speaking a foreign language! I had to have a G&T in the end, it was hysterical!'

'Sounds a hoot,' I agree drily.

'Anyway, we had a drink and a chat. It was nice,' Alec adds, smiling over at Lauren.

'So, you have a lot in common?' I ask, trying to sound unconcerned.

'Some things,' Lauren nods, glancing at Alec.

'Oh … good.' I keep my voice neutral, but I'm fighting an almost irresistible urge to take off a pump and smack them both on the backs of their heads with it. I slump back into my seat and focus on the scenery, trying to understand why I keep having these extreme reactions when I don't even particularly like Alec. Especially not now that he's being so friendly with Lauren. Perhaps I just need a break. Maybe visiting Jane is a good idea.

Arriving back at The Laurels, I head to the kitchen for a dose of Mrs Crumpton's medicinal reassurance, but she's gone home. I sit down at the table feeling lost without her and glance at the corner where Donald hangs out.

'Any ideas?' I ask him, feeling a bit silly. It's not like he's going to answer, and I'd be terrified if he did. I collect the bottle of wine and glasses Mrs Crumpton left out on the dresser and head back to the drawing room where Alec and Lauren are chatting comfortably.

I pour everyone a generous glass and Alec raises his in a toast. 'To another task,' he says, his eyes latched onto mine.

'Not that I really got to do it,' complains Lauren, 'but it had its moments.' She smiles at Alec and takes a swig of her wine. 'Perhaps you can take me to a proper club sometime, to make up for it?'

I take too big a gulp and it goes down the wrong way, so I don't hear his response. When I stop coughing and spluttering, Alec turns to me. 'So, how did you like dancing with Jane?'

'It was great, actually. She helped me a lot.'

'She seemed like the perfect partner for you,' says Lauren, and I bite my tongue because she and I both know she's staking her claim for Alec.

'She is,' I agree, suddenly tired, and I realise this is the first night Alec hasn't disappeared off to the study. It would seem it's not so necessary for him to work now that Lauren's here. I guess that tells me everything I need to know. Watching them both, I take another sip, and listen as Alec and Lauren discuss what they might do tomorrow. As they talk about the local pub, I have to pull myself back from the brink of sleep.

'I'm going to bed,' I say, getting up abruptly, and Alec looks at me, taken aback. 'I'm tired,' I explain, and Lauren smiles.

'Sleep tight. Don't let the bedbugs bite,' she says cheerfully.

'You, too,' I answer, and I see a flash of excitement in her eyes – but I don't think it's the bedbugs she wants biting her.

'Goodnight,' says Alec, sounding comfortable and relaxed.

'Goodnight,' I say quietly, and leave them together in the drawing room. I wend my way up the stairs, reminding myself of the futility of standing between Lauren and her conquests. A roadroller has nothing on her: a roadroller would only leave you flattened. Lauren would leave bits of you scattered far and wide.

Typically, as soon as I climb into bed I'm not sleepy. I try reading, but it doesn't have its usual soporific effect, and as I reach the last page I'm just as awake as when I started. Putting the book aside, I lie back and think about the task. I'm surprised I enjoyed it so much. I'd have thought dancing would prove to be my Waterloo, and it might have been if it wasn't for Jane. She was so patient and kind, but I get the feeling that's only part of why Donald chose her. I think he wanted me to meet her for some other reason, because judging from what I saw, Alec could easily have taken me dancing.

The stairs creak, and I just make out Lauren and Alec saying goodnight on the landing. I may as well admit it to myself: this is what I've been waiting for. Unable to resist seeing what's going on, I go out to use the bathroom and am almost bowled over by Lauren hurtling out of her bedroom. I try not to let my eyes bulge as I take in her lurid red baby-doll nightdress.

'Oh, it's you,' she says, looking at me and folding her arms. 'I thought you were asleep?' The hint of accusation in her tone isn't lost on me.

I smile, feeling positively puritanical in my plaid cotton pyjama bottoms and camisole top. 'I need the bathroom.'

Lauren rolls her eyes and flounces back into her room, closing the door.

When I come back a few minutes later, all is quiet. I get back in bed, but I'm unable to stop replaying the incident. I turn over, kicking off the sheets that have become knotted around my legs, and try to relax every muscle. I'm just about to drop off when I hear the squeak of a door opening. Immediately, I'm wide awake. It takes only a few seconds for a second door to open.

'Fancy meeting you here,' I hear Lauren say out on the landing.

I don't catch Alec's reply, but Lauren's giggle comes through loud and clear. I pull a pillow over my head, but it doesn't block out the image of Lauren twirling her finger in the hem of her red nightdress, with him looking like Christmas has come early. *Aaargh!* I lie still, but even from under the pillow I hear a door close. Just one. I roll over, fighting unwanted images of frills and lace, rosebuds and bows, thighs and cleavage. Alec, taut and muscled, just wearing his pyjama bottoms . . . I go hot and cold and turn onto my back, trying to both hear and not hear what's going on. This is not healthy.

I turn on my light and dig out my phone and headphones. Then I set a playlist going, and flick through my reading app for something comforting. I dismiss *Great Expectations*, *Northanger Abbey*, *Pride and Prejudice* and *A Room with a View* as all being a bit too close to the bone right now. I settle on *The Hobbit* – I don't remember anything too romantic in that – and, lying back in the pillows, I read into the small hours, finally falling asleep somewhere near dawn.

16

I wake up late and, staring blearily at the clock, see I've left hardly any time to get to Jane's. Groaning, I roll out of bed, and race to get ready. On the plus side, it's a relief to run out of the house, shouting that I'm late for Jane, rather than experience all the coy awkwardness of the morning after their night before. The downside is that I am a little hungry. Luckily I have an old cereal bar in the glove compartment, so I munch on that as I make sense of Jane's directions and set off.

I pull up in front of Jane's stately pile with my mouth hanging open, because if I thought The Laurels was impressive, it has nothing on this place. This estate was really built to subdue the masses, with its wide sweeping drive and enormous, ornate frontage, and I'm guessing from the sheer quantity of balustrades and roof cresting that at one time it had the luxury of its own stonemason and blacksmith hammering away in a workshop around the back.

I clamber out of the car, conscious that my denim shorts and T-shirt are not exactly in keeping with my illustrious surroundings, but it's not like I have a handy cocktail dress tucked in my bag, so I guess they'll have to do. I crunch across the gravel, feeling like it's my first day at school, but I haven't even reached the wide sweep of steps before Jane opens the front door.

'Hannah!' she says delightedly, coming down and giving me a huge hug. 'You found the place, then?'

'Yes.' I'm not admitting that I nearly drove away again when I saw the size of it. 'Thanks for inviting me.'

'You're welcome,' says Jane, matching my politeness, then leans in. 'The trick is not to be intimidated.'

'Thanks, but this is a *big* house.' I laugh nervously.

'I know, but I'm still me, and I'd do anything for Donald. Besides, I like you.' I relax a little. 'Come on, I'll show you the living room.' She takes my hand and leads me up the steps and through a grand entrance hall that probably emptied an entire quarry of its marble, and into a house-sized living room worthy of its own open days.

'In here will do,' she says, with a dismissive flap of her hand, and starts shoving priceless pieces of furniture out of the way. I bend to help, but an annoyed cough makes me turn. A butler with shiny shoes and a possibly permanently affronted expression gives me a stern look.

I hesitate, but Jane draws herself up to her full height. 'We need room to waltz,' she says firmly, though I detect a hint of defensiveness in her tone. The butler surveys our attempts, flares his nostrils, and takes over.

Jane crosses her arms and plonks herself down on one of the pushed-back sofas looking irritated. I perch on another, waiting for him to finish squaring everything off and leave.

'We don't get on,' Jane says flatly as soon as the door closes. 'He thinks I should know my place, but like I've told him, I'm perfectly capable of managing things myself. I'm not a porcelain doll!'

'Perhaps he's worried about his job,' I suggest. Jane looks at me, taken aback. 'If you always do what he feels he's been hired to do, he might feel a bit . . . superfluous?'

'Hmm. You might be right.' She nods slowly. All trace of her irritation disappears, and she laughs. 'Donald could always make me see things differently, too.'

'How did you meet Donald? I've been dying to ask since we first met.'

She smiles. 'It's a long story and I have been given special instructions about that.'

'Is it to do with a task?'

'Yes, and Donald was very particular about it. He said it wouldn't help if you received information out of order, so I'm afraid you'll have to wait.'

I know better than to push it. 'OK, so what do we do now?'

Jane stands up. 'We practise and then we have some tea.'

'Sounds good,' I agree, and she opens an antique cupboard concealing a very modern sound system and puts on a waltz. It streams out of multiple speakers, as clear as if there's a full philharmonic orchestra in the room with us, and Jane moves to the centre of the carpet and beckons to me. 'Do you remember the steps, or would you like to go over them?'

'Let's go over them again,' I say, and we make a start.

After an hour, I'm confident with the basic waltz and Jane's even shown me some salsa steps. She's ecstatic about my progress, possibly because I've only stepped on her foot once.

'Well done! I knew you'd be an excellent student. Let's have some tea,' she says, and the butler, who's probably been lurking about outside the door, sweeps in. Jane waits graciously as he repositions the furniture and lays out a full afternoon tea complete with crumpets. She makes a big show of thanking him. We exchange a conspiratorial smile, which turns into a laugh as my stomach groans loudly.

'Help yourself,' says Jane, pouring the tea.

I take a crumpet and start buttering it. 'Thanks, I'm starving,' I say and chomp into its delicious warmth.

'Yes, it's surprisingly hard work,' says Jane, taking one herself. 'You're doing really well, though, and it won't be long before you're ready for something a bit more complicated. Did Donald want you to learn anything in particular?'

'Not really.' I swallow. 'His letter just mentioned the dance class, and he seemed to think I'd be hooked after that.' To my own surprise, I realise I am.

'Sounds like Donald. Did he suggest dancing with Alec?'

Suddenly self-conscious, I look down at my plate. 'No.'

'Oh?' Jane seems surprised. 'He struck me as an accomplished dancer. I wonder why Donald chose me when Alec is available.'

'You're much better to learn with!' Jane looks up, startled by my vehemence.

'But you would *like* to dance with Alec?' she asks perceptively.

I picture myself stomping about on his feet like an enthusiastic hippo, and I don't mean one of the dancing ones from *Fantasia*. 'No.'

Jane gives my hand a little squeeze. 'Oh dear. You've fallen for him, haven't you?'

I stare at her, desperate to deny it, but the words stick in my throat. 'It's nothing like that . . . not really . . . he and my sister are . . .' but I haven't a clue how to explain, and it makes me uncomfortable even to try. I look at Jane, caught without an explanation. 'It's complicated.' I'm only just realising how true that is.

'Would you like to talk about it?'

'I don't know. To be honest I just want to focus on the tasks, but it isn't that simple.'

'It never is,' Jane agrees sadly. 'Feelings muscle their way in, and once they're there, they act like a constant tripwire.'

A lot like sisters.

Jane sips her tea, shaking her head, and I give her a furtive glance. I really do want to tell someone and Jane's so lovely . . .

'I didn't even think I liked him,' I begin hesitantly. 'In fact, it was awful in the beginning – and at the funeral he was so suspicious and judgemental – but as we've worked on the tasks we've got to know each other, and I can see he was just worried about Donald, and me being a gold-digger – which I'm not, obviously. Anyway, we were getting on better and better, and the day before yesterday, he kissed me.'

Jane's hand lands on top of mine. 'He kissed you?'

'Yes. Right in the middle of a task.' I can't help blushing. 'But it can't have been that good, because he pulled away and acted like it was a massive mistake. And now I don't know how I feel, or whether he likes me at all. It's ruined everything.'

Jane taps her fingers on her mouth thoughtfully. 'It sounds like it was spontaneous. I wonder why he backed away?'

'I wish I knew, and I haven't been able to ask him because then Lauren came to stay, and now he seems more interested in her. And what's worse, last night I think he and she might have . . .' I look down and see my hands are shaking.

Jane shakes her head. 'I can tell you here and now that if he chooses your sister over you, he doesn't deserve you.'

'She's more fun than I am.'

Jane's eyes focus on me. 'Donald didn't think so.'

I hug her verdict to myself and sigh. 'I know, and I should be happy with that and concentrate on the tasks, but even Donald's letters are frustrating. It's like I'm constantly waiting for the next thing, and it's never what I expect!'

Jane laughs. 'Donald hated to be predictable. It was part of his charm. But you're coping with the tasks? At least, for the most part?'

I bite my lip, not sure if I should say anything, but she did say if I ever needed to talk . . . I take a deep breath. 'There is one unexpected hitch.'

Jane gestures for me to continue.

'Do you remember the old lady who spat in Donald's grave?' Jane's eyes dart to mine. 'Well, she came to visit us a few days ago.'

'Mrs Jennings?' asks Jane quietly. 'What did she want?' Both her recognition and urgency surprise me.

'She told us that Donald ruined her social standing and she wants . . . revenge.' It sounds a bit overdramatic, but Jane's reaction says it's not.

'What kind of revenge?'

I shift uneasily, starting to suspect that Jane knows something. 'She wants us to reject his will to ruin his plans, because apparently he ruined hers? "An eye for an eye" is how she put it.'

'And if you don't?'

'She said she'll expose Donald's secrets to the tabloids. Apparently there are some fairly well-known people involved.'

Jane blanches. 'And are you going to turn down his will?' she asks, but I can't quite tell whether she thinks I should.

'We don't want to. Donald worked really hard to set everything up, but there are so many unanswered questions. Like, is Mrs Jennings dangerous? Is there really anything worrying in Donald's past? If so, how much does she know? Until we answer those questions, we don't know what to do.'

Jane looks pale, but calm. 'What do you have to go on?'

'She told us that Donald kept her quiet using some sort of blackmail. We're hoping that Donald's letters might reveal what happened. Apart from that . . .' I shrug. 'Do you know anything that could help?'

Jane shakes her head. 'I don't know much, but I can tell you that Mrs Jennings *is* dangerous. She knew Donald in London and, from what I've heard, she's adept at both acquiring information and using it against people. Has she given you any kind of deadline?'

'No. She said she's leaving us to think about it – stew might be a better word.'

Jane's mouth is a hard line. 'Sounds like her. OK, I'll see what I can find out, but I definitely don't know what Donald had on her.'

'Do you know what he did to upset her? Perhaps we can work from there?'

Jane shakes her head. 'He never told me.'

We sit miserably for a few moments. 'Is Mrs Jennings really that bad?'

Jane hesitates. 'Yes, but leave it with me.'

I check my watch awkwardly, knowing I've completely destroyed the mood. 'I should probably be getting back to Lauren. Thanks for having me.'

Jane escorts me out to my car and hugs me again. 'Call me if you hear anything, or even if you just need a chat.'

'I will, and I'm really sorry to have worried you with this.'

'Don't be. I'm here to help you,' she assures me. I close my car door and roll down the window. 'But keep me informed,' she adds seriously.

'I will,' I promise. 'And thanks again.'

'Any time,' she says, but as I drive off, I know I've ruined her day.

17

Back at The Laurels, no one's home. I go up to my room to find a book and see another of Donald's envelopes propped against my bedside lamp. The inscription reads, 'For Hannah. The Fifth Task. To be given after her first dance class – task four being an ongoing project.' I decide to take it outside.

Sitting down on the garden bench, I take a moment to appreciate the view before tearing open the envelope. There are more pages than in his previous letters. I unfold them and start to read.

My Dearest Hannah,
    I wish I could have taught you to dance! Unfortunately, it wasn't meant to be, but Jane will be excellent. She was a joy to teach, and will be very supportive, I'm sure.

I hesitate as Jane's words about being twirled around the bedroom floor come back to me, and a little piece of jigsaw falls into place.

    I myself learnt to dance when I was sixteen. My mother saw a flyer on the church noticeboard advertising dance lessons, so one evening she dressed me in a shirt and tie, shoehorned Betty into a dress, and hurried us down the high street to the village hall. My friends were there, too, grumbling and tugging at their collars as the local girls twisted their fingers in their skirts, and whispered behind their hands. It looked as if all our mothers had made a pact.

The teacher, a very prim and Welsh Mrs Jones, taught us the basic steps, with the girls in one row and the boys in another. I remember her desperate attempts to convince the boys to make even a token effort, while the girls, though far more willing, giggled incessantly and had to be told repeatedly to keep quiet.

Each week we were marched down to the village hall, and made to go through the same boring routine. I memorised the steps so I could stare out of the window and was rarely told off, while my friends, whose feet were of the clodhopping two-left variety, received the majority of Mrs Jones' tongue-lashings.

Then came the week that Mrs Jones decided we should dance with a girl. The girls went quiet for the first time in weeks, and I'm convinced the panic emanating from the boys seasoned the wood of the building. It was an intimidating atmosphere, and yet I remember looking along the line, searching for one face. It became imperative that I dance with her and none of the other frivolous nonentities that frosted the room. I was searching for Judith. Judith with her generous brown curls, pale skin, dark eyes and full lips. She was seventeen (older than me) and not silly. Before I even realised what I was doing, I walked across the room, stunning the boys around me, and asked her to dance.

Mercifully, she didn't giggle. She smiled as if she had been waiting for me and took my hand, and we stepped onto the dance floor together. My heart sang as the fear of rejection washed away, and I have only a vague recollection of anything other than how she looked as she held up her arms and placed a hand on my shoulder. My lead emboldened the girls, who refused to be left unclaimed. They hauled bewildered boys onto the floor and the music began.

We rocked about the room, accompanied by the scratchy recording of a waltz and Mrs Jones' delighted applause. I have never been so glad to remember anything in my life. I didn't step on her toes and I didn't fumble. Our magical bubble drifted around the room, everyone swirling around us, until finally it was popped by Jimmy Bartle, of go-karting fame, who cannoned into us with a determined girl called Mavis. He and Mavis had been having a battle of wills over who should lead. Mavis, being superior in both persistence and height, had won. Unfortunately, she didn't look where she was going and led them on a collision course with us, and due to the power struggle, their momentum was considerable. They barged into us, full force, knocking us completely off our feet, and I watched as Judith began to fall. I had no other thought than to save her, and I swung her around so that she fell on top of me, hoping she wouldn't hurt herself. She almost knocked the wind out of me. The waltz whined on, her curls obscured my vision, but I both heard and felt the shocked silence around us. Judith propped herself up on her hands and looked down at me with mischief in her eyes, but it was only a moment before Mrs Jones yanked her away, glaring at me accusingly as if expecting me to explain. That our compromising position had alarmed her was obvious, and after that, further practising in lines ensued.

That was the starting point of my relationship with Judith.

I engineered our next meeting. I knew where she lived, so I sat on a wall down the street for what must have been hours. She eventually rewarded me by walking past with her friends. She gave just a flicker of a glance through her lashes as she passed, but when they had turned the corner, she ran back and whispered for me to meet her by the river the following day.

I hardly slept. I imagined so much, and yet didn't know what to expect. I was so disappointed when I woke the next morning to find that it was raining. With no other method of contacting her, I went anyway, refusing to believe that she wouldn't go. I waited under a tree, feeling hopeless, with the leaves dropping heavy drips on me, but refusing to leave. And do you know what? She came. She was soaked through, with her hair clinging to her face and neck, but nothing could dampen that smile. I can see it even now.

There was no greeting, shyness or uncertainty. She joined me under the tree, took my face in her hands and kissed me full on the mouth. I looked at her eyelids, amazed that anyone could be so uninhibited, and my insides melted. The kiss was long, warm and damp from the rain. The world was gone. When we finally came up for air, she laughed with an exhilaration that was dizzying. She was so free of the gaucherie that inflicted our friends. She seemed ethereal, amazing and different, like a tropical bird next to starlings. And from that day on, I was hers and everything changed. From then on, the only thrill-seeking I wanted to do was with her. And with her, everything was a thrill; stargazing, swimming, picnics, even reading aloud was breathtaking when it was done with her. That summer 'I put away childish things', and spent all the time I could with her.

So here is your next task, to be done, as I did it, at the same time as learning to dance: you must stargaze. As you do so, try to understand what Judith and I had, and what our time together was like. See if you can find a hint of that magic, because for me it was the most blissful time I have ever known.

Gloriously yours,
Uncle Donald

I sit very still, remembering my own kiss in the rain. It was magical, right up to the point Alec froze and swam away. But even that couldn't obliterate the feeling.

I stare up at the sky and watch a flock of sparrows swooping about and coming in to land all together in a bush, then taking off again almost immediately, moving to a tree. The sparrows shift from tree to tree, inspecting the entire garden, before flying off as the terrace door swings open. Lauren's laughter trickles down to me like an ice-cold stream.

'There you are,' she says, skipping down the steps with Alec following just behind. I move along the bench so they can join me. Alec smiles at me tentatively, and I feel a tightening in my chest as I'm struck by how gorgeous he looks in his blue shirt, with the sun's rays emphasising the strong line of his jaw.

'We saw your car, but there was no answer in the house, so we thought you must be out here,' he says.

I nod, smiling back in a way I hope looks natural. 'Yes, I just got back from visiting Jane, and the garden looked so lovely . . . Have you been anywhere nice?'

'Alec took me to the pub and taught me to play pool,' says Lauren. She doesn't meet my eye, because Nicholas had a pool table when we were growing up, and she always beat us hollow.

I glance at Alec. 'Is she any good?' I ask him.

'Yes,' he says frowning a little as he takes a seat. 'How was dance practice?'

Lauren squeezes in between us, and I move up against the arm of the bench. 'Fine.'

Alec's eyes drop to Donald's letter. 'I see you found it,' he says, and Lauren squints slightly, her head tipping to one side as she tries to read the exposed page. I carefully fold it and put it back in its envelope.

'Yes, thanks. I thought I'd see what the next task is.'

'So what is it – snowboarding? Parachute jumping? A quick jaunt up Everest?' asks Alec, smiling.

'Or a trip to a spa?' suggests Lauren hopefully.

I shake my head. 'No, it's stargazing.'

'Interesting. Anything to factor in?' asks Alec, ever practical.

I look down, realising I can't explain about Donald's feelings for Judith with Lauren here. 'Not really.'

'Well, that doesn't sound too hard,' says Lauren, turning to Alec. 'Out in the dark, trying to spot Orion's pants.' She gives a deep-throated giggle, and Alex gives a small smile. I push down a flicker of annoyance on Donald's behalf, but then Lauren's sense of humour never did align with mine. 'We should go tonight!' she says suddenly. 'Look at the sky – it's completely clear, no clouds. And weren't you saying, Alec, how you wanted to get through the tasks quickly?' Lauren gives me a sly glance, and I can't help but feel stung. Is he that desperate to get rid of me? 'We could take hot chocolate,' she adds, turning back to him.

'I suppose we *could* go this evening,' says Alec uncertainly, looking at me for a decision. We all look up at the sky. 'I do know a good place, but we'd need to drive.'

'I'll drive,' says Lauren predictably. 'But we might need jumpers. You can lend me one, can't you Alec?'

Alec's still waiting for my answer, but I avoid his eyes, staring instead at Donald's folded-up letter and wondering if Lauren coming along fits with what he would have wanted.

'Do you want to go tonight?' Alec asks, his voice soft, and I finally meet his eyes.

I shrug. 'Let's get it done,' I say, surprised to see something flit across his face – irritation, annoyance at my lack of enthusiasm, sadness, hurt? I'm not quite sure which, since he's anything but an open book.

'OK, let's leave at nine. I'll bring hot chocolate,' he says getting up, and strides up the steps with Lauren hard on his heels.

I stay where I am and stare at the view, wondering what he was thinking. Was he hoping to spend time alone with Lauren? If so, he should know that won't happen on a task.

I try not to think too much about the evening ahead. Or Alec. Or Lauren. Donald chose me. That should be enough. But I can't help hoping that Lauren needs to be back at work soon.

18

Parking by a field gate, Lauren turns off the engine and she and Alec get out, leaving me to locate the lever and let myself out of the back. I look up at the night sky and stretch.

'What a perfect spot,' sighs Lauren. 'So romantic.' Since Alec has his head in the boot retrieving the plastic-backed picnic blanket, her comment is wasted on me.

Opening the gate, we set off up the hill, but we haven't gone ten steps before Lauren stumbles, giving a little cry of distress. I offer her a hand, but she grabs Alec's without asking and we set off again with them arm in arm. I follow them, trying not to feel like a third wheel on a bicycle made for two.

We reach the top, and I take in the rolling hills, dotted with farms and hamlets, patterned with field boundaries, and punctuated by dark patches of trees. Above us are a few scattered, wispy clouds sporting moonlit silver-linings. I think there's a message there.

I turn around to see that Alec has laid out the picnic blanket and Lauren has already made herself comfortable and is lying right in the middle of it.

Alec stretches out on his back next to her. It feels odd joining them, but I need to see the sky, so I lie down on Lauren's other side, crossing my ankles primly, and adjusting my position so that a hummock doesn't dig into my kidneys.

'The North Star,' cries Lauren, startling me. 'And the Big Dipper!' she adds, pointing.

I stare up and try to get my bearings.

'Ursa Minor,' offers Alec.

'Where?' asks Lauren, shifting over to follow the line of his arm.

'There – coming off Polaris. Your turn, Hannah.'

'Milky Way.' It's a great stripe of stars across the sky. 'And there's a satellite,' I add, pointing at the slow-moving dot of light.

'That's not fair, it's my turn and you just had two,' says Lauren reproachfully. There's a long silence as Lauren scans the sky, making irritated little huffing sounds. I clamp my lips together, careful to keep anything else I spot for my turn. 'I can't see anything,' she says finally. 'Alec, do you see anything?'

'Orion's Belt?' offers Alec quietly.

'Well done!' says Lauren. 'So, I suppose I can have the rest of Orion?' she asks, giving a flirtatious laugh and snuggling up to him. I wish I could see if he's as keen to cuddle up to her, but I have a lot more room now, so I suppose that's one positive. I make myself more comfortable, carefully ignoring what that means, and focus on the constellations – trying to pick one out.

'Hannah, it's your turn,' says Alec after a few minutes.

'Unless I'm allowed the moon, I haven't got anything,' I say.

'I can't help thinking we should know more constellations than that,' says Alec after a while.

'It is a bit disappointing,' I agree.

'Hang on.' Lauren props herself up on her elbow and takes out her phone. She studies a webpage and reads out the descriptions of Cassiopeia, Canis Major and Taurus, and we all lie back again, waiting for our eyes to adjust.

I'm staring hard, desperate to spot them before Lauren . . . and then stop. What am I doing? This isn't my task. My task is to understand how Donald felt stargazing with Judith, and imagine how blissful this might be with someone I love, not play pin-the-name-on-the-star with Lauren.

I stop searching the sky and let my eyes relax. I take in the magnificence of the cosmos wheeling above me, trying to comprehend the great depth between the stars, and remembering that the points of light are suns in their own right. I envisage the endless universe domed over me, travelling from the start to the end of time. It takes my breath away and yet, amazing as it seems, a few moments ago I was blind to it. I almost want to laugh at how utterly absurd that is. Maybe that's part of what Donald wanted me to understand with this task: perspective.

'Cassiopeia,' shouts Lauren triumphantly.

Let her win the naming game – it isn't important. I don't even care that I'm marooned over here as they snuggle, because above me is infinity and beneath me is the entire planet Earth. I'm poised between the two, balanced. I almost want to hold someone's hand in case I skitter off. I feel a pang of regret that I can't, but I'm happy that Donald could.

I imagine his hand resting gently in Judith's, the two of them lying there, staring up at the sky, excited by each other's proximity in the privacy of darkness. There would have been no desperate competition to throw out names, just wonderment and then velvet, sensuous kissing against the extraordinary backdrop of the night's sky. Perhaps even the sky disappeared in that all-encompassing moment as they only had eyes for each other—

'Taurus!' calls Alec on Lauren's other side, then points out what he thinks might be Gemini, but they have to check on Lauren's phone, and we're all temporarily blinded.

As I wait for my night-vision to return, a quote from Oscar Wilde's play *Lady Windermere's Fan* – one of my favourites – comes to mind. 'We are all in the gutter, but some of us are looking at the stars.'

A tiny streak of light zips across an inch of sky.

'Shooting star!' Alec and I call out together and laugh.

'Make a wish,' I add quietly.

'I wish I weren't so cold,' complains Lauren, bringing us back to Earth with a definite bump.

'Time for hot chocolate?' suggests Alec, propping himself up on one elbow. Somewhere out in the darkness a fox gives an eerie yelp, and Lauren answers with a little cry. Even I shiver.

'Definitely,' says Lauren, and Alec gives us both a hand up. I fold the blanket, noticing that Lauren hasn't let go of his hand, and she keeps a determined grasp on it all the way down. I follow at a discreet distance and, seeing another shooting star, make a very quiet wish of my own.

I'm lying on my bed fully clothed and reading, when there's a tap on the door.

'Come in!' I call, expecting Lauren, but it's Alec.

'Next one,' he says, holding up Donald's letter. He puts it on the bed next to my brushed cotton pyjama bottoms and stares at them. I hope he isn't comparing them with Lauren's red nightdress.

'Thanks,' I say, leaning over to pick it up and disturbing his perusal of my pyjamas, but as I read Donald's writing I feel a pang of unhappiness. 'Task six already,' I say sadly.

Alec looks at me questioningly.

'I just wish we didn't have to race through them so fast,' I explain, watching closely for his reaction.

'I know what you mean, but unfortunately, what with Mrs Jennings . . .'

'We have to rush,' I agree. 'But I still want to do them justice.' I wish I could explain how difficult this seems with Lauren tagging along.

Alec perches on the edge of my bed, his eyes searching mine, and I wonder if he can read my thoughts. 'We could always go stargazing again sometime.'

I look down, discomfited by how much I want that. 'After we've done some research – our knowledge of the constellations was woeful,' I say, trying to inject some humour to hide that I'm imagining being out in the dark under the stars with him.

'Yes,' he says very quietly. 'Perhaps we could go when there's a meteor shower? It would be good to see that.' He smiles, leaning just a tiny bit closer, and I can feel the air crackling between us.

The hall floor creaks, and the moment, like a fairytale glass slipper, shatters into a thousand pieces. I look down, almost hating him for casting the spell.

'Goodnight,' I say firmly, and give him a nod of dismissal.

He stares at me for an uncomfortably long moment, a crease forming between his brows, then sighing, he gets up. 'Goodnight, Hannah,' he says, and as he opens my door, I catch a glimpse of Lauren dressed in a cream lace negligée. How much sexy nightwear has she packed?

'Are you coming to say goodnight to me, too?' she asks Alec.

'I wasn't really saying goodnight to Hannah, just giving her the next task.' Why is he trying so hard to reassure her? 'Goodnight, Hannah,' he says again, and closes the door.

I sit very still for a few minutes, then I sit down at the desk and pick up my pen, hoping to recapture the sense of wonder that assailed me when I was lying beneath the stars. But only words like 'idiot', 'fool' and 'dickhead' spring to mind. I sigh and put down my pen, giving it up as a bad job for tonight. I slowly change into my pyjamas. Taking my toothbrush and toothpaste, I open the door into the hall and stop dead. Lauren has her arms wrapped around Alec's neck and she's kissing him. Alec has his back to me, but he's not pushing her away.

Everything slows down and my heart stops. The door knocks against the wall behind me, acting like the play button on a movie and everything starts up again. Alec flinches from Lauren and turns to stare at me, Lauren smiles triumphantly and I turn on my heel, closing my door quietly behind me.

I stand with my back to it, staring up at the pendant light and struggling to breathe.

Someone knocks on the other side, and I move to perch on the bed. There's a giggle from Lauren and, unable to get enough air, I transfer my attention to the floor. It almost feels like I've been winded.

'Hannah?' calls Alec, and knocks again.

'Good night,' I force out. 'I'm going to sleep now!' There's a long silence and then the floor creaks as they walk away.

Left on my own, I count to slow down my breathing. It was just the shock, I think, because though I guessed they were having some sort of fling, or relationship, or whatever, I'm coming to realise that knowing is very different from suspecting. Apart from anything else, knowing seems to involve nausea and light-headedness.

Donald's letter crinkles under my hand and I look down, still seeing Lauren wrapped around Alec as if it's imprinted on my retina. I blink away the image and pick up the envelope. Wasn't I desperate to find out what happened to Judith? Wasn't I curious to know why they didn't end up together? I climb into bed and struggle to get the letter out of its envelope. Then I take a deep, steadying breath, and start.

My Dearest Hannah,

Did you feel it? Did you feel the stillness, the beauty and the enchantment? Did you sense the universe revolving quietly around you, and feel yourself being tugged gently back towards the Earth's core? Did you see more stars than you have ever seen in your life? Was it amazing?

If so, I'm glad.

If not, don't worry. Perhaps the weather wasn't good, or maybe my feelings for Judith heightened it all. Love changes everything. I'm told artists chase that view of the world via mind-altering drugs, and having experienced it, I can see why. So while Judith did it for me, I have no doubt someone will do the same for you. So promise me that, when you do fall in love, you will take them stargazing. And for now, at least, you have a baseline from which to understand the difference someone as important as Judith can make to how you see the world.

Back to my history. After that day at the river, Judith became my entire world. I spent my days working like an automaton in my father's shop, which sold everything from tools and hardware to material, ribbons and cotton, and I spent every other waking moment I could with Judith. We had to meet in secret because our parents wouldn't approve – her family being higher up the social scale than mine and Judith being older. But these matters didn't bother us. We lived for the moments we were together, which were wonderful and precious.

Inevitably, our time together never seemed enough, and we began to take greater risks. Then, one day, Betty and her friends saw us. I'm guessing we were in the distance, as I never saw her, but she recognised us and told her friends. That night she teased me at the dinner table right in front of our parents, and in a moment of pure malice, revealed I was seeing Judith. I remember Betty drinking in their shock and dismay, and languishing in my horror.

'Betty. Room. Now!' growled my father, and Betty swaggered out.

She knew I was in trouble, but I often wonder if she knew how much. You see, from my parents' perspective, I was committing social suicide, not just for myself, but for our whole family. Judith's family were considered high ranking in the village, and were good customers, too. They received deferential, almost reverential, treatment from the rest of the community, and they expected Judith, their only child, to marry well. I wasn't even on their radar for her, and if I ruined Judith's reputation, her parents would bury mine.

I know that now, but at the time I could see only how unfair they were being. I told them they underestimated my feelings, and I ranted at them for not believing I was good enough for Judith. I told them Judith and I would rather die than be separated (very Romeo and Juliet), and they went very quiet, and sent me to bed so they could discuss our fate.

It was an hour later that my mother came up and sat on the end of my bed. She told me our best hope was to try and contain the matter. In her words, they had to 'nip it in the bud', before the matter became known. They hoped to 'sweep it under the carpet' and never speak of it. After she left, I lay in the darkness, furious and bewildered.

But Betty had told her friends, and they had told their families, and by the next morning the whole village knew that Judith was seeing the shopkeeper's son. Nothing could keep a lid on the story and my parents decided we had to brazen it out. I was made to work in the shop that day, with my father saying it was better if they got the gossip out of their system. It was awful. I watched the clock, playing the part of the dutiful well-turned-out son, being meticulously polite and carefully deaf to everyone's comments. I held my temper and worked quietly until I could escape to meet Judith.

I had to talk to her. I had to tell her what they were going to try to do. I rushed to the river, terrified her parents wouldn't let her come. I was overjoyed when I saw her waiting for me by the water. I ran and held her tightly in my arms, but after a moment, I realised her arms had not wrapped around me. I let go and stared at her.

'Secret's out,' she said, smiling regretfully.

'Betty saw us,' I told her.

Her face showed a flicker of annoyance, almost pain, and then she shook it off, like a horse shaking off a fly. 'It couldn't last. It was only a summer fling,' she said, smiling once again.

I still remember the shock as her words hit me – 'summer fling'. In that moment I understood that I had simply been her bit of rough, or whatever posh households call it, and her resignation told me that, while I had cherished images of us growing old together, she had always known she would marry someone else. In a ridiculous turnabout, I was her childish thing to put away. She would now grow up and marry someone else, while I stayed by the river.

'But I love you,' I said – one of the few times I have ever used those words – and she petted me like a dog.

'They said I could come and say goodbye, but now we have to move on, do as we were intended.' I listened as her parents' words poured from her mouth. 'It's over.'

I tried to stay upright as I realised she had no intention of fighting for us; she had no thoughts of us running away together. It was just over, as she had always known it would be.

She kissed me one last time and I stood, frozen, as she walked away. She never looked back. I have since wondered whether she was crying, but at the time I thought she was as hard as nails and I almost hated her. Almost.

After that, life had to return to some semblance of normality. I went back to working in the shop. She went back to her life. Her parents steered clear of us, never using our shop, and no one mentioned that we had ever been so much as friends. It was painful, but I continued to work, though now I did so like a machine. I read in my spare time and walked a lot on my own. I thought of her, but never sought out news about her, as each new piece of information was a penetrating wound.

The months grew into a year, and not long after she turned eighteen, I heard on the grapevine that Judith had become engaged to a colonel, who was much older than her. Her family were very proud of the match, and it was the talk of the village. Feeling the threat had passed, they even started to use our shop again, though they never sent Judith. They smiled and nodded, acknowledging our lack of fuss, and none of us ever mentioned the affair. It was like a crime that no one wanted brought up.

One year became two, and I grew taller, more muscular and assured. Now eighteen, I was handsome (even if I say so myself), and well read. I was always well turned out, polite and well mannered. The girls began to flock, not that I paid them any attention, and my parents started to worry. They hated that I kept to myself and treated Betty as if she were dead. They told me life moved on and that it wasn't really Betty's fault. It would always have ended, they assured me. They urged me to try walking out with other girls, and for their benefit, I tried, but none of them interested me.

Then I met a girl called Mabel. She was quiet and didn't expect anything from me. She didn't giggle, which was a mercy, and I found her soothing. She kept my parents happy without making any demands on me. By my standards, she was good company.

Then one day, as we were walking by the river, I asked her what she was thinking. I don't know why I asked, perhaps it was because she was so quiet, but it was a defining moment because she told me every thought in her head. I remember the shock. She told me how she was actually attracted to Jimmy Bartle (remember him?) who never looked twice at her, how she liked me, but was sad for me, that she was worried about her sister's baby, how she couldn't like making jam because she was scared of the hot sugar, and so many odd and varied things that I found it amazing that so much could be whizzing around behind her quiet countenance. She fascinated me.

After that, we spent hours together. She educated me in her thoughts and feelings, what she liked and disliked, dreamed and feared, and I helped her to get Jimmy's attention by going *out with her and making it clear what a wonderful person I thought she was. Jimmy began to take notice, and when I insisted she throw me over very publicly, which was not in her nature to do, he very soon showed his interest. I was pleased for them when they started courting, and I was very careful not to make him jealous, making do with the gossip I heard in the shop. What I heard made me very happy.*

They eventually married, you know, and had six children. They are content and are still very good friends of mine, and I admit their happiness is precious to me. You know them as Jim and May.

Every year since then, May has sent me a pot of jam. It arrives, unmarked, and it always makes me smile. To be honest, I'm very glad I shall never have to see the year when it doesn't arrive.

Your next task is to visit the theatre in London. Now doesn't that sound like fun? Why London? Because that is where my story goes next. You will find out more after that.

Reminiscently yours,
Uncle Donald

As I finish reading, I shake my head at myself. Here's me, getting all het up over one kiss with Alec, when Donald had it so much worse: Judith actually married someone else! He must have been devastated. I actually think he had a lucky escape, because even though I know he loved her, I can't help disliking Judith – she seems callous and unfeeling. But then I guess neither of them had much choice, in the circumstances.

As for Grandma Betty, I know Judith and Donald's relationship would probably have ended anyway, but I'm starting to think of her not so much as Blast-off Betty, but as Blabbermouth Betty. And given what I know now, I'm no longer surprised Donald and Alec took such pains to make a backhanded reference to her lack of trustworthiness and loyalty in the eulogy. I can't even say I blame them.

And Jim and May – if anything, I love them even more now that I know Donald's history with them, and I can just imagine Jim grinning impishly in motorbike goggles.

I lie back, my head swimming with everything he's told me, and focus on the best bit: a trip to the theatre. I can't imagine a better task. I adore the theatre and I've seen everything from Shakespeare to Sweeney Todd, Tennessee Williams through to Agatha Christie. Going to the theatre was always my birthday treat, so for once this task is completely within my comfort zone. It's just what I need.

Though, now I come to think of it, wasn't Donald aiming to expand my horizons? Have I unintentionally ruined one of the tasks? I flush guiltily. I suppose I could pretend it's my first time, and try to experience it like I've never been before? I've never been with Alec . . .

I picture the two of us sat in the red velvet seats with the lights going down and the curtain going up, but then my stomach does a little dip as I imagine Lauren there as well, smooching up on Alec's other side. I have to face it – now that they're together, she's bound to join us. I close my eyes, trying to keep a lid on my disappointment, then take a deep breath. I'll make the best of it – for Donald.

19

I trail down to breakfast, bracing myself for Lauren and Alec's happy faces, and almost fall over Lauren's case at the foot of the stairs. Checking no one's about, I give it an experimental lift, and it's gloriously heavy. I put it down again and feel like I'm going to float up in the air. I quickly hunt for any reason for the case being here, other than Lauren going home, and come up with nothing.

'Good morning!' I trill as I enter the dining room. Lauren smiles at me, but Alec is hunched over his plate and doesn't even look up.

I sit down and Mrs Crumpton comes in and dumps a bowl of porridge in front of me.

'How can you eat that stuff?' demands Lauren, cradling her cup of coffee, and Mrs Crumpton leaves without comment.

'Have you tried it?' I ask, liberally pouring golden syrup over it and reaching for the cream. 'And isn't breakfast the most important meal of the day?' Mum and Dad nag her about this constantly, and Lauren pulls a face.

Mrs Crumpton comes in with my coffee, and I put a spoonful of porridge in my mouth.

'Mmm, it's delicious. You should try some, Lauren. Breakfast of champions!'

Lauren's eyes narrow, but Mrs Crumpton gives a trace of a smile as she walks out.

'So, I have some bad news,' Lauren says, glancing at Alec, but he's still staring moodily into his breakfast. 'My landlord called and there's been a leak in the flat above mine. I need to assess the damage, so I have to go.'

'I hope nothing's ruined,' I say, feeling a bit guilty now.

Lauren shrugs. 'They said they caught it quickly, but they need me to make sure none of my personal property is damaged for the insurance claim.' She pouts, glancing at Alec again. He gives absolutely no reaction, so I guess he already knows.

I eat another spoonful of porridge. 'So, when do you set off?'

'Pretty soon.'

I was hoping for an estimate in minutes, perhaps even seconds, but she's still sipping her coffee, so I concentrate on my breakfast.

'So, what's your next task? Will it wait for me to get back?' she asks, fixing me with a look.

I stare at her. She's not serious, is she? 'It's complicated actually, and I don't have all the details – which reminds me Alec, I'll need to have a chat with you after Lauren's gone.'

Alec nods mutely.

Lauren grimaces, but for once she doesn't force the issue. 'In that case, I suppose I had better be going.' I hurry to finish my porridge in case she's waiting for me, and push my bowl away. Lauren gives Alec a long glance. 'Coming to see me off?'

'No, I'll let you sisters have a proper goodbye.' His tone is frosty and my heart lifts.

'Well then, I guess this is our goodbye.' She leans in and gives him a long lingering kiss on the cheek, and as she gets up she smirks at me. Alec has gone bright red, and he flashes me an uneasy glance as he picks up his coffee. Lauren flaunts a delighted smile as I follow her out to the hall.

'See you, then,' she says absently, and I shrug, never sure what to say in these moments of artificial sisterly affection. I contemplate hugging her, then pick up her case. 'I'll carry it out for you,' I offer, though it weighs an absolute ton.

'Thanks.'

We stroll out – or rather, she strolls, and I stagger – and as I heave her case into her boot she gets in. I stand back, ready for her to drive off, but her window buzzes down. I plaster on a quick smile and go to her window.

'I'll give Mum and Dad your love,' Lauren says.

'Thanks.'

'And I'll be back to see how you're getting on. I have unfinished business,' she says, glancing back at the house. 'And now that we've kissed . . .' She gives me a loaded look that smacks into me at ninety miles an hour.

'Drive carefully,' I say weakly, and somehow manage to hold onto my smile as, with a scattering of gravel and a cursory wave, she drives away.

I stand very still.

Alec and Lauren aren't my problem – I'm here for Donald and the tasks, I remind myself. It's almost becoming a mantra.

I take a deep breath right down to my toes to release the tension, and realise I haven't breathed properly for days. I walk slowly back to the breakfast room and pick up my coffee from the table. Lauren's gone. I finally allow a forgotten calm to settle over me, and let out a relieved sigh.

'Are we good?' asks Alec, probably worried about it being awkward with him seeing my sister. Not sure how to answer, I watch him for a moment. But the truth is, if I want to do justice to Donald's hard work, I have to be fine with it.

'Sure,' I agree, despite my every cell screaming to the contrary.

Alec frowns at me doubtfully, and I attempt a reassuring smile.

Mrs Crumpton bustles in. 'Has she gone?' she asks, collecting up the plates.

'Yes, back to her flat and her recruitment job.' I say, turning from Alec's interrogatory gaze.

Mrs Crumpton nods approvingly. Alec gives a little grunt, and Mrs Crumpton turns her beady eye on him.

'And *you've* no reason to be pleased with yourself,' she says firmly.

'What did I do?' he asks indignantly.

She gives him a penetrating look, smiles at me and carries out the dishes.

'She used to like me before you came,' he says accusingly, but I can tell he's only half-serious. 'Tell me about the next task,' he says, deftly changing the subject.

'We have to go to the theatre in London,' I say, unable to keep the excitement out of my voice. 'I'm hoping you know more?'

Alec nods knowingly. 'Yes, Donald told me about this one.' He gives a ghost of his old smile and looks at his watch. 'Let me check the theatre times, and depending on when it's on, we could take the train down today and stay overnight?'

Overnight? 'Erm, great,' I say, though I'm unsure how I feel about that. 'What are we going to see?'

'Didn't Donald say?'

I shake my head.

Alec's eyes narrow speculatively. 'Oh, well let me have a quick look and I'll get back to you.'

'But what are we going to see?'

'Just a minute,' he says, heading off to Donald's study. I'm still sipping my coffee when he comes back. 'You're in luck,' he says with a grin. 'It's on tonight, and since Donald had an arrangement with the theatre, I've been able to get tickets. We'll need to catch a train to London this afternoon, though.'

If we go this afternoon, we'll definitely be going without Lauren. 'And you're sure can book the train tickets and a hotel?' I ask, desperate not to have my hopes dashed.

Alec nods. 'I've already booked the hotel, and I'll do the train now.'

'So, what are we going to see?' I ask again.

'Oh, didn't I say? How odd.' He picks up his coffee, and grinning, he heads back to the study.

'But what is it?' I call after him.

He laughs. 'You might want to pack,' he calls, and I growl.

20

We've been on the train for over an hour now, and Alec has already tried several times to talk to me about Lauren. Mostly I've deflected him with a change of topic.

'Last night with Lauren—' he says starting again, and I realise it's time for me to close the subject, because if he wants to know my feelings about whether he and Lauren are right for each other, he can go boil his head. And if he wants to know her feelings for him, he can go boil the rest of himself as well.

'It isn't any of my business what the two of you get up to.'

'But I just want to check—' says Alec.

'We're fine,' I say firmly. 'You're fine, I'm fine, Lauren's fine and honestly, I'd really rather not discuss it.' I resolutely lift my book, but I still catch him giving me searching glances in my peripheral vision.

Arriving in London it's a relief to have the distraction of getting off the train and into a taxi, and as we arrive at our hotel I'm almost fizzing with excitement. We check in and, as we grin at the incongruity of the smart porter carrying my tatty holdall into the lift, there's a hint of how we used to be.

We follow the porter to my room first, and I stop dead in the doorway. It's huge! I swallow my amazement and try to look serene as I take in the modern furnishings, massive TV and white sheets. Alec's eyes are crinkling – he knows I love it. I want to explore, but the porter is showing me the television, flicking through the channels, and pointing out the phone. I want to discover it all for myself and glare at Alec, who coughs pointedly. Luckily, the porter gets the message and they head off to Alec's room.

Left on my own, I wait for the door to click closed, and throw myself onto the gargantuan, pristine bed, feeling wonderfully grand and shabby all at the same time. I throw my arms wide and make a snow angel in the swathes of Egyptian cotton, loving the fact that my fingers can't reach the edge.

There's a tentative knock at the door and I struggle upright. 'Come in,' I call.

Alec comes in and starts at the state of the bed. 'Have you been jumping on it?' he asks gravely.

'I couldn't help it. It was just so perfect and big and mine!'

'Not so perfect now!' he says, shaking his head and breaking into a grin. 'I just came to say our tickets are booked for an hour's time, so if you want to get ready and meet me down in the lobby, we should leave in forty minutes.'

'I'll see you down there,' I say cheerfully, and then wonder if I'm supposed to act like this is a date. I frown, then dismiss the thought. It's a task – end of. I'll treat it as if I'm going with Donald.

I've changed, done my hair and make-up, and I'm ready to accept whatever Donald has arranged for me. I take the lift down to the lobby and check my watch. I'm only a few minutes late, but that's the lady's prerogative, isn't it? Or is that only for weddings?

'Hi,' says Alec, getting up from one of the plush lobby sofas and coming over to meet me in a crisp clean shirt and jacket. He has a languid grace that I've never fully appreciated before, and my heartbeat picks up.

'Hi,' I say, feeling oddly shy.

'You look lovely,' he says.

I glance down at the dress I've put on, glad I've made the

effort, and resist the urge to say 'this old thing?' 'Thanks,' I say instead.

'Ready?' he asks, offering his arm, and he escorts me out to a waiting taxi.

I watch the London streets whizz by, and after a short ride we pull up outside a theatre with *Romeo and Juliet* emblazoned across its billboards. My stomach sinks. It's not that I don't love it – of course I do – but I've seen it so many times, including twice with school and once in Stratford-upon-Avon performed by the RSC.

As Alec pays the driver, I read the poster to see which company it is, hoping to salvage something from my disappointment, and I'm brought up short by the name of a ballet company. Only now does it sink in that the lovers on the poster are wearing ballet shoes. This is Prokofiev's *Romeo and Juliet*! It's nothing like the versions I've seen before.

'It's a ballet?' I ask Alec.

'Yes. Have you been to one before?'

'No, never. I haven't even seen one on TV.' It's not the sort of thing my family watches.

'Another new experience, then,' he says smiling, taking me inside.

I realise he's right, and although a small part of me is worried I won't like it, another part is pleased that I haven't inadvertently ruined one of Donald's experiences.

Alec escorts me up the foyer stairs, and I'm about to go through the large double doors into the auditorium when he redirects me along a narrow corridor, up some even narrower steps and in through a small door on our left-hand side. My breath catches as I see the auditorium and realise we're in a box. I rush forward as an usher greets Alec, and look down over the balcony. A sea of people are seated below us and I can see straight into the pit where the orchestra are tuning up. To my right is the stage and I'm so close I could almost touch the curtain. I sit down on a springy red velvet chair feeling both overwhelmed and conspicuous.

Alec sidles between the seats and hands me a programme. 'Why the ballet?' I ask.

'Donald loved it and thought you might like it. Or perhaps "hoped" might be a better word. He always said you could tell whether someone had a soul by how they reacted to a ballet.'

'Oh,' I say, a little taken aback. What happens if I don't like it?

'Don't worry,' says Alec, perhaps seeing the concern on my face. 'I won't tell anyone if you hate it – and I'm sure it wouldn't mean you don't have a soul. Plus, I'm pretty sure he was joking. But he was insistent about you seeing *Romeo and Juliet*, so here we are.'

I suddenly realise that Donald mentioned the play in his letter, and lean forward to tell Alec, but the lights are dimming and the orchestra are starting to play the introduction to Act 1, so I settle back in my seat.

The music wraps around us as the curtain rises and the first dancers come on stage. I watch, transfixed, as the story I know so well unfolds in front of me. The passion is just as raw and Romeo and Juliet's love is just as tangible in the dancers' movements as it is in words – if not more so. At one point I sneak a glance at Alec, but he's so immersed in the story that he doesn't even notice. I rest my cheek on the balcony rail, quickly slipping back into the action, and I almost feel yanked off the stage when the curtain comes down and the lights go up for the interval.

I blink, dazed.

Alec touches my shoulder. 'Would you like a drink?'

I stretch and nod. We make our way out to the busy bar, and I wait to one side as Alec finally makes it to the front of the queue and returns with two glasses.

'Are you enjoying it?' he asks, handing me a white wine.

'It's amazing! I didn't think it would be so intense.'

'They are very good,' he says knowledgeably.

'You've been to the ballet before, then?'

'I used to go with my grandmother. She loved the ballet, the theatre and the opera.' From the look on his face I can see that he did, too. 'None of the rest of our family appreciated it, and she used to say she wasn't going to have some philistine sat next to her yawning and snoring for two hours when she could have me.'

I sip my wine, and we watch the people milling around us.

'It sounds nice,' I say.

'It was,' he agrees, and we people-watch until the bell rings for the second half.

As soon as the curtain goes up, I'm pulled straight back into the action and before I know it, Juliet is waking to find Romeo dead and Alec's handing me a tissue. I take it, wiping my eyes as I will Romeo to wake up. It doesn't matter that I know it's hopeless; I can't help it. I feel Alec's hand slip into mine and give a little squeeze. I glance at him and he smiles sadly. Back on the stage, Juliet takes the knife and stabs herself in the chest, and I barely manage to stop myself gasping. In her last dying moments she reaches for her dead beloved and I stare, grief stricken.

The curtain falls. The audience breaks into heartfelt applause. I realise my hand is clamped closed around Alec's. Embarrassed, I let go, and slowly begin to clap, finally getting a hold of myself as the curtain goes up again. I sniff and clap louder as the performers bow, and as Romeo and Juliet come forward, I get to my feet with the rest of the audience to give them a standing ovation. Who knew that, even without words, it could be so powerful?

When the curtain has gone down for the last time, Alec leads me out into the street, where the fine drizzle and street lights finally bring us back from Verona and Mantua.

We don't talk much in the taxi back, and as Alec walks me to my room, neither of us has anything to say. The atmosphere is strangely charged, and we slow as we approach my door.

I take out my key card and fiddle with it. 'Thanks for taking me. It was wonderful.'

'I'm really glad you enjoyed it. Donald would be ecstatic. No need to worry about your soul!' He looks down at me. He's standing slightly too close, but I don't move away. I clear my throat.

'We've completed another task,' I say as casually as I can manage.

'Yes. You can have the next letter in the morning, if you like?'

I'm already thinking about the next part of Donald's story and I'm not sure I can wait. I look up at Alec. 'Or you could give it to me tonight? What do you think?' I ask.

Alec's frown deepens, and I'm about to ask whether he could pop back to his room and get it, when his lips land on mine.

I jerk back and before I know what I'm doing, my palm collides sharply with his cheek.

'What the hell was that for?' he shouts, clutching his face, his eyes wide.

'What do you mean, "what the hell was that for?",' I demand, shocked at what I've just done. 'That was for kissing me!'

'But I thought that's what you meant by all that "give it to me tonight" talk.'

'What? I meant the bloody letter. It wasn't some innuendo, you moron!'

'How the hell was I supposed to know?'

'You've been all over my sister for the last few days!'

His hand drops away. There's a livid hand-print on his cheek, but it isn't half as livid as I am.

'What?' he demands.

'You heard! We're not interchangeable, you know.' I'm glaring at him so furiously he steps back.

'I didn't think you were! Is this because she kissed me?'

'Oh, *she* kissed *you*, did she?'

'Yes, actually, she did. She caught me completely off guard and you opened your door while I was still trying to figure out how to disentangle myself without upsetting her. I thought you knew that. Lauren said she'd explain.'

'Really?' I say, my voice dripping with disbelief. 'That's the first I've heard of it, and you have to admit you weren't exactly fighting her off when I saw you.'

'I was caught by surprise!'

'Look what just happened when you caught *me* by surprise!'

'Are you suggesting I should have slapped Lauren?'

'Of course not, but you could have tried harder to stop her, and you spent a whole lot of time with her for someone who isn't interested.'

'I was doing you a favour.'

'Thank you *very* much,' I say, my voice heavy with sarcasm.

'I don't mean . . .' Alec pushes his hands distractedly through his hair, and looks up and down the corridor, then back at me. 'She's your sister, I was trying to make her feel welcome.'

I reduce my voice to a hiss as a door opens further down the corridor. 'Then you did a hell of a job!'

We glare at each other as the other guests leave their room, wait for the lift and get in. Finally the lift doors close behind them.

'For God's sake, she's your sister!' Alec shouts.

'I know! What do you want? Applause?'

'I didn't mean that. I meant I wouldn't . . .' Alec closes his eyes. 'I'm sure your sister is very nice and everything, and perhaps she is a lot like the other women I've been with—'

'Oh, whoop-di-doo!' I say, and a porter who has just come around the corner retreats the way he came. Seeing him, I suddenly realise how futile and ridiculous this all is. 'Oh, for God's sake, it doesn't matter. Just leave it.' I turn to go into my room.

'You're not even going to let me explain?' Alec demands.

'No, because it's been a really long, emotional day, and I've had enough,' I say, trying to keep the wobble out of my voice.

'Give me five minutes.'

'No, all you need to say is that you will not be kissing me again, and I think we're both already pretty clear on that.'

'Damn right,' he mutters.

I flush with fresh anger and hurt. 'Goodnight,' I say, my voice cracking. I look down at the key card, which I've almost bent in half, and stab it into the slot seven or eight times, trying different ways round until the light goes green. I give him one last withering look and storm into my room, slamming the door in his face. Or at least I try to, but the stupid thing has a slow-close mechanism, so it doesn't quite have the desired effect.

It finally clunks shut and there's silence. Part of me expects him to calm down and try to say sorry, but he doesn't knock. After a few minutes, I realise he must have gone to his room.

'Bloody hell,' I say out loud, and feeling suddenly limp, I kick off my shoes and collapse onto the soft sheets of the bed, staring up at the ceiling.

How dare he kiss me after Lauren. And why would he want to after his remorse last time? He's never explained. He's never apologised, and yet he tries to kiss me again? Tears slide down my temples and pool in my ears, but I don't know if they're from anger or hurt. I get up, take a few deep breaths to calm myself, and go to wash my face, savouring the cool, cleansing effect of the water. I scrub my face dry with a soft white towel, and sit on the edge of the bath for I don't know how long, staring at nothing in particular, lost in my own head. After a while I start to feel cold, and suddenly all I want is to be nestled in bed.

Coming back into the bedroom, I see an envelope has been pushed under the door. It's one of Donald's – Alec must have been here while I was in the bathroom. I bend to pick it up and turn it over to see Alec's writing scrawled across the back.

'I'm going home. Do what the hell you like. Alec.'

I stumble back to sit on the bed. It's almost like he's slapped me. Is he serious? He's leaving me here alone?

I reread his scrawl, unable to understand why he thinks he has any right to be angry. He kissed Lauren. Or she kissed him . . .

Unsure what to believe, I slide my finger under the flap and take out Donald's letter, vowing that if it's anything like the one about Billy, I'm going home, no matter what Mrs Crumpton says, or how much work Donald put into everything. I pull in a deep breath and start reading.

My Dearest Hannah,

London – what a place! It has a wealth of everything in its extremes: joy and hopelessness, parties and loneliness, high life and poverty. It is both heaven and hell in equal measure. Where the country is stable, safe and peaceful, London is the opposite. I both love and hate London, though perhaps love just tips the scales.

What have you made of London so far? I'm hoping you have seen the bright side that I saw when I first moved there. The hotels, the theatres and through the ballet I hope you experienced what it feels like to be in love – short of you actually falling in love, it was the best way I could think of for you to encounter that sensation in all its glory and heartache. But let me begin where my story left off, or nothing will make any sense at all:

In the early months of 1963, when I was nineteen, and about six months after my happy arrangement with Mabel, a typewritten envelope arrived for me with a London postmark. My parents didn't open it as it was addressed to me and looked official, but I knew it was from Judith just by being in the same room as it. I took it to my bedroom, tore it open and read it with such shaking hands that I had to reread it twice to make any sense of it. The gist was that she was asking me to come to see her in London. She said she needed me, and, of course, I went.

I packed a few things in a bag, took my earnings, and caught a bus and a train. Then, from a bustling London train terminus, I took a taxicab to Judith. She had rooms at a respected hotel – her husband thinking that living in London and experiencing the capital's high life would entertain Judith while he travelled.

What I saw in her face when I arrived worried me. Having first checked the hall for busybodies, she swept me into her room and held me very tightly. Then she kissed me so desperately and disarmingly that we got carried away and tumbled into bed together. Our love-making was short, I will admit, but very sweet, and afterwards as she lay in my arms, she cried and told me everything.

She told me how grown-up she had felt getting engaged; how much she had enjoyed the presents and the courtship, how big the wedding was and how she had basked in the glow of her friends' envy. Then she told me of her wedding night. She had expected it to be wonderful – a rite of passage, a blossoming into womanhood with fireworks and confetti – but what she'd experienced was painful and horrible, and above all, lonely. She told me she hadn't felt deflowered but defiled, and when he went to sleep, she had cried silently into her pillow wishing that *we had been together first. Their times together still weren't good, she confided. She didn't feel nurtured or cosseted, but like she was performing a loathed and most unpleasant duty.*

Then she described how, after their honeymoon, the army set and their wives had swallowed them up. She really hated those wives. They felt duty-bound to induct her into 'the way things are'. They laughed at her naivety as they opened her eyes to the brutal realities of their husbands' mistresses, their children at boarding school, and all their outward show. She said their bile burned her every time they met, but her lowest point came when they met to play tennis. A lady was pointed out to her, a Mrs Anderson – older, but still lovely. She was another man's wife . . . and her own husband's mistress.

Her downfall complete and unable to talk to her husband, family or friends, she did the one thing she felt she could. She sought out someone trustworthy. She wrote to me, taking care to type the letter to give it the greatest chance of reaching me unread.

And that is how my affair with Judith began.

Complete another task and I'll tell you more.

Anticipatingly yours,

Uncle Donald

I close my eyes trying to absorb it all, and then I turn the letter over. There's nothing more. I check the envelope and then drop to my knees, feeling around on the floor in case the task has fallen out. I open the door and check the hall for a second envelope or a Post-it note that has peeled off, but there's nothing. I let the door close, realising there's no task – no next move, or instructions for what to do next. Did Donald forget?

What am I supposed to do? I'm in London by myself and I'm not even sure if the room is paid for. An edge of panic starts to creep in, and I take a few deep, calming breaths. I have to think practically. I'll have to pay for a whole night now regardless, so I might as well stick it out and hope that Alec returns. And if he doesn't . . .

'Then he's a bastard,' I announce to the room, though I know he isn't really . . . even if he did kiss Lauren, which he says he didn't.

I think back on our argument and his insistence that Lauren had said she'd explain, and sit down on the bed as a nasty suspicion steals over me. I think back to this morning: the furtive look he gave me at breakfast and how he left me and Lauren to have a sisterly goodbye. And then there are the questions I was asking myself earlier. Why would Alec try to kiss me again if it was so awful the first time? Reasonable conclusion: he wouldn't. Why would he kiss me if he was involved with Lauren? Reasonable conclusion: he wouldn't. *Or* he's actually a bastard and he would. I wait for this to ring true, but it doesn't. Perhaps it would have done a few weeks ago, but I know him better now. He's a good person, and he's never lied to me unless at Donald's instigation. So why would he think she explained about the kiss when she didn't? Has Lauren been messing with me? I think back over all the times I've seen them together and mentally stumble over their kiss goodbye. Would Lauren really kiss his cheek if they were dating? She's practically suctioned the face off past boyfriends, even in front of our parents.

I put my head in my hands. Oh, shit. There is a reasonable chance that I've been wrong about him and Lauren. Part of me leaps at the possibility, while the other part is searching for a rock to hide under.

I glance at my mobile, wondering if I should give him a chance to explain, or whether I should let him cool off first. I suppose I could call Lauren and try to get the story from the horse's mouth, but I doubt she'll be honest with me, and besides, her gloating will be unbearable.

And there's still the issue of paying for all this. I stare hopelessly at the room. I can't call my parents – they've already helped me out enough financially and asking them to pay for an expensive London hotel room would really take the biscuit. I pick up my purse and search through the compartments, hoping for a stray twenty-pound note or five. Instead, I find Mr Sanderson's business card. I suppose, if I haven't sorted anything out by morning, I could give him a call and see if he can do anything.

I close my eyes, amazed that I am in a London hotel room contemplating calling my solicitor. What is my life coming to?

One thing's for sure, nothing can be done before morning. I pick up the remote and switch on the TV. There's nothing good on so I settle for a documentary on space and after changing into my pyjamas, I snuggle down under the covers to learn how black holes are made. I watch the swirling mass of galaxies, and do my best not to picture my relationship with Alec disappearing down this ultimate plughole, but I can't help it. There's no way of rescuing it now.

21

I wake with a start and roll onto my back. My mouth is dry, my head aches, and my eyes feel like they've been peeled by an amateur kitchen hand. For a moment I wonder if the banging I'm hearing is just the pounding in my head, but then I realise there's someone knocking at the door. I clamber out of bed. Hearing yet another knock, I picture a disgruntled porter standing in the hallway, tapping his foot and looking at his watch.

'I'm just packing,' I shout. 'I'll be down in a minute.'

There's another knock, and I tiptoe over to peek through the spyhole. Jane's standing outside looking up and down the corridor. I give my heart a second to slow down.

'Hello Hannah,' she calls. 'It's Jane. Can I come in?'

'Yes, of course! Sorry,' I say, turning on the light and yanking open the door. 'I thought you were hotel security.' Jane gives me a confused look. 'I didn't know you were coming,' I try to explain. 'Not that I'm not happy to see you – I am,' I add quickly, rubbing my eyes and ushering her in.

'I'm here for your next task. Didn't Alec tell you?'

'No, and Donald didn't mention anything in his letter, either. I thought he'd forgotten.'

'No, he didn't forget – I'm here to take you out for the day.' She looks at me doubtfully. 'Would you like a shower first?' she asks tactfully, and I catch sight of my tangled hair and panda eyes in the mirror.

'Er, yes,' I agree sheepishly. I pick up a bath towel and some underwear and stumble into the bathroom. 'Make yourself comfortable,' I call.

The shower is heavenly and I can't help taking a few extra minutes under the hot water, before emerging in a hotel dressing gown with make-up done and hair brushed. The curtains are now open and Jane is tucking into some pancakes. She gestures that I should do the same, but my heart stops at the thought of the bill. My credit card probably won't take the strain of the basics, let alone extras.

'You'll need your strength,' she prompts.

'I'll just ring the front desk and find out when I have to check out and how much the bill is.' And whether they'll let me work it off as a chambermaid.

'Don't worry about the checkout time – Donald wouldn't begrudge you an extra night in a hotel, and as for the bill, it's all being settled through the solicitor.'

'Is it?' I stop mid-reach and slump down into a chair, my head lolling back in relief – a puppet with its strings cut.

Jane laughs. 'Of course it is; it's part of the will. Why, were you worried?'

'A little,' I confess.

'I'm surprised Alec didn't put your mind at rest, but then I expect it didn't occur to him that you might worry.'

'We had a row,' I explain as I pull my jeans on under the dressing gown. 'He went home.'

'Oh. Was it over your sister, by any chance?' she asks sympathetically.

'Sort of.' I throw off the dressing gown and pull a top over my head, shaking my hair out of the collar.

'Have some breakfast,' says Jane, pushing a plate towards me. I load on a couple of pancakes, some syrup and some strawberries and perch on a desk chair. 'Well, I wouldn't worry about it. It was an argument waiting to happen.'

'Was it?'

'With you and your sister interested in the same man? Of course it was.'

I blink, unsure of how to respond, and eat a pancake. 'So, what are we doing today?' I ask, more to change the subject than anything else.

'Sightseeing,' says Jane. 'Sort of.'

'Really?'

Jane nods, puts her teacup back on the tray and glances at my empty plate. 'Ready to find out what I have planned?' she asks, and I detect a hint of a challenge in her words.

'Absolutely! Do I need anything?'

'Just yourself,' she says, and I grab my purse and follow her out of the room.

London with Jane is an experience! She whisks me straight into a taxi and our first stop is a hairdressing salon.

'They've squeezed you in as a favour,' Jane whispers as we go in. 'Marlene is a marvel, but I may have overstated your need a little.'

'In what way?'

'Marlene loves a desperate case, so please ignore everything I say for the next half hour.'

'Desperate—?' But before I can ask more, a woman with her hair shorn up one side and an angular bob on the other comes over holding out her arms.

'Jaaaaane!' she drawls, and pulls Jane to her with both hands. 'How are you?' Without waiting for an answer her eyes fall on me. 'Oh I see what you mean! Darling, when was the last time you had a professional cut?' Leading me through the salon by the hand she lands me in an empty torture chair and rotates me so I'm facing the mirror. She grips my head from behind, her cheek almost pressed against mine and we both study my reflection.

'When did you last have a colour, a cut, or a restyle?' she asks seriously.

'Umm . . . I . . .' If she'd said trim, I might have been able to answer.

'Don't ask, Marlene,' Jane replies for me, but I don't think she's coming to my rescue. Her mouth is twisting just as much as Marlene's as they both contemplate my apparently disastrous hair. I frown at her, and she gives me a flicker of a wink.

'The colour?' Marlene asks Jane.

'Natural,' says Jane.

'I can see that!' She holds up a piece of my mousy brown hair like it's a blunt-ended paintbrush liberated from a children's nursery. 'Split ends,' she decrees. 'Awful cut. No life.' She drops it and looks at me sternly in the mirror. 'Darling, what would you like?'

Feeling like I've been strapped to the tracks with a train due, I glance at Jane, who shrugs.

'Any colour preferences, cut, style?' asks Marlene, waiting.

Oh what the hell, I've wanted to dye my hair for years, but suspecting I might dip-dye my forehead, or accidentally turn my hair green like Anne of Green Gables, I've always chickened out. 'Could I try a chestnut colour?' I ask shyly.

We all wait as Marlene squints at me, her head tipping first one way and then the other. 'Yes,' she says, nodding. 'A lovely rich brown with reddish highlights? And a modern bob cut, with the hair nice and short at the back.'

I stare at her in the mirror, desperately hoping she won't shave one side of my head.

'No, not like mine,' says Marlene, shaking her head. 'No, for you we go symmetrical!' She turns to Jane, her eyes flicking heavenward, and I half expect her to say 'muggles!'

'You stay here and I'll buy you some make-up,' Jane says, like I have a choice, and snaps a quick photo of me on her phone. My mouth is half open so I probably look like a surprised goldfish.

Marlene hands her a vivid loop of fake hair. 'This will be her colour afterwards, so match the make-up to that.' I stare at it. It's bright.

'Thanks, Marlene. Get comfortable,' Jane says to me, handing me a glossy magazine from a stack on the side, and as Marlene zips away to talk to someone at the front of the salon, Jane bends down to my ear. 'Trust her, she's a genius.' Then, pocketing the loop of hair, she abandons me to the mercy of Marlene, who comes back looking scarily determined and calls a minion to come and wash, then colour, my hair.

By the time Jane comes back, Marlene is wielding a blow-dryer and refusing to let me look in the mirror.

'Darling, it has to be a grand reveal – it's such a change!' I'm hoping for ugly duckling to swan, not lamb to mutton, so I look anxiously at Jane as Marlene swings me round to face her. 'Ta-dah! What do you think?' Marlene asks her, holding her hands out like a magician.

Jane beams at me. 'Marlene, you're a miracle worker!'

Marlene spins my chair so I'm facing the mirror, and I stare at myself. I touch my hair, watching my reflection do the same. My hair is so short and bright. I look like a confident, vibrant woman – who admittedly needs a better make-up regime, but still . . . it's so different. Tears prick my eyes as I realise just how much I needed this, and I don't just mean the makeover, but the whole experience of being made to feel special.

I glance at Jane who nods encouragingly, though she looks a bit concerned about my reaction.

I pat her arm. 'Ignore me, I'm just being silly. I love it. It's amazing.'

Jane grins at Marlene who nods in satisfaction, and Jane takes out her purse. I open my mouth to protest, but Jane shakes her head firmly as Marlene disappears off with her credit card. 'Today's on Donald,' she says firmly, and I smile gratefully, unable to stop myself tentatively touching the short hair at the back of my neck. It's almost spiky.

Jane inspects my hair from different angles. 'It's a big change, but a good one, and sometimes we need to shed our old selves to let the new one flourish.'

'Let go of the past and embrace the future?' I ask.

'Or maybe see the opportunities of the present in a new light,' she suggests, a small smile playing on her mouth.

'Thanks, Marlene,' says Jane, as Marlene comes back with a handheld card reader. 'As always, you've worked wonders,' she says, typing in her pin.

'Yes, thank you so much,' I agree fervently, glancing again at my unfamiliar reflection.

Marlene slips her arm around my shoulders. 'My pleasure. I love a good makeover! Now go,' she whispers urgently, handing back Jane's card. 'My boring "give-me-the-same-as-last-time" eleven thirty has been waiting for twenty minutes!' And with a last squeeze, we're bustled out past a sour-faced woman and into the street.

'You look fantastic,' Marlene shouts after us, causing several people to turn and look at me. Well, I suppose it's one form of advertising.

'Lunch?' asks Jane and, somewhat dazed by the whole experience, I follow her into a taxi.

We end up down a tiny cobbled street that becomes too narrow for the taxi to go any further, and Jane takes me through a small pedestrian gap that leads right onto the bank of the Thames. A sharp right has us standing outside a small hidden cafe with tables on the waterfront.

'Make-up, scarves and sunglasses,' Jane says, handing me a shiny cardboard bag with tissue paper-wrapped packages inside. 'Open them later.'

'Thank you!'

'My pleasure. Now, lunch and then we have London to see.'

After lunch we start with Tate Modern, but we don't stroll thoughtfully from piece to piece, umming and ahhing. Instead, Jane insists we take turns interviewing each other about each piece as if we are the artists, making ridiculous claims about our motivations and muses, and I laugh so hard I almost see my lunch again.

Next we view London from the top of The Shard, with a competition over who can name the most landmarks – which degenerates into chaos as we start shouting out attractions that aren't even in London.

We eat ice creams in St James's Park while spotting secret agents and trying to guess their country of origin, mission and code name – which earns us a few confused looks from said potential spies.

Finally, we end up at Covent Garden Market looking for the most outrageous item of headwear. Jane wins with a snood with savage teeth printed on it.

Happy and exhausted, we collapse at a table outside a cafe and order some pasta.

'Shame, I think it really suits me,' says Jane holding up the snood, which she bought for her nephew. 'Still, he'll love it and his mum will hate it, so job done!'

'How old is he?' I ask, picturing an eight-year-old charging about in a cowboy outfit, the snood concealing his identity as he holds up relations with a plastic gun and demands their lollies or their life.

'Thirty-seven.'

'Oh,' I say, and stifle a giggle. 'So I've been trying to figure out today's task, but there doesn't seem to be a theme beyond "London"?'

Jane puts down her orange juice. 'You're half-right. Donald always said London had two sides. He wanted you to see the wonderful, extraordinary and amusing side of London. The details of how to achieve that were up to me.'

'Well, I've loved it. It's been the best day out ever.'

Jane pats my hand. 'Good. I was a little worried I might not do the task justice, but after meeting you, I felt sure it would work out.'

'Thank you. It's been brilliant.'

'You're welcome.' She settles back into her seat. 'Now, would you like a lift back to Donald's or would you prefer to go back on the train?'

It's just after five. I think of the train crammed with commuters, and suppress a shudder. 'I'd love a lift.'

'Excellent,' she says, and we head back to the hotel to collect my things and her car.

22

'It doesn't look like anyone's in,' says Jane as we pull up in front of The Laurels a few hours later.

I glance up at all the darkened windows. 'Don't worry. Mrs Crumpton has told me where the spare key is kept.'

'Are you sure? Because you can stay at mine if you'd like?'

'No thanks, I'm fine,' and I realise I mean it. I feel like I've arrived home, and it doesn't bother me in the least to be here by myself.

Jane helps me collect my bags from her boot and, after removing the key from under a quartz rock, I give her a hug.

'Thanks so much for today. It was exactly what I needed.'

She laughs, squeezing me before letting go. 'I've loved every minute of it. In fact, I think we should do it again sometime, don't you?' she beams as she gets back in her car.

'I'd love that,' I say, grinning, and stand back and wave as she drives off.

Once through the door I call out just to double-check there's no one in. There's no reply, so I head to the kitchen, make myself a cup of tea and marvel at just how at home I feel here. Part of it is the people – Donald leading me through the tasks, wanting me to have good experiences and love everyone he loves, Jane helping me, and also Mrs Crumpton making sure we behave ourselves. I look down at a plastic box of apple strudel she's made, with the words 'Eat me!' scrawled on the lid in Sharpie. Very Lewis Carroll, and I can imagine her writing it, knowing full well how much I'd appreciate it. But I also love the house. I love that Donald has a spot on the kitchen ceiling, and still seems to be here, ready to take his walking stick from the oriental jar by the front door. And I love how Donald is becoming more human, fallible, accepting and wonderful with every letter. I already feel like I've known him my whole life.

And Alec?

I stare at the kitchen wall trying to puzzle out my feelings. Yes, I like that Alec's here, too, because despite everything, he loved Donald and he's helped me, even though to begin with he didn't want to. I couldn't have done the tasks without him, and I wouldn't have wanted to, even if I'd known how it was going to turn out.

Having somehow managed to make myself feel melancholy, I pick up my tea, head upstairs and empty the bag Jane gave me onto the bed. I carefully unwrap each item, feeling like it's Christmas morning (only without the supersized turkey and family friction), and gaze at the chic selection. I take the Jackie Onassis-style sunglasses to the mirror, almost doing a double take as I see my hair, and slide them on. They suit me perfectly, and I silently thank Jane for being so clever. Next, I apply some of the eye make-up to see how it looks with my new hair. Starting to enjoy myself now, I tune the radio to Radio 1 and bob about to the music as I try on the soft aquamarine and midnight-blue scarves with several of my tops, marvelling at how my new hair sings against them. Perching the sunglasses on top of my head, I pose in front of the wardrobe mirror – and freeze as someone behind me clears their throat.

I spin around to find Alec in the doorway, with Lauren standing just behind him, eyes wide.

'Oh, hello,' I say, attempting to be friendly, but my smile falters as Lauren sniggers. I blush beetroot-red.

'Wow, exotic!' she says, and I suddenly feel like I'm five years old again, caught in my mother's high heels and scarlet lipstick. I let the scarf slide off my shoulders, and quickly remove my sunglasses. 'I've never imagined you as a conker-coloured hair kind of girl, but it suits you better than I'd have thought.'

'Er, thanks,' I say, though it doesn't feel like a compliment.

'It's a whole new you,' she adds patronisingly. 'Well, well. Aren't you brave!'

'Thanks,' I say again, my tone flat, and Alec looks suspiciously from me to Lauren.

'Nice, isn't it?' Lauren asks him, smiling sweetly.

'Lovely,' he agrees, frowning at Lauren before meeting my eyes. 'Truly,' he adds, his voice softer. There's a pause and Lauren clears her throat, eyeing us both beadily. Alec seems to come to. 'I came to give you this,' he says, handing me Donald's next letter. 'And also to say sorry for leaving you in London last night. Did you have a good time with Jane?'

'Er yes, brilliant, thanks. I was just trying on some things she got me today.' I glance at Lauren.

'They're nice,' says Alec awkwardly, and I realise this conversation is excruciating, not because of our argument, or my makeover, but because Lauren is standing there listening to our every word.

I turn to her, folding my arms across my chest. 'So, how come you're back?' I ask, trying to sound breezy.

'The painters are redecorating my bathroom and I thought, where can I stay while the work is being done? And the obvious solution was here!'

'Not our parents' house?' I ask innocently.

'No,' she says firmly.

'But we're going to be busy with the tasks, so it won't be very interesting for you.'

'*You* may be busy with the tasks, but poor Alec has just been hanging about here all day. I've been keeping him company, haven't I Alec?'

Our eyes shift to Alec, but his mouth is a hard line.

'Is Mrs Crumpton OK with Lauren staying?' I ask, and Alec's frown deepens.

'She left just after Lauren arrived, saying there'd be no dinner today, so I took Lauren to the pub.' I guess that answers my question.

'Yes, he invited me out to dinner,' agrees Lauren, smiling slyly at me.

'It was just food and a round of pool,' he says firmly. 'As friends.'

I raise my eyebrows at Lauren, but she rolls her eyes. 'You say that now,' she says coyly.

'Yes, I do.' Alec turns to me, and suddenly smiles. 'By the way, I love the hair – it looks great.'

I blush, then wonder if I clash with my new colour. 'Thanks.'

'Jeez!' mumbles Lauren. 'Are we going to stand around in Hannah's doorway all evening?'

'Yes, I should change,' I agree, remembering the heavy eye make-up I've put on.

'We'll see you downstairs,' says Alec.

I move forward to close the door behind them, and hear Lauren's parting shot: 'I know it's brave, but I'm not sure it suits her.'

Then I just catch Alec's calm but firm reply: 'No? Well I think she looks amazing.'

I can't help grinning as I tear open the envelope, and start to read.

My Dearest Hannah,

London with Jane – how I would love to do that again! I hope you had a wonderful time. Jane wouldn't tell me what she had planned, but she assured me it would be a whirlwind of activity and that she would do me proud. 'Make her love it' was the only instruction I gave her, so I'm hoping that you now understand why I adore the place. Like me, it is never dull once you know how to make the most of what's there. And also, like me, having a sense of humour is essential!

So, back to what happened with Judith. Prepare yourself!

I'm sure, if I'd had an ounce of decency or self-respect, I would have left Judith to her fate in London. She'd made her bed, so to speak. But I didn't. We began a relationship where she was my world and I was her consolation. Of course there were practicalities to be considered, and to support this new life I took any number of small jobs from hotel porter to desk clerk, doorman to barman. In between my many shifts we were together, but always careful to keep away from prying eyes.

To maintain appearances, Judith kept up her attendance with the army wives, and coped much better knowing she had someone to relate it all to afterwards. There were of course occasions when her husband returned; his presence keeping us apart while he was in town. But as soon as he left, we resumed our courtship with all the gusto of parted lovers.

But how long can such all-consuming passion stay hidden? A little over eighteen months, in our case, but as before in our village back home, I think it was inevitable that we would eventually be discovered, especially since Judith was now so much more content. The unfortunate part was that we were discovered by someone ruthless and very dangerous indeed: Mrs Jennings.

My breath catches in my throat at the sight of her name, and I feel myself go cold, just as I always did at the entry of the Child Catcher in *Chitty Chitty Bang Bang* when I was a child.

Like with Betty, we never did find out where she first saw us, but see us she did and that changed everything, because Mrs Jennings, though relatively new to London and Judith's circle of wives, immediately understood the nature of our relationship. And what's more, she knew exactly how she wanted to make use of this information.

The first we knew of it was when she called in on Judith one afternoon, just as if she were calling on a friend. Over tea and cake Mrs Jennings genteelly informed Judith that she knew exactly what was going on. She confided that of course she quite understood and would stay silent, but the price for her silence was for Judith to share!

I wasn't at this first meeting, so I'll never know how Judith reacted. My reaction was one of horror – Judith was my one and only, and the idea of sleeping with anyone else left me cold. But Judith begged me. She told me that her marriage and her social position depended on it. I listened, dumbfounded, unable to believe she could bear to ask this of me. The more she pleaded, the more I felt I didn't know her at all; her being able to share with so little thought for me. She argued that it was the same as me sharing her with her husband. She said that this way Mrs Jennings couldn't blackmail or tell on us. I kept my opinions over the blackmail issue to myself.

Unfortunately, before we could discuss the matter further, Judith's husband arrived unexpectedly and whisked her off to their country residence. I was left alone in London with Mrs Jennings, and she was very determined.

She found me wherever I went, presumably on Judith's information, and began flirting, persuading and cajoling. Perhaps unsurprisingly for someone willing to blackmail, Mrs Jennings was very charming. It's true that she made it clear that I had no choice if I wanted to keep Judith's marriage intact, but she told me that she also wanted me to be happy about it. She wanted me to be, at least partly, sleeping with her of my own volition.

In the end, having been wooed and flattered, I received a panicked letter from Judith telling me she was pregnant, that it wasn't mine, and that I had to sleep with Mrs Jennings or risk ruining everything she had worked for. I will spare you the tortured details of that letter, but it drove me to drink. Mrs Jennings, who I suspect had been having me followed, found me in a bar, took me to a hotel and persuaded me, in my drink-addled state, that I should take revenge on Judith. She convinced me that Judith would be horrified if I actually went through with it. Mrs Jennings said Judith would feel betrayed, and at the time her words made perfect sense. But afterwards, in the sober light of day, I realised I had done exactly what both Judith and Mrs Jennings wanted. The only person I had disappointed was myself.

But once it was done, there was no going back. Mrs Jennings, being very happy with the service, paid me handsomely for my attentions. She decided that, not only was I worth every penny, but that I would be more available if I didn't work. So that put me into a very specific category.

Do I shock you, Hannah? Well, wait, there's more.

Mrs Jennings, as previously described, was dangerous, and although she never linked me to Judith, over time she began to tell of her 'gigolo'. Word got out, and Mrs Jennings dangled me in front of her friends with the information that she had a hold over me, and could keep me to heel. At which point, I became the toy boy of the wives that Judith so despised. I became their pampered pet with ever-growing financial means, while Judith lived in the country and had babies. And using me, Mrs Jennings gained power over an increasing number of women.

Of course there were drawbacks. There were women who were not to my taste, theatre visits where only half the play was

watched before I was expected to perform. There were the hours
of dull conversation, before being pounced on as if by a raven-
ous panther.

But there were also compensations. The exhilaration of
evading returning husbands, for example – yes, I really did
hide in wardrobes and climb down drainpipes half-naked. In
fact, a policeman caught me once and said that, considering
how little I was wearing, he could tell I wasn't a burglar. He
allowed me on my way with the smirk of a man composing a
vastly exaggerated tale for his colleagues.

In truth I spent several years in these pursuits. I was thirty
before anything changed, and in the intervening years I rarely
saw Judith. She either travelled with her husband or stayed at
home with her children. But life was good, and contrary to
expectation I soon owned a flat in one of the more affluent
areas of London – which suited everyone.

More after your next task, for which I would request that
you join Jane for lunch.
Surprisingly yours,
Uncle Donald

At last, the truth. A gigolo. Forced to be one, but a gigolo
nonetheless. It's almost too far-fetched to believe. I tap the
letter against my lips, going back over all my memories of
Donald: his manner, his life choices, his lack of family –
and it all starts to make sense. Jane's warning about Mrs
Jennings also slots into place. Mrs Jennings must have dirt
on plenty of people – and given what she did to Donald
and Judith, she has no qualms about using it to her
advantage.

But how is Jane involved? Is she at risk? I'll have to ask
tomorrow, but if she is, I have to convince everyone to turn
down Donald's will, and I have no idea how I'm going to do
that without explaining why.

Still, first things first, Alec needs to know what the next task is, and I'm not going to let Lauren make me stay up here all evening.

Taking care to hide the letter in the window seat with the others, I brush my hair, surprised by how my first few brush strokes fly off at the end as I get used to my new shorter style, and use a wet wipe to remove a little of the eye make-up. I stare at my reflection trying to get used to my new look, loving how my hair's still sleek from the hairdressers. It's been a day of revelations, but I'm not about to let that faze me. I turn out the light and head downstairs to the drawing room.

I'm about to push open the drawing room door, when Lauren barks out, 'You can't be serious!'

My hand jerks away from the door as if it's electrified. I should walk away, but I hover a fraction closer to listen.

'I'm perfectly serious,' Alec says, his voice calm and quiet. 'No means no. You're just refusing to accept it.'

'Is this still about the kiss, because I told you in the pub, she's just *saying* I didn't explain. *She's* the liar, not me. You know that, don't you?' My hand reaches for the doorknob, but with great restraint I manage to swallow back my derisive snort and stay put.

'I know when someone's lying to me,' says Alec evenly, and even from here I can hear the certainty in his voice. 'And my answer is still an emphatic "no"; even more so than when you kissed me, in fact.'

'Oh, I see. You've fallen for her little act – "Lauren's so mean",' she says, mimicking me unflatteringly. 'But Hannah lies to get what she wants, you know. She plays the goody two shoes, then paints me as the bad guy. It's a means to an end, and it obviously worked on Donald, but I didn't realise you'd been taken in by it, too.'

I grit my teeth at the injustice.

'Oh, I haven't fallen for anything and I haven't been taken in,' says Alec, an edge to his tone now.

'Well, good, because I'd hate for you not to know the truth.'

'Thanks, but I'm perfectly aware of the truth.'

Hang on, what? What truth? Blood courses through my body as a suspicion nudges me.

'Now, would you like some wine,' Alec asks Lauren, 'because I believe this conversation has come to its natural conclusion,' and his voice changes as he gets up.

I pull back and run to the kitchen on tiptoes, take a plate from the cupboard, and just manage to open the plastic strudel box before Alec comes in.

'Strudel? It's delicious,' I offer, lifting out a slice. I take a large bite, breathing heavily and puffing pastry crumbs everywhere.

Alec watches me, looking amused as I struggle to chew. I don't think my guilty flush helps.

'Mrs C's apple strudel is legendary,' he says, with a smile that shoots a shiver down my spine. 'Glass of wine to go with it?' he asks, holding the bottle to his forearm like a wine waiter.

I swallow with difficulty and grin. 'Do you two want company?' I ask innocently.

'Yes,' he says, frowning back up the corridor towards the drawing room.

'In that case, yes please.'

He waits for me to finish my slice of strudel, and we stroll back together, taking an extra glass for Lauren. On seeing me her eyes narrow, but she quickly recovers herself and smiles.

'I'll be leaving in the morning,' she says, faking an airy tone. 'I'm going to stay at Mum and Dad's. It's far more convenient for my flat.'

Not sure what to say, I hold out the glass. 'Wine?' I offer.

She looks from me to Alec. 'No, I'll have an early night. Good night, Hannah,' she says, completely ignoring him.

'Did you know you have pastry crumbs all down your top?' and giving me a haughty look, she walks out.

Frowning slightly, I brush off the crumbs. 'Well, she's not happy.'

'No. I think that's down to me.' Alec looks into my eyes, and I smile ruefully.

'You can't take all the credit. There's some sibling rivalry mixed in there too – she's angry that Donald chose me.'

'But that's not your fault.'

'From her standpoint, it is. She's still annoyed I was born. I reckon my parents should have prepared her better for my arrival.'

Settling into an armchair, Alec stares thoughtfully into his wine. 'Which begs the question of whether it's nature or nurture that turns siblings into rivals.'

I think of Cain and Abel, Grandma Betty and Uncle Donald and even Mum and Aunty Pam, who wouldn't voluntarily spend any time together. 'I guess it depends on whether you are talking about specific people or siblings in general?'

Alec nods, watching me over his glass. 'When Donald was telling me about Betty, he said there was always an undercurrent of enmity between them, but that they might have weathered that if there hadn't been an unforgivable deed on Betty's part.'

I nod slowly, knowing the deed he means. 'I think that's true of me and Lauren, too.'

Alec's eyes meet mine. 'So did you get on when you were small?'

I pull a face. 'Not really, but it got worse in our teens.'

'Was there an unforgivable deed?' He looks at me with an intensity I'm not used to. 'Of course, you don't have to tell me,' he says, and smiles.

'I know. It's just that I've never told anyone,' and oddly, I want to tell him. I take a sip of wine, and tuck my feet up under me. 'When I was seventeen I wrote a book – right through from beginning to end. It took me months and I was very proud of it. I thought it was raw and genuine and well . . .' I can't help laughing, '. . . I would think that now that I can't check.'

'What happened to it?'

'Well, to understand that, you need to know what happened just before.' Alec nods for me to continue. 'It was my parents' anniversary. Lauren came home from university for a special dinner they'd planned at a posh restaurant. It was meant to be the four of us, but that morning Lauren bumped into an old flame outside our house, and he invited her out. I saw the whole thing, so it was no real surprise when she put on a show of being virtually at death's door with the worst head-ache ever, begging to be left at home.

'We went without her, but dinner was miserable because Mum began imagining Lauren might have meningitis. Dad and I tried to say it was probably a migraine, but she'd heard that students had a higher chance of contracting meningitis and couldn't relax. So, I weighed up the alternatives and decided honesty was the best course of action. I told them about Lauren's date, vainly hoping we could laugh about it and have a nice evening, but Dad was furious. He insisted we leave immediately, and of course when we got home, Lauren was nowhere to be found.

'It was a tense, frosty evening, with the three of us sat wait-ing in the living room and Mum and Dad glaring at me because I'd covered for Lauren. Then, when Lauren arrived home, dressed to the nines and trying to pretend she'd just been out for medicine, all hell broke loose. I couldn't even look at Lauren, but I knew her eyes were burning holes into me.

'The next day I went to school. While I was out Lauren rummaged through my things, looking for some way to pay me back, and found Dad's old laptop. I hadn't told her about my book, but she'd seen me typing away often enough, so she opened it up and read the start.' I glance at the floor and take a deep breath. 'Then hit delete. When I got home there was a space on the screen where the folder had been. I confronted her about it, and she said she'd read the start of my "poisonous little diatribe", saw that my main character didn't like her sister, and erased the entire thing. We both knew it was an excuse. This was all about payback and she'd been thorough. She'd deleted it from the computer's recycle bin and even wiped the backup copy from the memory stick I'd left carelessly on my desk. I was devastated.'

I finally look at Alec. His jaw is slack with horror.

'The irony is that there was only one mention of my character even having a sister in the entire book.' I try to sound casual, but even now, the memory stings.

'Did you tell your parents what she did?'

'There didn't seem much point. We were already in enough trouble, and Lauren would have claimed I'd written a three-hundred-page attack on her. I couldn't prove I hadn't, so . . .'

'Did you rewrite it?'

'I tried, but it all seemed so pointless after all that hard work going down the drain. I found it very hard to write anything for a long time. But like anything you love . . .' I think briefly of Donald and Judith, '. . . you come back to it.'

Alec shakes his head. 'I can't believe she did—' he stops with a slight clenching of his jaw muscles. 'Actually, scratch that, I really can, but I don't know how you didn't pull her hair out by the roots and kick her down the stairs. Honestly, if it had been me . . .'

I take a deep, cleansing breath. 'I was furious,' I admit. 'I screamed I'd never forgive her, like in *Little Women*.' Alec looks at me questioningly. 'You know, when Amy burns Jo's manuscript?' but Alec shakes his head, so I wave the reference away. 'And, if I'm honest, I'm not sure I ever have really forgiven her.' I shrug. 'Anyway, that's what happened between me and Lauren.'

'Enough to break any sibling bonds. But I admire you for still writing. Donald would have, too, though something tells me he already had a fair idea about your strength and determination.'

I shrug, suddenly embarrassed. 'I haven't got anywhere with it – I'm not published, despite sending stuff off,' I explain. He surveys me speculatively, a slight smile on his lips, and I feel a sudden need to change the subject. 'I actually came down to tell you about the next task.'

'Oh?'

'It's lunch with Jane.'

Alec's eyebrows flick up. 'Donald said that was a task, but didn't you do that today?'

'We did, but I have a feeling this one's slightly different.'

He nods. 'Well, I'm not invited, so I'll research Mrs Jennings while you swan off and have lunch with Jane.' His tone is teasing, but his eyes are still intense.

'A PA's work is never done,' I say lightly.

He smiles and looks at his empty glass. 'It will be over all too soon,' he says sadly, but before I can ask him what he means he gets up. 'Time for bed?' he asks, holding out his hand. I stare up at him, my pulse quickening.

'Aren't you tired?' he asks, and I almost laugh. He's just offering to help me up.

'Yes, I am.' I get to my feet, pluck his wine glass from his hand and carry them through to the kitchen. But as I rinse the glasses, I rest against the sink for a moment, thinking about Alec researching away tomorrow. I can't help feeling guilty about not being able to reveal the contents of Donald's letters, but what would Alec think if he knew? Would it ruin his opinion of Donald? I can't be responsible for that, not after everything he said in the study the other night.

I upend the glasses on the draining board, and watch the water drain back to the sink.

No, it has to be Donald's choice. I turn out the kitchen lights and go to bed before I change my mind.

23

It's very quiet at the breakfast table. Lauren left first thing without saying goodbye and after everything I told Alec last night, I'm suffering from a distinct sense of having over-shared. I smile shyly at him as I pour cream over my porridge. He nods, cradling his coffee, and I dig in. As soon as I've finished, I get up and call Jane to let her know about the task. She's comfortingly relaxed about it.

'Of course,' she says. 'I'm meeting someone at the race-track today, but we could have lunch there, if you're OK with that?'

I look down at my trousers and top. 'Isn't it all Pimm's and big hats?'

'Heavens no, this isn't Ascot – just a normal day. Come dressed as you are.' She's so keen it's hard to be anything but happy.

'I'd love to.'

'Excellent,' she says, and after taking down some direc-tions, I drive over to meet her.

It isn't the hat parade I feared it would be, and I quickly spot Jane. She introduces me to the marshals and staff, who clearly know her well, and while Jane has a quick word with the trainer she promised to meet, one of the horse owners explains betting to me. I'm not sure I completely get it, but thanks to their guidance I go through the new experience of placing three small bets ready for the after-noon's races.

It's soon lunchtime, and after saying goodbye to the horse owner, we take a table in a secluded corner of the restaurant. With food ordered and elderflower pressé in our glasses, Jane takes a deep breath and looks me in the eye.

'I'm going to tell you about how I met Donald. Try not to judge,' she says.

I shake my head. 'I won't, and I already know a lot of what happened with Mrs Jennings, if that helps? It was in the letter I read last night.'

Jane seems to take courage from this. 'OK, well, it also helps if you understand that I was very young when I married. It wasn't unusual then, but I think that I was also young for my age – or perhaps "sheltered" would be a better description.' She glances at me. 'He was older than me, which was thought to be a good thing, but for me it was a disaster. Let's just say that on my wedding night I was supposed to blossom into a woman.' Jane straightens the knives and forks nervously. 'I didn't.' She purses her lips together for a moment and continues. 'The whole experience was horrid, and after that night, I never wanted to do it again. The following months were awful. I was an emotional wreck and my husband couldn't stand the sight of me.

'Then I met Donald. I was at a dreadful tea party, where men's wives gathered to pick like vultures over the carcasses of each other's marriages. I'd adopted my usual tactic of sitting in a corner and drinking tea without uttering a word, waiting for the moment I could leave, when a lady approached me. Her name was Judith.'

I snatch a breath in recognition, but though Jane looks up, she doesn't stop.

'She sat next to me and talked to me, even though I didn't reply, and she became determined to sort me out. She did that by introducing me to Donald.'

She pauses, and I know she needs a moment.

'At first it seemed strange that he was there, because husbands weren't allowed. In fact, there were no other men there at all, but somehow, Donald was the exception. I remember watching him; how he moved among them, complimenting them, sitting where he wanted, and how they treated him as an adored son or a favourite nephew. The true relationship, I only discovered later. Then, on about my third tea party with them, Judith introduced us. She did it significantly, almost heavy-handedly, and then drifted away leaving us together.'

Jane pauses as our food is served, and we watch the waiter weave his way between the tables back to the kitchens.

'Donald's first words to me were extraordinarily perceptive.' She looks at me. 'He asked me, "Do you just hate London, or do you hate everywhere?" In that second I knew I hated everywhere. I hated everyone. I even despised myself for not being what my husband wanted. But his question left me flustered. I tried to cover it up by asking whether anyone could truly like London, and he smiled. He told me that everyone could like London, it just depended on how well you did it.' Jane smiles. 'Then he took my hand and said, "I'll show you if you like", and seeing I had nothing left to lose, I agreed. That was the beginning.'

We both eat some of our food and look out of the window at the race course, watching the horses gallop past.

'What did you do?' I ask.

'We toured London – a bit like we did yesterday, but without the stop at the hairdressers,' she adds with a smile. 'He took me to gardens and galleries, museums and restaurants. It was fun and silly, and even though we saw the other ladies sometimes, no one took me aside and told me we shouldn't be out together, which in retrospect seems strange, but then I guess it was what they expected. I think they enjoyed watching our relationship unfold. As for my husband – he didn't object either, though perhaps he had given up on me by then. So in a strange way, it was sort of *allowed* by everyone.'

Jane looks at me, checking that I understand, and I nod.

'Donald helped me enjoy myself for the first time since my wedding. He took me dancing and taught me the tango. He took me to clubs and increasingly disreputable places, and gradually increased the danger and exhilaration, until one night he took me to a hotel.'

Pushing her plate aside, Jane picks up a spoon and fiddles with it.

I put my hand on hers. 'You don't have to tell me if it's too personal.'

Jane shakes her head. 'You need to understand, and I know it will stay between us.' She takes a deep breath. 'It wasn't what I expected,' she admits looking at me again. 'I knew why we were there, and I was so nervous. I felt like I couldn't refuse after all he'd done, and yet I knew I'd be committing adultery. I felt cornered, but the strangest thing happened – he didn't even ask. Don't you think that's odd?'

I nod. It certainly wasn't what I was expecting.

'He promised me he would never ask me to do that, and I suddenly knew I could trust him. So we played like kittens, bathed each other, read to each other, ate food in each other's arms. We did a million different things, making us more and more intimate and yet we didn't make love.' Jane pauses, staring into the middle distance. 'He taught me to relax and let go of my inhibitions and that anything that happened was my choice. It was . . . magical.' Jane suddenly laughs. 'I even tried burlesque!

'We spent a lot of nights like that, and he waited until I wanted to. Only then did we actually go through with it. And by being so kind and careful, he taught me to share, be confident and know what I want. It's the most precious gift anyone has ever given me.'

I see the hint of a smile, but there's also sorrow in her expression – a slightly sad Mona Lisa gazing into the distance.

'Needless to say, I was a very different person afterwards – more confident, content and determined – but my husband never asked about my time with Donald. He must have known a certain amount, but bless him, the old duffer knew I was happier, so we began again. We bought our current house, moved out of London and forged a marriage out of the carnage of our nuptials. That was back in 1974, when I was just twenty-two, and we've been happy ever since.'

Jane smiles at me, looking more relaxed. 'So, you see, Donald changed my life. I love him for that, but it had its time and we remained friends. I miss him terribly.' Tears brim in her eyes, but she doesn't let them fall. I grip her hand.

'It must all seem rather sordid to you, but that's what Donald wanted you to know.'

I shake my head. 'If anything, I'm a bit envious. Not of Donald, exactly,' I explain, 'but of having someone fun like that? It's never been like that for me.'

'It will be. You just have to find the right person.'

'And there's the problem,' I say, pulling a face and rolling my eyes exaggeratedly, lightening the mood.

'Perhaps,' says Jane with an enigmatic smile, finishing her drink. 'In the meantime, shall we go and see how our horses do?'

Realising Jane needs a change of scene after unburdening herself, I agree and follow her out to the stands where, over the course of the afternoon, I win enough on the third race to more than cover the loss I made on the first two. As my horse crosses the line, I leap about like a kangaroo, while Jane's composure suggests she wins regularly.

As I drive back to The Laurels, I mull over what Jane said. I see how Donald helped her to be a happier person, and then, perhaps even more impressively, let her move on. And didn't he do something similar for Mabel – or May, as I know her? Did Donald do the same for Judith? Was she happier in her marriage because of Donald? Was this Uncle Donald's gift – he helped people shine?

My thoughts clank to a stop as, pulling into the parking area, I see the chauffeur-driven Mercedes hunkered down in front of the portico. Mrs Jennings must be here.

I park up, and Alec meets me in the hall looking stressed. 'Good, you're back!'

'How long's she been here?' I whisper, wincing as I quietly place my keys and mobile on the hall table.

'About half an hour. She refused to leave without seeing you – said she'd wait. And she heard the car, so now she knows you're here, you'll need to go straight in.'

I nod, but I know a lot more about Mrs Jennings and why she's here than Alec does. Also, I think I might need to push her a little to find out what she's planning. I look up at Alec, worried by how he'll take this. 'Can you do me a favour?'

'Yes?'

'Wait out here.'

Alec looks confused. 'Why?'

'Because I'm going to try something which may or may not work, and I can't afford for her to see your reaction to the things I say.'

'I could come in and not react?'

I shake my head. 'There are things you don't know.' The word 'gigolo' bounces around inside my head. 'I'll tell you afterwards, but there's no time now.'

'Well, I'll stay within calling distance, then,' he says doubtfully.

I grip his hand for a moment and, drawing strength from all the commanding characters I've read, from Ladies Bracknell to Catherine de Bourgh, I walk into the drawing room. 'Mrs Jennings! You should have called to say you were coming.'

Mrs Jennings and her bug-eyed dog look up in bizarre synchronisation. 'And given you a chance to sidle out?' she asks shrewdly.

I manage to keep my smile in place. 'So how can I help you?'

'I've come for an answer,' she states.

'To . . .?' I'm smiling as sweetly as I can manage.

'Don't play games with me, young lady – you know why I'm here. Are you going to turn down Donald's will, or not?'

I take a seat and regard her seriously. 'Before I decide, can you explain a little more? Perhaps unveil a secret or two so I know what I'm dealing with?' I think my nonchalant act is going well.

Mrs Jennings gives me a long, haughty look. 'You want me to reveal Donald's secrets to you, now? Why would I do that?'

I shrug. 'To help me decide? After all, we might be shocked by very different things. If he just addressed a duchess by the wrong title, for example, I'm hardly going to care.'

Her eyes narrow, but then her head tips slightly to one side like a bird. 'All right, I'll tell you what your uncle was really like, but on your head be it.' She pauses significantly, savouring the moment. 'Your uncle was a male prostitute – a gigolo, if you will.'

'I know,' I say agreeably, pleased to see the surprise on her face.

'A gigolo involved in sordid affairs with married women,' she persists, getting annoyed.

'Yes,' I agree calmly.

'A large list of high-society, well-to-do women whose reputations will be ruined by any scandal.'

I smile and shrug. 'It's not like I know them.'

'And you don't seem surprised,' she says, her annoyance turning to suspicion.

'No.'

'So, he told you.' I nod, and just as I think I might have won a point, a smile spreads across her face. 'Did he tell you about the girls?'

'What girls?' I ask before I can stop myself, and her smile beds itself in.

'He didn't tell you about his little sideline? How interesting, but then I suppose he wouldn't.' She strokes her dog's ears, taking her time.

'Why don't you tell me about it?' I say casually, but I'm starting to sweat.

'Certainly!' She settles into her seat as if she's going to tell me a bedtime story. 'In the seventies there was a fashion for the more influential families in London to prepare their daughters for society in a very special way. It was one of the best-kept secrets in high society. Let's just say that, once they came of age, their mummies and daddies wanted their little darlings to have the ability to climb the social ladder without attaching too much weight to sex. They wanted them to understand sex as the tool it can be, so they got in a fixer – a person with whom their daughters had no emotional attachment – to teach them how to use their sexuality for the advancement of their social aspirations. That . . .' she pauses significantly, 'is what Donald was paid to do.'

I don't know if that's true, but from what I've learnt about Donald, inspiring a mercenary attitude in others sounds like the last thing he'd want to do.

I quickly decide to go with total disbelief. 'He's told me everything, so I know *that's* not true.'

She gives a derisive laugh. 'That's a very poor bluff. Of course he hasn't told you "everything". If he had, you would know all about me, and you don't.'

'I do know some things about you, but I still don't believe

you. Parents don't do that kind of thing.' We stare hard at each other.

'They do, you know. I can name ten girls off the top of my head,' and she casually reels off a list of names that mean nothing to me until she mentions Jane, and I know Jane's relationship with Donald was nothing like that! Mrs Jennings is throwing out random names to make her list longer.

'Jane was married,' I say accusingly. Mrs Jennings focuses on me like a king cobra and, as a slow smile creeps onto her face, I could kick myself.

'You know Jane?' she asks, and my heart and stomach plummet as if dropped down a well. I almost hear the 'plunk' as they hit the water far below. 'I haven't seen Jane in years. Oh, do call her and ask her to join us!'

I stare at her, trying not to look as aghast as I feel. I open my mouth, hoping to extricate Jane somehow. 'I – I don't think that's necessary.'

'But I insist! Call her this very minute.'

'No, I'd hate to bother her, and I'm sure we can sort this out between us. We can discuss Donald's will . . . I'm sure I can persuade my family . . .' After all, what's five hundred pounds apiece? I could probably pay them all back if I had to.

'Call her,' says Mrs Jennings, her voice edged with steel. 'She's very much a part of this, and she'll explain everything in a way you can understand.' Mrs Jennings gives a little shooing gesture with her free hand. 'Go on,' she insists, and I head into the hall, feeling the discarded personas of Lady Bracknell and Lady Catherine de Bourgh tangle around my feet.

Alec gets up from where he's been sitting on the stairs. 'What's happening?'

I feel so ashamed I can barely look at him. 'I have to call Jane. I've dropped her in it with Mrs Jennings.'

He hands me my mobile, possibly hoping I'll say more, but I hold my finger to my lips and point back to the drawing room to show that Mrs Jennings is probably listening. He nods as I select Jane's number and hold the phone to my ear. I can only think of one way to help her right now, and I prepare myself to have a very one-sided conversation.

'Hello, is that Jane?' I ask as someone answers.

'Yes, Hannah it's me.'

'That's such a shame,' I say, keeping my tone flat.

'Hannah, what's going on?'

'In that case do you have any idea when she'll be back?'

'Are you all right? Is this to do with Mrs Jennings?'

Thank heavens she's understood so quickly. 'Yes, can you give her a message please?'

'Tell me.'

'I have a Mrs Jennings here, who would like to see her again at her earliest convenience.'

'I can come right now?' offers Jane.

'No, that's the message, and I will let Mrs Jennings know that Jane can't be contacted until tomorrow.'

'Do you need time, is that it?' asks Jane.

'Yes, thank you.'

'Phone me when you can.'

'Goodbye.'

'Good luck. Sounds like you need it,' says Jane and I hang up, feeling a surge of shame at the fact she's being so sympathetic.

Alec holds my hand as I take a few deep breaths, and I nod to show him I'm OK. As I re-enter the drawing room, I just catch Mrs Jennings sitting back down, so my suspicions about her listening were correct.

'I'm afraid Jane isn't available,' I tell her calmly. 'Perhaps tomorrow.'

Mrs Jennings watches me for a few seconds and I hold my nerve.

'No matter, let's say tomorrow morning at 10 a.m. sharp. Make sure Jane is here, and bear in mind that I will drag Donald, Jane and quite a few other people through the mud if either of you let me down.'

'I'll be here,' I assure her. 'Though I can't speak for Jane, of course.'

'She'll come,' says Mrs Jennings with chilling certainty. Taking a firm hold on her dog, she stands and looks down at me as I fail to do the accepted thing and get up to show her out. She gives a little 'Hm!', and leaves.

I sit holding my breath, and only relax when I hear the front door slam.

'She's gone,' says Alec, coming in. 'I think you'd better tell me what's been going on.' There's unmistakable reproach in his voice.

'I couldn't tell you with Lauren here,' I say feebly.

Alec pours me a whisky and puts it in my hand. I take a sip as he sits down opposite me, fixing me with a no-nonsense expression.

'Who is Mrs Jennings, and why is she so set against Donald?' he asks.

I stare at Alec, unsure if this is going to change his opinion of Donald and, praying that Donald will forgive me for revealing his secrets given the circumstances. 'I think the best way to describe her would be as his madam.'

'How old fashioned,' says Alec, his lip twitching.

'No, I mean in the Hollywood sense. You know, how prostitutes have pimps?'

I wait for the penny to drop.

'She was Donald's pimp,' I prompt.

'And Donald was her . . . what? Merchandise?' Alec asks incredulously.

I nod, but I still think he's waiting for the punchline.

'He was sort of forced into it by Mrs Jennings threatening someone he cared about.'

'Bloody hell!' He pushes his hands through his hair, making it stand up at odd angles. 'But I guess that would make him do it. He's always been fiercely loyal,' says Alec, frowning as he tries to make sense of it. 'And if there was no other option . . .'

'There wasn't,' I assure him.

Alec rubs the back of his neck distractedly. 'So the secrets she mentioned are to do with that?'

I nod. 'Through him she gained power over a lot of influential women in London.'

'Sounds like she had quite the racket going. But why is she so against him? What did Donald do to upset her?'

'I don't know, but I think he managed to leave her somehow, and from what Mrs Jennings said about blackmail, I'm guessing he discovered something that stopped her in her tracks, but I don't know what and nor does Jane.'

'And Jane's involved somehow?'

I nod, feeling terrible that I'm now breaking Jane's confidence, too.

'And she'll be affected if Mrs Jennings carries out her threats?'

I nod again.

'So, we need to find out what Donald discovered,' concludes Alec. 'And our best hope for that is Donald's letters.'

'Exactly,' I agree, my eyes finally meeting his.

'Did you complete the lunch task with Jane?'

'Yes.'

Alec smiles. 'Then keep your fingers crossed while I get the next letter.'

His hope is infectious, and as he bounds out of the room, I pray it's that simple.

Alec comes back in and hands me the letter.
I tear it open and read.

My Dearest Hannah,

Toy boys are only that when they have younger, firmer flesh than the husbands they replace. After that, they make the inevitable transition to escort. However, the year I turned thirty, my life took a different turn, and as had so often been the case, Judith was the cause of it.

She returned to London in January 1974, quite beautifully pregnant with her third child, and asked to see me. Not in my usual capacity, she explained, but she had a favour to ask: she had a new friend who needed my services.

It transpired that there was a new wife on the circuit who was not adapting. Judith explained how the grief of separation from her family, and the impatience of her older and sexually frustrated husband had left her friend drowning, and the wives were repeatedly ducking her, much as they had Judith.

I could easily believe it, for though I liked them individually, these women found the sport of someone insecure too much to resist. Judith, remembering exactly how that felt, wanted me to step in, and as she explained the situation, I deduced that she meant for me to seduce the girl. I wasn't sure to what ends, or whether it was a good idea, but I agreed to meet her socially, nothing more.

It was a strange meeting. The wives watched like hungry lions spying a gazelle in their clearing, and everyone seemed to know what was going on, except the person it was aimed at. The gazelle sat on a sofa, barely lifting her eyes from the carpet, and seemed so brittle she might break if she moved.

I sat next to her, and everyone held their breath. I glanced around the room, and one by one the wives returned to their conversations, and I was at last able to ask the poor woman how she liked London. I waited. Her eyes lifted to mine, showing she hated it, but more than that, the hopelessness of her situation was clear on her face and I could see what Judith said was true: she was drowning. If ever my heart went out to someone, it was then. Never had I seen someone so hurt. I wanted to help her, but I was being watched.

'It only takes a little knowledge to make London fun,' I assured her. 'I could show you,' I offered, my skin crawling at how the wives smiled at each other. 'What do you have to lose?' I asked, desperate to get her away from them and out in the open.

She looked into my eyes for a long moment as if searching for sincerity. I don't know if she found it, but she answered me.

'Nothing,' she acknowledged sadly, with a tentative, but genuine smile.

I loved her from that smile, and I don't mean lustfully. I loved her as a friend and from that moment, making her life as good as it could possibly be became the most important thing to me.

'Then let me show you,' I offered.

The wives exchanged looks, convinced of their own cleverness, and I've no doubt the scenario played out exactly as they'd hoped. Judith, too, was pleased, and I saw her as one of them for the first time, which changed everything. For I finally admitted to myself that, although I loved Judith passionately, I did not always like her. This young woman, on the other hand, I liked from beginning to end, and I wanted to protect her from them all.

So I took the young woman under my wing and taught her how to enjoy London, how to dance, cope with the wives, and most importantly, how to enjoy herself. I watched her blossom and grow in confidence, and I was pleased when my work was done, because she was happy and her husband came to value her. To this day, my work with her remains one of the things I

*am most proud of, and she will always be one of my closest
friends.*

*For your next task you must read three Isadora Layton
novels. You will find them in my study. Any three will do,
though I recommend* Milady's Lover, The Greedy Governor
and The Resident Gigolo.

Musingly yours,
Uncle Donald

I refold the letter carefully.

'So?' asks Alec.

I shake my head. 'I already knew most of this. There's nothing new.' I bite my lip, noticing that Donald didn't mention Jane by name anywhere in his letter. But even though Donald hasn't written her name, given the promise I just made to Jane that this would all stay between us, I still don't feel right handing the letter over to Alec without her express permission. Alec watches me slide it into its envelope and put it to one side, but he doesn't look annoyed, merely resigned.

'So there's just two letters left that might tell us about Mrs Jennings,' says Alec thoughtfully. 'And I only have one of them.'

'Where's the other?'

'Mr Sanderson held on to it.'

'And we can't open the letter we have?'

Alec frowns, biting his bottom lip as he contemplates my request, but then he shakes his head. 'No, I'm sorry, not until you've completed the task. Donald was very insistent about that. What is the next task, by the way?'

'To read three Isadora Layton novels.'

Despite our current situation, Alec surprises me with a laugh. 'You'll find a whole stack of them in the study. Go and have a look. Do you want help choosing?'

I hold up the letter. 'Donald made recommendations. I

must phone Jane back first, though. She'll be wondering what happened. I was just hoping Donald's letter might give me some good news to pass on.'

'Maybe the next one,' says Alec optimistically, and I go to phone Jane.

Jane is so understanding about my slip-up and about having to come at ten tomorrow that I feel even more terrible, but I haven't got the time to wallow. After saying goodbye, I head straight for the study, and just as Alec said, there is a whole shelf of Isadora Layton books. I check Donald's letter and pull out the three he recommended, pausing for a moment to examine their bawdy covers.

'Why these?' I ask, holding them up as I join Alec in the drawing room.

'Just read them,' he advises with a small smile. 'All will become clear. How was Jane?'

'Lovely, considering,' I say guiltily. 'She's going to contact her friends in London to see if they've heard anything incriminating about Mrs Jennings, and said she'll meet us here before ten tomorrow.'

Alec nods, and I slump into a seat. I frown at the woman on the cover of *Milady's Lover*, pouting as her lover cups her corseted breast. It feels odd curling up with a book, what with everything that's going on right now, but I guess reading these is important. I try to shake off the air of impending doom, and turn to page one.

The story is about a girl who is unhappily married to a fat old aristocrat. The girl takes her husband's valet as her lover and they fall in love. The husband, finding out, sets about separating them. He eventually succeeds, but only by threatening their lives. The writing isn't particularly refined, but the plot is good, and I find myself enjoying it even though I have to speed-read my way through.

As I reach the end, Alec puts a sandwich, a plate of sliced fruit and a glass of wine next to me.

'Mrs Crumpton went home early,' he explains, and looking at the time, I see we're late for dinner. I put the book aside and stretch.

'What do you think?' he asks, taking a seat and tucking into his sandwich.

'It's fun. I don't normally read this kind of book, but it's surprisingly . . .'

'What?' asks Alec.

'Gripping?' I suggest, and take a bite of the ham and salad sandwich.

Alec laughs. 'Pure, indulgent, swashbuckling fun was how Donald put it.'

'Yes, but I still don't know why he wanted me to read them. Surely they must have some significance?'

'You'll figure it out,' he says. 'Give it time.'

'The one thing we don't have,' I huff. 'Couldn't you just tell me?'

Alec shakes his head. 'Not a chance.'

I pick up *The Greedy Governor*, frowning, and while Alec settles back to look through some paperwork, I start to read.

This one is about a man who forces women, besides his wife, to be his lovers. He has something over each woman, but they find out about each other and conspire to kill him. They succeed, but not before he kills one of the girls in a most horrifying manner. I can't help sniffing as I feel their grief, and Alec kindly pops a box of tissues next to me before carrying on with his work. Finishing the last page, I let my head roll back against the seat, feeling emotionally exhausted.

'You OK?' Alec asks, and I nod numbly.

Wishing I could sleep, I rub my eyes, stretch and yawn. 'I'm going to take this last one up to bed,' I say, picking up the third book, and preparing myself to be put through the emotional wringer once more. Alec nods. I say goodnight and leave him to his paperwork.

Once in bed, I brace myself for the next book, but *The Resident Gigolo* proves to be a far more light-hearted account of a man trying to please the many women living in a stately home. He has to juggle his attentions, approaches and times, at which point something about the turn of phrase, and how Donald wrote about his time in London, clicks into place.

I almost drop the book. Donald *is* Isadora Layton. This is his life glamourised and exaggerated, pushed back in time and spilled onto the page. I don't know why I didn't see it before. I must have been blind! But dare I really think that Mrs Jennings is the inspiration for the Greedy Governor, and is Milady perhaps Jane? Smiling to myself, I finish the book and put it on my bedside table. I turn out the light and lie in the darkness, just hearing Alec play his guitar very quietly in his room.

As I listen, I think back, remembering Donald's interest in my aspirations to become a writer and his choosing me starts to make a bit more sense. We had writing in common. Pleased by this thought, I turn over and listen to Alec play 'Imagine' and 'Eleanor Rigby', and during a particularly beautiful rendition of 'Stand by Me', I finally fall asleep.

24

My dreams are a mishmash of scenes from Donald's books, interspersed with leering images of Mrs Jennings, and I wake up very early and stare anxiously at the ceiling. I haven't a clue what we're going to do about her. There's still Donald's letter, of course, but unless it's a dossier of recordings, photographs and microfilms proving that Mrs Jennings is an archcriminal, I don't see how it can help.

Wanting at least to find out, I tiptoe down the hall to see if Alec is up. I tap on his door just loudly enough for him to hear, if he's awake, but there's no answer. I return to my room, but am too anxious to go back to bed, so I pull on some clothes and head out for a walk.

I trudge down the gravel drive and along towards the church, stopping to look over the church wall at the graveyard. It's beautifully tranquil with the early morning sun on it, and since the church gates are open, I wander in to visit Donald's grave.

His brand new headstone is easy to find, as it's rudely pristine amongst the sea of weathered stones. I stand back to read the inscription, and can't help smiling:

Donald Makepiece
1944-2018
Dramatic in life,
Provocative in death,
I was magnificent.
Sorry you missed me!

I perch on a conveniently bench-height tomb, picking at the yellow lichen clogging up its letters, and mull over the possibilities of how to handle Mrs Jennings. Trouble is, what with her chauffeur waiting outside, our options are limited.

I close my eyes, letting the sun warm my face, and concentrate on being mindful instead. I sit very still, breathing in and out, trying to be calm . . . like the calm before the storm. I take a deep breath and empty my thoughts . . . the deep breath before the onslaught! No, relax. I pull back my shoulders . . . like the sea pulling back before the tsunami wave hits.

Wow, this really isn't helping.

I jump down off the tomb, and give Donald's grave one last look.

'I really hope you've written something useful in this next letter,' I tell him, and go for a brisk walk around the village before heading back to The Laurels.

Arriving back, I find Alec pacing about the front hall talking on his mobile.

'Hannah,' he says, sighing with relief. He hands me his phone, mouthing that it's Jane, and I hurry to take it.

'Hello?' I say.

'Alec thought you'd bolted,' says Jane, giving an uneasy laugh.

'No, I just went for a walk.'

'Oh, well, I've contacted several people from my London days, but they haven't uncovered anything useful. What about you? Any news from the task?'

'I completed it last night, but I haven't read the letter yet.' I look pointedly at Alec, who dashes off. 'I'll phone you when I've read it, shall I?'

'Yes, please,' and with uncharacteristic curtness, Jane disconnects.

Infused with her sense of urgency, I meet Alec coming back from the study. He looks at me expectantly, holding back the envelope.

'I read the books,' I assure him.

'And . . .?' he asks.

'Donald is Isadora Layton.'

'Good,' he says, finally handing me the letter. 'You read that while I make us some coffee.'

I follow him into the kitchen and sit down at the table, really hoping that Donald's going to give us the necessary weaponry, because anything less than a fully equipped, mission-ready tank just isn't going to cut it.

My Dearest Hannah,

Though the wives instigated it, my arrangement with Jane had been a thorn in their sides, as perhaps unwisely, I hadn't bothered to hide my preference for her. This annoyed Judith, of course, but seeing as she had chosen her husband over me, this didn't concern me. Mrs Jennings, however, hated it, and though I didn't realise it at the time, she held on to this grudge even after Jane had left London.

It was during the summer of 1976 that Mrs Jennings summoned the wives and me to afternoon tea to meet her niece, Theresa. Mrs Jennings explained to us that, to mark Theresa's eighteenth birthday, she intended to launch her on society in a modern day 'coming out'. She wanted it to be opulent and grand, and expected each of us to come up with ideas. Theresa, meanwhile, sat and listened with the smug confidence of a girl with a private education and obscenely rich relations. I could tell immediately that people were pawns to her, and I loathed her on sight. I knew my place, however, so I was the consummate showman all afternoon, alternately scandalising and complimenting the wives in turn.

As everyone left, Mrs Jennings held me back to speak with me. It turned out that she wanted me to perform the same service for Theresa as I had for Jane. I had been expecting something of the sort, but I was surprised at how angry I felt to hear Jane and Theresa mentioned in the same breath. I was perhaps unwisely cold as I explained to Mrs Jennings that I would not do that for Theresa, and that Theresa was not a distraught wife, but an overconfident debutante (at least, I hope those were words I used) who did not need my help. Mrs Jennings was equally chilly as she told me I would do as I was told. I countered that we were not suited. She said it didn't matter; I was merely a rite of passage. Our conversation went downhill from there, and she threatened Judith.

I think Mrs Jennings was surprised at how little effect her threat had on me. You see, I had been thinking for a while that Judith had too much control over my life, so I set my face and told Mrs Jennings to do her worst, pointing out that I could do her just as much damage in return. Mrs Jennings laughed at my temerity. 'I don't think so,' she said, and because Theresa chose that moment to sweep in, she sent me away.

I heard nothing for two days – no rumours, no threats – then Mrs Jennings sent for me again. I was late, just to annoy her, and I was shown in to find her scolding her cook. Mrs Jennings was dangerously angry and I remember her words even now:

'I don't care if your husband needs you. I pay you, which means I own you. You will cook for Theresa's party, and you will do it to the very best of your ability or I will make sure your name and your food is poison to every household in London.'

Then Mrs Jennings turned to me. 'As for you – you will also do as you're told or Jane will suffer the consequences!'

I was totally unprepared for this low blow and shock rolled off me as if I had been shot. Poor Jane: manipulated into an affair, and having rebuilt her marriage and moved away was now to be used as a hostage in one of Mrs Jennings' sordid power plays. Anger seared through me, hot and dangerous, cauterising all fear as I realised this was my future – to be whipped like a dog by my loyalties.

I looked at the cook and she looked at me, and I saw the same impotent fury reflected back. I have never felt such unity with a person I've never spoken to before, and with mute agreement, strong because of each other, we turned to face Mrs Jennings.

'No,' we said together and walked out.

'I hope the devil finds you,' shouted the cook, and I closed the door. Even though she was only a couple of years younger than me, I took her hand and we ran away from the house like children into the park opposite, only stopping when we had turned several corners and found a bench.

The cook was shaking. Tears ran down her face and I didn't feel too steady myself as I started to panic about what might happen to Jane, so we sat down and I handed her my handkerchief. When she had calmed down a little, the cook said she was crying because she was angry, and I wasn't to get any silly ideas about her being weak. She was just furious, she explained, and glared at me, daring me to say different. I liked her immediately.

I asked her what had happened and she told me how her husband, a tube driver, had struck a man who'd jumped in front of his train. It had taken hours to clean up the mess, and her husband had lost his nerve and his job, and now suffered from claustrophobia, agoraphobia and nightmares. He needed help, she explained, and they had waited for months for an appointment with a specialist they were seeing that afternoon. She had to take him, she explained, because he wouldn't leave the house without her. Mrs Jennings, though having previously agreed to the time off, had forgotten, and therefore refused to allow her to go with the results I had seen.

She shook her head with a grim smile. 'At least now I can take my husband to his appointment.' Her expression suggested that what lay ahead would be very difficult. Realising this, I offered my help and she accepted, with the stern warning that she only did so because she'd do anything for her husband.

That afternoon was an education. She was an abrasive woman, but I watched her manage her nervy husband so gently, without ever mentioning her own problems. I called taxis and helped support him as she kept up a constant stream of comments and admonishments that kept him calm. Over that afternoon I gained a true respect for that stern cook, who was resilient and real. What was more, she knew who I was and what I did, but never mentioned it. And though we were very different people from dissimilar backgrounds, we were sailors caught in the same storm, and it was she who hatched the plan to save both us and Jane. It was a very good plan, and the next day we visited Mrs Jennings.

Mrs Jennings welcomed us, expecting to crush our spirits beneath her heel. Her confidence suggested she would make us pay handsomely and she expected us to grovel. It was only as we stood our ground that she realised we were not there to apologise. She listened to our proposal with growing incredulity, and could barely contain her indignation when we told her we were leaving. We warned her that, if there were any reprisals, we would embarrass her by telling everyone what we knew about Mr Jennings.

We knew this would work, because even though Mrs Jennings was powerful, she detested the thought of anyone sniggering behind her back, and she realised that, while she could condemn one of us as spreading malicious gossip, two of her closest assets spreading the same tale would be a very different matter. I told her that if she wanted to give Mrs Crumpton—

I almost drop the letter.

— *a glowing reference, then all the better.*

Mrs Jennings looked like a rat caught in a trap – for between us, we knew everything about her. There was no way out, but she relaxed slightly when she realised we only wanted a reference. We weren't blackmailing her, just persuading her to be a decent person, with no room for reprisals.

Whether she thought us honest or stupid, she never said, and to be fair, it was a glowing reference, though it was never used. We left London, sold my flat and bought The Laurels. And this is where we settled. I wrote novels as Isadora Layton (as you should by now have discovered), and Mrs Crumpton took on the role of cook/housekeeper, while her husband became my gardener – an undemanding role that suited him – until he died a few years ago.

Your final task is with the solicitor, but please show Alec these letters, if you haven't already, as for him they will have their own significance. Also, consider how well you and Alec are suited. I know you didn't get on at that first meeting, but knowing you both, I feel sure you could make each other very happy.

Beneficially yours,
Uncle Donald

'Well?' asks Alec, handing me a mug of coffee.

I drag my eyes away from the letter and stare up at him. 'Mrs Crumpton knows what happened in London.'

'What? Are you sure?'

'She was there.'

'Then why hasn't she said anything?' he asks, his voice rising.

'I don't know. Maybe she didn't think it was important?' I suggest.

'But she's seen how worried we've been. She knows Mrs Jennings has been here. Why hasn't she told us what she knows?'

I shake my head helplessly. I don't know what to tell him.

'Well, when she arrives, we'll ask her,' says Alec firmly.

'When does she usually get here?'

'Soon,' he says, pacing irritably around the kitchen.

I bite my lip anxiously, feeling sweaty and totally unprepared for Mrs Jennings' visit, but if Mrs Crumpton knows something then we need to be ready. 'OK, well, if she does know something, shouldn't Jane hear it, too?' Alec nods. 'Could you call her and ask her to come as soon as possible, while I run upstairs and take a quick shower?'

Alec agrees, still glowering. 'And then, when she arrives, we'll ask Mrs Crumpton what she's been playing at.'

'Sounds like a plan,' I agree, but as I turn to go, he reaches out and grabs my hand. I turn, startled, and glance down at it, warm and strong in mine.

'We'll beat Mrs Jennings,' he says, looking earnestly into my eyes, and I'm caught staring into his as if the meaning of life and the universe might be found there.

I nod, unable to speak, sincerely hoping he's right, and he drops my hand so we can both make a start.

I come back downstairs feeling clean, fresh and a little more ready to face Mrs Jennings. Alec gestures towards the kitchen to let me know that Mrs Crumpton has arrived, and realising we probably don't have time to wait for Jane, I follow him through.

Mrs Crumpton is scouring the cooker as if she's scrubbing away the sins of the world, and I clear my throat uncomfortably.

'Mrs Crumpton?' I begin in clipped tones. 'Could we please speak to you for a minute?'

Mrs Crumpton turns with the scourer still in her hand, and for once her suspicious expression is justified.

'Mrs Jennings is coming here at ten and I understand you've been keeping something from us?' I say, trying to sound businesslike.

274

I expect her to be defensive, but she sags back against the cooker. 'Oh, thank God,' she says with all the relief of Atlas putting down the world. 'Donald said only to tell you in the direst need, but what with your sister stayin' and that Jennings woman poppin' in as the fancy took 'er, I thought I'd miss the right moment, but 'ere we are.'

'Here we are,' I agree, and we all jump as the doorbell rings.

'That'll be Jane,' says Alec, mildly amused. Mrs Crumpton gives me an enquiring look, and I bite my lip.

'I let slip to Mrs Jennings that I knew her, and now Jane's been pulled into this, too,' I explain.

Mrs Crumpton's frown deepens. 'I'll make some tea and bring it through,' she says. 'You go an' say hello, and then you can tell me what's been goin' on.'

I meet Jane in the hall and give her a hug. 'Thanks for coming.'

'Was there something in Donald's letter? Because my London friends didn't turn up anything that wasn't common knowledge,' she says anxiously.

'Yes . . . perhaps. At least, we think so. Mrs Crumpton was there when it all blew up between Donald and Mrs Jennings—'

'And she can help us?' interrupts Jane hopefully, not in the least annoyed. She's a better person than I am!

'We don't know, yet,' I clarify, not wanting to get her hopes up, and we all stare at Mrs Crumpton as she comes past with the tray.

Mrs Crumpton cocks an eyebrow at us. 'Come on, then,' she says, and we follow her into the drawing room. 'Before anyone asks,' she begins, eyeing me and Alec with disfavour, 'he –' she gestures at the ceiling (Donald apparently having a position in here as well as in the kitchen) '– said I might need to help if Mrs Jennings crawled out of the woodwork, but that I had to wait until it was necessary or I might ruin everythin'.'

'How?' I demand. 'Surely putting a stop to Mrs Jennings can only be a good thing.'

'Well tell me this, then. How would you have felt if you knew what Donald did in London before you knew anythin' else about 'im?' Mrs Crumpton's beady eye pierces through me, harpooning my soul. 'Would you have walked away? If you had, what then? It wasn't like I could get you back once you'd gone. It would all 'ave been over, with Donald's plans ruined, and we couldn't even be sure she'd try anythin' in the first place.'

I shrink a little under her biting certainty, and glance at Jane, who is nibbling her lip. Alec is staring at me anxiously. How come I'm suddenly the one under interrogation?

'I might not have done,' I say quietly.

'I couldn't take that chance,' says Mrs Crumpton decidedly. 'And Donald knew that.'

I glance at Alec, who gives me a sympathetic smile. 'So, what happened in London?' he asks, shifting the attention back to Mrs Crumpton.

Unwilling to be rushed, Mrs Crumpton purses her lips and pours the tea. 'What do you know already?'

I hold up Donald's letter. 'Perhaps it will help if I read this out. Do you mind?' I ask Mrs Crumpton. 'It's about the day you met.'

'Fire away,' she says, and careful to skip any mention of Jane, I read out the relevant section, sensing Alec and Jane's attention shift as Donald reveals the identity of Mrs Jennings' cook.

'I always wondered where you came from,' says Jane. 'You arrived with him at The Laurels, and he wouldn't hear a word said against you. You were as thick as thieves, and yet I'd never seen you before. I thought you must be a relative.'

'No fear!' scoffs Mrs Crumpton, making us all laugh, and releasing some of the tension.

'So, *do* you know something that will stop Mrs Jennings?' asks Alec.

'Hopefully,' says Mrs Crumpton. 'But first I need to know why she asked *you* 'ere,' she says, looking at Jane.

Jane glances nervously at Alec. 'I had a . . . fling, for want of a better word, with Donald.' She blushes, but neither Alec nor Mrs Crumpton show the slightest surprise, and I'm guessing Mrs Crumpton suspected as much from Mrs Jennings' threats all those years ago.

Mrs Crumpton nods. 'Right, what you all need to know is the truth about Mrs Jennings' husband. That's what we had over 'er.' We all wait for her to continue, but she glances at her watch. 'What time did you say she's comin'?'

'Ten o'clock. We've still got over twenty minutes,' says Alec.

'Oh no you don't,' says Mrs Crumpton standing up. 'When I worked for 'er, whenever she wanted people on their toes, she always turned up fifteen minutes early. Boasted about it, she did, to one of 'er nasty friends who came to tea. "Catch them on the hop", she said, and I don't see why she'd change 'er ways.'

'We need a plan,' I say quickly.

Mrs Crumpton purses her lips. 'Stop panickin',' she says scornfully. 'Now, she'll have been plannin' this for months, if not years, and she'll have a whole set of things to try until she finds the one that has you cowerin'. The trick is: don't cower, and don't show weakness. Now, my problem is that I need to hear what she says, but since I'm staff and should be in the kitchen, that could be tricky.' Mrs Crumpton frowns hard. 'But seein' as she didn't recognise me—'

'How could she not recognise you?' I ask.

Mrs Crumpton huffs at my interruption. 'It was a long time ago.'

'How old were you?' I ask curiously.

'I was eighteen when I started with 'er. I wasn't cook to begin with, though, nor married until a few years in, but I learnt from Old Cook and took over when she was sacked.' She stares into the middle distance, looking into the past. 'I 'ad long hair back then and I used to have ever such crooked teeth. They were my definin' feature, you might say. I never did smile, but when we came here Donald sent me to a dental surgeon. Still, I didn't think I'd changed that much,' she says, coming back to the present. 'And after twelve years in 'er service, I was a bit offended, to be honest with you.'

'Twelve years?' I blurt out, then boggle at the thought that Mrs Crumpton smiles more than she used to.

Mrs Crumpton shakes her head. 'I know. A bit insultin' really – but it might be useful. That doesn't solve the problem of me hearin' what she says, though.' There's reproach in her voice for me taking her off topic.

'May I make a suggestion?' asks Jane. 'What if you and I arrive together? Won't Mrs Jennings assume you are some sort of chaperone? And it won't look odd if you stay in the room.'

A slow smile spreads across Mrs Crumpton's face. 'That could work.'

'But Mrs Jennings saw you here before,' I point out.

Mrs Crumpton dismisses this with a clipped shake of her head. 'Doesn't matter, staff are all the same to 'er – even after twelve years. But you learn a lot about a person over that amount of time,' says Mrs Crumpton, a satisfied expression on her face.

'Shouldn't we go?' asks Jane, anxiously checking the clock.

'Might as well, though the hob isn't finished,' says Mrs Crumpton regretfully. 'But we can't have that woman thinkin' she's won, now, can we?'

'But we still don't know what you have on her,' I say, following them into the hall. 'Are you sure Mrs Jennings will back down?'

'She'll run for the high hills if she knows what's good for 'er,' mutters Mrs Crumpton, disappearing off to the kitchen to get her bag.

I stare at Jane, feeling a little panicked, and I can see she feels the same.

We trail into the kitchen where Mrs Crumpton is re-laying the tea tray.

'Right, you two,' says Mrs Crumpton, addressing me and Jane. 'Neither of you back down, look scared or agree to anythin'. Let 'er use up all 'er threats, and only then will I step in, understand?'

Jane and I nod. Alec comes in behind us.

'Hot water in the teapot when she comes,' Mrs Crumpton says to him. 'Can't have her noticin' anythin's different.' There's a determined gleam in Mrs Crumpton's eyes, and I get the impression she's enjoying herself. She focuses on Jane's anxious face. 'It's Mrs Jennings that should be worried, not you. So, are we going, or lettin' the grass grow?'

'Going,' agrees Jane meekly, and follows Mrs Crumpton out of the house, leaving me and Alec waiting nervously for Mrs Jennings.

25

Alec and I wander listlessly into the drawing room and sit down, but neither of us can relax.

'God, I hope she knows something really shocking,' I say with feeling.

'Mrs Crumpton has never let me or Donald down,' says Alec, fiddling with a coaster.

'Then let's hope she doesn't start now.' I check the time and jump as the doorbell rings.

'It seems Mrs Crumpton knows what she's talking about,' says Alec, tapping the face of his watch. We go out to the hall together and Alec opens the front door.

Mrs Jennings sweeps in clutching her dog, and eyes me head to toe. 'Good, I'm glad you have the sense to face me, but whether you have the intelligence to accept my offer remains to be seen.'

Remembering Mrs Crumpton's advice, I look her in the eye. 'Good morning to you, too.'

'No Jane?' she asks, looking around as if Jane might be playing hide and seek.

'It's not ten, yet,' I point out, and she smiles tightly.

'Please go through,' says Alec, indicating the drawing room, and I follow her in and take a seat, while Alec goes to sort out the teapot.

'So, you said you weren't the sole heir,' says Mrs Jennings conversationally, though we both know this isn't a polite enquiry.

'No,' I say, and happily leave a long silence as she waits for my sense of duty to make me fill it with the answer she wants. She can wait all day as far as I'm concerned.

'So, tell me, how are Donald's affairs settled?' she finally asks.

I just have to keep blocking her moves, like in chess. 'I've absolutely no idea.'

Her eyebrows flick up. 'Why not?'

'I'm just a distant relation.'

'And yet you know a lot about his past . . . though not everything. And you are friends with Jane,' she adds thoughtfully. 'She's happily married, I believe?'

I'm digging myself into a hole whichever way I answer that, so I let the underlying threat to Jane's marriage lie like an open grave between us.

'Yes, Donald was always fond of Jane,' she adds. 'And you like her, too?'

I glance at the door, wishing Alec would hurry up with the tea. 'Of course.'

'Oh, isn't that . . .' she hesitates, and words like 'useful', 'convenient' and 'handy' all elbow their way into my thoughts, '. . . nice,' she finishes blandly. She smiles as Alec comes in with the tray. 'Handsome *and* practical. You would have been quite my type,' she says as he places the tray on the coffee table. Knowing what she did to Donald, I struggle to maintain a calm expression as I get up to pour the tea. I hand her a cup, and the doorbell rings.

'Ah, here's Jane,' she says with satisfaction, and I glance at Alec, who goes to answer it. Mrs Jennings puts her cup on a side table, ruffles her dog's ears and smiles beatifically as Jane walks in.

'Jane, it's been a long time.' She gestures for Jane to sit down and motions for me to pour more tea.

'It has,' agrees Jane, and neither of us comment as Mrs Crumpton comes in and quietly seats herself in an upright chair near the door. Mrs Jennings gives her a curious glance. 'So, why did you want to see me?' asks Jane hurriedly, diverting Mrs Jennings' attention. 'Hannah didn't seem to know.'

Mrs Jennings breathes out a beneficent sigh. 'I thought it high time I settled some old scores. After all, you took something precious that wasn't yours,' she says, her smile faltering as a fleeting expression of hurt crosses her face.

Jane looks at her blankly. 'I never took anything from you.'

Mrs Jennings' lips tremble and she purses them together, taking a moment to regain her self-control. Her eyes turn steel-hard as she focuses on Jane. 'You took Donald.'

Jane glances perplexedly at me, and I'd grab her hand if I could. I try to warn her to hold it together with my eyes. 'I was under the impression that my time with Donald was a gift; a gift of his own choosing,' she says, turning back to Mrs Jennings.

'He was mine. It was of my choosing. Nothing was his choice!' cries Mrs Jennings, glaring at Jane. Then, adjusting her posture, she adds calmly, 'He was never the same after you, and I will never forgive you for that.' She strokes her dog, her eyes narrowing infinitesimally as she studies Jane.

'Your choice, of course,' replies Jane coolly. 'But it still doesn't explain why I'm here.'

'You're here for two reasons. One is to explain to . . .' Mrs Jennings stares at me, obviously flummoxed.

'Hannah,' I supply unhappily.

'. . . Hannah that she would be well advised to do as I say, and secondly in order to witness that I have won.'

'Won?' asks Jane.

'Yes! I have outlived Donald, and now that he's dead, either his final wishes will not be carried out or the truth will come out. All those smug, hypocritical marriages will be revealed as the shams they are, including yours, and everything Donald worked so hard to protect will be ruined. I win,' she says simply, smiling with malicious satisfaction.

'Except that you don't,' says Jane. 'Not yet.' She glances at me and I nod, trying to look unconcerned, while desperately hoping Mrs Crumpton's ammunition is worth all the faith we're putting in it.

Mrs Jennings regards Jane with mild puzzlement. 'If you're trying to appeal to my better nature, you're wasting your time, Jane. I'm self-aware enough to know that I don't have one.'

'No, I wouldn't bother trying. No, I was referring to the fact that you lied to Hannah.'

Mrs Jennings laughs. 'Embellished a little, perhaps. A little poetic licence—'

'You lied,' says Jane flatly. 'Donald never went near young girls. The only one who wanted him to was you.'

'And he's told me about everything else,' I add, glancing at Alec, who gives me an approving wink.

Mrs Jennings titters contemptuously. 'We've already established that you don't know a thing about me.'

'That was yesterday. We've learnt a lot since then.' I hold up Donald's letter like a trophy. 'Donald told me himself.'

'We know all about Theresa,' says Jane, 'and why he left. So I'll tell you what happens now. You say nothing about Donald, the marriages you mentioned remain intact, the people you threatened will not suffer, and Donald's money will go exactly where he intended.'

Jane and I give each other a satisfied nod, and for a second I think we've got her. Then Mrs Jennings smiles. I hate it when she does that.

'That letter proves nothing. It's just the ramblings of a jilted lover. I'll deny everything, and since there's no proof . . .' She dismisses the tattered remains of our defence with a flick of her wrist. 'Whereas I can have you all named and shamed in the newspapers without the least difficulty. I can picture it now, "Wife of famous MP involved in sordid sex scandal",' she says as if reading out a headline. 'You remember Margo?' Mrs Jennings asks Jane. 'And then there's your husband – he was a district judge, wasn't he?' Jane looks like she's struggling to breathe. 'Oh yes, the papers will be all over it. And then Donald can be investigated for immoral earnings, and the government will seize his assets.' Mrs Jennings focuses on me. 'Do you really want to put everyone through all that just because you won't ignore Donald's final wishes?'

'You don't have the right—' begins Alec, but Mrs Jennings holds up her hand to silence him.

'Stay quiet and you may come out of this unscathed,' she warns him chillingly. 'I asked you a question, Hannah – are you going to do as I say?'

Jane stays absolutely still, and out of the corner of my eye I see Mrs Crumpton shake her head ever so slightly.

'No,' I answer quietly, hoping Jane will forgive me.

'No?' Mrs Jennings laughs in disbelief. 'Jane, are you going to let this young woman ruin your life?'

Jane doesn't flinch. 'I stand by Hannah's decision,' she says bravely.

'Commendable, but misguided . . .' begins Mrs Jennings, and behind her, Mrs Crumpton quietly gets up and comes to sit on the sofa beside me. 'And what do you think you're doing?' asks Mrs Jennings coldly.

'Joinin' the conversation,' says Mrs Crumpton, pouring herself a cup of tea. She takes a sip, winces, gives Alec a disgusted look and puts it back on the tray.

Mrs Jennings looks on, flabbergasted. 'Jane, your *friend* needs to be put back in her stall,' she spits, but though Jane and I shoot each other wide-eyed glances, we stay quiet.

Mrs Crumpton looks Mrs Jennings in the eye. 'Are you talkin' about me? Because the only old nag round 'ere is you, and I wouldn't even use you for glue.'

Mrs Jennings gapes as if she's been struck. 'How dare you! Jane, muzzle your watchdog or I'll make your life a misery.'

'I thought you were doin' that already,' says Mrs Crumpton. 'But I wouldn't start threatening people.'

'And why not?'

'Because *Mr* Jennings will be mentioned, that's why, and I know how you'd hate that. I might even contact 'im and ask 'im to visit. Never did get that divorce, did you?'

Mrs Jennings' eyes bore holes into Mrs Crumpton. 'Who *are* you?' she demands. 'What makes you think you have even the faintest right to speak to me?'

'Twelve years of service should earn me at least five minutes, don't you think?'

Mrs Jennings still looks mystified.

'What, don't you recognise me? And me your cook for so many years? Shocking it is. I'm hurt,' mocks Mrs Crumpton. 'It's Mrs Crumpton, but you always called me "Cook"!'

Mrs Jennings shakes her head. 'You can't be. If you were her, you'd be dead!'

'The cheek of you! I might not have all your la-di-dah lotions and posh clothes, but I'm younger than you.'

Mrs Jennings stares at Mrs Crumpton, and I can see she's trying to peel back the years. 'But . . . but you were dowdy and worn. And the teeth!'

'Watch it!' snaps Mrs Crumpton. 'Or I might start talkin' about *Mr* Jennings.'

Mrs Jennings face loses some of its colour. 'I will not have that man's name mentioned!' she hisses furiously.

'Why not? It seems to me like you've been sayin' a whole lot of things you shouldn't. Some of which are downright lies.'

There's a flicker of uncertainty in Mrs Jennings' eyes.

'Didn't you accuse Donald of doin' the very thing he refused to do for you? And now you want to ruin his good name with it? Shame on you!' declares Mrs Crumpton, her tone even more frightening than when she said it to me.

'"Good name"? You know what he did for a living – he didn't *have* a good name, and besides, he deserves it. It's poetic justice!'

'About *Mr* Jennings—' begins Mrs Crumpton.

'I told you not to say that man's name!' bleats Mrs Jennings, clutching her dog to her chest, her bottom lip trembling.

'No? Well I'm about to, unless you take back every word you just said. In fact, I might do some embellishing of my own. Like that your husband is now a famous drag queen livin' in Milan an' performin' on stage every night in six-inch heels under the stage name Fanny Maybe.'

Jane gasps, Alec claps his hands together and I gape mutely.

Mrs Jennings' eyes widen and dart between us. Without her bravado she looks twenty years older. 'You wouldn't dare – not with everything I have on you.'

'Perhaps I wouldn't under normal circumstances,' agrees Mrs Crumpton. 'But if you was to carry out those threats you talked about—'

'No one would believe you.'

Jane smiles. 'They might if I tell all my London friends and ask them to vouch for it. Plus, it's easy enough to add a little backstory. Didn't I hear that he has a marvellous repertoire of Abba songs?'

'His "Dancing Queen" is a must-see,' agrees Alec.

'And he knows all of Barbra Streisand's music off by heart,' I add.

Mrs Jennings is lost for words. 'You're all perverted,' she finally manages.

'And you're a bigot,' adds Mrs Crumpton without rancour. 'So, do we have a deal?'

Mrs Jennings' mouth tightens. 'There must be no more

talk of Mr Jennings in any form, to anyone, from any of you!' she stipulates, looking formidable once more.

Mrs Crumpton folds her arms. 'I'll make this agreement: it'll go no further than me, Hannah, Alec and Lady Jane 'ere, so long as you leave all Donald's friends and family be and never mention any of them ever again.'

Mrs Jennings stares malevolently at Mrs Crumpton, like a toad squatting in a hole, but finally relents. 'I never should have written you such a good reference,' she mutters darkly.

Mrs Crumpton shakes her head. 'It never made no difference either way. So, seein' as we're all agreed?' she asks, checking with Jane, Alec and me, and we all nod. Mrs Jennings looks slightly ill, but she dips her head once. 'In that case, I'll show you out.'

We all stand, none of us daring to say a word in case we break the spell. Mrs Crumpton escorts Mrs Jennings from the room, and we hear her call out, 'Goodbye. Don't come again.'

Mrs Crumpton comes back in. 'Good riddance to bad rubbish!' she says triumphantly, and we burst out laughing.

'I can see your skills extend beyond just managing Donald,' says Jane when she can finally speak.

'That one needed a firm 'and,' agrees Mrs Crumpton.

'So can you tell us the real story about Mr Jennings?' I ask. 'What's the big secret?'

Mrs Crumpton regards us speculatively. 'I'll tell you, though it's against servants' etiquette – "What's heard be'ind closed doors, stays be'ind closed doors", an' all that.' She pauses. 'But in this case, there should be more than just me that knows it. After all, it's the only thing that does the trick with that woman, and she needs to be kept in order.'

None of us disagree.

'The truth is, in my first year of service, back when she was with her 'usband, she found 'im in bed with another man. Mortified, she was. Screamed and shouted and said some 'orrible things. So he told 'er how she'd always revolted 'im. How she bullied and complained, nagged and was so awful she completely put him off women. Not that I think it's true. Some people are just born different – nothin' wrong with that. But he really had a go at 'er, and made 'er that upset that I think it accounts for some of how she's been since. Not that she was nice before,' Mrs Crumpton adds frowning.

'Blimey!' says Alec.

'Yes,' sighs Mrs Crumpton. 'Trouble is, word got out, and what with him bein' high up in the military, he was busted down to *Mr* Jennings and booted out of the officers' mess faster than you could say "dress uniform". It was a different time, you see,' she explains, shaking her head sadly, and I start to see why Mrs Crumpton's references to 'Mr' Jennings were so effective. 'Anyway, a bit of a cover-up happened, an' they left in hush-hush circumstances without it goin' too much further, but it was still a bit of a comedown for 'er. Proper shamin', and she couldn't bear the sight of anyone who knew.'

'What happened then?' I ask.

'They went their separate ways. He went off to Italy with his "friend", with no intention of comin' back, and she set herself up in London with 'er family's money – a complete clean slate . . . not that it stayed clean, mind. But she's always been that afraid of him coming back, ruining 'er new life and everyone findin' out and sniggerin', so I knew what to do if she ever got out of 'and.'

'And you're still in contact with Mr Jennings?' asks Alec.

'No, but she wasn't to know that. But she's that ashamed of what happened and has been trying to make up for it ever since by being the big "I am". Explains a lot, I reckon.'

'Mmm,' agrees Jane. 'But why didn't you or Donald reveal all this years ago?'

'He wouldn't hear of it. Said 'e didn't want to hurt 'er. He said it took two whiskies to explain everythin' wrong with that woman, and one evenin' we had two whiskies.'

'You're telling me he understood her?' I ask incredulously.

Mrs Crumpton nods. 'One night, we sat out in the dark on the terrace and he explained it all. Told me he reckoned that Mrs Jennings was desperate to be loved, but was frightened that she was unlovable, and that afraid of bein' hurt, she wanted someone she could control. That's where Donald came in.

'Trouble was, even though she could control 'im, Donald didn't love 'er, much as she loved 'im, and she hated that he made her feel so weak. So she sent 'im to other women to prove to 'erself that she was above love and didn't need 'im, and she held on to that power and told 'im who to be with and when. So you can see what a mess Mr Jennings left be'ind?'

We nod.

'Donald felt sorry for 'er,' says Mrs Crumpton, shaking her head. 'Said she'd been through enough, and that he could never betray 'er unless she forced 'im. But attacking those 'e loved, and that included me,' she reminds us all firmly, 'was not allowed. He told me I was to stop 'er, and I 'ave.'

'But why attack him now, after all this time, and once Donald has gone?' I ask.

'Do you think that woman could ever forgive and forget, 'specially someone who left 'er? Someone she was frightened she had chased away? Someone she could punish in the place of her 'usband?' Mrs Crumpton gives me a penetrating look.

'Wow, I guess not,' I breathe, amazed at how all Mrs Jennings' spiteful actions suddenly make sense.

'Well, now you know,' says Mrs Crumpton.

I shake my head in wonder. 'I almost feel sorry for her.'

'Don't waste your breath,' snaps Mrs Crumpton. 'She'd eat babies if someone told 'er they were good for the skin!'

Jane stifles a shocked laugh. 'That's more like the Mrs Jennings I know. But thank you for coming to our rescue. I could almost kiss you.'

'Best not,' says Mrs Crumpton, draining the last drops of her tea and putting the cup back down with a grimace. 'Though a nice cuppa wouldn't go amiss.' She lifts the lid on the teapot and looks inside. 'I don't know what you two did to this pot, but I don't fancy it.'

'I think the milk curdled when Mrs Jennings came in,' I giggle.

'Wouldn't surprise me,' mutters Jane. 'Milk turning sour, locusts, boils, the lot.'

'Well, let's make another pot,' says Mrs Crumpton. 'I'm parched.'

26

There's almost a party atmosphere as, with a fresh pot of tea and some oatmeal cookies, we all settle down in the drawing room to recover. Mrs Crumpton regales us with some of Donald's antics at The Laurels, and Jane describes Donald's wonderfully dreadful behaviour in London. It's all very relaxed and I love that, after years of only passing Mrs Crumpton in the hall, Jane seems to have neatly sidestepped Mrs Crumpton's usual reservations and jumped straight into being one of the family. So much so that, when Mrs Crumpton talks about making us all some lunch, Jane follows her into the kitchen leaving me and Alec in the drawing room.

Alec smiles at me. 'It never occurred to me that they would get on so well. In fact, I'm not sure they'd have ever spoken more than two words to each other if it weren't for this whole Mrs Jennings thing.'

'No,' I agree. 'It's an unexpected silver lining. So, what do we do now that the pressure's off?'

Alec gives me a long look, a warm smile sneaking onto his lips as if he's considering his options. 'Let's tackle the last task,' he says, playing safe. 'But take our time over it. Did Donald say what it was in his letter?'

'No.' I take it out of my pocket and read the last few lines. 'Apparently Mr Sanderson has it. But he does say that he wants you to read his letters.'

'OK. Should I start with that one?'

I glance down at Donald's suggestion that Alec and I could make each other happy. 'No. I think you should read them in order, like I did.'

Alec raises his eyebrows expectantly, so, keeping the last letter with me, I go and collect the full set. He's waiting at the foot of the stairs as I come back down, and I hand him the small stack of envelopes, carefully tucking the last one at the back, and follow him into the drawing room. I watch as he takes out the first letter.

'Donald said they would have their own special relevance to you,' I say.

'Really? How intriguing,' he says, and makes himself comfortable in an armchair, while I curl up in another.

He skims the first few letters without a hint of emotion – he could be reading a dishwasher manual for all the effect they're having on him – but I keep a careful track of his progress, and as he reads the letter about Billy, his forehead creases. Now reading with avid concentration, I watch the emotions flit across his face as he reads about Judith, May, Mrs Jennings, turning the pages quicker and quicker as he gets to Jane, Mrs Crumpton and finally the end.

I smile cautiously as he folds the final letter and puts it back in its envelope. I can tell he's shocked, but I don't know what by – I thought I'd passed on a lot of the salient points as we went along, with the rest being covered today.

'Are you OK?' I ask, and his eyes finally meet mine.

'Judith was my grandmother,' he says quietly.

My mouth drops open. '*Donald's* Judith? The Judith he loved who led him to London? *She* was your grandmother?'

Alec nods, still looking dazed. 'I didn't even know they knew each other. Neither of them ever said a word, not even when I applied for the job.' He fixes me with a piercing look. 'Should I have guessed?'

I shake my head. 'I don't think so. I mean, how hard is it to say "I have a friend in the country who needs an assistant", rather than show you a magazine advert?'

Alec nods numbly. 'Now I understand why she was so confident I'd get the job, despite me having no experience or references. I turned up with the flu for heaven's sake. Who gives someone a job when they turn up with the flu?' he asks in disbelief.

'Yes, but that meant you couldn't leave, and they got to know you . . .'

But Alec isn't listening. 'He didn't even say anything when she died.'

'She died?' I feel a jolt of sympathy for Donald, and then for Alec. Given that Donald told me practically everything else, him not telling me that she died suggests it really hurt him. 'When?'

'Two years ago. Donald even came to the funeral. I thought he was just being nice, but he must have needed to say goodbye just as much as I did. I should have guessed then.'

'Why? He'd have gone with you anyway, wouldn't he?'

'Perhaps, but he wouldn't have been mopping away torrents of tears or got quite so drunk at the wake.'

I picture Donald singing about 'Spanish Ladies', or even giving 'Hey Jude' a go, but one look at Alec tells me this isn't the time to joke.

'It really annoyed me that he'd been drinking,' says Alec. 'I called him a taxi and made him leave before he caused a scene. The next day, he told me he'd been feeling his own mortality, but now I know the truth . . .' He stares at the stack of letters, his eyes bright. 'He loved her. Even after everything she did. I don't know how I feel about that.'

He's looking so bewildered, I find it easy to push aside my own feelings about Judith. I perch on the arm of his chair and take his hand. 'The way I read it, Donald loved her, and despite how it all turned out, he didn't regret any of it.'

Alec stares at me. 'Perhaps.' He pulls his hand away, runs it through his hair and shifts irritably in his seat. 'But it's not only that – it's his whole time in London! I was his typist, proofreader, copy checker and it never even occurred to me that any of those situations could be real – I thought they all came from his imagination.'

'Reading his books, I think most of what he wrote about did come from his imagination. And no one would suspect another person of being quite so much larger than life.'

Alec glances at me sceptically. 'Even Donald?'

'OK, perhaps Donald,' I admit. 'But the reality won't have been as romantic as he described in his novels – and you have to remember he was doing something people looked down on. He was hardly going to wave a scarlet flag in your face and shout, "Look, I was a gigolo". Who knows how you would have responded? And before you give yourself any more of a hard time, you weren't about to jump to the correct conclusions while reading about his swashbuckling heroes, either.'

'I suppose not.' Alec glowers at the letters for a moment or two. 'I suppose it was all quite squalid, really.'

I'm caught by a sudden urge to defend Donald. 'Some of it was, I expect, but then you have to realise that he changed quite a few people's lives for the better despite, and perhaps because of, what he did for a living.'

'Jane?' he asks.

'And Jim and May, Mrs Crumpton, her husband, and Judith. And even yours and mine,' I add, remembering Donald's intimation that we should get together. 'And those are just the ones we know about.'

Alec rubs his forehead. 'You're right. And he's still the same person. I suppose I just need to come to terms with it all.'

'Yes, you do,' I agree.

We sit in silence and I glance at the letters, slightly relieved that Donald's suggestion about us being well suited seems to have got lost somewhere among all the other revelations. But like a forgotten pin at a dress fitting, it's needling me and I can't stop thinking about it. What will I say if Alec does ask me about it? 'Yes, isn't it funny that Donald thought that?' 'No, I didn't see that coming either.' 'Well, of course I know the kiss was an impulse' ... not that this explains Alec's second attempt to kiss me.

Alec suddenly gets up and checks his watch. 'I should phone Mr Sanderson and see when he can fit us in.' I glance up at Alec. 'We need to get the last task,' he reminds me.

'Yes. I wonder why Donald gave it to Mr Sanderson?'

'Ah,' says Alec. 'This bit needs to be official.'

I stare at him, unsure what to make of that, and a grin spreads across his face. 'I'll call Mr Sanderson,' he says.

'Please!' I say, resisting the urge to throw a cushion at him, and I'm glad to see he's over the initial shock of finding out about Judith and Donald.

Luckily for my rampaging curiosity, Mr Sanderson can squeeze us in during the afternoon. So, after a leisurely lunch of homemade leek and potato soup in the kitchen with Jane and Mrs Crumpton, Alec escorts me down to the village.

We arrive early, and I take a seat in the reception area. Alec remains standing, supposedly examining a print of the church, but I get the feeling he's almost as tense as I am.

Mr Sanderson lets a client out, and shaking our hands, he welcomes us into his office. He takes a large file from his cabinet and opens it on his desk. An envelope, clearly labelled 'For Hannah. The Last Task' is sat on the top, and Mr Sanderson contemplates us both seriously over the top of his glasses.

'So, the last one,' he says. 'And in record time, too,' he adds with raised eyebrows.

'There have been reasons for that,' I say, feeling I should explain myself.

'Ah yes,' agrees Mr Sanderson, consulting his notes. 'Mrs Jennings. Any further problems on that front?'

'Nothing we couldn't handle,' says Alec, dismissing the terrifying twenty-four hours with just a few words and giving me a conspiratorial look.

Mr Sanderson graces us with a small smile. 'Excellent. In that case, let's pursue the matter in hand, shall we?' He holds out the envelope, but as I reach for it he twitches it back slightly. 'Your uncle left your final task with me because, as he put it, it lets the cat out of the bag. It is, however, imperative that you complete the task he mentions before you consider yourself in possession.'

I look from Mr Sanderson to Alec, and see the same expectant look on both their faces.

'Understood,' I say, and Mr Sanderson hands me the envelope. I slide my finger under the flap and start to read with growing incredulity.

My Dearest Hannah,

My story is almost done. You know all about my past: how I came to own The Laurels, how Mrs Crumpton came to be my wonderful housekeeper and how Jane, Jim and May became my very dearest friends. I am hoping they are now as dear to you as they have been to me. Alec can tell his own story, but the most pertinent point is that Judith was his grandmother. Taking him on as my personal assistant was my last favour to her, and one I never lived to regret. She knew that would be the case, and my time with Alec was her final gift.

So, all that remains to be done is for you to complete the circle and for me to bring you fully up to date with my life. How is that to be achieved, you may ask? I have had a brainwave!

For your last task, you will host a party very similar to the one where I met you. You will invite all your family, and let them know you have an announcement to make. When they arrive, I want you to stand up in front of them all and inform them that you are my heir and have inherited both my wealth and The Laurels.

I gasp. I feel a little dizzy, but I don't stop reading.

I can imagine you are surprised – at least I hope so! But let me assure you I am certain I have chosen wisely, and if you have made it this far through the tasks, you have proved yourself worthy.

You may be wondering why I didn't choose Alec. I'll admit I did consider him, but Alec inherited his grandmother's estate, which is far grander and more prodigious than my own. And I couldn't let Judith outshine me, even in death! I am pleased to know that, in your eyes, at least, I will always reign supreme, because you have my side of the story.

In passing on The Laurels to you, there is, however, one pitfall I am anxious to avoid: I do not want to drive a wedge between you and your family. I don't want you to live here missing out on knowing important people, as I missed out on knowing you and Albert better. So don't be scared, and invite them. Be proud of who you are, accept what you have achieved, and stay unshakeable in what you want to do. Manage that, and you will be bullet-proof to their comments.

Added to that, I would like you to be honest about how they treat you. It is almost always a mistake to hide other people's unkindness. If you are protecting a third party, perhaps it is excusable, but if you are protecting your aggressor from exposure, don't think for a moment they will ever stop or thank you. So be brave, Hannah, as that is the theme for this final task. Take the bull by the horns, and realise that it is up to them to

*come to terms with your inheritance, not your duty to apologise
for it. Remember this and stand tall.*

*To misquote the wonderful J.K. Rowling, 'It takes a great
deal of bravery to stand up to our enemies, but just as much,' in
fact, probably more, 'to stand up to our family'. So I bid you
good luck in this final task.*

Bravely yours,
Uncle Donald

I sit very still. Can it be real? The idea of owning The Laurels
gilds every thought like the sun breaking through on a rainy
day. Is it really possible? I stare at Alec, expecting him to
answer my unspoken questions. He grins at me, and I look
from him to Mr Sanderson.

'Am I really inheriting The Laurels?' I whisper.

Mr Sanderson nods. 'Yes.'

'It isn't some kind of joke?'

'I assure you I would never allow a joke of that kind,' says
Mr Sanderson evenly.

'But you're certain? I mean, you're really, really sure?'

Mr Sanderson steeples his fingers and looks at me over the
top of them. 'I asked your uncle several times if he was really
intending to leave all his worldly goods to a relation he had met
only once, and he told me firmly that it was up to him what he
did with his property, and that, yes, he was more than certain.
Seeing my incredulity, however, he had his mental acuity
measured and a certificate issued to provide sufficient protec-
tion against detractors. As it turns out, that came in useful, but
to answer you more fully, I have in my possession all the paperwork necessary to transfer the ownership of The Laurels over
to you. I only require the say-so from Alec concerning this
final task and we will start the process.'

There's a knock at the door and Mr Sanderson's secretary
puts his head around the door to ask him a question about

another client. Mr Sanderson sniffs irritably, looks at us apologetically, then gets up and follows him out.

'Why me?' I ask, turning to Alec, feeling that Mr Sanderson didn't cover that point. 'Not that I'm not grateful – I really am! But why me?'

'Donald said he knew as soon as he met you. He said he knew, just like he did with Jane, although at the time I didn't know what he meant by that.'

'But Jane's wonderful. Jane's gorgeous and genuine and kind!' My voice sounds cross, but I don't know how to change it.

Alec grins at me. 'Yes. And he saw all those qualities in you on the day of the party. He saw how dignified you were when you were attacked, how open and honest you were when he asked you to be, and how you never muscled your way into the limelight – and then, when he caught a glimpse of your wicked sense of humour, that was that. He knew.'

'Did you know, too?' I ask, hanging my insecurities out like laundry.

'No,' he says, looking a bit shamefaced. 'I thought you were all circling around like vultures, waiting for him to die so you could enjoy the spoils.' Remembering Lauren's words before we even met Donald, and Aunty Pam saying at the graveside that they couldn't leave yet because of the will reading, I can't help thinking his suspicions were justified. 'But I soon saw what he meant,' Alec assures me.

'Did you? When?'

Alec laughs, but his eyes are kind, and he lifts his hand to cradle my cheek. My skin tingles under his fingertips and a blush rushes to my face. 'Honestly? I had my first suspicion when you came back from visiting Jim and May. You were so indignant and decent, outraged and so obviously caught between laughing at yourself and fury.' Alec shakes his head, smiling at the memory, but I can't figure out if we are still talking about Donald choosing me – or something else. 'But I suppose I knew properly when we were at the ballet. I saw just how vulnerable and honest you were and . . . Smack! No coming back from it.'

My breath quickens. Is he really saying what I think he's saying?

'But by then, of course,' he continues, his hand dropping from my cheek, 'I'd been rude to you and tried to make you jealous by flirting with Lauren – yes, I admit it now, and I'm sorry, but blimey I paid for it, if that's any consolation?' His eyes lock onto mine, beseeching me to understand. 'Lauren kept ambushing me, and the one time I failed to fend her off . . .' Alec's head drops, and I think we're both picturing Lauren kissing him. 'Well, let's just say, I thought you'd never speak to me again.'

I stare at my hands, hardly daring to breathe as I reframe everything from Alec's sly glances, monitoring my reaction when he spoke with Lauren, to Lauren springing out of her room, disappointed to find it was me. Even her clamping hold on Alec morphs into a desperate attempt to keep him to heel, while Alec, even during the stargazing, never forgot I was there, despite all of Lauren's best efforts.

I look into his eyes, which are kind and perhaps a little afraid, and . . . everything swims. Black dots flash in my vision. A sudden wave of nausea sweeps over me and I plunge my head between my knees before I faint, throw up or, heaven forbid, both. Did I forget to breathe? Am I swooning, like in one of Donald's novels? God, how embarrassing.

Alec bends down to my level. 'Are you OK?' he asks anxiously.

'Fine, just give me a minute,' I rasp. I should be leaping around singing, not staring at the floor trying to keep hold of my lunch.

Alec sits up as Mr Sanderson comes back in.

'Is she all right?' Mr Sanderson asks. 'Is it not all as she expected?'

I try to sit up, but another wave of queasiness sends me back down again.

'I think it's just shock,' says Alec. 'I'm not sure she expected to inherit Donald's *whole* estate.'

Not to mention having Alec almost declare himself. But it's true, I wasn't expecting Donald's whole estate, or to be able to stay at The Laurels. *Owning* The Laurels! How could that possibly have faded into the background? It just doesn't seem real. And imagine how furious Donald would be to be upstaged by Alec at this crucial moment! I suppress a grin as I picture Donald ranting about on the ceiling above us, yelling 'Not now!' at Alec, and I dutifully focus on the amazing thing Donald has done for me.

'What *were* you expecting?' asks Mr Sanderson, bewildered.

'Five hundred pounds, like everyone else,' I whisper, getting my breathing under control.

'Ah! In that case, I do see. I'll just get her some water,' Mr Sanderson whispers to Alec.

While Mr Sanderson is gone, Alec explains about Judith's estate and how it's looked after by a trust. I'm desperate to get him back onto the subject of us, but now's not the time.

'. . . so Donald helped me sort it all out, but when it came to his own will, Donald accused me of putting him in a difficult position, because now he had no one to transform in the name of "making a difference".'

I take some slow deep breaths and finally manage to sit up. 'So that's why he arranged the party?' I ask, cottoning on.

'Yes, he wanted to find someone to make a difference to, and he found you.'

'Well, he's certainly made a difference!' I say, an edge of hysteria to my voice. With The Laurels as my home, Alec,

Jane and Mrs Crumpton as my friends, and a chance to write – everything's been completely transformed.

Mr Sanderson returns with a glass of water and hands it to me. 'Feeling better?'

'Much better, thank you.'

He shakes his head sadly. 'It never occurred to me that you might not know about the possibility of inheriting the house. If it had . . .'

I smile, still unable to believe any of it's true.

'Well, no harm done,' says Mr Sanderson irritably, and as I sip my water, he starts to explain the complexities of changing over the ownership of The Laurels, paying inheritance tax and filing for probate. I sit quietly and nod every so often. Very little of what he says goes in, but the dull legal monologue is surprisingly soothing, and gives me a chance to come to terms with the wonderful thing Donald has done for me. I'm going to own The Laurels: live there, write and be happy – it's extraordinary.

'. . . so all that should be comparatively straightforward,' concludes Mr Sanderson, raising his eyebrows. 'A lot simpler than writing the will,' he adds with a reminiscent shudder. 'So, when you've finished that final task, everything can be put in motion.'

'So, just invite my family and announce I'm inheriting?' I ask, grimacing at this forgotten fly in the ointment. I let out a slow breath. My family. Right now, I think I'd rather face Mrs Jennings again.

'Exactly so,' agrees Mr Sanderson.

I glance at Alec. 'Do I have to invite them all, or will a token selection do?'

'All of them, I'm afraid,' says Alec. 'As close as you can get to the original party.'

I pull a face. 'Could be tricky. I'm not their favourite person, but if I invite them for afternoon tea they might come, just out of curiosity. Do you think Mrs Crumpton would mind catering?'

'We'll ask her,' says Alec.

Mr Sanderson nods briskly, and I can tell he's trying to hurry us along. He hands me an envelope labelled 'Upon Completion'. 'The final letter for when you have successfully completed this last task. Good luck,' he says, and we leave him carefully closing the file and putting it back in his filing cabinet.

Walking back, I glance shyly at Alec. 'So, you're Judith's heir?'

Alec looks a little sheepish. 'Yes, and you're Donald's.'

'Why don't you tell anyone?'

He shrugs. 'People act oddly when they find out I'm rich – especially women.'

Lauren would have welded herself to him if she'd known Alec was rich as well as good-looking. 'But isn't it a bit hypo-critical of Donald to want me to broadcast that I'm an heiress when he helped you keep your inheritance a secret?' I can think of several reasons for keeping it to myself – Lauren being one of them.

'Ah, but you see, my family knows,' he points out. 'I just keep it to myself when I meet new people.'

We walk along in silence for a while, until I slow to a stop. Alec looks at me curiously.

I look up at him, afraid to even start. I take a deep breath. 'So, when you said in Mr Sanderson's office that you "knew properly" after the ballet, what did you mean, exactly?'

Alec looks away and shifts his weight. 'I knew that I had fallen for you,' he says to the pavement. 'Do you feel the same way about me?' He looks at me searchingly.

I can't stop myself smiling, and his expression moves to echo mine. 'Yes,' I say simply. 'But why didn't you say some-thing?' I ask, half-irritated. 'Why did you kiss me in the river, and again in London, and not explain?'

He turns, suppresses a smile, and blows out a breath. 'Fair questions,' he says, taking my hand in his and we start walking again. 'For one thing, Donald made me promise to help you through the tasks. He wanted me to look after you like a sister because, from what he saw of your family, he didn't think they'd be very helpful.' He's not wrong. Alec stops and looks anxiously at me. 'I was under strict orders to support you and not cause you stress or distress,' he explains. 'That worked out well! By the third task I couldn't stop myself kissing you.'

I've thought about that kiss a lot, and the words 'stress and distress' do cover what happened afterwards. I take a deep breath. 'And that's why you dropped me and bolted for the car?'

Alec shrugs.

'Why didn't you just tell me?'

'Because I was just as shocked as you were – I had no idea whether what I was feeling was genuine, or a manifestation of grief. I just knew I wasn't thinking clearly. Then afterwards, what with Mrs Jennings and Lauren . . .'

I try not to react to the thought of him entwined with Lauren, but it's tricky. 'So, what did happen between you and Lauren?'

He sighs heavily. 'When she first arrived, I was angry with myself for kissing you, angry at you for being angry at me, and I'm ashamed to say I was nice to her. Perhaps a little overly nice,' he concedes, 'but I was trying to see if you had any feelings for me. I'm not proud of it. But you didn't react, and then Lauren became this rampant flirt, clamping onto my arm and laughing at everything I said. I found her quite alarming, to be honest.'

'And then she kissed you,' I can't help prompting.

'Yes. *She* kissed *me*,' he stresses. 'Believe me, there was nothing at all from my side. I explained that to her, and how it would make things difficult if you got the wrong impression, and she said she quite understood. She said she'd explain everything to you, and stupidly, I accepted what she said at face value.' He sighs and shakes his head.

Passing the churchyard, I spot Donald's grave. 'You can see how it looked from my perspective—'

Alec stops and looks at me earnestly. 'The only person I chose to kiss was you – and I wasn't even supposed to.'

'The lure of forbidden fruit,' I comment drily as we start walking again.

'No, just you.'

'Then in London?' I ask.

'In London, everything went wrong, and then on my way back I realised something awful. What if you failed to complete the tasks because of me, or something I did? What if you walked away because I'd upset you? I could have ruined everything for you, for Donald, for me, even for Mrs Crumpton! And it wasn't like I could tell you The Laurels was at stake without invalidating the will or letting Donald down – it was crucial you didn't know until the tasks were completed.'

'So you backed off?'

Alec nods. 'But only because I was worried you might lose your inheritance. Plus, I could see how angry you were and I didn't want to make it worse.'

'So where does that leave us now?' I ask, stopping under the laurel bushes on the drive.

Alec looks down into my eyes and even in the cool shade I feel my insides melting. 'You know how I feel about you, so I guess it's up to you.'

'Is it?' I ask, my heart beating faster and my voice barely above a whisper.

'Yes,' he says softly. 'Though perhaps you should leave deciding until after we've completed this final task. That would be more in keeping with Donald's instructions to me, at least.'

It makes sense, but I don't want to leave everything hanging in the balance until then. 'How about, once we're through this final task, we go on a date? I mean, I know a lot of what we've done could be construed as dates, and we've been living in the same house, but I don't think it's the same when you are being told to go by an elderly relative from beyond the grave.'

'No,' he agrees, breaking into a grin. 'It's not the same, and a date is a great idea. But can I be given one allowance between now and then?'

'What?'

'Just let me kiss you. I have spent so long stopping myself, it would be a massive relief to be able to.'

Rather than answering, I stand on my tiptoes and lift my chin. He wraps his arms around me. Looking deeply into my eyes he slowly and deliberately lowers his lips onto mine as if savouring every last second and as soon as they touch I melt into the kiss just as I did at the river. The laurels swirl and every sense between us heightens as the world falls away. After a long while we break apart, a little breathless.

'Damn it, let's get your relatives here,' he growls, holding me so close that our noses are almost touching. He delicately brushes away a stray strand of hair from my temple, then touches his lips to my cheek.

'Agreed,' I breathe, and grin as I imagine Lauren's reaction if she knew this was one of our motivations for having them visit. Alec grins too, and letting me go with one last look of tenderness, he leads me inside to find Mrs Crumpton.

27

Mrs Crumpton is oddly pleased about staying on at The Laurels given that Donald has left her enough money to retire. I even spot her scuffing away a tear as if it has no business being there. 'I can't stand the idea of havin' nothing to do,' she explains, then instantly regrets it when we ask her to cater for a tea party in three days' time.

Still, she agrees, and I phone and invite everyone, with nerves fluttering in my stomach for each and every phone call. Mum and Dad accept immediately, and also agree on Lauren's behalf – which I think is pretty brave of them. Grandma Betty complains that it's a long way, but I can tell she's curious about what I've been up to, and is just keeping me on my toes. The most difficult person to convince is Aunty Pam. I try buttering her up, which doesn't work, but she finally agrees when I tell her there'll be a special announcement – she'd hate to be the only person not to know something. Thankfully, she says she'll make Nicholas come, too.

The next few days skip by in a flurry of activity, with me frequently having to pinch myself to believe this could soon be my home. I keep catching myself grinning at unexpected moments. Alec and I shop, tidy and generally do as we're told by Mrs Crumpton to make the place ready. In between times, we go out for walks, and sometimes I write and Alec plays his guitar. I also read more Isadora Layton novels, which I'm not ashamed to say I find completely addictive. In the evenings,

Alec is keen to hear what I think about them, and we debate endlessly over which parts are fiction and which are based on Donald's actual experiences. It's sometimes difficult to know if we are still discussing Donald, or obliquely referring to us, but it's lovely – flirty and full of a promise that makes my stomach turn cartwheels whenever I think about it.

This morning, knowing my family are coming today, my stomach has shrunk to the size of a pea. I'm unable to capture any of the happiness I've been feeling over the last few days, and I wander into the kitchen to find Mrs Crumpton grimly stirring porridge, and Alec sat at the table moodily nursing a cup of instant coffee.

Mrs Crumpton gives me a curt nod. 'Mornin',' she says, leaving off the 'good'. 'It's today, then,' she adds, giving the ceiling a hard look. 'What time are they gettin' 'ere?'

'Two.'

'I've made cakes,' she says, jerking her head at the sideboard where three cakes are cooling. 'An' I'll be makin' scones and biscuits. If you want porridge, help yourself.'

I take a clean bowl and ladle out some porridge as Mrs Crumpton gets on with removing the cake tins and peeling off the baking paper.

'Nervous?' asks Alec as I sit down opposite him.

'A bit, but I keep reminding myself that I shouldn't feel ashamed or guilty about Donald choosing me. So long as I remember that, I should be OK.'

'And you never know, they might be happy for you,' he says.

'Hmm,' I say doubtfully. 'Acceptance would be a start.'

Alec's head dips in acknowledgement. 'I guess that's more reasonable to expect. My family weren't too happy about my grandmother choosing me, either, but since she and I always had a special bond, it wasn't much of a shock.' His face darkens. 'There were a few snide comments about me now being able to squat in my own property, but apart from that they pretty much kept their thoughts to themselves. How do you think your family will react?'

'Honestly? They'll be shocked, but how that will manifest itself, we'll just have to wait and see.'

'Fair enough. So, what do you want to do this morning?'

I glance over at Mrs Crumpton. 'Well, seeing as this is a team effort, what would be most helpful?'

Mrs Crumpton presses her lips together in thought. 'Wash up, then give the place a good vacuuming. That would be a real help.'

I grin at Alec. 'Do you want to wash or dry?'

The house is ready. Mrs Crumpton has an amazing array of baking waiting on wire racks in the kitchen and I've come upstairs to run a brush through my hair. I look in the mirror and decide I'm pretty much ready, so after rereading Donald's instructions, I put the letter in my pocket for luck and head downstairs.

'You look lovely,' says Alec as I come into the drawing room.

'Thanks, so do you.' He's made an effort – his blue shirt is crisp, and he's used something in his hair. He looks down at himself and shrugs. I don't think he has a clue how sexy he is.

'How are you feeling?' he asks, and all my worries flip up like cardboard gunmen at a shooting range.

'Umm, OK?' I say, but my voice is unnaturally high. In fact, I'm feeling a lot like I did before Mrs Jennings came that last time. Alec smiles and wraps his strong arms around me, resting his head against my hair. A little of my tension seeps away and is replaced by something quite different. He pulls back slightly and, almost as if he can't help himself, kisses my lips, butterfly-light. My breath catches and I look up at him.

'Let's get this done, first,' I say firmly, not wanting to greet everyone looking flushed, and he chuckles and lets go.

'Just remember, it doesn't matter how this goes, you just have to get through it.'

I nod, but I want to prove myself – perhaps even make myself proud. What was it Donald wrote? Stand tall, and something about being bullet-proof?

There's a crunch of car tyres on the gravel outside, and I pat the letter for luck before going with Alec to the front door.

I glance at him before opening it. 'Ready?' I ask.

'Donald asked me the exact same thing on the day I first met you.'

'Like uncle, like niece,' I laugh, and taking this as a good omen, I pull open the front door.

Grandma Betty and Grandpa Albert are already parked. Uncle Nigel is pulling in beside them and Nicholas's Porsche has just come into the parking area – so I'm guessing he didn't take Donald's advice to ditch it.

Watching them all, I remember my first impressions of The Laurels and realise I'm now standing in Donald's place. I try to imagine what he saw. Uncle Nigel is crouched, peering at his front bumper, probably checking for dings from the gravel. Aunty Pam is stood looking as if her lips have been pursed for so long they've fused. Nicholas looks as conceited as ever. Grandpa Albert is gazing at the garden, and Grandma Betty is waiting for him to open her car door. Aunty Pam eventually helps her out.

It's quite a performance, and Alec's watching them with wry amusement. His eyes meet mine, and we exchange smiles.

'Hannah!' calls Grandma Betty as if she's summoning a dog. I turn, shocked to find my perception of her has completely changed. She's no longer Blast-off Betty, my unassailable grandmother who's always been able to make me feel small; she's Donald's go-kart-busting, treacherous little sister.

'Yes?' I say, standing a little taller, and using a commanding voice that I wouldn't have dared try on her a few weeks ago.

An uneasy smile flickers onto her lips and she squints slightly. 'You've changed your hair!'

'Yes.' My voice is calm.

'Hmm. Can you now tell me why you have invited us here today?' I might be imagining it, but I think her tone is slightly less militant.

Aunty Pam's head pops up, looking at me like a meerkat.

'All will become clear,' I say cheerily. 'Do come in.' It's odd saying that, knowing this will soon be my home.

I stand a little more erect as Aunty Pam accosts me. 'Well, Hannah, we've come. It was against my better judgement after how you treated Nicholas, but we've decided to give you the benefit of the doubt.'

I feel like I've been given a little kick up the behind, but if she's expecting me to look shamefaced she's going to be disappointed. 'Thank you. I know it can't have been easy given that you are under the mistaken impression that I told Donald about Nicholas's adoption.' My eyes slide over to where he's schmoozing Grandma Betty.

'Ugh, well,' says Aunty Pam, looking less certain now.

'Never mind. How about you go in and make yourself comfortable.' I hold out my hand to show the way, and Aunty Pam, Uncle Nigel, Nicholas and Grandma Betty all make their way in.

'Nicely done,' Alec whispers.

Grandpa Albert is the only one left outside, and he's rummaging about in the boot of his car. I stroll over to see what he's doing, and he brings out a pair of wellies.

'Ah, Hannah!' he says as if he's surprised to see me here. 'I thought I might take a look at the garden, if that's all right?'

'Of course, but would it be OK if you came in to hear my announcement first?'

'Oh? Absolutely,' he agrees sadly, putting his wellies back in the boot.

'No, keep them out. It'll only take a few minutes, and after that – help yourself.' I'm pleased to see the smile return to his face. 'Bringing wellies was a good idea.'

'They're a compromise,' he explains, examining them as if they're an odd invention. 'I'm allowed to "grub about in the garden", so long as I don't "ruin my trousers and shoes".'

'That's good. How are things with the allotment?'

A look of rapture spreads across his face. 'Wonderful! I go there most days and I've been sowing carrots, beetroot, runner beans, radishes, fennel . . . Well, I don't want to bore you with it all, but I love it down there. The chap on the neighbouring plot is marvellous. He's called John. We share flasks of tea.'

'Sounds great. Does Grandma Betty go with you?'

The mischievous smirk takes years off Grandpa Albert. 'She followed me down there once, but John said she was stunting the plants speaking like that. She's not been down since. Mind if I leave these in the porch?' he asks, holding up the wellies.

'Not at all. And come in for tea and cake later if you like . . . or there's a door around the side. I'm sure Mrs Crumpton will give you a mug of tea and some biscuits.' I'm confident she won't mind as I'm guessing her husband probably did the same.

'Lovely,' says Grandpa Albert and, hearing another car, heads off into the house, leaving me to welcome Lauren and my parents.

As Dad parks, Alec strolls over to join me. Mum looks worried, and Lauren is eyeing me from the back seat with an expression that would, a few centuries ago, have landed her on a ducking stool.

'Hello,' I say as they get out.

'Hannah?' Mum says, her eyes wide. 'You look amazing.'

'Thanks.' I beam and give her a hug.

'Lauren told us you were . . .' Mum glances at Lauren.

'Yes?' I prompt.

'Stressed,' finishes Mum, in a way that tells me this isn't at all what Lauren said. 'And when you invited everyone, I thought there must be something wrong.'

'There's nothing wrong. There's just some news. But I'll tell you all about it inside. Hi Dad. Lauren,' I add.

Lauren glances at Alec then looks away, and Dad gives me a hug.

'Hello, darling. Love the hair. Everyone else inside?' he asks, then grimaces at Uncle Nigel's Land Rover.

'Yes, everyone's here.'

'In that case, shall we head in?' His expression suggests he'd rather not, but he and Mum bravely troop inside. As we turn to follow, the back of Alec's hand brushes against mine and lingers there for a fraction of a second. I glance involuntarily up at him, and he grins at me.

'Jesus!' mutters Lauren. 'Pass the sick bag.'

I stare at her, and seeing the spiteful look in her eyes, I suddenly realise that all the times I've watched her play tonsil-hockey with her boyfriends was for show – she was just trying to make me feel small and insignificant. But what I have with Alec is real, and from that tiny touch, she knows it.

I grin at her and just manage to resist the temptation to chirp 'happy, smiling faces', before taking Alec's hand, and going inside.

Entering the drawing room, we're greeted with a glacial silence. I stare at my tense, tight-lipped family, and realise that this is what Donald was faced with a few months ago.

'Oh look, it's a Poirot-style showdown,' says Lauren, pushing past us and taking a seat.

'Hopefully without the murder,' I murmur to Alec, and he winks at me.

I hesitate, wondering how to begin, then Donald's words come back to me. I smile at everyone. 'I'm sure you're wondering why I asked you here today,' I say, and a frisson of anticipation runs through the room. 'Well, I wanted to tell you about Uncle Donald's will. You may, or may not know that Uncle Donald left me a series of tasks to complete with Alec, with the promise of an undisclosed reward at the end. The tasks ranged from apple scrumping, through go-karting and dancing, to attending the theatre and stargazing. After completing each task I learnt a little more about Uncle Donald's past and who he was. It was an amazing education and . . . well . . . I have now completed the tasks . . .' I look around at their expectant faces, 'and I have discovered from the solicitor that I am going to inherit this house.'

There's an astonished intake of breath.

'I bloody knew it!' says Nicholas almost immediately.

Then there's a moment of shocked silence – clearly no one else did.

'So, this is *your* house?' asks Grandma Betty. 'Donald left his house to *you*?'

'Did he, darling?' asks Mum. Dad's mouth is half-open.

'Yes, though it isn't mine quite yet. We have to go through probate.'

'And what about his money?' demands Nicholas. 'Do you get all that as well?'

Alec's glowering hard at Nicholas, but Donald said I shouldn't be ashamed or apologetic, so I'm not going to be.

'Yes,' I say, looking him straight in the eye.

'So you got all Donald's money after telling him I was adopted,' he states, breathing heavily. Everyone's eyes are on me, and I feel my self-confidence waver a little under Nicholas's certainty. Then Donald's words come to me as if through a medium. 'Don't let people make you feel insignificant – always remember they don't have the right.'

I look Nicholas firmly in the eye. 'No, Nicholas,' I say evenly. 'I didn't tell him, and the only underhanded thing that happened was you trying to have Uncle Donald declared mentally unfit and have me disinherited.'

There's a profound silence, save for chairs creaking as everyone turns to look at Nicholas. He shifts uncomfortably.

'Why would you do that?' demands Dad, staring daggers at Nicholas.

'What made you think you had the right?' adds Grandma Betty, looking dangerously like she's re-evaluating her own arrangements. Everyone else just stares at Nicholas.

'Well, who leaves their money to a woman they've met only once? It's completely ridiculous, and if it hadn't been for Hannah it would have been mine! *I'm* the first male in line. *I* was the natural choice of heir before she stuck her oar in.'

'But that's not how it works,' says Dad. 'Grandma Betty would have been the next of kin if he'd died intestate.'

'And are you trying to imply you had more right to Donald's money than Hannah simply because you're male?' demands Grandma Betty, her neck lengthening and eyes protruding. Now that's how you do Lady Catherine de Bourgh!

'Yes, are you?' demand Mum and Dad in unison.

'She could still invest,' chimes Aunty Pam, her desperate voice cutting through the awkward silence.

'What?' I ask.

'You could invest in Nicholas's clinic,' she says earnestly.

'That's true,' says Nicholas, turning to look at me. 'You could. So, will you?'

Alec's jaw has locked and I smile at him. A wordless reassurance passes between us and he relaxes back against the bookcase as I turn back to Nicholas. 'Before I answer you, Nicholas, tell me this: if our roles were reversed and you had inherited everything from Donald, would you give me any money?'

Nicholas grunts out a laugh. 'The circumstances would be completely different.'

'In what way?' I ask, and wait as his eyes dart between the various members of our family.

'I'd be—'

'Just a minute, why should you get money from Hannah and not me?' demands Lauren. She eyes me speculatively. 'I'm your sister,' she points out, as if this is some strong form of currency. I glance at Alec, who rolls his eyes.

'Hang on! Why should *any* of you get any money?' asks Dad.

'She's the one who got pots of money for nothing,' complains Aunty Pam.

'Donald chose her,' says Dad.

'And who says it was for nothing?' asks Mum.

'Oh, now we're getting to the bottom of it,' says Nicholas, his nose wrinkling. 'But at least we finally understand how she influenced Donald.'

'Don't be disgusting, Nicholas,' snarls Mum. 'I meant she did the tasks. And that they liked each other, and got on well when they met.'

'I think you had it right the first time,' mutters Nicholas waspishly, and everyone erupts.

I share a quiet look with Alec, and notice that Grandpa Albert has already escaped out of the door. I stare at the arguing rabble that is my family.

'WILL EVERYBODY PLEASE BE QUIET,' I shout, glaring at them until there's silence. 'That's enough. Now, there are a few things we need to clear up because no one expected me to inherit, least of all me.'

'It was blatantly obvious to me,' mumbles Nicholas, and Aunty Pam, Uncle Nigel and Grandma Betty all start to speak at once. I hold up my hand, raise an eyebrow and, to my surprise, they fall silent. Perhaps I'd have made a good school teacher, after all.

'I inherited because Uncle Donald and I got on well and we had things in common. There was nothing seedy about it,' I say, fixing Nicholas with a hard look.

'What on earth did you have in common?' asks Lauren, pouting in disbelief.

'He wrote novels for a living, and that's what I want to do.'

'And who told him that?' asks Lauren, giving me a critical look.

'I told him over lunch at the party.'

'Since when have you wanted to be a writer?' asks Dad, not unkindly, but everyone else stares at me like I must have conned Uncle Donald.

'Since always,' I say quietly. 'It's been my ambition to write novels for years, and now that I have the means, I'm going to write one.'

'I seriously doubt it,' says Lauren contemptuously. 'You'll just waste everyone's time and lose interest halfway through, like you always do.'

'You of all people should know I'm telling the truth about wanting to write, Lauren,' I say, unable to keep the anger out of my voice.

'Why? Because of that pathetic little book you wrote in your teens?'

'Yes.'

'I didn't know you wrote a book,' says Mum, surprised.

'No, you wouldn't. And just so we're clear, it wasn't pathetic or little. It was full-length, and Lauren deleted it.' I look her in the eye. 'On purpose.'

'What?' asks Dad. His voice is quiet, but his shock radiates through the room. He turns to Lauren, his eyes demanding an explanation.

'It was a dismal story about a woman being held back by her sister. Of course I deleted it,' snaps Lauren, but her reddening cheeks show that she's not quite as convinced of being in the right as she'd like us to believe.

'No it wasn't. There was only one mention of a sibling in the entire book!'

'Well you would say that, wouldn't you,' says Lauren angrily. 'And I wasn't going to read the whole thing just to be repeatedly insulted, now, was I?'

'So, in other words, you didn't give it a chance?'

'It was a diatribe!'

'I don't care if it was a political assassination of all you hold dear,' barks Dad, startling us both. 'How dare you do that to your sister? I'm *appalled* at you, Lauren!'

We both stare at him and I'm almost as shocked as she is. He's only spoken to her like that once before, and after that she deleted my book. I'm wide-eyed as Dad turns to me. 'So, is that why you changed your university applications from English to history in sixth form?' I nod mutely. 'And why you went back to study English as a mature student?'

'Yes,' I say, finding my voice.

'I always wondered what that was all about,' he says, shaking his head.

'But how did you find time to write a book?' asks Mum.

Lauren glares at me, threatening me with her eyes, but I take courage from Donald's letter.

'You know all those times I was supposedly at home with Lauren when you and Dad went out?' Mum's face falls as she realises what's coming.

Lauren's eyes narrow. 'You little shit!' she says before I can say.

'Jesus, Lauren!' says Nicholas, and noticing everyone's horrified faces, Lauren juts out her chin and stalks from the room with her nose in the air, closing the door loudly behind her.

'Well!' says Grandma Betty.

Alec drifts over and puts his arm around my waist, and I let my head rest briefly against his shoulder. 'Perhaps I should get everyone a drink,' he whispers, and slips out.

Dad comes over and gives me a hug. 'I'm sorry, darling. I had no idea.'

Mum looks at the door Alec just went through and back at me. 'Are you and he . . .?'

'Yes, I think we are.' I can't help smiling.

'And he isn't just interested in you because of Donald's money?' she asks, her shoulders rising fretfully.

'Mum, I can guarantee that isn't the case.' I smile as Alec comes back in with a tray of glasses and a big jug of Pimm's clinking with ice cubes.

'Mrs Crumpton had a tray ready,' he says, his eyes widening significantly at her magical foresight, and starts pouring.

Glancing around, I hope it does the trick, because they all seem more uncomfortable than ever. I resist the urge to check my watch. Alec smiles up at me and indicates the drinks are poured.

'Grab a glass, everyone,' I urge, handing them out, and after a few minutes I'm relieved to see the Pimm's is working its magic. They start chatting, possibly discussing the appalling show Lauren and I have just put on, or Nicholas's underhandedness, but at least it's a start.

Grandma Betty beckons me over to the sofa and I sit down beside her. She looks at me curiously, as though she's seeing me properly for the first time. 'Hannah,' she says, after a moment's considered thought. 'I am starting to see why Donald chose you, and I'm glad to see that it suits you. But I feel compelled to warn you that there are certain aspects of his life . . .'

I lay my hand on top of hers. Not being a tactile person, this startles her into silence. 'You don't need to worry. I know all about his past.'

'Are you sure?' she asks.

'Absolutely certain. He trusted me enough to tell me pretty much everything, and though I appreciate your warning, you don't need to worry – I know all about Judith, him leaving home and his time in London.'

A slight flush comes to Grandma Betty's cheeks. She assesses me for a few moments and I hold her gaze. For the first time in my life, she's the one to break eye contact. 'Very well. In that case I wish you every happiness,' she says finally. 'And you, young lady,' she says, seeing Lauren creep back in, 'owe your sister an apology.'

Lauren shifts uncomfortably under Grandma Betty's scrutiny, then her chin lifts and she smiles at me, though the warmth doesn't quite reach her eyes. 'Hannah, I'm sorry for deleting your book,' she says with commendable gravity. Of course I don't believe she's sorry at all, but for my parents' sake, I give her a curt nod, and watch as Mum and Dad's faces relax.

After a slight pause, everyone gets back to their conversations, and I join Alec, who pours me another Pimm's.

'You're getting your wish,' he whispers, handing me the glass.

I colour slightly, remembering the wish I made on the shooting star, where he and I . . . but then I grasp what he's talking about. He's right – everyone now seems to have accepted the idea of me being an heiress, and thankfully seem to be over their initial wave of outrage and resentment. Except for Lauren – though she has quite a few things to be upset about right now, and there's only ever been a thin veil covering those sour grapes. But if it hadn't been for Donald's face-it-and-brazen-it-out last task, there might have been months of grumbling and bad feeling behind closed doors. As it is, I think we can all now move past it.

I grin at Alec and he rests his arm around my shoulders, almost causing Lauren's mask of repentant civility to slip. Luckily, Mrs Crumpton chooses this moment to bring in the cakes and scones, distracting everyone with her excellent culinary skills, and Alec goes to help her.

As Mrs Crumpton starts pouring tea, Mum comes over and leans in close. 'Who is that?' she whispers.

'That's Mrs Crumpton.'

'Oh! Lauren told me about her. Is she staying on?'

'Yes,' I say cheerfully. 'For as long as she wants; a bit like tenure – or the housekeeper's equivalent, anyway.'

Mum quails a little as Mrs Crumpton, hearing her name mentioned, treats her to a degree of scrutiny. 'Is that one of Donald's stipulations?' whispers Mum.

'No, it's one of mine.' I grin at Mrs C, and she gives me a glimmer of a smile.

Mum looks from Mrs Crumpton to me. 'You've really fitted in here,' she says, surprised. 'Well done, darling.' She drifts off to get a piece of cake and sit by Lauren, who leans into her, already playing for sympathy – but for once it doesn't rankle. It seems Donald was right; hiding her unkindness only made me feel substandard and vulnerable, but now everything's in the open, the little things don't hurt.

I take a slice of date and apple cake and go to have a chat with Dad and Grandma Betty joins us in order to hear all about the different tasks. And then I start to mingle, with everyone wanting to hear more about what I've been up to and telling me their own news. I even chat with Nicholas, who seems to have finally accepted that he's behaved badly, and I wish him good luck with the clinic. Despite the unpromising start, it's turned into a pleasant afternoon.

Before I know it, it's time for everyone to go. Alec puts his arm around me as we stand on the drive waving them off. Lauren, I notice, focuses determinedly on her phone, and Alec gives me a little squeeze.

'Well done,' he says, planting a kiss on my temple as Mum and Dad's car, the last to leave, pulls out onto the main road. 'That went really well.'

'It did, didn't it,' I agree, grinning.

Hearing the chink of crockery inside, I wrinkle my nose at him. 'We should help clear up.'

Alec nods, looking resigned. He takes my hand and we almost collide with Mrs Crumpton and her tray of dirty plates as we stroll into the hall.

'I fed your grandpa in the kitchen. Nice man,' she says. 'There are dish cloths and tea towels waitin' in 'ere for both of you,' she adds crisply, before heading off towards the kitchen.

'We're on our way, Mrs C,' says Alec, stealing a quick kiss from me while her back is turned.

'Don't get distracted! Washin' up!' shouts Mrs Crumpton. She must have eyes in the back of her head.

'I look forward to continuing this later,' mutters Alec in my ear, eliciting a little shiver of anticipation. He pecks me chastely on the cheek and holds on to my hand for just a second longer before letting me go so that I can collect more dirty crockery from the drawing room. I grin to myself as I feel him watching me walk away before he heads towards the washing up.

Later that evening, Alec and I are sat in front of the fire in the study, cradling a glass of whisky each. Alec gives me a small reassuring smile as I put my glass aside and pick up Donald's last letter. A sudden sadness sweeps over me as I realise there won't be any more. I hold it for a couple of seconds, savouring the moment, then carefully peel it open.

My Dearest Hannah,

Do you remember that at my party you asked what advice I would give you? I've thought long and hard, weighing up what I told you, and I've come to the conclusion that I gave you excellent advice. The only thing I forgot to say was that you should put it all into action right away. Be brave now, do what you want to do now, and never allow anyone to make you feel insignificant. This was the purpose behind your final task: I wanted you to stand up to your family now. I didn't want you to wait. I only hope it went well.

Either way, we are at the end of our journey together. You have tried many of the best things I have experienced during my lifetime, and stood up to your family at the start of your life rather than at the end, which is the one thing I wish I'd done, so our time together is complete. It is now up to you to shape your life into exactly what you want it to be, so be brave. If you wish to write, then you should now have a wealth of experience, to inform your writing. If not, then I am still pleased you are in a good place going forward, and know that whatever you choose, I wish you joy.

As for your inheritance, The Laurels is now yours, barring all the final trumpery and bureaucracy that Dingbat Sanderson will no doubt muster. But remember that with money comes great responsibility, and responsibility for those around you. And remember, money is not the only currency. As we know from Mrs Jennings, people will do almost anything if you give them the right incentive. The trick is to make it a worthy one.

So my dearest Hannah, bravo, and bravo to me, too! Planning how to open your mind to new experiences has been a delight that has enriched my final months, and for that I thank you. Plus, perhaps, I should give a nod to Alec, Jane and Mrs Crumpton. (Mr Sanderson was paid, so he can thank himself.)

All that is left for me to do is to tell you to live well, and please know that I die happy in the knowledge that the world is a far less interesting place without me!

Forever yours,

Uncle Donald

I hand the letter to Alec and he reads it through.

'Is he asking me to look after Mrs Crumpton?' I ask as he hands it back.

'And me, and Jane, and Jim and May, I expect,' he adds with a small smile.

'OK,' I say, and curl my feet up under me.

'So, which part of Donald's life are you going to write about in your novel?' asks Alec.

'All of it, of course. Sort of. With the names changed to protect the innocent.'

'What about the guilty?' he asks solemnly.

'Them, too, I suppose.'

'Well, if you need a proofreader, typist or general factotum, I know of one that's free.'

'Not all that free, I hope! I've booked him for a date.'

Alec grins and reaches across the gap between our two chairs. He takes my hand, lifts it to his lips and kisses my fingertips, sending small tingles pulsing up my arm, then kisses my palm. My eyes close for a second.

'So, what would you like to do on our first date?' he asks, holding my hand to his cheek, and I feel a hint of stubble. 'Any ideas, or would you like to go the traditional route and go out for dinner?'

'I know exactly what I'd like to do, if you don't mind?'

'Not at all. What were you thinking?'

'Something special,' I say, and press my lips together to show that he's going to have to wait and see.

On the same hilltop, but with far more space on the blanket, Alec and I gaze up at the stars, hand in hand. Neither of us needs to say a word. We lie still, absorbing the starlight, and experience all the things that Donald hoped we would feel the first time. We stare up at the cosmos, hearing only the wind rustling in the trees, aware of the Earth rotating beneath us as the stars expand away into the never-ending universe way over our heads.

Alec breathes out a contented sigh, and his fingers intertwine with mine. His hand is warm and soft, and this small contact feels strangely intimate in the darkness. I glance over at him, and it's as he rolls onto his side, and his lips brush mine oh-so-gently, that I learn exactly how blissful stargazing can be.

ACKNOWLEDGEMENTS

I have been fortunate enough to be part of an amazing team whose combined and unrelenting support helped crystallise this story into a book I am very proud of. It absolutely would not have been the same without them.

In particular, I'd like to say a big thank you to my wonderful editor, Thorne Ryan, and everyone at Hodder & Stoughton who have made publishing this book so enjoyable. Also, my special thanks to my literary agent, Jo Bell from The Bell Lomax Moreton Agency, who has been both reassuring and diligent throughout.

My husband and children have been brilliant – their energy, patience and enthusiasm when trialling plot lines, testing ideas and being guinea pigs for my early drafts, was truly invaluable.

And finally, my deepest gratitude to an unsung, dearly departed hero, whose generous guidance and skilful encouragement all those years ago sowed those first seeds for my becoming a writer. His belief and confidence have stayed with me, and will continue to do so.